A Mermaid's Kiss

Joey W. Hill

BERKLEY SENSATION, NEW YORK

THE BERKLEY PUBLISHING GROUP
Published by the Penguin Group
Penguin Group (USA) Inc.
375 Hudson Street, New York, New York 10014, USA
Penguin Group (Canada), 90 Eglinton Avenue East, Suite 700, Toronto, Ontario M4P 2Y3, Canada
(a division of Pearson Penguin Canada Inc.) • Penguin Books Ltd., 80 Strand, London WC2R 0RL,
England • Penguin Ireland, 25 St. Stephen's Green, Dublin 2, Ireland (a division of Penguin
Books Ltd.) • Penguin Group (Australia), 707 Collins Street, Melbourne, Victoria 3008, Australia
(a division of Pearson Australia Group Pty. Ltd.) • Penguin Books India Pvt. Ltd., 11 Community
Centre, Panchsheel Park, New Delhi—110 017, India • Penguin Group (NZ), 67 Apollo Drive,
Rosedale, Auckland 0632, New Zealand (a division of Pearson New Zealand Ltd.) • Penguin Books,
Rosebank Office Park, 181 Jan Smuts Avenue, Parktown North 2193, South Africa • Penguin China,
B7 Jaiming Center, 27 East Third Ring Road North, Chaoyang District, Beijing 100020, China

Penguin Books Ltd., Registered Offices: 80 Strand, London WC2R 0RL, England

This is a work of fiction. Names, characters, places, and incidents either are the product of the author's
imagination or are used fictitiously, and any resemblance to actual persons, living or dead, business
establishments, events, or locales is entirely coincidental. The publisher does not have any control over
and does not assume any responsibility for author or third-party websites or their content.

A MERMAID'S KISS

A Berkley Sensation Book / published by arrangement with the author

PUBLISHING HISTORY
Berkley Sensation trade paperback edition / November 2008
Berkley Sensation mass-market edition / December 2012

Copyright © 2008 by Joey W. Hill.
Excerpt from *A Witch's Beauty* by Joey W. Hill copyright © 2009 by Joey W. Hill.
Cover art by Don Sipley.
Cover design by George Long.
Cover hand lettering by Ron Zinn.
Interior text design by Tiffany Estreicher.

ISBN: 978-0-425-25111-9

BERKLEY SENSATION®
Berkley Sensation Books are published by The Berkley Publishing Group,
a division of Penguin Group (USA) Inc.,
375 Hudson Street, New York, New York 10014.
BERKLEY SENSATION® is a registered trademark of Penguin Group (USA) Inc.
The "B" design is a trademark of Penguin Group (USA) Inc.

PRINTED IN THE UNITED STATES OF AMERICA

10 9 8 7 6 5 4 3 2 1

ALWAYS LEARNING   **PEARSON**

To the angels who fight for us all,
risking their precious spark to give ours a chance.

To the soldiers.

One

*The function of the wing is to take what is heavy
and raise it up into the region above where the
gods dwell. Of all things connected with the body
it has the greatest affinity with the divine.*
—PLATO

LIGHTNING flashed, the sky unnaturally dark. His doing, or
his enemies'? He couldn't tell anymore. But bloodlust required instinct, not thought, and pain could be ignored. As he
roared his fury, the resulting heat that shot through his sword
blade illuminated his surroundings. A hundred shadows con-
verging, almost indistinguishable from the black clouds, but
the nearest one was close enough to become an opponent. The
Dark One's death scream made Jonah's lips curl in a satisfied,
feral smile, despite the foul taste of the creature's blood splat-
tered across his mouth.

Good or evil, what did it matter? It all came down to this
in the end—battle. Those who were the best would be left
standing, if luck and skill held.

But the Lady didn't stand with them on this ground. He
fought for Her, but he never sensed Her presence in this. It was
that lonely thought that defeated him, took his attention for a
blink and let his enemies strike the sword from his hand. It
went end over end through the heavens, arcing and then arrowing down toward earth. He spun, twisted. The sweep of the
battle-axe he couldn't evade was a dull gleam among a malevolent tapestry of red eyes and bared fangs.

Perhaps they'd aimed for the spine, intending to cleave him
in half. An irony, since that reflected his mind these days. But
instead they severed one of his wings. Struck it from him with

a terrible hollow *thunk* like the chopping of a tree. A bolt of agony rocketed through his upper body, numbing his legs and arms for a key moment.

Balance gone, he hurtled down among them. Jonah struck out, snarling, fighting with bare fists. Blood ran down his back, dripping onto his thighs as brutal talons tore at the open wound.

Using the last reservoir of concentration he had, he electrified the air around him. The shattering flash jolted his own muscles and nerve endings, wrenching a hoarse cry from his throat that was lost in their shrieks. But the smell of burning flesh was grimly sweet.

He was falling free, spiraling down and down, unable to control anything as he dropped for miles, his one wing making the descent an unpredictable, wild twisting that tore away his ability to stay conscious.

It didn't matter. He'd prefer death to dismemberment. Another lightning flash, not his this time, outlined the demonic forms of his attackers. A few had recovered enough to dive after him. They would try to take him alive, he knew. And then all Hell would break loose. Literally.

When his body fell into the sea, his velocity sent up a plume like a geyser. As he hit, the wake would impact the shoreline a few miles away, like a storm surge. Coming out of nowhere, it would baffle the ever ignorant and oblivious humans.

A pebble dropped in a pond could create ripples, affecting everything it touched in subtle but undeniable ways.

The fall of an angel could drown the very heart of Earth.

———

As a flash of lightning struck the ocean surface thirty feet above, Anna paused, her hand resting on the whale's side. The subsequent boom of thunder was powerful enough to send a vibration through the rippling water. The humpback made a keening noise, but did not stop, her dark flank moving at a sedate but determined pace under Anna's fingers, moving forward and away.

She'd been traveling with the migrating pod tonight, seeking peace in the nighttime world. Until the storm blew up, she'd been able to look up and see every star, the light of the moon reflected by the floating plankton. In the shadows of the coral reefs, the fish slept, their bodies swaying in the current. Yes, the ocean had its own rhythm, an echoing, pulsing murmur, but something was different about it now, almost as if it had paused, just like Anna, ear cocked for something that wasn't quite right.

The clouds had blown in swiftly, thickening around the moon, covering the pale orb, casting their shadows on the sea as the flat panel of it built into a moving panorama of turbulent waves. Raindrops struck so fast and hard they stippled the flow. Though she'd sought tranquility tonight, Anna had to admit the ocean now reflected more of her true mood.

Of course, the sea was ever moving and changing, unlike her relationship with her own kind. She wondered that anyone sought the company of mermaids, then chided herself for the uncharitable thought. But by the Goddess, she didn't go to the palace that often. Was it too much to ask her cousins not to be so insular and self-centered? She'd just wanted to see them, and they acted like they wanted her gone within minutes of her arrival.

Maybe she should have phrased it differently. *Hello, all. I'm visiting because I'll be dead in eleven months. Just thought I'd let you know I'll miss you.*

But she wouldn't, would she? She missed what they'd never given her, and she'd hoped for one fleeting moment of that, now that her time was getting short.

She wouldn't regret tying their hair in knots while they slept before she slipped away. Or pressing her hand and forehead for one long moment against the solid door to Neptune's throne room.

At another resonant clap of thunder, she turned, glad for the distraction from her disturbing thoughts. No, something *did* feel odd, as if the plates had shifted, sending a seismic wave through the water like a startling pulse of pressure. Surely the whales had detected it?

When Anna saw the whale's mate holding back, testing their surroundings as Anna'd been doing, she knew he had sensed the strangeness as well. No wonder the pod was moving at night. She'd thought it unusual, but until now they'd seemed so placid, unhurried. But whales tended to anticipate things. The mother must be moving the baby to safety while her mate guarded her back. Anna wondered what it would be like to have someone like that.

Oh, Great Lady, she did *not* want to think about that, either. She was alone. She would always be alone. It was time to make peace with it, with all of it. And really, she had been fine for all these years, knowing. It was just that now, there was nothing—

She cried out as an object shot down through the water before her, seizing her in the turbulence. When something slashed against her hand, she convulsively closed her fingers on it as she was somersaulted backward. Though a somersault suggested a circular pattern, predictable in its track, she was twisted, upended and thrown while the sea boiled and heaved as if the projectile had been a bullet striking the ocean's heart.

Ramming into a coral reef, she was punctured by the sharp edges. Then the wake seized her and dragged her body along the coral, pulling several scales loose from her sensitive tail. Her left tail fin was spliced, wresting a full scream from her.

When the wave passed and she was floating clear, a fine mist of her own blood swirled about her like the inky passing of a squid. Trembling, Anna saw she still held what she'd reflexively clutched, the blood from her hand flowing around it.

It was a feather.

But not just any feather. She forced herself to keep her wits about her and hold on to it, for it was obvious this did not belong to a seagull or swan haplessly plunging to earth. It had an iridescent, milky gleam, with a blue aura that shone even though it was detached from its owner. She swallowed, her eyes wide, her scrapes forgotten as she realized what it must be.

An angel's feather.

There were fanciful things said of angels. Like how a merchild might see one at night, winging through the sky like a shooting star. If that should happen, the child should only chance a look and then duck her head, make her wish. If one had the remarkable experience of being in the presence of an angel, speaking was forbidden, unless the angel commanded it. Otherwise, the tongue would simply disintegrate in your presumptuous throat.

An angel was the highest echelon after the Goddess Herself, doing Her will. Lords of the air, the skies, even the earth and water. Nothing limited them but the Lady. They could be agents of destruction or life, depending on Her will, reapers or saviors.

Humans were the only species that treated the existence of angels as belief instead of fact. It was grimly amusing how many real things humans considered myth or wishful thinking. Or nightmares. No one knew why the Deity allowed humans to exist in such childish ignorance of what the rest of them knew. Though Anna, who was as much a part of the human world as that of the merpeople, had her theories.

While she knew angels existed, she might have scoffed at some of the stories, for no one she knew had interacted with one in any significant way for decades, but her great-aunt, Neptune's sister, had been saved by an angel. It was still one of the most vivid memories of the old merwoman's life, though it had happened when she was little more than a child. Trapped in a lost shrimp net, she'd fallen into the Abyss, a series of reefs and caverns that went down so far no one knew how deep they were. Currents had taken her into the caverns, tumbling her over and over. She'd fought the net until, exhausted, she'd resigned herself to her own death, for the more she struggled, the deeper into the tunnels she was carried.

Then she'd found herself in a place of fire. Heat, far below where heat existed in the ocean. Instead of dying by fire, Aunt Judith, or Jude as they all called her, had been untangled and led out of the place by an angel. He'd been so beautiful that whenever she remembered him, she cried at the memory. Jude had been blind ever since, a sea creature dependent on others to be her eyes. While she thought the angel had taken her sight to keep her from coming back, she bore him no ill will for it.

"He cut himself when he helped free me from the net. I remember his blood was blue, like the sky . . ."

The feather Anna held was stained with that blue. The water could not dislodge the fluid, as if the feather refused to release an intrinsic part of itself, realizing its surroundings were not where it belonged.

Perhaps the blood was simply from where the feather had gotten pulled out. Though thinking of an angel being plucked like a chicken seemed almost . . . sacrilegious. But they *weren't* gods. Just incredibly powerful beings compared to everyone else, like whales to plankton. But they could be harmed, couldn't they?

She was sure that was a thought that most . . . no, *no* mermaid had ever had. Underscoring yet another reason why she was out here by herself.

What if the sudden storm above was one of the battles between angels and the Dark Ones? Everyone knew they were happening more frequently of late, creating violent weather patterns that made her glad she could seek the shelter of the ocean depths.

Yes, angels were beings of terrible power. Their ways were a mystery, but they were essential to the balance and protection of everything. Anna hesitated, watching the track of bubbles from the unknown missile settle, disperse, while the ocean still heaved uneasily.

No, she should follow the whales. Stay out of this. Whatever *this* was.

Then she saw the wing.

Except for the ethereal glow, she might have thought it a manta ray, the lazy flow of its wings rippling like a blanket dropped into the water, or the long strands of her vain cousins' hair, moving like thick ribbons of silken seaweed.

But it was turning in uneven circles, heading down, down. It had the same blue fluid not only clinging to it, but drifting around it in a way that reminded her of how her own blood had clouded at the coral reef. Only, an angel's blood simply made the wing more beautiful, colors of sky and moonlight together, pieces of the firmament severed and drifting in her world.

She was swimming toward it before she could consider the wisdom of doing so. As she did, she realized she was by herself. A glance showed all other sea life had vacated the area. It was as if she'd found herself in a quiet oceanic chamber where she faced a challenge that called to her alone.

She caught the wing in her arms as it came down. It startled her, for it had such substance, a weight that started to take her down with it. It felt limblike, the arch and spine covered with layer upon layer of feathers. The feathers tickled her bare back, drifted over her breasts, the line of her bare stomach, the nip of her waist. As she turned with it, bemused, the elongated tip curved around her hip. As if the wing were holding her, as much as she was holding it.

She realized then that she was warm. Not a warmth caused by temperature—this sensation came from the inside. It called up a vision of strength, protection. A sense of . . . connection, making her acutely aware of the loneliness she always carried within her, like a vital but despised essential organ. The warmth helped soothe it, the feathers whispering over her cheek and her lips like a lover's regard. Understanding, acceptance, love. And more than that.

Her mouth suddenly felt needy for something . . . a kiss, the heat of another's mouth. Firm lips on hers, demanding pressure, coaxing hers open, filling her. It was a startling and yet languorous yearning, like the first press of a lover's body. Not that she had much knowledge of such things, but this sensation made her feel as if she did, and her fingers curled into the feathers, holding them as she would a man's hair. Was it her imagination, or did the curve of the wing where the bone held its shape feel like an arm, drawing her closer?

It must be the power of that incandescent light, the magical heat of it. She realized abruptly she was sinking with the wing, had been the whole time she was experiencing that heady feeling that seemed to make her aware of all the parts of herself that could stir a lover. Her mouth, her throat, her grasping fingers, the undulation of her hips . . .

Even as the wave of sensations amazed and confused her, a tingling sense of unease penetrated them, warning her that the pleasurable light was struggling, fading somehow.

There was also a definite urgency to its downward motion that couldn't be explained by the weight of waterlogged feathers, mainly because they did not appear waterlogged at all, floating as easily as the tendrils of her own hair. And didn't birds—or birdlike creatures— have hollow, nearly weightless bones?

The wing had maneuvered her off the white sand bottom, down to the nearest shelf another thirty feet below, then to a finger seventy feet below that. From here, she could see one more shelf, and then the ocean tipped off into a much deeper cavern, so deep she was startled out of her reverie by a sense of vertigo. While she could see the wall of coral, covered with tube sponges and sea fans, below that things became much murkier, until it went into complete black, where the light from above wouldn't penetrate, and the water grew far, far colder. There were no reassuring whorls of warmth. They were over the Abyss.

The wing had seduced her like a siren, and sea creatures knew all about the danger of sirens.

Wriggling out of its grasp, she leaped away from it. Because of her sudden surge of apprehension, she whipped around, half expecting pursuit.

It did appear to hesitate, but she told herself it was just the waters she'd stirred, holding it in a momentary vortex. When it drifted down and landed on an outcropping of rock, it began to slide, tumble, toward the edge of the Abyss. As it drifted in that direction, a hunger grew in her heart that she couldn't explain. A need not only to grasp *it* in her hands again, but the creature to whom it belonged.

Danger . . .

The sonorous call reverberated through the waters, the whales signaling one another, the message picked up and carried by a school of fish that exploded out of the edge of the pit and cut past her on all sides.

The instinctive spear of terror through her vitals made her look up. She couldn't see anything, but somewhere above her, she sensed dark, shifting . . . monsters. There. Red lights, glowing at a distance like signal lights from boats. Red eyes, a color she shouldn't be able to distinguish at this depth unless it belonged to something that contradicted natural law.

Every creature had a honed fight-or-flight sense, necessary to live in a world governed by survival of the fittest. But this was more than the alarm caused by a predator's impersonal hunger closing in on her. This was personal, creeping into the marrow of her bones, a dark, anxious poison spreading out from her internal organs. Even as she was able to identify that the intent was to paralyze her with her own fear, she could not seem to counter it, which made it even more terrifying.

Leave him . . . You cannot help him . . . No concern of yours . . . He cares nothing for your pathetic kind . . .

Dark Ones. The enemies of the angels, of every life-form. The power of the compulsion was overwhelming, and it was not a single voice, but many, a malevolent force. As she struggled against it, she managed to throw up a weak protection spell, enough to give herself the space to realize they were not targeting her specifically, but any creature in range that might be giving their target aid.

She couldn't stand against Dark Ones, and she knew nothing of the battles angels fought. Why should she defy the will of that voice of darkness?

As Anna watched the wing make its tumble, she realized it was being drawn to its master, like an innocent child betraying its parent. It was just an amorphous glow now, falling into darkness, like a candle being extinguished. The darkness of the Abyss was total. Final. It would swallow the wing.

The owner of that wing was unprotected, wounded. She was as sure of that as she was that much of the fear battering her senses was real, not just the magical effect of his pursuers.

Abruptly she shot forward, using the powerful propulsion of her midnight blue tail to send her over the edge and arrow down into the Abyss. Seizing the floating wing, she increased the speed of its descent, taking it down, herself with it.

Take me to your master. We must save him if we can.

Two

IT got much colder, very quickly. As she descended, Anna tried not to think of the increasing darkness, the shadows melting together as the light was left behind, heralding the total blackness that waited below. She gripped the wing as if it represented a life-or-death oath she'd taken.

When the curve of her tail touched the edge of another precipice, it startled her. The wing slowly, slowly settled. As it did, she realized it was covering a shape partially illuminated by the wing's fading internal light. When it shifted, the light grew stronger, making her realize it had blanketed another wing whose light was brighter, for it was still attached to its owner.

She floated closer, hovering over him. His eyes were closed and there was a cut on his face, the blue line of severed flesh a smaller version of the alarmingly large open wound on his back, staining the other wing and his skin. Beneath it, he was bruised, covered in welts as if he'd been beaten, clawed. She swallowed.

Another good current, and he would roll over the edge of this outcropping and fall even deeper, to where the temperature could drop beyond what she could bear. But there was nowhere to hide here.

She glanced up. They were coming. In the unnatural despair hovering just at the edge of her consciousness, she could sense them. Scattered, but descending. And they had no intention of helping him, whatever they were.

The wing was drifting, so she reached out to grasp it, only to realize it *wasn't* drifting. It was . . . shifting. Shifting to align itself with the wound in his back.

Then the wing brushed her. Since she was bent over the angel, it curved around her, pulling her down, low, lower. She tried to free herself, but before she could she was lying upon the side of the inert creature as the wing folded itself around its host. Her alarm eased as Anna realized she was simply inside the wingspan as it curved inward.

She was almost afraid to look into his face at this close range, but curiosity won out over good sense. With that one look she understood why her great-aunt had wept in remembrance.

He was unnaturally beautiful. No, that was wrong. He was as perfect as Nature could make him, and nothing could make anything as Nature did. While her cousins always sought to make themselves more beautiful, as if that were the main reason for existence, one underwater orchid blossom emerging from a crevice of coral put them all to shame.

It hurt the heart to look at something as beautiful as this, so perfect that it was almost an emotion in a physical form. Despite the danger pursuing them, for a moment she was absolutely still, amazed she was close enough to touch. A high, fine brow. Such a straight, straight nose. His hair was dark, so dark it blended with the nearly night color of the water and made her jump when it whispered over her upper arms. As it waved over his face, brushing those sculpted features, she saw the strands of varying lengths formed a shoulder-length mane. One piece apparently had been braided to keep the rest from his line of sight, for it was already half unraveled. The clean-shaven line of his jaw made it almost impossible for her to resist the desire to reach out and touch his face, see what it felt like, smooth skin, chiseled bone. The texture of his mouth. She remembered the way the wing had made her imagine a man's mouth upon hers, and her body unexpectedly tightened all along where it lay against his. She wanted him, but in ways that went far beyond physical and emotional understanding.

She needed to be a part of him. His beauty spoke of light, a light so pure it would burn away the body while the soul clung to it, willing to become ash to be within its presence.

And she would never feel alone again.

This was some strange compulsion, a different, much more pleasurable form of what the dark creatures had tried to impose on her mind. Anna shook it off with effort and focused on the immediate problem, the insane thing she was about to do. Roll them both deeper into the Abyss.

When she curled her arms around his upper body, it was a reach. He had broad shoulders, necessary to support those wings, she was sure. A wide chest. Unlike human flesh, which felt cold and slippery beneath the water, or sea creatures, which felt soft and sleek, he was somewhere in between—hard muscle and warm, smooth skin. It reassured her, because she'd been uncertain if he would be affected by depth pressures the way humans were. The wing obligingly stayed curled over her. Would it stay with her? Could she hold him as they fell, or would she lose him in the darkness?

As his heart beat against hers, she tightened her arms around him. Closing her eyes, she had to will herself to pay attention to what she was trying to do and not just lie there, clinging blissfully to him until death came to take them both.

She felt her way through the feathers to his side, his waist, an easier holding point. Using her tail, she pushed against the ground, her bare hip bone pressing into his leg. All he wore was a belted, short half tunic that rippled with the water's movement, and she felt the hard muscle of his thigh.

"Come on," she whispered desperately. "We must move." They had to go deeper, where his light wouldn't be seen. The overwhelming warmth she felt from him was being poisoned by the artificial despair creeping more deeply into her mind. His enemies were too close.

Slowly, despite the weight of the wings, he began to turn, taking them over the edge. She pushed harder with her tail, wanting to fall clear enough that they wouldn't bounce off the sharp edges of the coral. *Come on.* They had to go deeper, deeper.

She was already deeper than she'd been before, and Goddess, but the water was cold. So cold. And dark. His light was the only light. As they tumbled together, with her wrapped in his wing and wrapped around him, she realized she could lose her sense of direction, go down when she meant to go up, and never find her way to the surface again. The reality of that brought another terrifying thought. When she was lost in the darkness, it wouldn't matter to anyone. No one.

But nothingness would mean no more pain or loneliness, she reminded herself. Ridicule, inadequacy. Staring from cruel eyes. Callous comments that made her angry but gave her anger nowhere to go because it was pointless. All of that would dissolve in the Abyss, like the tar pits where Ice Age creatures were destroyed. No more . . . anything.

Oh, God. She didn't want to die. The red lights were too close. They were going to catch up to them.

No! The wing tightened around her hips and Anna held the wounded angel's weight closer, felt him living against her. *Think about him, Anna.* How mighty and fine he must look up in the sky, his wings spread. Protecting. Existing.

How was she going to hide his light?

Praying the Dark Ones were following the light and not the essence of the man himself—Soul Finder magic—she sent out a small tendril of magic herself, so insignificant in comparison to what she held and what followed them that she hoped it would warrant no more notice than a floating cloud of foam to a shark. Many sharks.

Come to me. She issued the command in her mind urgently.

Like fireflies of the sea they came, puncturing the darkness. The fish of the Abyss were a variety of unusual shapes and sizes that blended well with their surreal world and lived without fear in the void. They approached from various directions, in small groups and then one blessedly large school.

Their glow reminded her that light came from within. She would fear no darkness. If they caught him, they would kill him . . . or worse. She would not permit that.

She summoned the fish so they moved with them, weaving in and out until the two of them were part of a school of many different, iridescent colors, but primarily white and silver. As they dropped, she and her precious burden blended, a part of their travels.

Stay with me. She held the simple, pure minds as she sensed the darkness getting closer, looking. Oh, Goddess, probing. She wouldn't let herself panic, for if she did, the fish would scatter. *Focus on me. It does not seek you.*

When the probing collective mind found her, touched her, the fear and despair were like being rammed face-first into the steel side of an unexpected shipwreck. The emotions were so strong that for a moment she was disoriented, terrified, thinking the monsters had appeared all around her.

These are not your emotions. They're using you, manipulating you.

She shoved out of them with a fierce burst of resistance. She had enough unnatural factors shaping her destiny, thank you very much. No one was taking a single decision from her that was within her power to make.

Fortunately a push of current, an even colder surge, took hold at that key moment, rolled them left when the fish would have startled away in that direction, a reaction to the disturbance in her mind. Steadying them, she held the compulsion magic with renewed vigor, joining her mind with the school's as well as focusing on blending her body, and the body of the angel to whom she clung, among their physical shapes.

Just a school of fish . . . seeking dinner from the water. Seeking . . .

Her knuckles made contact with the canyon wall. While many places were too steep for anything to get a purchase, some things grew and lived in the crevices beneath the crags. The soft, wavy touch of sea fans, the quick, startling stab of some type of blenny, seeing if she was food before the creature pulled back in again. Clinging to the trunk of a sea fan, she let it anchor her and her burden. Her meager magical abilities were exhausted, so the fish swam away. Her arm ached with holding him. The severed wing helped, snugged in as it was around them both, but she sensed its sentience was connected to its master and would eventually fail if she did not find them a resting place.

Practically, she knew she didn't stand a chance against an old, blind and wounded Dark One, let alone how many she sensed were after this angel. She would find and enter a tunnel, she told herself. She would go down deep enough to get him out of range of the senses of the evil creatures following them. If she could do that, perhaps they would decide he'd drifted with the current and was no longer in the area.

And then you'll both die because you'll get stuck or lost or there will be horrible things waiting for you . . .

Making herself move along the cliff face, she followed it by touch alone, trying not to let her panic be fueled by the fact that all light except that from the faint glow of the wings had disappeared.

Once, she had discovered a travel postcard floating in the water. It was the place the humans called the Grand Canyon. Aunt Jude had told Anna these underwater cliffs had also felt the touch of sun, thousands of years ago. The world was so old, old as the Lady Herself. Older than this filth that was trying to take what she had found.

Finding a crevice wide enough for the two of them, she discovered it led into a narrow tunnel. As she followed it, tugging on her burden, she tried not to think about her lack of options if she took them down a fissure with no exit, where she could be trapped by what pursued him.

There was no greater terror for a sea creature than to be immobilized. The lack of ability to move was a sure death, a waiting death—the worst kind. Which was why Anna had such admiration for Jude, who held on to her sanity for the hours she spent tangled in that net.

Holding on to that thought, she kept moving forward, trying to keep track of her orientation with one hand on the wall, though the cold fear in her vitals told her she wasn't sure if she was going up or down anymore. All she knew was that there was now rock on all sides, the occasional conical shape of a stalagmite or stalactite, a reminder of Aunt Jude's words regarding the land-based history of these caverns. Had she thought the open pit of the Abyss dark? This was true darkness, the kind that could tug one toward madness in no time. Once, she hit a wall. It made her yelp in startled fear and she almost went back. Then, thinking carefully, collecting herself enough to feel around, she realized it was a turn in the tunnel and began to follow it in a new direction.

At one point, the rock became smooth, and pinpricks of

light started to come through the glittering flecks of minerals embedded in the tunnel sides. While it provided illumination, it was too small to give more than meager comfort, so she imagined the water here as a Caribbean crystal blue touched by the sun.

Her muscles were burning. Her tail propelled her for swimming, so she was unused to straining her arms and shoulders this way. But stopping was not an option.

The minerals disappeared, taking the illusion of light with them as the tunnel turned once more. Despite that, she kept following, obeying the compulsion to outrun whatever might be behind them, knowing by instinct that was the priority above all other things.

There. It was gone. She drifted to a halt, using her tail as a wedge between the walls to hold them in place while she waited, probing. Yes, the artificial hopelessness was gone, bringing a keen sense of relief. They'd lost them.

But instead of bringing in a rush of comfort as she'd hoped, rational thought returned, bringing terror with it. She'd long ago lost track of the direction she was going, the turns she'd made. What had she been thinking? Had she been thinking at all when she made the decision to do this?

Even as panic rose in her breast, she recognized it as the most deadly enemy she'd faced yet. A creature could quickly seal its own death warrant by giving in to mindless flight instinct. But her energy to resist had been sapped by those evil things as well as the physical effort of moving the large angel. She was where she'd never been before . . . a place that had been part of the nightmares of her childhood. Despite herself, she returned to the idea that the Abyss seemed not only capable of swallowing their physical bodies, but even the memory of their existence. In such a desolate place, maybe even the Creator could forget them.

She choked back a sob. She wanted to turn back, take them back, but she didn't know which way *was* back. It didn't matter. She'd just swim, the faster the better. Anything was better than not moving.

When the wing brushed the center of her back, at first she paid it no mind, but then she realized it wasn't the creature's wing. It was the angel's hand, his arm coming inside the circle of the wing to take a sure clasp around her, bringing her close against a body that was firm, warm. Alive.

It's all right. Be still and let me think, little one.

The relief she felt, not to be alone in this empty pit, almost made her sag against him before she remembered she was holding him up. Even though the voice was wholly inside her head, it reassured, not only because of the pitched velvet of it, but because of the command. It was a thought with no fear in it. No uncertainty. And an additional quality that unexpectedly distracted her from their immediate problem.

His hand moved along her back, then down to the curve of her hip, which was layered in tight scales that felt every movement of his touch. Her sensitive side fins feathered against his fingers.

A mermaid. A young mermaid, come to my aid. His hand went up, tangled in her loose hair. *A maid in truth.*

So he knew her kind, enough to know that the unmated girls wore their hair down. Then he found his way around to her mouth, and that thought skittered off somewhere, forgotten.

Despite the cold and fear, nerve endings activated like the sea fans agitated by the stimulation of an irresistible current. She eagerly embraced it, because it made the terror retreat enough so she could think again.

"They're close," she managed. "If they see your light . . ." She spoke in the way of mermaids, a combination of sounds that vibrated through the water, because she wasn't sure if he could hear her thoughts. She also didn't know if he knew her language, but she needn't have worried. He didn't seem to have any problem understanding her.

She was able to feel his head nod, once. Sensed him probing their surroundings in some way. Despite that and the firm command in his mind-voice, she wondered if he would remain cognizant. While she didn't want to hear it, pain and effort were there, in a strained note underneath his thoughts. His next words confirmed it, bringing back her fear.

Another mile down, there will be an outcropping shaped like a dragon's head. Do you know what a dragon is?

She nodded.

Good. Use it as your marker. Its mouth leads to a series of caverns. There should be light there. And warmth. But it is a long way. Far, far down into its belly. Too far.

She felt his attention on her, though she couldn't see the features of his face.

You know . . . there are no female angels.

She wasn't sure what he meant by that. "Save your strength, my lord. We will get you to safety."

You are beautiful and kind. But it is best to leave me. Let me die and save yourself. There are many angels, and only one of you.

He couldn't know how true those last words were. Could he?

When she turned her head, her temple brushed his face, his jaw. At that moment, his other hand raised, and a soft blue light emitted from his palm, giving her a brief flash of dim light that almost made her sob in relief. His eyes had opened, the remarkable sweep of thick lashes now revealing his dark eyes. All dark. He had no whites, so the way he gazed at her was peculiar, animallike. She couldn't tell his thoughts from them, or if he was having any thoughts at all.

She wanted to push away the thought that she would be descending even farther into the darkness and freezing cold, and that he might be delirious. She sensed no fear in him, though he must know better than she what followed them.

I am quite conscious and rational . . . but I see you need proof.

His head descended and his lips, his mouth, were on hers. A turn of events that completely immobilized her. It wasn't kissing, not exactly. It was as if he was tasting her, for his tongue traced hers, his lips coaxing hers apart as she'd first imagined.

Had she been cold? It seemed fire now swept her. She'd been holding him in the role of protector, but now she was pressed against him, one of his arms tightly around her body, making it clear who was the far stronger of the two of them. The one most capable of taking charge, keeping fears at bay.

She soared through those clouds of distracting thoughts and into a blue sky of something else. This was wanting and feeling and needing . . . ecstasy and sorrow together in that odd way, balancing release with never-ending yearning, leaving one in a strange confusion of joy. Her fingers crept up, wondrously touching the place where their lips met. His curved, and then his teeth nipped at her, making her start. Astonishingly, she almost laughed.

A convulsion went through him, disrupting the moment, making her heart leap into her throat. "My lord—"

Consciousness deserted him once more, his lips drifting along her jaw. Anna had never felt so awake in her life.

Three

E VEN as she wondered if there'd been a deliberate magic in that kiss, given to bolster her courage, she chose to believe his words, because to do otherwise was to lose her mind. Still, she felt a wave of relief when she found by touch the outcropping he'd described, though she ripped her palm open again on the sharp rock edges of the "dragon's" fangs. She entered its mouth into a blind nothingness. Keeping her arms around her angel's body as if she were moving a broad barrel, she swam onward anyway, glad the broken wing had curved around her shoulders and hip so she didn't have to worry about holding on to it. It was still emitting a separate warmth and reassurance, but as the fissure narrowed until she could put an arm out and feel the rock on either side, things became somewhat cumbersome, negotiating the direction with one severed wing and one attached one, the large male unable to aid her as she tried to keep him from getting knocked against the walls.

She almost screamed her frustration when the tunnel turned downward again. At first it was a gradual slope, but then it became harrowingly steep, until they were descending as if down a hollow tube going to the center of the earth. The water got cold again. Colder. At one point, she was barely moving, her limbs so weighed down with him and the freezing temperature. Her fingers and tail scrabbled against the sides, helping to push him downward. Did he realize that if it got too cold, she could die? They would remain here, a wall of bone and decaying flesh warning anyone else foolish enough to do something like this. Goddess, what a horrid thought.

He was wounded, gravely so. How could she be sure of him?

I am quite conscious and rational . . . but I see you need proof.

The fiery warmth in her belly, kindled by that kiss, re-ignited just in memory, spurring her onward.

The Abyss was mysterious, uncharted. So were angels. Certainly they'd used the honeycomb of caverns, right? After all, while it was filled with unknown dangers to the rest of them, what in the sea could hurt an angel?

Of course, the truth of that had nearly caught them. She prayed they'd successfully thrown his enemies off their trail, for contemplating a confrontation with them down here was just more than she could handle right now. When his body tried to slide out of her arms once again, she braced herself against the wall, holding him. She was sure her blood was staining his perfect wings. When tears pricked her eyes, Anna closed them, trying to focus.

Far, far down into its belly. Too far.

Whenever she'd had to face the unthinkable, she'd told herself if there was no way to retreat, then she had to make the unthinkable possible. This was one of those times. She couldn't go back. She *could* do this. She would do this. There was no going back.

He would die without her. *Let me die . . .*

No, by Neptune's Trident. She would not. And she wasn't dying here, either. This wasn't how she was going to go, damn it.

When her tail encountered a flat surface, and moving water pushed against her face, telling her the tunnel had become horizontal again and was widening, she sobbed in relief. She was able to switch arms and swim forward, using the additional propulsion offered by a wider sweep of her tail. And then, the darkness began to have shapes. Rock formations in the walls, the curve of the tunnel on all sides. *Light.* There was light coming from somewhere. Sea fans with waving tendrils and myriad corals began to blanket the walls again, scraping at her knuckles. Bless the Lady, the water was getting warmer. Much warmer. As the tunnel directed her up, she pushed against the wall with her free arm as well as pumped with her tail, suddenly desperate to know that what she was seeing, sensing, was true and not some odd type of mirage in this watery desert devoid of any familiar navigation marks.

As her head broke the surface of the water, she drew a deep, shuddering breath in the airbell, using her lungs instead of her gills. It was an open cavern. The closer walls were lined with rivulets of orange, silver and blue, like the inside of a creature's body—the mysterious multicolored strata of the earth. Imprints of small fossils of fish thousands of years gone were embedded in the rock. There were flat ledges above the waterline here, places to get dry.

But it was the far wall that made her draw in her breath and hold it. On one wall, stretching as far as the wall reached, was a dragon. She stared at the skeletal remains preserved perfectly in the rock. His head was thrown back as if in a defiant roar; the forest of widespread wings forever pressed into the strata. While she knew the position had to be how the animal had lain when he died, the impression of him frozen in a moment of terrible beauty and power could not be discarded.

Managing to get the angel to a sloped ledge, she hooked her elbow on it, shuddering as she tried to get her breath back. She didn't dare take too long, however. The temptation was too great to simply hold on to the ledge and lay her head down, give in to her fatigue. The wounded wing still curved around her shoulders, so that her hand could rest on the slope of his back. Great Lady, but he was just so many beautiful lines of muscle. It made her fingers itch, the desire to stroke him.

Anyone she knew would have gasped at her thought. But they hadn't been on the other side of that kiss, which had created a wealth of very irreverent thoughts. He could only blame himself for tempting her to sacrilege.

Now that they were partially above water, his wing seemed to be trying to reconnect to that wounded area again. A shudder ran through his unconscious body, a sign of pain.

"Sshh . . ." She stroked the line of his shoulder blade next to the wound, though she wondered if she was talking to him or the wing. "Wait until we can figure out what to do about that. Just wait. You're hurting him."

While he'd shown no discomfort with his environment, he was wounded, and she couldn't imagine a creature of the skies would prefer to stay immersed in water indefinitely. He needed to be out of the wet.

Getting him up on the ledge proved to be enormously difficult, however. In the water, he'd been unwieldy but buoyant. Rolling him out onto the ledge required bringing him out of the water, and that transformed his body into more than two hundred pounds of heavy muscle and limp weight. Did she just a moment ago admire that smooth muscle? Now she cursed the pounds it added. And then there were those wings. One attached, one not, though the latter was clinging fast to both him and her, impeding progress so she almost also cursed the very thing that had helped her so much until now.

At last she got him onto the rock by awkwardly shape-shifting into her human form. Holding on to him precariously, she scrambled onto the rocks, scooted backward on her bottom and heaved him up with unfeminine grunts and swear words. But when it was done, he lay on the flat shelf, only his feet and calves still dipped in the water.

Since he was turned halfway on his side, that awful wound was now fully visible, making her heart thud faster. It was a jagged tear from his shoulder blade down to the base of his rib cage, revealing the gleam of bone. He needed healing. No wonder he'd been unable to maintain consciousness long.

But in the attempt to escape his pursuers, she'd taken him far beyond where healing help might be found. That realization swept her exhausted mind with renewed desolation.

She would have to catch her breath and figure that out. For now, she dragged herself closer and tried to study him without getting distracted by his great beauty or unnerved by his wounds. Or the enormity of what he was, what she'd done.

Hesitantly, she reached out and arranged his severed wing next to him. It seemed to be having more difficulty moving when fully out of the water. The feathers were at least water-logged. The wing still attached seemed to have some shedding ability that was allowing it to dry quickly, perhaps some type of internal warming mechanism of his body the other one could not utilize. Not sure what she was doing, but wanting to do something, Anna used her fingers to stroke the wet from each feather of the detached wing. Since one feather was layered over the next, it became a slow, methodical exercise, almost meditative. She let it guide her, help her steady herself so she could figure out what to do next.

Each feather gleamed after her passage, the water beading on her fingers. She kept trying to straighten the whole wing, but the more she stroked, the more it curled toward her, until she was coiled in the thing again, wrestling with it. Absurdly, she found herself almost laughing despite the seriousness of the moment. It was like it was trying to make her not worry, wrapping her up, teasing and tickling her with the feathers.

"Enough," she admonished at last, shrugging free. She turned her attention to the angel himself. Tentatively, she reached out and stroked the wet hair out of his face. Anna noted again how strong a face it was, a countenance that showed, even in unconsciousness, that the scope of his world and responsibilities was far, far beyond hers.

A firm, square jaw, held resolute even against oblivion. His lashes fanned his cheeks, drops clinging to them, so she brushed those with her fingertips, too. Most mermen didn't have beards, and apparently neither did this angel. There were fine dark threads of hair on his chest that formed a gleaming arrow down his belly to where the waist strap of the half tunic held the brief garment belted on him. Now out of the water, the red silken fabric clung to his upper thighs and groin area, nearly transparent. Angels had . . . well, they apparently had sex organs, just as most males. She didn't know why that should surprise her, after that kiss and the spiral of feelings it had detonated. A man didn't kiss like that if he didn't have a reason to *want* to kiss like that.

At the silliness of the thought, she had to suppress a hysterical giggle. She snatched her hand back when he shifted. What was she doing? This was an *angel*. A terrible warrior of the sky, one to whom they all owed absolute obedience and allegiance, awe and respect. Servants of the Light, whose will was not to be refused. She was touching his hair like some lovesick girl, feathering through it with her fingers, letting her thumb graze his temple, the prominent slope of his cheekbone. She'd just had her hand on his chest, fingering the dark, fine covering of hair, wondering what it would be like to let her fingertip follow that silken line, trace the diagonal ropes of muscles angling in the same direction at his waist.

She couldn't help but wonder, though. Did *anyone* touch him this way? He'd said there were no female angels. Surely someone loved him. Or did angels share love with another? Perhaps all their love was for the Creator, but there was something so virile about him, so . . . Her cheeks tinged as her thoughts strayed into earthy areas. He seemed made for such things. Did he mate in the skies? Was that what rainbows were, the consummations of angels? Or perhaps it was the flashes of heat lightning, the cleansing touch of fresh rain in the spring. Who knew how the love of angels would manifest itself? She was dazzled by the possibilities.

Except for the wings, anatomically her charge was a large, muscular, very impressive humanoid male form, most of it revealed by the half tunic skirt despite an overlay of hardened straps like leather lying over the fabric, which made her think of it as a uniform of sorts, a battle skirt.

Daring again, she touched his mouth. She was aware of the curve of his wing around her, the feathers touching her calf, that warm, sensuous feeling.

"Mine." She said the word softly, wondering what it would be like if it were true. Perhaps, for just this little span of time, while she could claim the excuse of needing to build her strength again, she could pretend he was. There was no one around to be offended or laugh at her astounding presumption, the ridiculous nature of even entertaining such a thought. *Mine forever.*

She well knew she would never have anyone to call hers, let alone something like an angel. Aunt Jude had said angel lore claimed everyone had a guardian angel. As she'd said it, she'd stroked Anna's hair, smiled and said, "I think yours must be very busy."

Perhaps this unexpected attraction and devotion on her part was the involuntary effect the proximity of angels created in living creatures. Maybe that was the reason for all the forbidding stories. They had to keep mere mortal creatures at a safe distance. Otherwise, angels would be mobbed by all manner of amorous creatures, like human rock stars. Anna muffled a snort.

All right. Enough was enough. The humor died out of her, an effort at bravado, she knew, because there was only one she knew who had the healing skills to help an angel. Once she'd taken a brief rest, she would have to face the harrowing fact that she must brave the Abyss again, alone, try to retrace her steps and retrieve the seawitch.

Mina alone could help him.

Four

Whadheen had he stopped feeling? How many had died? Diego, Alexander . . . Ronin. Valiant, foolish Ronin. When had he started wondering if the cause, not the symptom, should be their focus? The *Lady's* focus. When had he started nursing the poison of betrayal in his breast, locked himself behind a mask of loyalty that no longer fit well, and so had brought upon himself the curse of utter loneliness?

My Lady, why have You forsaken my heart? Or have I forsaken Yours? Have I bathed in the blood of evil so long I understand nothing? Am I becoming as lost and unclean as what I fight?

In his dreams as well as his reality, he was buried in their filth. Flashing, brown saliva-stained fangs, empty red sockets for eyes. The stench of death and despair emanating from them, for their flesh was always rotting, hanging on the protrusions of jagged bones. Like scarecrows made out of the cadavers of angels. It was an image he couldn't shake, particularly after it had become one of his nightmares. The men he'd lost over the centuries, rising and becoming that which he fought, over and over again.

Then there was the roaring. It had gotten so it took days of meditation after the battle was over for blessed silence to reign in his mind again. Saliva, vomit and blood. There was no way to get clean from it.

At least in this last battle, his men had gotten free. By the time they realized he was not with them, it had been over.

He drifted. He was not in the clouds. He was in the earth. Deep within the earth. Under water. Under an ocean. Far, far from the skies. But among the pain that was starting to return to him in full, throbbing measure, he remembered something not as unpleasant. The vague sense of it close by gave him an annoying will to return to consciousness. He would have preferred to accept oblivion.

But there'd been a gentle touch, the simple press of a female body against him, her hands guiding him. Her heartbeat fast but her eyes concerned, determined. So determined. He'd never seen such great strength in a face so fragile. Reaching down inside him with those great violet eyes, wanting him to survive, willing to do the unthinkable to get him to safety. Sacrifice. Goodness.

As an angel, he was helpless not to respond to it.

Blinking, Jonah found himself looking at the rocky, multicolored terrain of a cavern ceiling. The warm air told him he'd directed her down deep enough, but not too deep. He had no more desire than the Dark Ones to attract Lucifer's attention. The cavern was one of the far outer honeycombs of his domain. While Jonah couldn't draw healing energy from it without catching Luc's notice, at least it was dry and warm. He'd have to use another energy source. Something close at hand.

He turned his gaze, and there she was.

―――――――

SHE hadn't wanted to leave him until he woke, for she didn't want him to think he'd been abandoned. Which was a ludicrous thought, considering that even wounded, he probably wielded more power than all the creatures in the ocean combined. But as a quarter hour passed and he hadn't moved, Anna knew she might have to leave him this way regardless.

She was so deep in such thoughts that when he shifted his head, she nearly stroked back ten feet like a startled guppy. She'd been sitting on the ledge, her feet in the water, watching him. She hadn't shifted back to mermaid, not knowing if her legs would be needed.

Until he moved his head, she couldn't tell he was looking at her. Without whites to his eyes, there was no way to detect shifts. Like a shark in some ways, every thought and potential action masked. But the language was there, rich and varied, just not comprehensible to her yet.

She thought about standing, but that seemed disrespectful with him supine like this. So instead, hesitantly, she turned, bringing her legs out of the water, folding them beneath her. Bending from the waist, she touched her forehead to the ground in respect. It felt odd, for she'd never offered her allegiance to anyone. But he was an angel. From the command in his expression, even when at rest, she suspected he was perhaps an angel more important than some others. Those horrible things had certainly been determined to find him.

She tensed as she heard his arm brush against the rock. Reaching out, he fingered a tendril of her hair coiled on the ground in front of her knees. She remained still, though it did odd things to her, feeling that slight pull as his fingertips gauged its texture. Then he turned his palm over, began to wrap it, shortening it, which would by necessity require her to come closer. Oddly, it almost made her smile, because it seemed a child's trick.

But she moved forward. When she dared to raise her gaze, Anna's humor fled. He was in pain. Sweat shone on his body and there was a tremor in the hand that held her tethered. She should have gone to Mina before he woke, had something she could offer to him . . .

"Come closer, little one. I need your help, if you freely offer it."

Well, that was something she never expected to hear from an angel's lips. Bowing her head, she dared to speak, hoping either that his words gave her permission or that the assertion that her tongue would burn to ash was an old wives' tale. "I am yours to command, my lord."

Anyone who'd ever told her about angels had said they were to be obeyed as if they were the Lady themselves. She'd always gone the opposite way in her life, respecting but resisting her great-grandsire's authority, living far outside the boundaries of the insular mermaid community. But she knew she'd do whatever this being required of her. There definitely must be something magical about him. With all the trouble she caused, she could almost hear King Neptune wryly asking if he could bottle it.

The angel shook his head, even as he continued to tug her forward. "I won't compel you to do this against your will. I need energy to heal my wing, to reattach it, and it is more energy than I have."

"I'm not so little," she assured him. "I can help."

A smile twitched at his mouth. Oh, dear Lady, what a smile did to his face, even if it didn't seem to reach those dark eyes. Grasping her hand, he drew her attention down. When he placed his palm against hers, he straightened their fingers and showed her the breadth of his palm, the lengths of his digits, dwarfing her own.

"Your heart has great courage, but your body is quite small. Another of the Lady's contradictions. What's your name?"

"Anna." She tried not to stare at the way their hands looked, palm to palm like that. "My name is Anna. My lord."

"Jonah," he responded. When he tensed, his mouth tightening, she curved her fingers into his, holding his hand through the spasm.

"Please, tell me how I can help. I can't bear to see you in pain."

His head tilted, and she sensed her words had startled him.

"Do you belong to another?"

The question hurt, though not as much as the answer. "No," she said.

"Then perhaps you can help. It is simple, old magic. Did you like it when I kissed you?"

One of Neptune's guards had taken her hand once, a formality to guide her at some official function. It had been years ago, before she'd left the palace for good. That touch, one of the few she'd had in her life, had lingered in her young mind, so powerfully that she'd developed a short crush on the guard, slinking around and watching him. Nearly eight years ago, and she remembered it still, that brush of flesh against flesh.

Yes. Oh, heavens, yes. A flush rose in her cheeks as she realized he might be able to read her thoughts, since he'd spoken to her inside her mind easily enough. "I was somewhat hoping you'd forgotten about that, my lord. I hope I didn't offend you."

"I believe I should ask that, seeing that it was *me* who kissed *you*." That light smile again, but his eyes were intent upon her face. "Female energy is strong, particularly when defending what they love, or when they are aroused. You are willing to defend me; that much is obvious, as you did not heed my wisdom and leave me. I cannot wield much magic here without attracting unpleasant attention, unless I use one of the most elemental of earth magics. Joining Magic."

"Joining . . . Oh." She looked down quickly to cover the sudden widening of her eyes. Their interlaced hands suddenly seemed to have far too similar a symbolism, his long fingers resting inside the tender creases of hers. "I . . . If that will help, of course, my lord." She bit down on her tongue, willing herself not to babble.

Shifting his grip so he was holding her shoulders, he drew her down to him. His hands were confident, holding her easily as he brought her close enough to his mouth that she felt dizzy. It made her chest hurt, so full of her reaction her skin felt stretched, sensitive. She wanted him to touch every part of it. Yet she was nervous, and couldn't help the instinct to pull back. He let her, his grip sliding to her hands, and she swallowed.

"Please forgive me, my lord," she stammered hastily. He was hurting. What was wrong with her? Her body was an easy thing to give, something that meant nothing to anyone but her. "I can do this. I am not refusing you—"

"*Sshh . . .*" He shook his head, squeezed her hands. Then he let go so one could lift toward her face. Something altered in his expression as he eased his hand onto her cheek, his fingertips seeking beneath her hair. His thumb passed over her cheek. Everything in her heated under his touch, liquefied. Her lips parted despite herself, making her uncertain of what her body was doing in uncontrolled reaction to that amazing touch.

"We're going to make something very clear here, little one. Anna. I do not command this of you. I don't wish you to fear me. Others fear me. Many others. And they should." A dangerous glint to his eyes, here, then gone before she could retreat, startled. But then something wistful went through his expression. "However, I think if this world was populated by more creatures like you, I would find myself with much time on my hands."

Anna put her hand tentatively on top of his, feeling the sensitive channels between *his* fingers, an intimate discovery, a vulnerability amid such obvious power. Faith, he was an odd being. Or perhaps she was the odd one. "I was told if you spoke to an angel before being given leave, your tongue would disintegrate."

His brow lifted. "Likely a rumor spread by one of my brethren who didn't want to encourage excessive chatter."

The brief, dry humor startled her, such that she giggled before she could stop herself. Reflexively, she put her hand over her mouth, but since their hands were interlocked, she managed to move his palm over her lips.

A jaw muscle tensed, pain or something else, she didn't know.

"Taste me, little mermaid," he said quietly. "See if I am something you can create magic with."

She parted her lips, touched his skin with the tip of her tongue. Heat, if heat had a taste. That sensual warmth, like what she'd felt from his wing, coursed through her whole body at just that miniscule contact. It went to every corner, into every organ and artery, driving away the sense of being damp in her human form that the cavern's unseen heat source couldn't completely dispel.

Since his attention appeared completely riveted upon her, she knew she should feel terribly self-conscious. Here was this powerful being, probably ancient compared to her, patiently waiting for her to decide if something as insignificant as her innocence was worth sacrificing to his healing. He was in pain, she reminded herself. That was all that mattered. She could help.

Pressing her face into the span of his hand, she let his fingers graze over her brow, her nose, then her lips. Recognizing her acquiescence, he began to ease her forward.

"Do you know anything about channeling, Anna?"

She nodded. "I have been tutored in the way magic works."

It had been necessary to learn because of her unusual shape-shifting abilities, and then there had been Mina's teachings as well. Anna had badgered her into it, and then absorbed as much as the seawitch would offer her.

"When we Join, I will direct the energy to my wing and the other internal wounds I have suffered. You may feel light-headed as I do this. Don't worry if you drop into sleep for a while."

He was speaking quietly, gently, as if he were explaining the mechanics of how to swim, or to fly. She found it unsettling, because what was fluttering in the pit of her stomach was not studentlike in the least. In fact, her female pride was ruffled, an unexpected reaction that discomfited her.

Am I simply a tool?

She didn't say the words, because it was a presumptuous question. He was in need, hunted, and this would help him regain his strength.

But it hurt a little. Probably because while he was unconscious she'd let herself have that ridiculous, over-in-a-blink fantasy of being his. His only. She'd had the silly impression she was special. She knew better than that.

"What do you need me to do?" she asked quietly.

He blinked, his dark eyes somehow softening and yet getting more intense at once, reflecting the fire that drew her even closer to the flame, to feel it spread over her body the way it was spreading inside.

"Just feel, Anna," he murmured. "Just feel, and do whatever you wish to bring yourself pleasure. Take off these garments you wear."

From a shipwreck she'd recovered a silken, nearly transparent purple scarf embroidered with silver threads. She'd added her own decorations of small shells and kept the garment tied over her breasts, knotted in the middle, the ends tied behind her neck. While mermaids didn't generally have a problem with modesty, most found it more comfortable to keep their breasts bound when swimming. Because of Anna's shape-shifting ability, she preferred to have something accessible for her lower body. Therefore, she also wore a similar scarf around the upper part of her hips. When she was in human form, it just barely covered the tops of her thighs and snugged down over her backside, but it gave her the decency needed to move on land to where she could get more appropriately concealing garments as a human.

Now she reached up and tried to unknot the scarf at her neck. The knot of course had contracted with the damp, and because of her nervousness, she was fumbling it. As she opened her mouth to say something awkward and incomprehensible, he threaded his hands along either side of her throat, his gaze holding her motionless. Her hands fell away, her lips pressed together, breath caught as he efficiently untied it, brought the ends forward and uncovered her upper body for his viewing.

Her breasts were neither overly large nor too small, a pleasing size that seemed to attract the eyes of other mermen, before those eyes quickly shifted. A nice pair of breasts was not enough to overlook her other drawbacks. But his eyes did not shift. He studied them closely, such that she felt the heat that emanated from him increase. Of course, at this point she didn't know if it was coming from him, or her.

Leaving the ends of the scarf trailing over her thighs, he unknotted the lower one, pulling that one completely away so she was naked except for the upper scarf's hold just below her breasts.

She'd never had any hair on her lower body like human women did, so the fleshy petals of her sex were there, unguarded. They felt somewhat swollen, and she shifted a bit. As a merwoman, her sex was completely concealed beneath overlapping scales, so she thought she probably felt more naked right now than even a human woman would normally feel.

His hands closed on her shoulders, brought her back down to lie upon his chest, her breasts making contact with smooth, firm skin. She drew in a breath at the sensation, and something sparked in his eyes.

"You are pure goodness. That's rare, Anna. Do you know that?"

This was rare. Once in a lifetime. So instead of responding, she closed her eyes, experiencing the way his hands held her that way, so powerful and yet so gentle. It made her breasts feel fuller as well, the nipples tightening and hardening, the contact between them and the hard muscles of his chest distracting to her senses. A swirl of sea horses was fluttering in her belly now, galloping madly.

When he moved his lips to her temple, she opened her eyes to see the curve of his throat just below her own mouth. Energy already seemed to be weaving around them from that one contact, and she shuddered as his attached wing curved around her, brushing her shoulders, settling over her hips, giving her reassurance in the caress. Slowly, she turned her head, her hair brushing him. One bare inch, then another. Vividly she remembered that earlier touch of his mouth on hers when they'd been in the cold darkness together. She wanted another like that. One that dispelled every fear or moment of desolate emptiness she'd ever experienced.

Impulsively, she tipped her head up to find his mouth. He hadn't burned her to ash for presumption yet, so she was willing to take the risk. He went still beneath the press of her lips. Not unresponsive, just utterly still, letting her get the "taste" of him, as he'd said.

His mouth was so firm, and the fact it was held so still now was arousing in itself, for she sensed him holding himself back with a certain level of effort, his fingers curling on her leg as she shyly nibbled, pressed. Tasted. Dragging her lips like one of his feathers over his cheek, the side of his nose.

On instinct, she placed her hand on the top edge of his wound, just behind his shoulder. When he flinched, the reaction shuddered through her, tightening her body, rocketing through her. He needed her. Only she could do this.

Something different and more aggressive roused inside of her. The light, uncertain way she was touching him seemed inadequate to the compressed feeling in her breast. One courteous hand from a guard she didn't even know was it, everything she'd ever had. She'd never been this close to anyone in her life, and she found herself on a knife edge of not wanting to hurry a single second and yet wanting to grab hold of something with both hands and tear it apart to get to the center of it. Whatever it was Jonah was offering seemed to have the weight and glow of treasure. And she wanted him to respond in kind, with the near-violent need surging up in her now.

She *should* hurry. He was suffering. But this might be the one and only time she got to feel something like this. *I'm sorry. I just can't hurry.*

"Take your time, Anna," he whispered. "My pain is eased by watching you discover your pleasure. Seeing what you will do next."

"You can read my mind?"

"Only when you speak directly to me. I like it when you do that." His mouth firmed, creating a sterner line from cheekbone to jaw that made those sea horses in her belly do somersaults. "I'll make certain we have speed when the moment calls for it."

This was a dream; she knew it. So before she woke, she was going to make sure she had the best memory ever to carry her through her waking hours. Maybe even into eternity, if the Lady was kind and allowed favorite memories to become the afterlife.

Anna knew she'd have no problem doing this forever. When she pressed against his mouth again, something else took over. Him. Apparently he'd decided that speed wasn't the only thing he'd control.

His lips moved onto hers, hot, parting and compelling her to do the same. When her lower body clenched like the coils of an eel, she felt a warm liquid on her thighs as his tongue penetrated her mouth. The sensation of want flattened her against him. She needed to feel the hard lines of his body press against the softness of hers. Yes, this was what she'd been craving, him to touch her in a way that was anything but gentle. Her one leg had been draped over his until he shifted, tilting her over his body. Catching his shoulders for support, she gasped as his thigh pressed between her legs, against moistness, flexing so her hips responded as if by instinct, rubbing her against him. When his hand went beneath the curve of his wing to grip her body, she moaned into his mouth as his large palm molded over her buttock, squeezing, taking possession. It gave the friction an even more delicious edge.

"Holy Mother," she breathed. Her fingers dug into his muscles. It was so hot in here now. She saw the flow of it coming off their skin, illuminating the chamber further. When she pushed impatiently against him, his lips curved in a male smile that didn't lessen the flames in his eyes. The flames gave her a surge of pleasurable anxiety even as the smile balanced it, made him familiar, a being like her. Though he was so much more.

She'd thought he was a fantasy, but she knew now she'd been wrong, for he wasn't even within the grasp of her wildest imaginings.

Part of her knew she should be holding on to a scrap of reason, something that would keep her anchored in reality in the midst of this. They were doing this to heal him, after all, not because he was wildly in love with her. But the part of her that had always hungered to rush out and truly touch, truly connect with another, to feel without words or even defined thought that the other being knew her, could want and love her, was imagining so much . . . so many possibilities and what-ifs that could never be. Dreams that goaded her as high emotionally as her body was going physically.

It didn't matter. Her soul resisted all restraint and admonitions anyway. When he discarded the battle skirt, his broad shaft caressed between her legs, against the cleft of her buttocks. His jaw was held tensely, as if he was somehow trying to restrain himself, while she strained forward. She'd never done this before, but she was a creature of water, air and earth. Even fire, at the moment. Those elementals knew where they were taking her. The power of instinct overrode fear.

"Touch me," he demanded. "Let me feel your small hands."

His long form was naked, powerful. Intimidating. Regardless, she wanted to see him. Lifting up so his sex could spear forward toward his belly, she couldn't help but draw in a breath at the breadth and length of him, for she knew enough to know where that beast was going to go. Still, she curled her hand around him, wondering, wanting to feel. He was steel and, like all of him, pure heat. His eyes closed, a shudder running through his body that jolted hers. He was reacting to her touch, sharing pleasure at it. As she tightened her grip, she was amazed when he thrust reflexively through her fingers and a fluid came from the tip. She ran her thumb over it, testing the feel of it, bringing it to her lips to taste. Salty. Like the sea, but of earth as well. *What would it be like to put my mouth there, taste you . . . ?*

"By the Lady, come here." Rearing up to a sitting position, he caught her waist in both hands, despite the pain she was sure it caused when she saw the tightening of his mouth, the flinch that rippled through his muscles.

"My lord—"

"Your innocence is going to incinerate me, little wanton." He overrode her concerns with his urgency. "Put your arms around my shoulders. Don't be afraid of hurting me."

She kept a cautious embrace near the severed area anyway, but lowered her face into his neck as he locked his arms around her waist and back, and shifted. The broad head of the shaft entered her sex, past the slick folds of flesh, moving slowly in. The inexorable grace of a dragon's head penetrating a hot, moist cave where the maiden waited. But she did not tremble in fear—much. He held her close and, Great Lady, he was so big. She was like a child, how easily he held her, the breadth of his shoulders under her fingers, and yet she felt like anything but a child. She felt stirred, heated, restless. She bit the firm skin of his shoulder when he rubbed her body against his arousal, for she could not bear the feel of it without a violent response. He growled, his hands on her hips taking her down. As wet and slick as she was, she was also tight and unbroken, so the sharp pain was inevitable as he took her down in one sure, long stroke.

She cried out, interrupting his groan of pleasure, and she was sorry for it, but, Neptune, it hurt. She blinked back tears, holding him, trying not to look at him. His hands slid up her back, gentle upon her but firm as he tried to pry her loose. She held more tightly, not wanting him to see her tears. She didn't want to do anything that might make him stop. For as much as she hurt, to be touched and held this way, part of his body . . . she'd never experience anything like it, again.

Don't stop. Please.

He flattened his palm on her back, giving in to her. As he tangled his fingers in her hair, he let that other hand fall to the rise of her buttocks, applying slight pressure to hold her in place. Her internal muscles were quivering, not sure how to move or adjust. His breath became somewhat erratic, though his voice was quiet, deep, resonating in her ear. There was some powerful emotion in his voice she couldn't comprehend, but she didn't sense it was displeasure.

"I knew you were inexperienced, but I didn't expect . . . You're untouched."

More true than he knew. *Untouchable*. She nodded, her cheek rubbing against his jaw, his fall of silken hair. When her hair dried in the sun, it dried like seaweed, unless she applied oils to it, rinsed away the salt. His was now dry but as feather-like as if it were underwater. She couldn't help inhaling it, a smell of pleasurable things she didn't recognize. She imagined them to be like sky or the clouds at elevations she'd never been. Perhaps he'd even gone close to the sun, caught the rays in his hands. How close could he get without being burned? The pulsing heat of his body was setting her on fire.

When he raised his head and cradled hers in his hand a moment, bringing them eye to eye, it was as if she'd stepped inside him. Anna was sure she could feel not just what he was, but who he was. And in that moment, the heart overwhelmed awe. He was like her . . . He needed, wanted. She could feel the beat of his heart, the rush of his blood, his desire and his determination mixed. Not so different from her after all.

"You should have told me, Anna."

"I said . . . I belonged to no one."

"So you did." There was a quiet, sensual amusement in his voice, but something else, too, something that made her insides quiver even more. "I suppose that means you belong to me now. At least for this moment."

May this moment never end.

She closed her eyes, knowing she shouldn't say such a thing, but she couldn't help thinking it. She wondered if he'd picked it up as a direct plea to him. However, he merely turned her face, cupping the back of her head still. She wouldn't open her eyes, but he brushed a kiss over both eyelids.

"I'm hurting you."

"No, my lord."

"Don't lie to me," he said mildly, though there was an underlying command to it that again suggested his high rank, that he was used to issuing orders. "I'll make it better. Will you trust me?"

Straightening, he held her away from him, his gaze coursing down her face and throat to her bare breasts, the pink tips that were too taut to ignore. "Don't move. You will wish to do so, but do not. Hold very, very still."

"I . . . I don't know if I can, my lord. The way it makes me feel . . ."

That look in his eyes again, telling her somehow her words pleased him. He nodded, took the edges of her scarf and crossed them over her abdomen.

"Put your hands behind your back, your wrists crossed."

She swallowed, another herd of sea horses stampeding, this time down even lower, making something clench hard and fierce between her legs. When she obeyed, he took the ends of the scarf behind her, tied her wrists so they were held back there, the crisscrossing of the garment over her front holding her up straight before him, as she sat upon his loins.

He leaned forward, still holding her securely so she would not sway and fall. Nor could she move her hips, which, despite the pain, she had an unexpected desire to do. Especially when his back curved, the one wing stretching out to balance him and allow him to bring his face closer to her breasts. Flexing his grip, he arched her back. In that same movement, he put his mouth over the right nipple.

Sensation exploded through her. She bucked instantly against the restraint, making it even more intense. What was this pleasure, liquid pleasure, just rushing all through her from that one place? From the wetness of his mouth on her skin, the firm suckling of it, drawing things tight, making her want to move. Oh, she had to move; it was unbearable not to . . . but he'd said . . .

He kept doing it, flicking her with his tongue, suckling, drawing her deep, easing up to lick, then biting again, making her cry out. When he moved to do it to the other one, she moaned, a breathy sound.

"Do not move, little one," he reminded her harshly, but she so wanted to disobey. The pain between her legs was dissolving into pure hot lava, and yet if it was possible she thought he'd gotten larger inside her. Wetness was spilling on her thighs.

"It will build inside you like the fiercest storm," he muttered against her. "The power of your desire rising over all else, until I will be just an instrument in the gale you've created, sweet mermaid."

Dipping lower, he gripped her buttock again. His fingers squeezed, their length making it possible to tease the cleft, which caused a shudder. She'd never imagined how sensitive the nerves were there. The throbbing pain ebbed like a fast-retreating tide as he suckled her like an infant, a curious image for such an erotic feeling, but it was as if the two images had a special power. Nourishing the man, nourishing the child . . . She hummed deep in her throat. She wanted to move in rhythm with his hands, because the pain had become something more than pain. He was doing marvelous things to her nipple, to her whole body. When he began to move her on him at last, she moaned in relief.

But it was still excruciating, a slow rise and fall, building, building, bringing an explosive heat closer and closer. Raising her, then taking her back down again, letting her feel the movement of him against her, inside and out. She was wet so deep inside now the passage was easy, even as he stretched the virgin opening, let her feel the way of it. And ah, Great Lady, the way he had her bound so she could only watch what he was doing to her, see the sway and quiver of her body and the way his eyes watched her every movement . . .

The spirals of energy closed in, reminding her there was another purpose to this. She tried to focus.

"I'll take care of it, Anna." His voice was a husky growl against her flesh. "Just let it build. I'll channel it."

Thank Goddess. She couldn't think.

The feathers of his attached wing rippled as if from a gust, fire flickering in the corners of her eyes. Lapping over the ledge, the water surged restlessly. A wavering energy crackled in the air around them, heat waves. They turned, swirled, closed in on them.

His biceps flexed, powerful and sure. That wonderful ridged head stroked inside her, to the point she was gasping in rhythm to her movements, keening low in her throat, a plea. Deep in, slow, tormenting drags out, and back in again. Visualizing the movement in her mind was as erotic and stirring as the actuality of it. Then there was the stimulation of his hands on her buttocks, the way he pressed the globes of flesh against the hard muscle of his thighs as he pushed her down, harder now. Making the flesh of her breasts wobble more freely, which seemed to arouse him further.

Taking one hand back to tangle in her hair again, he held her, controlling her movement as he began to thrust with consistent strength. But he was still holding back. She knew it because his body was quivering, every muscle drawn taut. His pain was part of their mutual pleasure.

"Don't . . . hold back, my lord," she managed over a moan. "I will be . . . all right."

"Not until you . . ." He didn't finish, instead renewing his assault on her breast with his mouth, flicking at the nipple with his tongue, firm lips moistening, drawing on her skin. Her fingers dug into the bonds around her wrists.

"What . . ."

"Let go," he growled. "Trust it. Trust me."

She knew what he was referring to, even if she didn't know what it was that surged from between her legs, rippled through her body, seized her in a paroxysm of sensation that took away all her control. Her head fell to his shoulder, pressing hard against the bone. Banding his arm around her, he held her on a fixed point in the universe as everything else spun faster and shattered. She let his command sweep over her. The mental images of what they looked like doing this drove her with as much force as his body. Fire racing, water surging . . .

The sea rushed up the rock ledge, splashed against her like sun-kissed surf blown in by the wind. The energy built to a great peak around them, the wind of it beginning to sing. When he briefly raised his head, his hair blew over his lips. She kissed them desperately, feeling the texture of the strands and his mouth at once. Their flesh was the only anchor to earth as this spiraling feeling tightened all her muscles, stroked her taut in his powerful arms and set off a series of spasms throughout her body, starting at the joining point between them.

Joining Magic.

She screamed with it. When he yanked her binding free, her arms came forward to grip his shoulders. Her hips slammed down, demanding more. For the first time in her life she was free, so very free, and yet she'd handed all control over to him. It made perfect sense in this perfect moment.

Her cry was as savage as that of the first creature who'd ever walked the earth, her head tipped back, fingers raking at his skin. She rode the wave of the passion as if she could see the whole world from the crest of it, and the view was enough to destroy her. She would explode into a million pieces, become part of the stars, the drops of the ocean, and she wouldn't care, because this was the answer to the ache of loneliness. This was the answer to everything.

He growled, just as primal, responding to her fierce need. Surging into her like a battering ram, he filled her completely, tight, hard, holding her. Anna didn't care about pain. She welcomed it, wanted to bleed for him and him only. Dramatic, romantic nonsense she nevertheless meant with her whole self. He'd given her this, the greatest happiness she'd known in her short life. It didn't matter that it might give him the ability to control the worst moment of her life as well. Control no longer mattered.

The elemental reactions gathered, swirled around them. His eyes glimmered with green sparks, blue and white flame. Some red as well. As the climax took her higher, higher, she was vaguely aware of the broken wing rising, aligning with his back, the energy they'd raised cycling into smaller spirals in that area. It was roaring through her veins, making her want to soar.

Because she sensed he was somehow still cushioning her from the full effect, protecting her, she fought through her own desire. "You need . . . all of it, my lord. Do not spare me. Let me . . . help heal you."

Then the power crashed over her. The blue light of his clotted blood became flame that speared out from the wound and blinded her. When he cried out, she heard the agony mixed with the throaty response to his own release. She clung to him, working her hips on him, emulating the motions he'd taught her, stroking him, trying to take the pain away, feeling the energy rushing through them both.

It thundered and roared, tossed her loose from all her preconceived notions of what her first time coupling with a man would be like. It went much higher, high enough that there was room for only one seed of doubt to mar the moment.

The reminder that the moment *was* more than her offering herself to a man. This was magic. For him. For his healing.

Just magic.

Five

JONAH considered the mysterious being lying in the curve of his arm, sleeping with all the uncomplicated exhaustion and moving trust of a child. Her sensual response had likewise been a curious mixture of shy innocence and the reckless, unbridled enthusiasm of what he'd called her. A wanton.

He'd been weak. Terribly weak. He'd chosen earth magic that could be concealed from all but Lucifer's most in-depth probe, because he had a disturbing need not to be found. Even so, he might have been able to make the magic work with one powerful kiss. He'd thought about trying it that way first, but her response had compelled him to take it far beyond that. He rationalized it by telling himself he'd not even been sure if the Joining Magic they could raise would be enough to aid him, but as her pinnacle rose, it had overwhelmed him like a summer storm. It wasn't just earth magic, but far more. Air, water, fire . . . they'd all surrounded him, infused him. In the center of that surprise, there'd been the overwhelming, completely unexpected response of his body to hers. Of his soul to hers, if he wanted to be honest. He'd wanted to bury more deeply into her, roll her over and take her the way he would if he was whole and there was no purpose to their Joining except their own desire. Her body beneath him, soft thighs spread, arms reaching, clinging as he drove into her. Faith, he was hardening again, just thinking of it. What was the matter with him?

He'd hurt her. He brushed fingertips over the smears of

blood that remained on her thighs. He'd taken her innocence, just taken it, no matter how gentle he'd tried to be. That should have been the right of her handfast, her mate. A frown crossed his brow at the thought of that. She said she belonged to no one. She was too young to be despairing about such a thing, but he'd detected the note of it in her voice, nonetheless. Not the dramatic despair of one who'd experienced the death of puppy love and was too young to realize love would come and go at this age. No, a serious, deep despair, as if her soul was old enough to know too much truth about what love was, and what it wasn't.

Merpeople were flocking creatures with a driving need to socialize with their own kind. But only their own kind. Not only did they have a staunch, conservative aversion to mixing in the affairs of non-mermaids, they also avoided dabbling in magic.

And while mermaids accepted sex as a natural act, they didn't do it indiscriminately. She'd given him her innocence either because her heart was that noble, or because she didn't feel it was a gift with any worth except to a wounded angel who needed it as an ingredient to a healing spell.

He blew gently on her cheek. Her lashes fluttered, her eyelids crinkling. When she turned her face into his chest, an unexpected smile curved his lips. An enigma. A mermaid who could take human form, who was an exceptional channel for magic . . . who was brave beyond her years, inquisitive in a way unusual for her cautious kind. Who also appeared to be quite alone in the world.

Her features were so fine, small. He put his finger up beside the line of her nose, just to judge, and it seemed the tip of his finger would almost cap it. Her lips were a tiny bow, and despite himself, he imagined what it would be like to stretch them . . .

While he knew human mythology suggested angels were above such things, that myth was not based on the warrior class of seraphim. The nourishing energy they required made carnality a vital part of their strength, one of the easiest and fastest ways to replenish their powers. Many of the humanoid races freely offered themselves, and he was all too aware that many felt they had no right to refuse an angel. While he tried not to take advantage of that, fortunately, not many had the desire to resist.

But as the years had passed, there was a lack of intimacy to such couplings that bothered him in a way he didn't care to examine too closely. He'd begun to prefer recharging by going into seclusion, drawing from the elements, a slower, meditative process, but one that met his needs on several different levels.

A twinge interrupted his musings, reminding him that he needed to be focusing on the problem with his wing. While it had reattached to his body with the magic, something was wrong. The fuse was not as strong as it should have been after such a powerful energy raising. His body possessed nowhere near the strength it needed to bear him aloft and back to the clouds, though his strength still far exceeded that of a humanoid male. And most definitely that of one little mermaid.

She had trusted him far more than he deserved. As Jonah gazed down into her face, all that waited for him outside of this cave dimmed. While he knew he was somewhat consciously choosing to push it all away, he had no problem getting lost in the contemplation of her body and ignoring whatever it was that had gone wrong with the healing.

He'd fought the Dark Ones for well over a thousand years, and they'd be around for another hundred millennia. He could take a day. Maybe two.

He wanted to savor her again, beast that he was. Joined with her, he'd felt something he hadn't felt in so long, so long he couldn't even remember what it was called. At the moment of pinnacle, he'd almost felt purified, the fires of passion burning past the crust of blood and loss on his soul to find there was still something worth saving beneath. Something worth the trust she displayed now, curled up against him.

As she started to stir, he gathered her to him and turned, putting her beneath him. Her lashes rose, reflecting a moment of sleepy confusion, her hands coming to rest on his shoulders, as light as her fins when she had a tail. He remembered their brush against his legs when she'd carried him through the water endlessly, even as her strength flagged. One of her fins had been split. Things had been hazy then, but he remembered more now. How much she had risked as the Dark Ones closed in. If they'd taken her, they would have tormented her, twisted her soul and drained it. Then they would have torn her apart. His fingers tightened on her delicate flesh.

A wistful smile coursed across her face. "You weren't a dream," she whispered.

Just like that, the softness of her breath touching his mouth, and Jonah knew he had to be inside of her again. If he didn't know her kind well, he'd think her an incubus. Except she'd helped heal him, with an amazing reservoir of power she likely didn't realize was exceptional. Or did she? He had much to learn of this one.

His hardened organ was nudging at her channel, the broad head between the tender lips of her nether mouth. A sweet, warm cunt, so wet and pleasing to him. Her eyes became wider, her lips parting to moisten, making his cock flex against her.

"Would you take me again?" He'd meant it to sound courtly, gentle, but it came out as a hoarse demand. He needed her, needed to be in her with an urgency that seemed as violent as the world in which he normally existed. He was approaching this almost the way he did a battle—conquer, overwhelm, immerse himself, until the only thing he was conscious of was the goal. The blood, the slashing . . . bodies shoved out of the way to get to the next one . . . While he pushed the disturbing images away, he couldn't prevent the tremor that went through his muscles.

Her fingers touched the ends of his hair, moved down over the skin stretched taut over his shoulders. That touch soothed, even as it aroused. Steadying him, while the urgency to be inside her rose even higher. When the tremor grew, like an electric current humming between them, her brow creased, her soft eyes growing softer.

"My lord does not need to ask. He may simply command."

She was *teasing* him, a cautious smile in her voice, a sparkle in those violet irises.

"I . . ." He fought past the base desire to do exactly that. "I will not take that choice from you."

"But you said I belong to you. And if that is true"—that tempting voice again, and by the Resurrection Trumpet, he was drowning in her eyes, in the light moisture of her lips, the hint of her tongue as she spoke—"then you can command

me. I submit my will to your care, and trust you fully with it."
Her eyes were serious now, her young face wholly intent. "It
is my wish for it to be so."

Holy Mother, where had such a creature come from? Without need of magic at the moment, he was Joining with her for
pleasure only. His sense of honor whispered that he needed to
make that clearer, give her the chance to demur at least. But at
her tremulous smile, he let his honor be damned and the gentle
light of her eyes be his consent.

"Then lift your legs, Anna, and lock them around my body.
Grip me hard, for I wish to plunge deeply. Are you sure?" At
her shift of gaze, he put a hand to her face, made her look at
him. "If I am your master, then you will not lie to me or hide
your pain."

"I am somewhat sore, my lord."

"Then my plunge will be gentle." Still holding her face so
he could keep her clear gaze upon him, watch every shift of
her expression, he started to ease in. Finding her tissues moistened, he was reassured at the proof their words had aroused
her the way his hands and mouth could and would do again.

Deeper. Deeper. Like the Abyss, only this was an oblivion
he would welcome. He knew his size and knew he'd gone far
enough when she tensed, but then she startled him by tightening her legs, lifting and trying to impale herself to the hilt,
her hands digging into his shoulders, her features taking the
pain, her eyes closing as she held on to him. Increasing the
grip of her arms around his shoulders, she buried her face into
his neck, her lips against his skin. He felt the feathers of her
eyelashes, like tiny wisps of down.

"Sshh . . ." His lust was nearly unbearable, but her desperation was greater. Easing her back, he settled his hand on
her throat to hold her there, stroking her, making her chin
lift. "It's not a race, little one. Not a challenge." Turning his
hand, he ran his knuckles over her breast, watched the nipple
tighten, watched her bite her lip. She contracted on him, and
he groaned.

When she reached up to him again, he couldn't bear it. He
had to pin her wrists above her head. Still she arched, pressing her open mouth to his chest, taking bites and licks, and her
wetness increased. Gliding deeper, he slid home, and there

was no stiffening this time as her body took him with a croon of pleasure from her lips.

Her tissues rippled around him, the more frenetic and unfocused press of her mouth against his chest warning him.

"That's it . . . Let me hear you . . ."

Gasps became soft noises that built in volume until she was crying out, her head back and mouth open, eyes glazed in a way that pushed him toward release quickly. She was not climaxing . . . She was far too sore for that. But it was as if the pleasure of feeling his every stroke was giving her tiny spasms she responded to with her voice, the writhing of her hips, and in turn shoved him harder and faster toward climax. As his thrusts pushed her along the flat rock that was their bed, he knew it couldn't be comfortable, but he was driven by the thought that if he plowed deeply enough, he could find the center of himself. As if somehow she held it deep in her womb . . .

In the end, he made sure she did climax, holding himself back until her release, reaching between them to find that tiny but powerful clitoral flesh, stroking and teasing until she was writhing, her eyes wide and wondering, mouth opening with satisfying gasps. The searing liquid heat of it arched her up further, produced a scream he swallowed in his mouth, letting it reverberate in his throat, the tightness in his chest. He sucked her voice into him like breath.

When they came down, he had her face framed in his hands and her tears were on his thumbs, tiny jewels. Pressing his lips against each one, he breathed hard on her flushed skin, trying not to crush her, but needing to feel the full length of her beneath him, every ripple and shift.

"You're all right?"

"Yes," she whispered. "I'm just happy."

For once.

The young woman didn't say the words, but Jonah read them in the quivering of her body. Again he felt a sense of shame for taking advantage of her innocence. Her tears humbled him to the point that he couldn't speak.

When she dashed them away self-consciously, he rose off her, taking her hand to draw her up to a sitting position. Easing down beside her, he was careful of the juncture of his wing, which was still tender to movement. Her brow creased in concern at his grimace.

"Are *you* all right?"

"It's healing."

"But didn't the magic we raised . . ."

"Yes," he assured her. "It just needs more time."

Again, he noted his own curious ambivalence about that. But if he couldn't fly, there was no reason to leave this place.

"Do you . . . eat?" Anna didn't like the sudden bleak distance in his expression, as if he were walking alone in an empty place where no soul should have to walk. So she blurted out the question, bringing him back to her.

At his odd look, she gave an awkward smile. "I wasn't sure if I needed to bring you food. I know little of angels, my lord, except that they rule the sky."

The angel considered her a moment. "The only food we eat is what this world would call manna, but I absorb energy in various ways." A flicker of his gaze over her still-flushed body told her one of the ways, made the flush deepen.

He smiled, reached out and twined a lock of her hair around his fingers, tugging on it. "If you tell me more of what you know of angels, I'll tell you what I know of mermaids. We'll find out if we've both been misinformed."

Anna lifted a shoulder. "I don't want to offend you with my ignorance, my lord." Actually, she just wanted him to keep talking so she could drink her fill of his voice, his expression, the long length of his body lying bare before her. There was an accent in his words, one she'd never heard. The syllables were rolled, but drawn out with a rich slowness that made it a sensual pleasure just to hear him talk. And wouldn't he think her mad if he heard that thought?

"Anna." His dark eyes drew her gaze reluctantly to his face. "I've been inside your body. I've kissed your breasts, felt the wetness of your lovely cunt on my fingertips. Goddess willing, I'll taste it on my lips sometime in the near future. So far, your ignorance has brought me nothing but intense pleasure."

She cleared her throat and tried to look like she'd taken his words in stride. When in fact her skin quivered from the spasm of sensation rocketing through the very area he'd just described putting his mouth on. "All right, then. I've heard angels can seduce any species to do their will."

"That one is false. Angels have no more seductive abilities than the males of any other species." He gave her a lofty look. "So I must be exceptional."

She opened her mouth, shut it. "My lord," she said stiffly.

He lay back on both elbows with a chuckle. His long, muscular body was still gleaming with sweat from their coupling as he rested inside the curve of one wing to favor the other. Despite his arrogance, she couldn't get enough of looking at him. Even as she had an outrageous desire to pinch him.

"You're not used to guarding your tongue, are you, little one?"

"No," she offered that easily enough. "Nep—my great-grandsire says I tend not to think before I speak."

"So what were you going to say, before you had your rare moment of reticence?" When she shifted her gaze to study the cave walls, the lines of the dragon's wings, he drew her attention back to him by reaching out and caressing her thigh, trapping the ends of her hair between his fingers. "Anna, if you don't tell me, I shall proceed to tell you, in great detail, many other reasons why you don't offend me, until you turn the color of a rose."

She narrowed her glance at him. "I was going to say you're exceptional only in your arrogance, my lord."

Oh, Goddess, she should have known better than that. The smile that spread across his features, which took away the shadows in his eyes and some of the pain lines around his mouth, was enough to make her lose the capacity for speech altogether.

"Let us make a pact, you and I. You will speak your mind to me, and I won't be offended. In fact the only way you could offend me was if you submitted to me because you felt overwhelmed, as if you had no choice." His expression sobered then, his mouth setting in the hint of a stern line that perversely ran shivers through her lower belly.

"I did feel overwhelmed, my lord. As if I had no choice. But when you looked at me, even the way you're doing now . . ." *I didn't ever want free will again. Only you.*

Oh, heavens. She'd said that directly to him, hadn't she?

"Anna." He stroked her skin with his fingertips so she had to look at him, despite her self-consciousness. "You only make me desire you more when you say and think such things. Come, stop worrying so much. It's just us here. We don't have to be who we normally are. Tell me something else you've heard about angels."

For some inexplicable reason that bothered her, as if this was simply an illusion to him, an interlude with no connection to reality. But of course, hadn't she herself thought this could be just a dream? She pushed it away. "There are no baby angels."

"True and false. Reproduction is important, but not the essential purpose of sex. Creation is, whether it's creation of a spiritual connection, dissemination of energy, a healing ritual to remake flesh, or creating new life. Angels often use Joining as a way of grounding ourselves after battle. And that's just a few of its purposes. There are no baby angels, no. But there are *necrilim*, those born of an angel and another species, usually human. They are rare, but exist."

Carry the child of an angel. An astounding thought. One she didn't even dare entertain.

"It is purposed when it is done," he said, a gentle tone to his voice. "An angel may choose to release his seed or not, when he reaches pinnacle."

"And you . . . ?" She blushed. "Forgive me, my lord."

"It's your body and your right to ask. No, I didn't. It would have been poor gratitude to take advantage of you like that, wouldn't it?"

In fact, it might not be unpleasant at all to have something to call her own, that might love her back and be a permanent memory of this amazing day. A day that would mean nothing at all to him the moment he left this cave. The darkness such a thought brought to her also brought to her the significance of what it would have meant to her if she had found herself with child. The beginning of the end. But the end was coming regardless, wasn't it? Some things were within her control; many things were not. The challenge of her life had always been figuring out which was which.

He studied her. "Little one." When she looked away, he

grasped a tendril of her hair, started wrapping it around a knuckle, tugging her body inexorably forward. "Look at me."

Anna couldn't. Wouldn't, but he was going to make it impossible, for he was winding, winding. She was going to have to wrap her hair up when she was around him—she could see that now. She tried bracing her arms, but then he simply reached out and pulled one of her wrists from beneath her, toppling her onto his chest. His hand still tangled in her hair, that arm still around her back, he used the other to cup her face, her chin, lift it.

She noted the cut on his face was gone, as was the mottled bruising on his skin. Only the worst wound, the wing, seemed to be causing any tenderness to him. His healing ability was astounding. When she finally stared into his eyes, they burned, and suddenly she knew angels *could* shatter something mortal. Burn out their eyes, take their tongues. Take their very will to live with just the power of their presence. His gaze was so dark, she felt she could fall into the heart of him; only it wasn't like the fearful cold of the Abyss. This was the darkness of being wrapped in something warm and safe, something one would never want to leave again.

"It was magic, Anna. But it was not *just* magic. You understand?"

"You promise?" It was out before she could call it back, knowing it for what it was. The question of an innocent, a child. But the woman could handle whatever came, if the child got the right answer to that one question.

It seemed to startle him, for something flickered in the depths of his eyes, but then his grip tightened on her face and he leaned in, so close she had to close her eyes, her lips quivering as he brushed them with his own.

"I promise. And an angel does not promise what is not true. Ever."

She nodded, eyes still closed. She could live with that. Over time she'd learned that small things could actually be big things, like a rock randomly coming to rest where it would anchor a much larger boulder. Those two words were what counted. Not what came after or changed later. This moment in time was inviolate, that one small gesture locking its truth in place for all time.

So she made herself smile against his fingers, opened her eyes to look at his mouth, his face. "I knew angels Joined with other creatures for energy. I didn't know they did it for pleasure as well."

The amusement that remained in his gaze made him appear mortal. Approachable. "All creatures feel desire, and love. Even arrogant creatures like angels. There are a few . . . They take Full Submission. It means they completely submit to the service of the Lady, and they pledge everything to Her. Their bodies, minds and souls. They don't eat, drink or seek carnal pleasure. She is the sum total of all they want, serving Her."

"Like priests, or monks."

He nodded.

"But I thought all angels serve Her."

"We do. But it is much like . . ." He frowned, thinking a bit, but then Anna got it.

"Like the knights of old, who fought for the Church, versus the priests. They serve in different ways."

"How do you know about that?"

She shrugged. "I've spent time in the human world. I've studied their history."

"So have I." The shadows were back in his eyes again, the dangerous set to his mouth that made him seem so formidable. But he regarded her curiously. "Won't someone be missing you? Your family? Your great-grandsire?"

"I don't stay in one place for long. They're used to my absences."

"So no one looks after you."

"I look after myself," she said with a trace of irritation. "I got you here."

"Despite my command to leave me."

"It wasn't a command," she protested.

Jonah snorted. "It most certainly was, and you ignored it."

She rose, went to the water. For a moment he thought she was going to dive, metamorphose into her other self and leave him there. Rising, he came up behind her, not yet touching her but standing just at her back. Feeling her hair brush his chest, his abdomen, he gazed down over the top of her head at the swell of her breasts, the pink tips so recently suckled. One was abraded from the fierceness with which he'd laved her, and that enduring mark gave him an odd sense of satisfaction.

"I'm not angry with you. I just didn't want you hurt on my behalf. I am grateful for your help." It was somewhat of a lie, he knew. The darkness had been welcoming, quiet. Even through the pain there'd been a lure to it that had almost made him want to forcibly resist her help.

But she'd been persistent. Thinking about it now, he realized it had reminded him of the presence of the Lady. That determined reassurance that spread from the heart into the rest of the body, bringing a calming peace. Creating a desire to be closer to Her, to step inside Her essence and never leave. When he'd surfaced enough to realize it was a mermaid, risking her life to take him to shelter, it had surprised him. Also thinking about it now, it angered him. In a sea full of creatures stronger, more capable, they'd allowed one young girl to risk her life and sanity for him.

He needed to send her away. She would be in danger here. He couldn't let his weaknesses cause her further harm.

"My lord?" Her voice was soft, her breath on his skin. He had both arms around her, one across her breasts, his forearm pressed to her beating heart, the other wrapped over her waist, holding her against him. His one undamaged wing had swept around and covered her in front, cocooning her. His feathers brushed their toes.

"Yes, Anna?"

She pressed her temple against his jaw, an unexpected gesture of comfort. After a pause, she spoke hesitantly. "I've seen your kind once or twice. At first, I thought I was seeing the wind moving the clouds under the eye of moonlight, but then it was like the glitter of green light that ripples over the sand's surface when you walk upon it. You know, where the weight of your foot ignites the creatures that make the light, telling you they're there and not illusion?"

When he nodded, she continued. "I was floating alone on the surface when they shimmered through the sky. Then they came down lower. Two or three of them."

He could feel her smile pull against his jaw as she recalled the beauty of it. "When the gulls play in the sky, they make it look so effortless, but this eclipsed even that. They danced, the three of them, whirling, twisting, as if they were able to ride the air and yet bend it at once so they could do the most remarkable things."

"Windwalkers," Jonah responded. "They guide the air currents. Alter the tide flow, send seed to the ground, scatter the ashes of things that need dispersal. They are happy creatures."

Apparently, something in his voice turned her regard to him. Under the scrutiny of those large violet eyes with silver rims around the irises, Jonah felt as if he'd been turned inside out. And the view was not pretty.

"There are others," he said gruffly. "Messengers. Healers. Guardians. Watchers."

"What kind of angel are you, my lord? If angels have so many tasks, what is yours?"

I am an angel of death. But he didn't say that. He was afraid if he did, something violent would come forth from him.

He brought destruction. The blood and ash of those he vanquished were part of what the Windwalkers dispersed, before they touched the earth. Swirled away into nothingness, as if the Dark Ones he destroyed never existed. Whereas the bodies of the angels they killed fell heavily to earth and had to be incinerated after the fact.

"What is your purpose, my lord?" she repeated, her head cocked, eyes curious.

Jonah withdrew his touch. "I am not a Windwalker," he said.

Walking away from her, he squatted, naked and pensive, at the water's edge, his functional wing automatically spreading to balance him as the other stayed in a protective half fold. "You've given me some of what you know of angels. Let me give you something I know about mermaids." His gaze rose and pinned her. "A mermaid can't shape-shift unless she is a descendant of the royal house of Neptune, from the bloodline of one particular daughter, cursed by her love for a mortal human."

Anna became very still, and the energy in the cave pressed in even more closely, making it harder for her to breathe. "That is true," she said at last.

He nodded. "It's time for you to go, little one. I cannot

endanger one of Neptune's children further. Particularly not one I'm sure he values like a jewel in his trident for her courage."

She blinked. "I don't understand."

Oh, of course you do, she told herself. *It was just magic to heal him, you ridiculous child. He's an angel. He's done with you now.*

Jonah rose, the shadow of his body making her traitorous limbs shudder in the remembrance of him on top of her, surrounding her as she held him. A fleeting impression, so fleeting she'd call it illusion except she'd learned long ago she couldn't permit herself that kind of cynicism and keep her sanity.

"It's too hazardous for you to be here if the Dark Ones are still seeking me. You've done more than anyone could have asked, and certainly more than I deserve."

She was not going to make a fool of herself. Anna looked down to see his fluids trickling down her leg, her body still flushed and swollen from his attentions. It almost overwhelmed her, then and there. She closed her hands into fists at her side, trying to hold it in.

"If there's nothing more you need, then, my lord." Forcing herself to swallow, she looked up and met his gaze squarely, though she had to firm a trembling chin. She could see understanding in his eyes, regret. If it masked pity for her naïveté, she might just die. "How long must you stay here before you can surface?"

"Awhile," he said vaguely. Then he turned away, bending to pick up the battle skirt that had been carelessly tossed aside in their passion. He wrapped it around his hips, belted it, though somehow the concealing garment just emphasized the sensual beauty of his body. If anything, it made him even more appealing, snugging in across his hips, the hem stopping so high on his bare, muscular thighs. Was her moisture on him? Of course it was.

Anna focused past it, tried to concentrate on a niggling sense of wrongness about his response, something that was pushing through her personal concerns. "Awhile, my lord?"

"Aye. I'll rest here a bit, little one. Perhaps more than that.

It's a quiet place. A good place." His gaze drifted to the spot where they'd lain. "Already with good memories."

While she was gratified a miniscule amount, her gaze traversed the damp cavern with its bare traces of heat coming from the fissures. It seemed lonely, barren, with the bones of the dragon and nothing else for company. But she was not an angel. What did she know of them other than what she'd learned in the past several hours?

What did she know of anything? She was hardly more than a child to one such as him, anyway. Except for those few moments when she'd been far more than a child.

To suit his purpose.

Six

Dᴀᴠɪᴅ sat cross-legged on a bank of clouds, staring down at the mist drifting across the alternating green and blue terrain of the earth's surface. Mostly, he focused on the blue area. He'd made the clouds solid beneath him in order to support his weight. He tried to keep that in the back of his mind, despite his other urgent concerns. He didn't want to have his thought flow interrupted by the sudden yank of gravity as he let his attention wander and found his seat had become like the diaphanous waves rolling below in translucent clusters.

He felt Lucifer approach, settle next to him, his black wings brushing David's carefully folded white ones in an affectionate greeting before Luc tucked them in and squatted, his toes curling onto a cloud sphere that formed at his behest and fit just beneath the curve of his feet as if he were an eagle atop the small gold ball of a flagpole.

"Show-off," David said absently, though the worry line of his brow didn't ease.

"I need not your opulent throne, youngling," Lucifer said, casting a glance at David's self-made chair. "But I suspect you've been holding vigil here awhile."

"Have you heard anything?"

"He is below the Line. That's all we know. He fought off an exceptional number of Dark Ones. His captains thought he'd gotten free with them. They are much distressed about it.

He was separated from the others. It was a fierce fight. Their numbers were great."

"Can't She . . ." David's voice trailed off as Lucifer looked toward him, dark eyes tinged with red. He had long black hair to his waist, his lean and strong body emanating power, great age and an intimidating level of wisdom he could quickly transform to censure if he felt it was warranted.

Since David had become an angel, he'd learned that the mysterious Lucifer was neither the fallen angel nor the horned specter of evil suggested by human religion. While that was reassuring, he *was* in charge of Hell, and no one crossed the Lord of the Underworld lightly.

"You know She will not offer help below the Line unless it is asked in a true manner. Even under the most terrible duress, he remains one of Her generals. Her Prime Legion Commander. All he would have to do is direct the merest wisp of a thought to Her and She would answer. If needed, She would send Raphael immediately to heal him. He has not called. Either he has no need of aid, or he is dead."

David lifted a shoulder. "The Dark Ones don't think he's dead. They're seeking him still."

"I know." For a moment, there was a grimness around Lucifer's mouth. "He and his angels, including you, defeated many, but there are always some that escape and must be hunted."

"If they capture a live angel, use his energy—"

"Jonah would destroy himself before he'd allow that to happen, no matter what his state," Luc said firmly. "You are worrying too much."

"As are you," David murmured. "Else you wouldn't have joined me here." He looked down at the blue patterns of the oceans. Even at this height, he could detect their movement, the vast deepness. "He drew some of them away from me, purposefully, to protect me."

"You are still learning, while he can handle many."

"I think he could obliterate them all with just his will," David said slowly, "but perhaps it was his state of mind that struck him from the sky."

Lucifer shifted to look at him. Like most angels, he and

Jonah had never been men, their souls part of the seraph from the beginning. Whereas David was a made angel, no more than thirty earth years. He'd been a human, his mortal life lost as a teenager, but his soul had been called to the service of the angels, as certain pure souls were, rather than to reincarnation.

Jonah had seen centuries of battle and Lucifer . . . well, his purpose was something different, but he'd certainly been around quite a while. However, David's quiet levelheadedness and his lack of ego made Lucifer give weight to the young angel's words.

"You have noticed his recent state."

"We spend time together, and he was getting . . . quieter. Sometimes I sensed something almost like despair in him." David met Lucifer's eyes. "He was lonely. Adrift. Luc, angels mate, don't they?"

Lucifer's gaze sharpened. "They do," he said cautiously. "Balance often comes in pairs, David. But time is far more relative for us, so for most angels it is centuries before the urge comes. We are all males, so those who desire females find their other halves outside of our species. And angels mate only once, no matter the life span of whom they choose."

"Like swans," David said thoughtfully.

"I've never thought to compare Jonah to a swan. Perhaps a rather irascible hawk. Ah, to Hades with it." Lucifer directed his piercing gaze down toward the sea. "I've known him a very long time. You have known him a very short time. And yet we both love him well, I think."

Reaching out, he pulled on a handful of feathers, nearly toppling David from his perch. "Come, chick. Do you feel like taking a swim?"

David rose, steadying his stance, his wings spreading out. "I do."

"Then let us go see what the ocean can tell us about our missing brother."

———

Joining Magic was just a tool. A manipulative, diabolical tool that drew out every ounce of energy from her soul and mind, creating the illusion that it formed a permanent binding to another. Now Anna knew why so many females had such sad crushes on the first male they lay with. Like she did.

It seemed the farther away she swam, the more she felt the need to return to him. No matter he'd all but brusquely ordered her to leave, and he certainly hadn't asked her to check with Mina about anything.

She told herself she was going to Mina to find out if there was anything else she should do to heal the angel, get him back into the skies, out of that cave. Beyond where she could reach him physically, which might help banish him from her mind.

And fish will fly.

In the odd order of things, she considered Mina her closest friend, more like family than the many cousins she had. Of course, Anna was beginning to suspect she had a weakness for believing relationships to be far more than the object of her affections did. Most likely, Mina had *never* thought of her as a sister. Maybe not even as a friend. But then, Mina maintained her solitude the way a skeleton guarded internal organs, single-mindedly determined in its function.

While at a more endurable level of water, Mina's home was still in the upper reaches of the Abyss. The forbidding pit was a perfect neighbor, to Mina's way of thinking. Most creatures, except those that lived in its darkness, avoided any prolonged proximity to it.

As she looked for that cave opening, Anna let herself rise out of the Abyss cautiously. She'd felt such a squeezing sense of relief when light began to permeate and she could once again see, recognize her surroundings. She was also relieved that she didn't feel the presence of the Dark Ones. Of course, without Jonah, she suspected they would ignore her. Much as angels would on a normal day. Just an inconsequential water creature, not significant in the elaborate machinations of Heaven and Hell.

Her bruised feelings couldn't deny that, at the last, Jonah had seemed reluctant for her to go. When she'd moved into the water and shifted back to her mermaid form, he'd told her how to get back to the main throat of the Abyss. Made her repeat the tunnel directions to him several times, apparently to assure himself she would not get disoriented again.

"If the Dark Ones are still out there, you'll feel them. And if you feel them, you go the other way. I forbid you to worry about me. I can handle myself, now that you've helped me heal my wing."

Though he himself had admitted the wing was not yet ready for prolonged flight, and she suspected from the careful way he moved that it impacted his balance.

She'd been hurt by his dismissal, but if she was going to be ruthless with herself, she knew that was her own doing. It had been magic, requested honestly and freely given. So she pushed aside the personal, female reaction and focused on what she was certain was far more important. Something more than the wing was wrong. She wanted to talk to Mina, who, of anyone, would be least likely to think her crazy.

"Are you completely insane?"

The hiss startled her, for it seemed to come at her from several directions at once. Anna yelped and spun, finding herself for one harrowing moment amid a tangling bed of black strips of cloth. They swept away from her like a man-o'-war's forest of tendrils as Mina drew back, pulling the cloak she always wore around her, guarding the true shape of her form. "Come in here, out of sight. It's not safe to be in the open near the Abyss right now."

Mina swam into the opening of her cave, which required careful maneuvering for it was camouflaged by myriad inhospitable forms of sea life, including a rampant garden of stinging fire coral. The only portion of her lower body visible beneath the cloak was two sleek black tentacles, each nearly six feet long, that helped propel her along and served as an extra pair of appendages when she needed them. While Mina was of the mermaid people, like Anna, she was also something more than that.

So many things that connected them, and yet they were the same things that kept their relationship a wary one at best. When she stopped inside the shadows of the cavern, Anna knew this was as far as they would go. She had never been deeper than fifty feet into Mina's home. But she was certain that was more than anyone else had been permitted.

Mina was just a handful of years older than she was, the only mercreature the merpeople preferred to see less than

Anna. It didn't keep them from seeking her out for her highly effective potions and spells, however. Anna had never asked her for either. Once she'd gotten old enough to go out alone and knew how Mina's story tied to hers, she'd tracked her down. Mina had threatened to turn her into a cat and let her drown if she didn't go away. Anna offered to help her gather plants in the more populated areas Mina didn't like. It took time, but eventually Mina agreed, and the uncertain bond had begun.

Now, seven years later, Anna was no more certain of her welcome at Mina's than she'd been the first time she'd come here. It just depended on Mina's mood. But Anna had learned not to take exception—much. Once or twice she'd caught the witch staring at her as if entranced, a chilling bloodlust in her vacant eyes. On those days, Mina had snapped out of it only to order her away, telling her never to return. But Anna always did.

Thinking about it now, Anna saw a similar connection between Mina's darkness and what she'd sensed in Jonah. As if he and Mina both were engaged in a personal struggle with demons they didn't care to discuss. She didn't know if Jonah's demons had been with him throughout his lifetime, but she knew Mina's had. So perhaps it was more appropriate than she'd first thought to seek Mina's help.

"What have you been doing?" Mina demanded.

"What do you mean?"

"The Dark Ones were loose and swarming about the ocean floor, seeking one of the winged ones. And it's all over you, his aura. You are fair glowing with it." Mina was already rummaging through her stores, reaching into crevices in the rock used for storage for her healing tonics and potions.

"He said I would be safe as long as I wasn't with him."

"Idiot."

"Mina," Anna gasped. "He's an angel."

"And an idiot. Here, drink this quickly. It will purge you and you'll be rid of that glow. Go on or I'll pour it down your throat."

Anna hesitated. "What do you mean, purge? Not . . . forget?"

Mina stopped, stared at her. "No," she said at last. "It's a cleansing, not a . . ."

"Cleansing. How . . . Does that mean . . ." He'd said he could voluntarily withhold his seed, but what if . . .

Mina peered at her. Now her gaze traveled more slowly over Anna, apparently seeing far more than auras.

"Anna, you lay with him."

"It was necessary, to heal him. He used Joining Magic." And then, inexplicably, Anna burst into tears.

_____

"I don't know why I did that," she said at last, when she was able to get herself under control.

"Crying in the ocean is a sad metaphor," Mina said cryptically. "And you do know. I see it all the time in those pathetic creatures that slink to me for love potions. You're feeling this wonderful yearning, but it makes you hurt at the same time. Like you've glimpsed the meaning of the universe, but you already know you can't hold on to it. It's mocking you. So tell me the full story, beginning to end."

Anna complied. She knew Mina enough to know the futility of arguing with her cynical assessment or taking affront at being lumped in with the "pathetic creatures." While she didn't dwell on their coupling, Mina asked her more questions about that than was comfortable, gazing at her with typical discomfiting shrewdness with her one visible crimson eye. The rest of her face, like most of the features of her body, was shadowed in the cowl and floating tendrils of that cloak, though Anna could see the pitted scarring that covered her cheek and jaw beneath the glittering eye.

When she finished, Mina raised a brow. "He _had_ to use Joining Magic. It was the only thing that would work," she mimicked. "Oh, that's rich. If I had an anemone for every time I'd heard that one . . ."

"Mina . . ." Anna let out a startled chuckle at the acid comment, but then shook her head. "I don't know if I can get him to leave."

The seawitch cocked her head. "Enamored of you as all that, is he?"

"No. _No._" Anna blanched. "Goddess, he's an angel, Mina. I'm not as daft as you think. It's just . . . It's almost like . . . When I found him, he wanted me to leave him. Just let him die. Then I got him to the cave, and it's like he's not interested in leaving it. *Ever.* Could his wound have affected his mind? He doesn't even seem to want his own kind to find him. I can't explain it. It's wrong, is all."

"So he doesn't want to return to the skies. Sometimes people get tired of what they're doing and want to do something different, at least for a little while. Those humans you are so fond of—what do you call it? They take a holiday."

"No, it's not that." Anna lifted her shoulder in a shrug, gave an unhappy laugh. "Though I'm not denying that *I* could be a holiday. Was a holiday," she corrected herself.

Mina gave her an impatient look. "Do I have to hold your hand through this, like a child? Get past it. Relationships would do far better if they weren't tied up with sex. Sex should be as basic as eating or shi—"

"Don't compare it to that."

"See what I mean? If it was just a bodily function, no one would get confused about whether or not they were in love. It wouldn't have anything to do with the body. Most of the potions I give are to simply deaden the sex drive. That tells people instantly whether they're thinking with their hearts or their hormones."

"I'm going. You're just making me depressed."

"It's never stopped you from hanging about endlessly before. And we're going back to see him now, anyway."

Anna bit off her irritated retort. "What?"

Mina rose and began to rummage through her stores again, tucking things away in the cloak. "You're many things, Anna. Impulsive, too open and loving. But you're *not* daft. Not in the least. The Dark Ones will be back very soon. They know he's still down here. And there's nothing the Dark Ones want so much as a captured angel."

"Why? To kill him?"

"No." Mina shook her head. "Far worse than that. To cut him open and take the Lady's power that resides in his chest. It would increase their own power exponentially and make his will their slave, as long as they hold his heart. He would fight for them."

Anna gave her a horrified look. "Why didn't you tell me sooner? He could be in danger. He could—"

"I wasn't going to tell you at all." The seawitch shrugged.

"It's not our concern. But then I figured you'd hear about it when it happened, and you'd be hanging about here again, blaming yourself and spreading your guilt heavy enough to suffocate me."

Anna counted to ten, figuring it would not be productive for her to reach out and try to strangle the witch. "So you're going back with me, because?" she asked between gritted teeth.

"Because without my help, you'll try to do something noble and stupid to save him and get yourself killed. Stay here. I'm going to go deeper into my cave and throw together some ingredients that may help him. Then we'll go evaluate his condition. If he won't go back to the skies, perhaps you can persuade him to go to the surface, somewhere not in the vicinity of where he originally landed. I can figure out a way to disguise him, not only from the Dark Ones, but from his own kind."

"His own kind? I don't understand."

"They're the best source of help for him, but he hasn't summoned them. Do you know why?" Mina asked it bluntly. "Angels are mighty beings, Anna, but that doesn't make them all good. You need to keep that in mind for your angel as well. He may be hiding for a reason that is not so angelic."

"No, he hasn't fallen from grace. I'm sure of it. It's . . ." Anna's brow furrowed. "You remember the male dolphin, the one whose brother was killed?"

"Yes. You followed him around the ocean, became his family until he was willing to integrate with a male pod again." Mina muttered something to herself and added another packet from her hidden stores to her person.

"He wanted to die," Anna said softly. "He saw nothing in the world to keep him. His loss hurt him so much, he just shut down, waiting for death."

"Your angel is not a dolphin, Anna." Mina shook her head. "Your capacity to love may be endless, but it can't always save the day. It's not going to be enough to save *you*, let alone everyone else."

Anna looked down, focusing for a long moment on the automatic, slow sway of her tail, keeping her stationary in the water. "Well then, on that day I'll no longer be a nuisance to you, will I?"

When she raised her gaze and met that of the seawitch, Anna thought she might have seen a flicker of regret, but she'd long ago learned her lesson about assigning regular emotions to Mina. "You may be right," she said at last. "But I must help him. When an angel falls out of the sky practically into your arms, how can that not be Fate?"

Mina gave a grudging grimace, turned away again. "Is he handsome?"

"Of course. I mean, he's an angel."

"His body . . . is it finely made?"

"Mina." Anna snorted at the glint in Mina's eye. Some of the tension loosened its band around her chest. "Now you're teasing me."

"I rarely get handsome, confident and powerful men in my cave. Never close enough to smell their skin, see their bodies move with such casual beauty." She was moving away into the recesses of the cave, the shadows swallowing her, but her voice still resonated. "The flow of muscle, the tensing of a buttock as they turn. The chance to stroke my finger down a line of ridged, tightly overlapping scales and find out what they conceal beneath them. Perhaps I simply wanted to know."

The evocative image was startling, powerful, particularly in combination with the mesmerizing tone with which Mina murmured it. The words echoed through the cavern, vibrating in the water against Anna's body. Now she wasn't sure if Mina was teasing or saying simple truth. With Mina, one never knew. And she'd certainly turned the conversation in a different direction, distracting Anna from more troublesome areas.

"Well? Keep talking; I can still hear you." Mina sounded farther away, suggesting that there were a few more twists and turns in the mysterious recesses of her home.

"He is very finely made," Anna said cautiously. Then the images Mina had painted spurred her own and she couldn't help herself. "Oh, Mina, I've never . . . He's so large and powerful. All of him is firm muscle. His arms and legs . . . His shoulders seem as broad as a ship's timbers. I know all angels are probably like that, but somehow, I just know he is more handsome, more beautiful than all of them. Goddess help me."

Mina reemerged, and her red eye blinked once, holding a

wealth of things Anna couldn't decipher. "I don't know if the Goddess will help you, Anna. But I'm going to."

_____

IF he meditated on it, Jonah could reach down, down, and feel the lick of flame of Lucifer's world below, so close. If he wanted to reach further, he knew he'd find the essence of Luc himself. Just as he could the Lady if he went in the opposite direction. As above, so below.

But he didn't. He preferred here, this place of stasis, below one Line and above the other. Disembodied, as if his soul had split.

He'd been on his side awhile, perhaps hours, studying the dragon's outline in the wall. At the lapping of the water, he adjusted his chin to see Anna's head break the surface, her long golden hair, which waved and wildly curled when dry, now slick along her skull and bare shoulders. His heart leaped in his throat, disregarding the fact she was ignoring his wish that she not return. No, not his wish. His command. It was not his wish at all.

Another being surfaced behind him and grasped the rock, gracefully lifting itself upon it, despite a strange cloak that made the being unrecognizable. And then he felt . . .

Dark One! It exploded through his system, tripping off all alarms. Here, where Anna was, where Anna could be harmed. Jonah launched himself off the ground, ignoring the searing pain that shot through his back, cursing the fact he almost stumbled from the unexpected lurch it caused. He still moved quickly enough that the creature only had time to let out a feminine shriek and throw herself backward as he reached for a sword that was not there. The fact he was unbalanced was the only thing that made his grip on her neck fall short. Otherwise, he was sure he could have snapped it in a heartbeat.

Then Anna was there, and before he could stop her, she'd flung herself over the sprawled creature, a bundle of rags and snarled black hair.

"Anna, get—"

"No!" Anna tucked her limbs around the Dark One's body like a mother bird with a precious egg. "Jonah, no! This is Mina. She's a seawitch. A healer."

"She's a Dark One."

"Half." Anna said it emphatically. "Her mother was a mermaid. She is my friend. She is not evil. Please, you're frightening her. Step back. Step away."

He struggled with it, gripped in the bloodlust that had been trained to rise to killing level at the barest hint of a Dark One. Only Anna's eyes disrupted it, the plea in her voice.

"Please, my lord. I have known her all my life."

At length, he stepped back, and Anna rose cautiously. Mina straightened to a sitting position. She had the hated red iris of the Dark One in the one eye he could see, almost the only feature of a horribly scarred face distinguishable in the folds of her cowl. That eye followed his every twitch just as closely as he was following hers. As he watched, she uttered several unfamiliar, harsh words. The hint of a serpentine pair of tentacles vanished, giving her the ability to stand on two legs, though he could only see her feet and ankles.

While Anna had said he'd frightened the witch, she didn't show it. Her face was an impassive mask. Stepping outside of the protection of Anna's body, the witch began to move to his left, studying his wound.

"The blade that did this. Did you see it?"

Jonah moved with her, instinctively keeping himself between her and Anna.

"My lord—"

"No, Anna. Stay where you are so he needn't worry about you."

He was surprised at the creature's admonition, and the careful scrutiny she was giving the wound, despite the fact he was making no attempt to help her examine it.

"It was an axe," he said gruffly.

"It was more than an axe." Mina took three deliberate steps forward. "If you are not too fainthearted to let me touch it, I believe the wound is poisoned. I can help."

"You would help an angel." He didn't bother to hide his derision.

"I would help Anna." Mina planted her feet.

"Your filth is not touching me."

"If you want to lie here and let it fester until you rot and die, ratty seagull," Mina responded, "that is no concern of mine."

"My lord, please. Mina." Anna threw an admonishing

glance between the two of them, then shifted back to Jonah. "She has come here to help you, I promise. Since I was born, Mina has done nothing but help and protect me."

Jonah knew he shouldn't be surprised. Loyalty was usually a close handfast of courage, and he already knew his mermaid had a foolish overabundance of the latter. Despite that, he had too much experience with Dark Ones to simply go on faith. "She's pretending friendship for the advantage it brings her, getting close to the house of Neptune."

Anna let out an inelegant snort at almost the same time Mina rolled her eyes, bemusing and irritating him at once. "Trust me, my lord," Anna said resolutely. "Being my friend brings *no one* an advantage."

"Except perhaps you," Mina offered in a dry tone, staring at Jonah with that hated gaze.

But now that he'd had a moment to adjust, he could tell there *was* something different about this Dark Spawn. His experience with the few that had managed to survive birth was that they were either wholly evil, unable to control or conceal their base nature, or so deformed they did not live long beyond two or three years.

It intrigued him to sense a duality of nature in this one, a strong darkness warring with a flickering light. While it didn't make him less repulsed by her or more trustful, he was more willing to tolerate her presence in the room with Anna. Within limits.

"My lord." Anna was speaking again. "If there is nothing I can say that can make you understand, I'm asking you to respect my judgment, out of courtesy for me. If you feel you owe me a moment of such regard," she added.

He cocked his head toward her, still keeping Mina in his peripheral vision. "Now, you're going for polite. Haughty. And using the fact that you saved my life to make me behave."

Anna opened her mouth, a flush staining her cheeks, but Jonah waved a hand. "The Goddess I serve is female, Anna. I am not unused to such tactics." At a sound from the dark creature to his left, he arched a brow at Mina. "Are you laughing at us, Dark Spawn?"

"I laugh at most everything, my lord," Mina said, the seriousness of her one visible eye altering not a bit.

"Mmm. I shall allow you to examine me." It took a tremendous effort to say it, but in truth, what did he care? What did he have to lose? Of course, that answer was in the cavern, just to his right, watching him with concern in her lovely face. He would not drag an innocent down with him. "I will do you no harm, for the moment."

"Do you promise?" Anna asked.

He shot a narrow look at her. "Using the truths I've told you against me is a woman's weapon as well."

When she blinked innocently, he blew out a breath. "I promise." It irritated him that the clearing of her expression pleased him, so his brow lowered, and he turned back to Mina, not bothering to mask the menace in his voice. "But keep in mind I have destroyed Dark Ones far more powerful than yourself. You cause Anna any kind of harm, you will not live to regret it."

"My exact sentiments toward you, my lord." Mina approached and examined the wound, the attachment of the wing, though she didn't touch him as expected. "You can't use it well, can you? The muscles are not fusing as they should."

He shook his head, wanting this over. Despite his agreement, his heart was thundering, his body tense, ready to react if the creature twitched in the wrong direction toward Anna, no matter the illogic of that, if the two had known each other for some time. But Dark Ones *were* wholly evil, and the creature stank of their blood, as well as a variety of other disturbing things.

Why couldn't she just leave so he could have Anna to himself? He wanted her safe. But more than that, notwithstanding the fact she shouldn't have returned at all, he found himself inappropriately glad about her disobedience.

"There definitely was a poison in the blade," the seawitch muttered. "Cleverly done, but not irreversible. I expect, my lord, their intent was to disable you for a prolonged period so they'd have a better chance of capturing you. Even now, they continue to look."

"And you brought her back down here—"

"She brought *me* here, my lord. You can take your ire out on her."

Anna opened her mouth, then closed it, suggesting there

was more to that story, but Jonah managed to throttle his reaction down to a glower as Mina continued.

"If you will sit down, I'll put you in a healing circle and use a simple spell to start the cleansing process. The poison can't kill you, but as long as it's in your system, it will hamper the wing's ability to heal."

When her attention flitted briefly toward Anna, Anna saw the unspoken message. *And it may be what is causing his mind to be affected so oddly.*

"Very well." Anna let out a relieved breath as Jonah took a seat, cross-legged on the flat, wide ledge, keeping Mina in his peripheral vision like a watchful lion as she began to gather loose rocks. Drawing a sharp tool out of the recesses of her clothing, she used it to break them down to a uniform size. As she began to build a circle around him, apparently satisfying him of her immediate intentions, he turned his gaze back to Anna. She'd taken up a position along the dragon's wall, her hips resting on the nervous hands she'd deliberately folded behind her back.

On one hand, she was glad his immediate thoughts had turned from murdering her friend. On the other hand, when he looked toward her, Anna realized how the position tilted her breasts up, drawing his attention even though her long hair tangled forward over her shoulders, impeding the view of her body to the juncture of her thighs.

It seemed out of place to be thinking of such things right now, but the way his eyes moved over her reminded her how recently she'd felt his body take hers. She found she could think of nothing else when he looked at her like this.

"Push your hair back, Anna."

Anna glanced toward Mina, who ignored them and continued arranging her rocks. Anna pushed the hair over one shoulder, then the other, feeling heat expand across her skin at his expression as she revealed herself. She wore the scarves at hip and breast again, but the way he studied her, she knew he was imagining in detail what she looked like without them, though in truth it didn't require much imagining. The upper scarf was snug over her breasts, revealing the dark smudges of nipple clearly, particularly with the fabric wet as it was now.

Mermaids were not shy about their bodies, but after what

they'd done earlier, she felt self-conscious. And she wasn't going to disrobe in front of Mina. Her gaze strayed to his lips, the line of his jaw . . . those dark, implacable eyes. Okay, maybe she might.

"I want you again."

Goddess help me.

"It's not a bad idea," Mina said efficiently before embarrassment could suffuse Anna. "You should perform Joining Magic daily with her, or whoever's available, to help you raise the energy. It will speed your recovery and reinforce what I'm about to do to drive out the poison. It's going to need reinforcement."

Or whoever's available . . . So matter of fact . . . so medical. To Mina it was apparently that simple. Whereas Anna's reaction to Jonah's gaze and the husky words were anything but. How did he manage to do this, penetrate her mind so her thoughts clenched and shivered with the possibilities, rousing as much as her body did to his attentions?

He seemed to care little about Mina's diagnosis. While his posture was stiff and alert, betraying his distaste of her proximity, he paid no attention beyond that to what she was doing. Picking up a rock, she began a chant. She lifted it over her head, turning in a four-point circle, and then put it down to start the same process with the next stone.

Would he take her with Mina present? Did their coupling mean so little? An impersonal receptacle for his lust, his healing? But he'd said it meant more. He'd promised.

Jonah reached out a hand. "Come sit with me, Anna. As long as it won't disrupt . . . your friend."

He tilted his head slightly in Mina's direction. The sea-witch merely lifted another rock. When Jonah glanced back at Anna, Mina slammed it against the back of his head.

Seven

THE green flash of the additional power she'd given the blow exploded in a shower of sparks.

Jonah toppled over, knocked out cold.

"Mina!" Anna shrieked, darting forward. "What are you—"

"Getting the two of you out of here." Kicking the rocks out of her way, Mina pulled a vial from the recesses of her cloak. "He'll stay here and let them kill him. You were right, you and your damn intuition." Mina uncorked the potion. "Hold his head up. I don't want him to choke."

As Anna hesitated, the seawitch's tone sharpened, impatient. "Anna, we don't have much time. I told you the Dark Ones are still looking for him. Well, they *are* looking for him. Meaning *now*. If he wasn't so infatuated with you, he probably would have felt them soon after I did, right when we got here."

"Why didn't you say—"

"Because I was evaluating the situation."

Anna locked gazes with the witch. "We didn't lead them back here, did we?"

"You mean, did *I* lead them here?" That crimson eye glinted. "Well, if he gets caught, you can assume I did. If I help him escape, then you'll have a different answer. But if you drag your anal fins and don't hold his head, you'll never really know, because they'll get us all."

Muttering, Anna bent, sliding her hand beneath Jonah's neck. "He is going to be *so* angry . . ."

"And alive." Mina poured the substance down his throat, massaged until she got the involuntary swallow. "But you're right. I'm glad I won't be around when he wakes." She ignored Anna's narrow look. "Come on. We've got to get him close enough to the surface that the pressure doesn't kill him when he physically changes to a human."

"*What?* What are you . . ."

"The potion I just gave him makes him human. Neither his own kind nor the Dark Ones will be able to detect him." Mina grunted, seizing Jonah under the arms, trampling one wing without care, and began to drag him toward the water. Anna was forced to help, despite the questions whirling in her mind.

"And what was that nonsense about performing Joining Magic every day?"

"You're not objecting, surely." Mina gave her an arch look as they heaved together. "It *will* help. He'll likely have a tantrum about this, so you'll have to convince him. Dance for him, sing for him, touch yourself to draw his desire."

"I'm not . . ." Anna had never blushed this much in front of Mina before, and it just added to her irritation. "I don't know how to act that way."

"For him, you do. It's in your eyes. Each time you Join with him, the magic will rise and you can channel it. You know enough to do it even if he won't. While it would be better if he'd participate, I wouldn't rely on his cooperation or participation. If you value him, you'll have to seduce or trick him into it."

They'd reached the water's edge. "You're right," Mina gasped. "He's a bloody ton of muscle. Mind me, now. Dawn to dusk, he'll be human. Dusk to dawn, an angel again. The potion will last about a week, enough to get him inland."

Dropping Jonah unceremoniously, the witch grasped Anna's arm to clap a hand over her forehead. Mina never touched her, so Anna was too startled to immediately react. Heat flashed across Mina's palm, and suddenly Anna was jumbling a set of images that rolled into the front of her mind like a bag of marbles scattered pell-mell there. "Mina—"

"It will settle in a moment. That's a mindmap. He needs to go to Desert Crossroads in Nevada. It's a place, not a town, and it's not on any human map. There's a man there, living on a magical fault line called Red Rock Schism. He can help heal your angel's deeper hurt, if your angel doesn't do it for himself."

"Mina." Anna planted herself, gripped Jonah when Mina started to roll him in. "Stop. Look at me."

The witch scowled. "We don't have time—"

"Tell me what in the name of Neptune is going on, damn it all." Anna managed, barely, not to shout. "Or . . . I'll hug you."

Mina drew back, horror flashing through her eyes. At another time, it would have made Anna laugh, but not now. She meant it, with all the grimness of a death threat.

"Fine. Just remember when the Dark Ones catch us, it's because *you* wanted to waste time chatting. When the Dark Ones first invaded the waters, I consulted my scrying mirror to find out what was happening. Your angel was isolated during a battle, and his wing was severed on purpose. Not just because he's any angel. Because he's Jonah."

"I know that. He told me his name."

Mina rolled her eyes. "Be quiet and listen. Jonah is what's called the Prime Legion Commander. He *leads* the angels that fight Dark Ones. The only angels more important than him are Full Submission angels, and I don't have time to explain what those are."

"He told me—"

"Shut up, for Neptune's sake. Do you know this place, this Nevada?"

"It's a state. Inland." As far as Anna knew, Mina had never left the sea, despite her own shape-shifting abilities. One of the many things the witch had never explained to her.

"This man . . . he's something like me," Mina continued. "Something called a shaman. Like a wizard. If the angel can't find a way back to himself, it appears he can help."

At Anna's look, Mina shrugged. "I know. It makes no sense to me, either, why a landlocked human wizard instead of the angel's own kind can help. But as I said, maybe what he needs can't be found among the angels. Now, let's go."

"I know there's more you're not telling me. I'm not—"

"That's enough for now. I mean it, Anna. We're out of time." Leaning over Jonah's body, Mina seized Anna's arm, shocking her with the grip of her hand, the bite of nails like claws in their sharpness. "This angel probably has the power to incinerate the world with barely a thought. Remember what I said. If the Dark Ones catch him alive, take his heart, they can enslave him. Do you want that?"

"No. But you don't care about that. You've never cared about what happens to anyone."

Anna knew Mina wasn't lying about them being out of time. The urgency coming off of her was palpable. But the answer she'd always wanted from the witch was behind this—she was sure of it. "Except me," she pressed. "You're doing this because I'm tied up with him somehow in this vision, aren't I?"

Mina started shoving at the unconscious angel again. "I can see the way you look at him. You're going to do that stupid thing you do, risking everything for one of your ridiculous compulsions. I'm duty bound to protect you, aren't I? Our shared curse and all." Mina's lips pulled back from her teeth, an unattractive feral snarl.

"You're duty bound not to cause me harm," Anna persisted. "That's different."

"If I don't protect you when I know you're in danger, it's the same thing. Now, stop arguing and get in the water before I turn you into a sponge."

"Nevada is a desert state," Anna said. "Far from the shoreline."

"Well, it's good you can become human, isn't it? Now, quickly, there are other rules. You must travel by Fate alone. You can't rent a car, or however you move around among the humans. Someone must pick you up."

"Or else what?"

Mina gave her a look that could have speared a fish. "Magic doesn't usually have the patience to explain itself, Anna. But ignore it at your own peril. Trust me."

At last Anna joined Jonah in the water, held on to him while the seawitch prepared to shift back to tentacles and gills. "I guess, at the very least, it makes practical sense," she considered doubtfully. "If I want to keep him safe until he recovers, he needs to go where they don't expect him to be. Why would they expect him to be on land, on his way to Nevada? It sounds ludicrous to *me*, so it may be beyond their imagining as well."

Mina nodded. "Neither the angels nor the Dark Ones know his whereabouts. But they all know he went into the sea. Nothing is farther from the sea than the desert. Even so, travel only by day, when he's human. Even that's going to be a risk, because his power signature is strong. The Dark Ones will track that signature. They won't be able to pin it on him during the day, but if they're in his vicinity when night falls, they might be able to find him. So stay undercover at night. No traveling.

"Now, mind me on this as well. Two days." She gave Anna a sharp look. "You head back toward the ocean after two days. I don't care if you've gotten there or not. You promise me."

"Do you care for me at all?" Anna asked abruptly. Reaching out, she snagged the witch's cloak, careful not to touch her skin, since she knew Mina hated that. "Tell me true, in case we never see one another again. Is it just the curse between us?"

"Anna, stop it. We don't have time for this."

"Yes," Anna said steadily, gazing at her. "We do. I'm twenty years old. You know we may never see one another again. Tell me, just this once. What is the truth between us?"

Mina drew back, and for a moment Anna saw both of her eyes. One red, emanating the dangerous malevolence of Mina's Dark sire. The other a sapphire blue, equally disturbing in its intensity, reminding Anna that Mina's mother had been one of the most feared seawitches in the ocean.

"As long as you insist on helping him, you're a target. I care not whether an angel lives or dies. But there's only one of you."

Anna stared at her. "Those were almost the first words he spoke to me. 'There are many angels. There is only one of you.'"

"Maybe he's not an idiot, after all. Stay safe, Anna. You're important."

Important to Mina? Or to this vision?

However, before she could ask another question, Mina shoved her under the water and dumped Jonah all the way in, on top of her. Anna thrashed beneath the weight of his body, sputtering and cursing, before she managed the transition back to mermaid and could use the balance of her tail to help her seize a portion of the unconscious angel. By that time Mina was in the water with her.

The seawitch watched Anna get her arms around the angel until she was holding him securely, as if she thought her world would end if she let him go. She told herself it didn't matter that she hadn't told Anna everything. The mermaid had an irritatingly overblown sense of responsibility as it was.

And Anna was right—her time was running out. Mina should be glad the mermaid would no longer be her responsibility.

Instead, one of the seeds of the vision came back to her, disturbing the seawitch more than she cared to admit.

She is the only one who can save him.

———

As Mina predicted, they'd talked too long. They weren't quite to the surface when the physical transformation began.

Anna was forced to a stop, her arm latched around Jonah's upper body as it writhed, convulsed in the grip of the potion's effect. As Mina held his legs, the wings slowly dissolved, a few handfuls of feathers drifting away on the current.

Like a sudden explosion, overwhelming desolation detonated through Anna. This plan would not work. It was going to fail. She was going to fail Jonah, and he would die.

Her gaze shot to Mina, frightened. Her friend's eyes had become wild, mouth taut. She gestured upward. "Ignore it. Keep going. I'll draw them off. Two days inland, Anna. Don't forget."

"But what if he won't go on without me?"

"That's his Fate. You can't make his choices, can you? Now promise me—"

Despair closed in, knocking Anna back like the blow from a strong wake. Only the fierce hold she had on Jonah's body kept him with her.

Mina gave her a searing look, seized an armful of glowing feathers, and flipped backward. She shot back down through the water like an arrow, away from Anna. Toward the source of those dark and hopeless feelings.

"Mina, no!" Anna fumbled her burden and began to sink.

No. They weren't getting him, not this way. She wouldn't let them compel her to surrender. Gritting her teeth, she seized

Jonah under the arms and started pumping upward as fast and hard as she could. Without the wings, it was actually easier.

Ten strokes later, her heart choked her as she realized he was now human. He had to *breathe*. Frantic, she stopped, hovered and closed her mouth over his, breathed. Gave him air from her lungs. Then stroked upward again. Up fifteen strokes, breathe for him, drop five.

And each time, despite the circumstances, she couldn't help but feel desire at the touch of his mouth. She had to focus to make sure she breathed into it instead of nibbling, tasting. By the time she made the surface, she was gasping, her vision gray. Her mermaid form allowed her to breathe with gills or lungs interchangeably, but she'd had to use her lungs to keep air in him. Now she drank in oxygen greedily, floating a moment and holding him to her side before she rolled him to his back and began to navigate toward the distant shore. They were a couple miles out, but she knew that shoreline, had swum toward it before. Cradling his jaw, she held his throat as she moved, keeping his mouth and nose above the waterline. His hair brushed her arm, and she hoped he wouldn't wake before they reached land. She didn't want him to realize his form had changed and he'd been betrayed while they were still in the water. He might just be piqued enough to drown himself. Or her.

The sense of the Dark Ones faded, telling her Mina had been successful in drawing them off. She swallowed over a jagged ache in her throat. *Please let her be all right.* Even while praying for that, she knew her bond with the seawitch was pathetic. Her one enduring relationship was with someone who despised the sight of her most of the time.

She kept on, fiercely focusing on her destination. While Mina had said as a human he would not be detectable as an angel, Anna didn't want anyone investigating why a mermaid was rescuing a stranded human out as far as this when there were no capsized boats in the area. She swam as fast as she could, pushing herself, holding on to him, praying for Mina.

———

JONAH surfaced slowly, feeling as if he were swimming through sand. Weighted down, but curiously weightless as well. Hazy. Nauseated. *Nausea?*

Though he was on his back, he managed to roll to his side before he started throwing up, an altogether astounding and unpleasant first-time experience that felt like his insides were being squeezed by a large, punishing fist. Fortunately, he was at the tide line. He convulsed, fighting against it as he would an enemy, but his body would not be denied.

When he finished, he rinsed out his mouth with seawater and rolled back, passed his hands over his eyes. The sun. He was above the water. But something was wrong. Everything seemed muted, as if his finely tuned senses had been stuffed with cotton. As he tried to struggle back to a sitting position, he found himself still off balance. He straightened out his wings to steady himself and . . .

He had no wings. *No wings.* Groping at his back, he twisted, turned and found out that not only were his wings gone, but he was wearing human clothes. A black cotton T-shirt, and a pair of jeans, both too snug over the musculature of his shoulders and thighs.

Then he became aware he was being watched.

She sat nearby, her back against a large piece of driftwood, hands tightly clasped in one nervous ball on her knees. He vaguely registered she also was wearing clothing. A light, gauzy top that stretched over her breasts, outlining the sweet points of her nipples. Slim straps over her shoulders. A skirt of similar fabric brushed her ankles in her bent-legged position, the hem rippling over the tops of her bare feet. Her golden brown hair was tied back, but of course it was so long the curly ends had blown forward, caressing her wrists, tangling them like restraints, holding her in that spot as if she were a captive awaiting his punishment.

"It's okay," she said quietly, as he made it to one knee and stared at her. "It's disorienting at first. When I go from legs to a tail and back again. But you adjust to it in time. And you won't have to get used to it for long—"

In two steps he was on her, seizing her shoulders, though he stumbled and fell to one knee again, his head spinning. She caught him, and they ended up tumbling together, her on top as he hit the sand. Cursing, he rolled to his side, taking her under him, holding her with bruising hands.

"What the hell did you let her do to me?"

"She was trying to save your life. The Dark Ones—"

"She is a Dark Spawn. Damn it, I never should have trusted her. Or you, a child stupid enough to think a Dark One can be your friend. I—"

"She may be dead because of you, my lord." Anna thrust hard against him, but of course he didn't budge. "Because of me. Because I brought her into this. She led the Dark Ones away from us."

"Perhaps that's what she wants you to think." He had no patience for her feelings right now. With disgust, he released her and managed to make it to his feet this time, though he had to fight the desire to lie back down. Because his voice was hoarse, he cleared it twice before he got the words out. "What did she do to me?"

"You're human." She flinched at his expression. "It's only temporary. At dusk, your true form will return. Until . . ." She bit it off and looked away. "It will return at dusk."

His eyes narrowed. Gods, his head felt like someone was pounding a mallet against it.

"Until what?"

When she didn't answer, he lunged out and grabbed her arm, this time managing not to topple over. If the little idiot had any sense, she would run. He wanted to break the sea-witch's neck, but at the moment anyone's might do. Instead, his little mermaid watched him like a captive in truth, unshed tears in her eyes, those hands still clenched.

Seizing both her wrists, he swayed alarmingly. She braced her feet, her fingers flexing as if she'd like to help steady him. To Hades with that. "Answer me, Anna."

"Until sunrise, my lord," she said at last, looking past his shoulder. "You are human during daylight, angel at night. Mina says the potion will last about a week, to give us time to get inland and confuse the Dark Ones as to your whereabouts. By the time it wears off, we'll be where they don't expect you to be."

"So we are to be wanderers, you and I?" As he gave her a shake, he tried not to care when she flinched again, this time at the brutal grip of his hands. Her forearms were like slender branches. She was so fragile. Even in this form, he could easily overpower her. And yet, she'd still tricked him into this . . . abomination.

"Did you hatch this plan with her?"

"No, my lord." Her jaw took on a stubborn set. "I didn't know of Mina's plan, but yes, I did help her when she told me the Dark Ones would be there any moment."

Jonah snorted. "I don't suppose it would have occurred to either of you to advise me of her plan before she executed it?"

Anna shook her head. "She didn't think you would agree. They were coming," she repeated. Was he mistaken or was she . . . gritting her teeth? Her words were coming out clipped, measured.

Jonah dropped his touch. "It would have been wiser for the two of you to leave. So I could deal with them and you would have been safe. You were utterly foolish."

"You would have been dead." Her gaze shot up to his face and he saw a surprising flash of fire. "I won't allow that. Not while I live. Not while I'm supposed to be taking care of you."

"Anna—"

"I *won't* allow it."

Her shout reverberated up and down the beach, stunning him into silence. She stood there, quivering with fury, her hands balled into fists, despite the fact he loomed over her like a mountain.

"You won't *allow* it, little one? *Who* do you think you're talking to?"

By Hades, she took another step forward, tilting her head to come almost nose to nose with him. "You wanted to die. You want them to kill you. You think I don't see it? That Mina and I don't recognize it? Well, I'm sorry, my lord, but it's your misfortune to have landed in the clutches of the two people in the whole ocean who know what it is to feel that way."

His rage struggled with his astonishment. She was standing fully in the blast zone of his fury, and not backing down a bit. He had captains smart enough to stay out of range when he was in a temper only half this fierce. No one of his own Legion had dared anything but respectful dissension with him for as long as he could remember.

From the shifting of her eyes, he could tell she knew the

ground beneath her was quicksand. And yet the little idiot wasn't done yet.

———————

ANNA couldn't stand it. She'd sat there, watching him vomit and struggle, seeing his horror and disorientation when he realized his wings were gone, an intrinsic part of who he was. Knowing she'd done this to him. Even wounded, as an angel, he'd been so fully in command. So perfect. He was an *angel*, the Prime Legion Commander, and she'd reduced him to this.

She'd known she wasn't in any way prepared to deal with this situation. But that never seemed to stop her from doing what she shouldn't do. Now she found herself well over her head, with only one compass to guide her. Mina's dark vision of what could happen if he fell into the hands of the Dark Ones. She had to do what she could to protect him. And since she had ridiculously little power of her own for such a task, she could only follow Mina's instructions. Trust the one being Jonah thought she was a fool to trust.

"You don't know anything." His jaw was held rigid. "You've lived for barely a blink of my life. You know nothing."

He could destroy her. At sunset, he would return to being an angel who could extinguish a life without a thought. Hades, even as a human he could snap her neck. And he was, as the humans liked to say, tremendously pissed off. But even beyond her self-doubt, she knew she was right about this one thing, and she told herself she wouldn't back away from it, no matter how much her stomach was quaking with nerves.

"*Let me die*. That was one of the first things you said." Anna took a breath, and reminded herself of how he'd been inside her, overwhelmed her with his mouth alone. She was part of him in her own mind, whether he cared to nurture that illusion himself or not. "I don't know the shape or reason for the darkness you carry in you, my lord, but I do know it's there, and that it's likely a greater danger to you than a Dark One. I won't let you throw your life away. Not if I can do anything to prevent it."

What *could* she do?

Touch him, make him desire you . . .

She'd never been . . . Well, obviously she had no experience in seducing a male. But she needed to try something different than arguing with an ancient being who would consider her measly twenty years of wisdom inconsequential. Knowing she was risking a humiliating rebuff or worse, with an awkward jerk she rose on her toes, aware the motion dragged the full softness of her breasts against his chest, as well as his knuckles, for his hands came up in reaction, locked on her wrists again.

It was a stretch, but she managed to reach his lips. Not a shy kiss this time. Leaning into him, she opened her mouth and sought the inside of his, tasting his tongue, wishing her hands could be free so she could bring his head down, grip his hair, delve deeper.

He wasn't holding her feet, though. She stepped in between his, her hip bone pressing the front of the snug jeans, her thigh rubbing the inside of his.

His hands slid from her wrists, seized her upper arms and pulled her off him, holding her with a rigid grip. He studied her, unsmiling, his firm mouth moist from hers. At first her stomach plummeted and she thought she'd failed miserably. But then she saw something in his gaze that made her shiver in her lower belly. While he was indeed in a dangerous mood, he was not unaffected by that kiss. The uncertain combination was more exciting than she expected it to be, though she couldn't explain why that was.

"Do you think to distract me, Anna?"

"No." She shook her head, though the sea horses in her chest pranced with cautious joy as he used the nickname. "I just . . . I wanted to remind you that there might be a good reason to stay around a few more days, until you go down in a blaze of glory under a hundred Dark Ones."

The comment was unexpected, ridiculous. She was trembling, but her chin was up. Jonah found his wrath simply couldn't hold before the combination of innocent sensuality and determination. Whatever the seawitch's motives, he wasn't so angry he couldn't see that Anna had sincerely meant to help. Faith, she was brave. Beautiful. She had a courage that would impress his toughest Legion commander. But she was so foolish to bait him. He would have to take her to task about that. Eventually.

This abysmal transition was temporary, if the seawitch had

told Anna the truth. And if she had, he'd just been granted a week of total invisibility. That was not entirely without appeal—more than he wanted to admit or explain to himself. In fact, the passion Anna had summoned from him, on several different levels, was as alive as he'd felt in a while.

"Where did you get these clothes?"

Anna blinked at the change of topic, then looked over her shoulder, toward a small cottage nestled in the dunes. He noted the next nearest one was about a mile down the beach. "That belongs to me, my lord. It's the place that Neptune set up for the daughters of Ariel."

"That's not what I meant." He indicated himself. "Why do you have a man's clothes?"

The implication and demand in his voice startled her. Surely he wasn't being possessive? When he'd first said, "You belong to me . . . for now," she'd loved the words in a very hard-to-explain way, such that she wouldn't dare to repeat them, for fear the independent Mina would ridicule her. Besides which, she'd known she'd simply woven those words into the elaborate fantasy of being part of him. The words had no enduring meaning. Much like what had brought them together in the cave.

Despite that bleak thought, the look in his eyes suggested he had meant his words of ownership quite literally. Though he had human eyes now, a white sclera around the dark brown iris, it made him no less overwhelming in his stillness when he watched her like he did now. She wet her lips. "The original legend. Ariel rescued the prince from the sea. It's one of our odd family traditions, my lord. We always keep a change of men's clothing in the house, for when the man of our dreams washes ashore. It's a stupid thing, but none of us has ever broken it."

Of course, every man who had spawned Arianne's next generation had been rescued in some fashion from the sea. As she had the thought, she blanched, and barely managed to keep herself from laying a palm over her flat stomach. He'd said he didn't . . . Of course not. He wasn't a human. He was an angel. Anna's tragedy had yet to happen. And yet, she couldn't imagine wanting another man after being with Jonah.

He nodded, apparently satisfied. "And the little beast you call a friend? Will she come here?"

That snapped her back to the present. Despite her attempt to remain calm, tears choked her throat. "I don't know, my lord. I was hoping she would come at least to the water's edge, so I'd know she was all right, but then she never comes to the surface. And I didn't . . . I couldn't leave you." Briefly she relayed how she and Mina had parted.

"I've been sitting here for two hours, watching you, wondering if she's alive or dead, if they've hurt her, and I've no way of helping her. Don't you see how much courage it took for her to come to you? She told me you *lead* the Dark Legion, and she is Dark Spawn. No one will help her, because I'm the only one . . ." She shook her head, turned away as he dropped his grip. "She's the only person I think of as a friend."

"You are so certain of her loyalty?"

"Yes. First off, it doesn't make any sense for her to betray you this way, my lord. She could have chosen not to warn us down in the caves. Even here, you've been out for two hours. Plenty of time for them to come for us if that was her intent."

"She was indifferent to my well-being, Anna. The mystery is what her feelings are for you." As she glanced back at him, surprised at his intuition, he inclined his head. "It was the only thing I sensed from her that saved her life when she came into the cave. Why does she feel such a strong compulsion to protect you?"

"You don't give her enough credit, my lord. Mina fights the darkness within her. She has had to fight it so hard and . . . It's difficult to explain, but she's the type of person who won't give up what she's worked so hard to earn."

"She refuses to give in to the evil because that's what it wants her to do?"

Anna allowed herself a slight smile. "She has a formidable contrary nature, my lord."

"I won't argue that. But there's more there. Why does she protect you? And why are you making me ask everything twice to get a straight answer? It's irritating."

Jonah arched a brow as Anna shot him a look, but she relented. "It's an ancient history between our two families. Even if she were wholly evil, which she isn't, she can't betray me." She looked toward the cottage. "We should get inside before night falls."

His piercing gaze told her he knew she was being evasive. It made her want to swim away, but of course she was on human legs now. For so long, she'd wanted someone to talk to, but she hadn't imagined having to talk about these types of things.

"Or perhaps we should go ahead and start our journey," she said casually. "Get farther away from the shoreline."

"Journey? A journey has a destination. Where are you supposed to take me?"

When Anna would have drawn away, that long arm outmatched her. He circled her wrist, drew her back to him. His grip this time had a different strategy, though no less capable of keeping her in place. Moving his thumb over her pulse made her gaze drag upward to linger on his mouth. His eyes were still so dark the pupil and iris were almost indistinguishable. She should have felt threatened by their intensity, but what responded inside her couldn't be called fear. Not exactly.

"If you don't tell me, I'm going to prove to you how unpleasant defying an angel can be." When his voice dropped to a silky murmur, her eyes widened as he drew her against his chest with one implacable arm, tipping her chin with the other hand. "*Where* are we going?"

She jumped when his hand lowered, covered one buttock. His gaze glittered, and she had the astonishing and unlikely thought it was amusement. "You're tempting me to warm this part of you, little mermaid. Speak."

Mina had told her to play the wanton, but when the full force of his dominant sexuality was upon her, it was all she could do to keep her head above water. Especially when drowning in him was so much more appealing.

But was he doing it deliberately? Manipulating her with seduction? Using her, as he had for the Joining Magic? Maybe. He wasn't being deceitful about it, though. He wasn't concealing his intent, his desire for information. This was a serious form of teasing, in a way too damn mesmerizing for her peace of mind.

Who was she to argue with his methods? This was certainly preferable to being shouted at. Which she expected was about to happen again. Briefly, she explained about the shaman, bracing herself for the storm clouds that gathered in his expression.

"A *human*? A human can drive out the poison?"

"Actually, my lord . . ." She made herself continue to look at him, though the frequent burning in her cheeks was turning them a permanent scarlet, she was sure. "The first tonic she gave you will drive out the poison if it is reinforced daily by . . . some type of energy raising. The shaman . . . His purpose is to heal your spirit."

"My spirit doesn't need any healing. Even if it did, no human would be involved." He eyed her with a sneer in his expression. And distrust was back as well.

No, she decided. He wouldn't use seduction as a tool. He had too much temperament to rely on charm. "You are very highly ranked, are you not, my lord?" She struggled for patience. "Yet you show no interest, no urgency to return to your kind. I'm sure there are those who care for you, and yet you also have no interest in letting them know you are alive. You don't want the Dark Ones to cause me harm, but you have no concern for your own value. Even with my meager skills, I feel the darkness inside you, a desolation. He can help heal it. Mina says so."

"And if I refuse to go? What if I have no interest in this plan your witch has concocted?" His eyes narrowed. "She may not serve the Dark Ones, but it doesn't mean she's not serving her own dark purposes. A prescription of daily Joining Magic," he mimicked. "That certainly motivates a young, attractive sexual innocent to keep me on the witch's quest, doesn't it? You've had a taste and you want more. She knows it. And she knows how distracting that would be."

Shock flooded Anna. Pulling her hand away before he could stop her, she stepped back. "That was just mean," she said in a tight voice. The hurt gathered in her throat, a painful lump. "Angels aren't supposed to be mean. I don't care who or what you are. I'm not some kind of . . . I . . . It was, to me, what we did . . . You make it sound dirty. I wasn't . . ." She shook her head, balled her hands into fists. "Here's an alternative plan, my lord. Sit here and brood until the Dark Ones come and make a meal of you."

Spinning on her heel, she prepared to stalk up to the cottage—and cry there.

"Anna."

When he grabbed at her arm, she rounded on him. Maybe she'd intended it, maybe not, but somehow her hand connected to the side of his face with a resounding *thwack* that left the imprint of her hand. The shock that crossed his face was matched only by the horror on hers.

Holy Goddess. She'd just struck an angel. An angel.

But he'd deserved it. He'd said . . .

"Anna. Stop." She was trying to pull away, and he was gathering her back to him, quelling her struggles without great effort. Why couldn't Mina have transformed him into a spindly, gawky teenager?

"I won't say I'm sorry."

"No, you won't. I will. I'm sorry. I apologize."

She stopped, startled, as his hand cupped her face, lifted her chin so she had to look at those dark eyes. Overwhelming her. "You *are* a sexual innocent, Anna."

"Oh, you—"

"No." This time he hauled her firmly back to him. When he sighed, the expansion of his broad chest nearly pushed her back a pace. "Be still for two seconds, or I *will* spank you. Listen to me. You're telling me we're going to seek the counsel of a mere human who thinks he knows what the world is, enough to work magic in it. And this is the plan of a half-breed Dark One who turned me into a human. I am furious, off balance, incredulous. And yes, more than a little confused in my own mind. Because here's the problem."

Taking her hand, he put it down between them, so Anna felt the rigid state of him. Her gaze flew back up to his face, her lips parting.

With relief, Jonah saw some of the hurt die out of her expression, replaced by wary curiosity about where he was going with this. Her heart was beginning to quicken, and he knew the pulse between her legs would synchronize, beating urgently for what he could give to her. He wanted to feel that rhythm of life against his cock, but first he owed her this.

His hand slid up, his thumb finding her nipple and making her moan softly. Closing his eyes, he forced himself to focus.

Goddess, it was as if he hadn't sated his lust in eons. What was it about her? Rationally, he knew it could be something the witch had done. But his heart knew differently, for an angel's heart knew truth.

"I'm off balance, because despite all that, I'm enthralled by the way your hair lies on your shoulders, how anger flashes in your eyes like heat lightning. The flush of your cheeks, the way your nipples have hardened against that thin shirt just from my barest touch." He folded his hand around her throat and cheek, tucked her head under his chin, and let sensuality give way to comfort.

When Anna let out a resigned sigh, coiled her arms around his upper body, he felt that curious relief again. "I'm angry, because in the midst of all these things, I want you. So I strike out at your desire for me, so new and clean. It's beautiful, Anna, a miraculous gift to any male you choose to bestow it upon." Though Jonah was damn glad it was him, for he couldn't tolerate the thought of anyone else. "I have become a coldhearted bastard, if I'll strike out at something that is pure goodness."

Picking up one of her hands, he ran his thumb over her fair skin, where bruises from his fingerprints were starting to show. "Perhaps my soul is more of their blood now than my own," he said quietly. When she made a startled noise of protest, he pressed his jaw down on her head, kept her where she was. "It doesn't matter. I'd rather go down with them than watch my soul disintegrate a piece at a time. Faith, the first time I've felt anything in so long is in your arms."

She was silent a moment, and then, amazingly gratified, he felt her arm tighten around him in reassurance. "I'm far from perfect, my lord. I have a bad temper. You might have noticed."

"I'm sure I haven't." He bit back a smile, tipped her chin again, gave her an even look. "Now, hear me. I'm used to commanding thousands of angels. I answer only to Michael and the Lady Herself. I'm a little bit out of my element, and these clothes chafe. Given all that, do you think, little general, that you could give me one night in your enchanted cottage to think this all through and let *me* make the decision of whether this journey should be taken?"

When she bit her lip, he shook his head. "It is my right to choose my destiny." As an afterthought, he added, "She's very resourceful, your witch. I'm sure she'll be fine."

Anna closed her eyes. "Don't be kind right now. You know you don't care about her."

"Maybe. But the fact that you do matters."

When she laid her head back down on his chest and nodded her acceptance of that, of all of it, Jonah sighed. It had been decades, maybe longer, since anyone had defied him over anything. And yet in barely a blink of time, less than a day, she'd developed a habit of it. It goaded something in him, arousing him, igniting him. Making things feel alive that he'd forgotten. Things that made him bend his head, kiss the side of her vulnerable neck. As he felt the little shiver go through her body, he ran his hand possessively down her back, feeling the shape of her.

"Show me your cottage," he commanded quietly.

Eight

EACH generation of the daughters of Arianne added touches that made the cottage her own. For that reason, Anna waited just inside the door, feeling nervous as Jonah stood in the center of the living area and turned slowly, examining everything.

It was not large. Sea creatures were not indoor dwellers. Her needs were small. A simple, quiet space to help her blend when she was human, give her privacy and the sense of something that belonged to her. Neptune could not offer her what her heart most desired, what would nurture her soul, but his was the greatest kindness that had ever been done for her by her own people.

She'd been here less than a few days ago, so the latest wild-flowers she'd collected inland on the roadside were still blooming. From her very first forays into the human world, she'd been enchanted with the many shapes and colors in which they came. Purple, white, gold, red. Shades of lavender, light pink, dark pink . . . An unbroken trio of dandelions, their soft white spheres waiting for the touch of the wind to make more of them.

The flowers had comforted her, this obvious connection between her two worlds. So many varieties of underwater flowers lived among meadows of sea grass, stroked to life by the currents. And they had a mirror in the earth element, where flowers grew wild among long, golden grass caressed by the wind.

Eventually she would take the dandelions to the door, purse her lips and gently blow, releasing them. When she stepped into this cottage, it was stasis, a fixed point in the universe. Stepping out, life in all its cycles, below the sea or upon the land, resumed again.

Because the hodgepodge of things she found in shipwrecks had likewise always fascinated her, perhaps it was natural that the myriad vases in which the wildflowers were placed had come from her intrigued prowlings of yard sales and junk shops. Things were quieter there, and people easier to be around, gliding like relaxed fish among a coral reef of unlikely treasures. In some of the vases, among the flowers, she'd inserted utensils she'd found. Everything from ornate scrollwork to flat, simple beaten spoons.

She didn't know the names of the styles. She could have gotten a book, studied them, but she was sated by simple absorption with the human need to create.

"This place is protected," Jonah noted at last, telling her that at least some of his magical training and abilities had not been affected by his transformation.

She nodded. "King Neptune reinforced it with cloaking spells and protections so that no one can approach unnoticed or penetrate the field with harm in mind. He's also woven an invisibility spell, so that those who detect magic won't detect anything out of the ordinary about the cottage unless they're inside the house itself. Which means they have to be let in, and therefore can't be anyone intending harm."

"Complicated. Not easy to do."

"No." She shook her head, moved to stand behind the sofa. The small living area in which he stood was open to the kitchen. A stairwell led to a balcony and a loft bedroom with a circular skylight so she could watch the stars. She could see the ocean out of the front panel of windows, and there was a small deck, a fountain into which she put her feet while sitting out there. That had been one of her improvements, so she could feel the water on her skin even though the ocean lay only about fifty yards away at high tide.

Regardless of what other improvements each daughter of

Arianne made, each one also added to the artwork along the unbroken back wall underneath the balcony. Like the men's clothing, there were so many traditions about the cottage hard to explain to anyone. Odd tributes to Arianne, things done because the women had no other family traditions, no permanent ties into any community. Their tenuous link to one another, mother to daughter through the generations, was therefore vitally important.

But as his gaze traveled the wall, noting the pictures, Anna felt the need to try to explain. Maybe because she wanted to tell someone who might just want to listen.

"Each daughter chooses a picture for the wall, something she feels belongs there. No other specification, just that indefinable feeling."

It had been started by the first inhabitant of the cottage, the true daughter of Arianne. A postcard, set in a large frame against a white matting, a small picture in a blank void. It was a snapshot, the stone statue of her mother, gazing with suffering, blank eyes toward the port that had held her dream.

"One person's tragedy and heartbreak becomes another's tourist attraction," he murmured. Jonah's gaze shifted down the row, past several other contributions, and then stopped on the picture Anna's mother had left.

A black box on a stale gray background. Defined, never changing. A prison. Anna hated looking at it. She'd often wished the compulsions that dictated so much of what happened or was done in this cottage were not so strong in her, so she could find the courage to pull it off the wall, throw it into the sea.

Then his attention shifted to the final picture. She'd found it in the back of a dusty antique shop, a painting done by an artist who'd never found fame, but had adapted a Romanticist style to come up with a different interpretation of the Little Mermaid's story. The mermaid was still in stone, but her prince had come. He stood in the water up to his thighs, his white horse just behind him. He was touching her face, and as he did so, the stone was melting. The picture showed the gray granite of her arm melting away as the pale white flesh and fingers lifted, reaching for him.

Jonah had moved closer and now he turned, his fingers on

the bottom of the frame. "If these are in order, this one is yours. Is this your heart's desire, Anna?"

Perceptive as he was, she shouldn't be surprised he understood more about the pictures than he should. One to remind them of the consequences of love. One recommending that hope for love—for anything—be abandoned. One refusing to do so. She looked at the picture, but more than that, she looked at his hand, the curve of his fingers, the bones of his wrist, the light covering of dark hair on his forearms, calling to mind instantly the way it felt to be in the span of his arms, the firm biceps pressing into her back.

His initial anger over his human transformation seemed to have ebbed, for now. Still, she knew she should be cautious with him. Unfortunately, that didn't seem possible for her. Mortal, he did not have the otherworldly beauty he had as an angel, but he was still a breathtaking male figure. The energy of him reached to all corners of the room, washing over her, making her want to close her eyes and just absorb him, take him in through all her senses, even as she wanted to keep looking. Those jeans . . . while she wouldn't say they were an improvement over the brevity of the battle skirt, which revealed so much of him, they were still not hard on the eyes, the way they fit. His dark hair lay on his shoulders, so black that it could not blend with the dark T-shirt.

She'd never been governed by lust. Perhaps it was because he'd broken down the door where it dwelled within her by taking her innocence, but she couldn't seem to stop her body's vibrating response to him.

"I want to see you fly again," she said softly. She wanted to see him soar, everything beauty and power should be, the way she was sure he flew when he didn't have an injured wing, or an injured heart. If she could help in some small way to make that happen, and was given the privilege of living long enough to see it, as she had seen the Windwalkers, then that would be enough.

One moment of perfect happiness could satisfy the soul forever, couldn't it? Particularly when that soul had always known such a thing to be a miracle beyond reach.

She wondered why she'd thought she wanted to tell him any of this, for now all she wanted was for him to do something so she wouldn't have to think about it anymore. So she took a step back, then another, moving to the first stair to the loft. His eyes watched her closely as she took the hem of her thin shirt and pulled it over her face, her hair lifting to funnel out the opening when she removed the garment.

"Stop."

She stopped, the gauzy fabric pressed against her lips, eyes and lashes. She could see him, a hazy, cloudy outline tinted in soft blue green dye as he came toward her. Her arms were tangled in the straps of the shirt, and he placed his hands just below her raised elbows, holding her that way as he bent, his breath caressing her. When his lips touched her mouth through the fabric, her own lips parted, moistening the threads. Her body swayed toward him, and he gathered handfuls of her hair, helping to remove the shirt so now she stood bare breasted before him. Untying the string holding the skirt, he loosened it, and she was naked, her clothes in a pool at his feet. Cupping her face, the side of her neck, he caressed the line of her throat. So slow, so sensual, a man fully aware of the power of his touch on a woman's skin, that vulnerable column.

As he gazed at her, the light of the setting sun turned the room gold, then rose, bathing them and their surroundings in rich color. He removed his shirt, tossed it to the side. Holding her breath, Anna watched as his chin tipped up, his eyes closing and hands tightening on her as his body rippled, the muscles quivering. Rose and gold became a wash of amber light, and the wings stretched behind him, the one spreading out, the other tentative, but able to join it partway, filling the small room with magic.

Slowly, his eyes opened and his chin came back down so his eyes could focus on her again with those dark, unreadable depths. He hadn't stopped touching her throughout, and now the energy that he'd had as a mere mortal had expanded exponentially. She was glad for the warding around the cottage, for otherwise surely there would be shards of it sparking outside the structure.

"Come here, Anna."

When she took a step down the stairs, he surprised her by catching her under her back and legs and lifting her in his arms, moving forward to take the steps to the balcony loft. He folded his wings carefully along his back, their points trailing him like a prince's cloak as he walked up the stairs, his eyes never leaving her face. "I would lie with you in the bed where you dream."

She couldn't think of anything she wanted more.

As he carried her up the stairs, Anna slid her arms around his shoulders, her fingertips buried in the arch of his wings. She wanted him to carry her forever. This weightlessness was . . . Oh, it felt so good to be carried, held close. It merged with the sweet anticipation in her stomach, the tiny fish that seemed to be darting everywhere, the restless press of her thighs, so aware of the grip of his hand there.

In addition to a bathroom, the two main things in the loft were her bed and the Jacuzzi pool she'd designed like a walled pond. He went directly for the bed, making those fish leap. Looking like a stretch of soft sand with its quilted brown coverlet, it was simple, wide and fortuitously long, taking up half the space. Shells she'd collected off the beach, pieces of dried coral and more flowers in vases were on the side tables and the ledge over it. Things to help keep her connected. A tiny watercolor of a mermaid she'd picked up at a traveling fair one night was there, too.

There was no lamp, for she preferred to stare out through the glass at night, watching the moonlit foam of the ocean sweep across the sand, hearing the muted rush of sound. Now he laid her down, bending over her. Her fingers curled around his upper arms, and she didn't let go. Putting one knee on the bed, he stretched out next to her, his hand settling on her bare waist, thumb idly tracing her stomach, her navel, making her thighs tremble.

"You've made yourself a nest here," he observed. "Tell me, little one. Why are you the only one left? Why are you so alone in the world?"

She reached up toward his face, but he caught her wrist, bent and kissed her palm, nuzzling her. "I want to be inside you again, Anna. Stretching your soft lips, feeling the hungry clutch of your body desiring mine. But you will tell me this first."

She closed her eyes. "That's bribery, my lord."

"So it is." The trace of a smile did not eradicate the seriousness from his face. "I won't harm you with the knowledge, I promise."

He understood. It twisted inside of her, a sweet pain. In the same breath that she'd felt the desire to tell him, she'd experienced the fear of having him react as so many others had, as those who'd known the story for centuries.

"The original seawitch, Mina's great-great-grandmother, gave my ancestor Arianne the spell of legs to win her heart's desire, the love of a prince."

When Jonah nodded, indicating his familiarity with that part, Anna was glad she didn't have to go back over the details. "Arianne failed and was turned to stone, as the legend and the reality go. But Neptune made a deal with the seawitch. He wouldn't kill her painfully, and she would turn Arianne back into a mermaid." Anna's lips twisted. "But something went wrong, and the seawitch couldn't lift the shape-shifting spell. Nor could Arianne control it. Throughout her life, she'd still shift unexpectedly from mermaid to human, and so had to live close to the land, else she would have drowned. Each time she shifted to human legs, she also experienced excruciating pain, as if stepping on razor blades when she walked. Even so, she danced on the beaches at night, remembering her prince. She left her daughter a letter that said the way he'd looked at her when she danced made the pain worth it to her."

"So who was the father of her child?"

Anna shook her head, curled her lip. "The prince, for all that he gave his love to another, had no problem lying with Arianne before he decided to leave her for his human bride. Arianne was carrying his child when she turned to stone. No one expected the child to live, but she did. It's been the pattern ever since. No daughter of Arianne has ever found the happiness of enduring love, but she always finds herself with child at some point. But each child, while inheriting the ability to become human, also had different unique . . . abilities. Curses."

Jonah frowned. "Why curses?"

Anna let her gaze drift toward the nightstand, to a pink flower among the others there. Delicate petals, fragile existence. But it lived, pushed up through the ground. Endured. If only for a short time, it was perfect.

"Because the abilities were involuntary and caused harm to themselves or those they loved. The first daughter, if she got excited in any way—too happy, too sad—she would violently disrupt the waters around her. Tidal waves, tsunamis, waterspouts. That was why Neptune built the cottage for her. As long as she wasn't in a large body of water, that wouldn't happen. But before that, she wrecked ships, created storms that took lives. She rescued one man from her devastation, and was able to love him long enough to get with child before he discovered her nature and couldn't accept it.

"Her daughter couldn't speak except in song. The sound of her singing voice would put whoever heard it into a deep sleep from which they wouldn't wake for days. Sometimes months. So she remained mute most of her life, desperately wishing to communicate, but only able to do so a moment or two before those to whom she wanted to talk so desperately were lost in slumber." Anna tried a smile, failed. "And so it goes.

"Neptune suspected it was a cruel irony orchestrated by the seawitch, because the deal between them included a blood oath that neither she nor her descendants would ever directly cause harm to Arianne or those descended from her again. But Mina told me the stone spell was never meant to be reversed and the magic simply took on an unpredictable life of its own."

"Are any of them alive now? Your mother? Her mother?"

"No." When she couldn't bring herself to say anything further, even at his questioning look, he bent and placed his lips on her neck, just below her ear. His nose brushed the outer curve, breath tickling the flesh there. At the wet heat of his mouth, her head tilted back, her nerves shimmering deliciously. "Ah, Goddess. You're evil."

His lips pulled in a smile against her, but it couldn't dislodge the heaviness in her chest, even under that sensation of response. "Tell me."

She'd just say it, and be done with it. He wanted to know, she'd tell him and they'd go on. Still, the words clogged in her throat. "We all die before we turn twenty-one, my lord."

Jonah stopped, lifted his head, all amusement fading out of his expression. Her gaze shifted to the ocean outside the window. "How old are you?"

She gave a half chuckle, and knew it was a bleak sound. "A fine time to decide I'm too young for you, my lord."

She wasn't surprised when he gripped her shoulders, lifted her to a sitting position. Her fingers had to curl into his thighs, though, to give her the courage to look into his face. "How old, Anna?" he repeated.

"I just turned twenty. So if I'm going to carry on the legend, I guess I better get pregnant soon."

"Don't." He made it a command. "What happened to your mother?"

When she shook her head, he eased her back to the bed and moved over her body, his knee pressing between hers. She opened to him. His eyes somehow got darker as Anna found herself submitting to his will so desperately, so easily. She could deny him nothing, even the words that had gotten trapped in her throat. He came down upon her, his chest pressed against her bare flesh, the denim and the length of him trapped beneath it rubbing against her aroused flesh. Anna drew in a breath, arched against him. Taking her wrists, he stretched both their arms out far to either side. With his arms being longer, he was able to lift his upper body to bend and kiss her sternum, just a brush of lips.

He made her feel vulnerable, holding her this way, and yet it made her want to strip her soul bare for him. She didn't understand why putting her in this open pose unlocked something inside her that a more protective posture would have kept closed, but it did, and she finally found her voice, a tremulous whisper in the darkness, feathering against the hair on his brow.

"She cut her throat right after I was born, with the knife that severed the cord between us. She asked my forgiveness, Mina told me." Anna stared blankly at that fall of hair over his forehead. "My mother said she couldn't bear to see her daughter suffer, but she didn't have the courage to end my life with hers."

"Holy Mother." When Jonah rested his brow on hers, Anna closed her eyes, feeling the heat of him, his strong features. His body pressed down on her further and she couldn't help herself. She raised her legs, coiled them around his thighs, her toes sliding down the inseam above his knees. "My lord . . ." *Please, take away the thoughts. I am going to keep talking until I shatter into pieces.*

But he didn't move, and she found herself speaking aloud again, the words pouring out of the locked memory chest that weighted her heart. "You asked about Mina. When that happened, Mina was young, no more than a child. While they were distracted, she . . . They said she captured my mother's blood, and made me swallow it, along with some of her own. Because it made me violently ill, Neptune had her thrown into the Abyss, weighted with chains. But then they discovered I lacked the type of destructive powers the other daughters had had. The midwife and healer who attended me said Mina had somehow discovered that being nursed on my mother's blood and that of the seawitch's line would give me some kind of protection. So Neptune had her fished out of the Abyss." She swallowed. "No one expected her to be alive. I was told her body was badly maimed by scavengers. I didn't see her again until I was older and sought her out, made her tolerate my company."

A faint smile touched her lips and now she was able to bring her gaze back to his penetrating one. "So you see, my lord, Mina risked her life to give me the life I have. I know she struggles with her darkness. But even if she doesn't think of it that way, she needs me to believe in her goodness. Because I'm the only one who does."

He remained silent, studying her as if she was the most fascinating thing he'd ever seen. After a few moments under that intent gaze, she couldn't bear it anymore. She began to strain against his hold. He stayed motionless, and that increased the need within her, released some of the pain and replaced it with the hard, needy anticipation of arousal. Something in his face told her he was waiting . . . wanting . . . She lifted her hips against the pressure of his, strained further, arched her throat, pressing her breasts against his chest. Offering. Begging with her movements.

His wings were at that half fold still, but they sheltered her from the remaining day's light, shading her, taking her into twilight as he bent at last, seizing her behind her nape and bringing her up against his mouth. No tenderness, startling in the way his mouth clashed with hers. But she just opened as far as she could for him, let him plunder, making urgent whimpers in the back of her throat. Her legs clamped over his hips, the muscular curves of buttocks. Her aggressive movement earned a warning growl. Her answer was to arch further, make small motions against his hard length, daring him to restrain her movements further.

He reached between them, figured out the workings of the pants, stood with sudden impatience to strip them off, then came back down upon her before she had more than a moment to miss his heat, the weight and hardness of him.

But she needed him to fill her, to be inside of her. Her heart and soul were suffocating; couldn't he see it?

"Jonah . . . my lord. Please don't let me feel this way."

His gaze flickered up to her. "Do you need the pain, little one?"

She nodded. "Make me not remember, my lord." *Make me forget I belong nowhere, not to the mermaids or to the humans, not to anyone.*

She knew those like Mina might scoff at the debasing idea of belonging to another. But when a soul was starved for touch, for connection, it would willingly enslave itself to the offering of love from another, even if only for a few moments. She would be his, as long as he would have her, and she would nourish herself on that brief time if she could. *How many of us have had the opportunity to be with an angel, after all?*

She'd been strong and independent the whole of her short life. There'd been no real choice in that, but she'd been bolstered by the example of Mina, by the wasted life of her mother. She'd never realized the danger of being held in the arms of a strong male who wanted to protect, to care. It was far more dangerous to her than anything else about Jonah. But like most things in her life, she made the conscious choice to embrace it as long as it was offered. She had too little time to waste it being afraid.

Rearing up against his touch, she bit him just above the circle of his nipple, tightening her legs on him. In response, he slid an arm around her waist and sheathed himself in her, hard, deep and fast, making her suck in a breath, utter a sharp cry of pleasure.

He pushed her back down and began to stroke inside her,

his eyes fierce, almost like the glinting red of a Dark One in the darkness of her cottage. "I will make you scream, sweet mermaid."

Jonah knew he'd kept her talking about the painful memories past the time he should have. She'd inherited a legacy of unfulfilled hopes, and he was likely to be yet another one of them. He hadn't even thanked her for saving his life. But he couldn't bring himself to do so until he knew that it had been worth saving or that it didn't bring more sorrow to her. However, he had not been alive as long as he had without learning to be resourceful, and there were things he could give her now other than his gratitude.

The flowers with which she surrounded herself were part of the key to her. Delicate, temporal, living with fierce, perfect and altogether fragile beauty in the moment. So he would give her that moment.

Sliding from her body despite her mewl of protest and his own aching hardness, he picked up one of the dandelions from the vase on the side table. Trailing it over her stomach, he watched some of the seeds dislodge, tickle her further. Then he bent, kissed the underside of her breast where the crease of its weight rested it over her rib cage. Lingered, tasted as she moved restlessly beneath him, tangled her fingers in his hair.

Lifting up, he stopped her so he could return the favor, combing out her hair with his fingers, loosening the tie that held it so he could spread it over the bed. It surprised her, he could tell, when he threaded her hands through it, tangling them, tying the strands over her wrists to keep her like that, open and trembling. Then he lifted one of her legs, supporting the calf in his hand, and guided it under his arm, resting her heel on his hip as he dragged the dandelion down, down . . .

Anna bit her lip at the feathery contact, and then a guttural cry came from her lips as he bent and replaced its touch with his own mouth.

"What are—"

"Taking you as high as you can go."

When he put his mouth fully over her hot, slick flesh, all the painful memories fled back into the darkness. Anna tugged on the quilt, working her hips against his face. His urging, rhythmic squeezes made her feel like she could bear no more, though she also wanted to ride his mouth forever. She rocked, cried out. When she looked up the slope of her body, his lashes fanned his cheeks as he watched the aroused state of her soaked sex with avid intent. It made her writhe even more insistently.

For his part, Jonah's noble intentions had fled and now he simply needed to take. As she lay so open below him, he was reminded of how she'd offered him everything on that first night, and he realized in himself the trait of a conqueror, taking as his due that which he might not deserve.

Whatever he gave her could not measure up to what her full submission gave to him. That thought gave him pause, and he studied it briefly from several angles before he pushed it away, lifted both her legs to his shoulders. Feeling her calves slide past the arches of his wings, he raised her light form, holding her for the deeper penetration of his mouth.

He'd forgotten the sweet, musky taste of a woman's cleft, the slick honey of it, the way she would respond to it if done well, as if she were being tossed on a stormy sea, her body moving as sinuously as the frothy waves.

One of the human legends of Ariel's demise had been her turning to seafoam, the supposed natural death for a mermaid, where the soul forever became a part of the sea. Now, as Anna undulated as she might if she were moving through the water, Jonah knew her heart was in the ocean, her soul deep in the sea. But it was a world that often didn't want her there. So she lived here, caught on the boundary of land and water, symbolic, like everything in this cottage. For all its quiet tranquility, he found he didn't like her being here, where all its traditions might make her believe this was the best she could hope for.

Except for that one picture. The one that said she hoped for something better.

As he came back up her body and sheathed himself again, pushing them both over the edge they needed, he knew he was going to embark on this journey with her. Not because he believed the seawitch, or that the darkness in his heart needed healing, but because suddenly the most important thing was that his little mermaid knew that someone believed in *her*.

And hellfire, he still couldn't bring himself to go back,

reach out to Lucifer or the Lady. Or any of them. What would
a week matter? Time was relative, when one was an angel.

———————

SHE woke alone. The thunder was shaking the house, coming
close together, flashes of lightning illuminating the cottage so
she could see him standing on the deck, the sliding glass door
open to the driving rain. His hair was plastered to his head, his
face tilted to the sky, the wings a heavy weight on his back.

She didn't dress, but moved down the stairs, stood in the
open door, stepped out behind him.

"Is it a battle?"

He shook his head, put his hand back without looking at
her. When she took it, he drew her forward, tucking her under
his wing so she could stand before him. He spoke in a quiet
murmur despite the rain because his jaw was along her temple
as they looked up together. "It's just a thunderstorm, little
one."

She could feel it from him, a thrumming tension. Anna
turned, tilted her face to him instead of to the sky.

Every line of his face was taut, his eyes . . . haunted. Something moved there, something that reminded her of what Mina
had said. *He leads the angels that fight Dark Ones* . . .

"Tell me of the other angels." She sought for something to
draw him out, not wanting him to dwell alone in the darkness
of his thoughts. "Your friends. Those you command."

A quiver ran through his muscles. "I can't." Bowing his
head, he brushed her temple and closed his eyes, even as her
arms came up around his neck. "When I think of them, I only
hear their screams. See the blood."

It took her a moment to digest the meaning behind his
words, and realize where his thoughts were. Not with the living he'd left behind to be here tonight, but with the dead who'd
left him.

"Choose one." Guided by intuition, she whispered it, as it
might come to him in a dream, where it was safe to remember.
"Something simple. Tell me the color of his hair."

He opened his eyes and stared at her, so intently he jumped
when the lightning flashed again. His fists clenched, but she
put her hands over his arms to remind him she was there when
the snarl of the thunder came, as it always did.

"Ronin had bright gold hair," he said in the thunder's aftermath, the rush of the rain closing them into a still space where she was conscious of his breath on her cheek, the mist on his lashes that might not be from the water dripping from his brow. He shook his head, his lids squeezing shut again, then reopening. "He was inordinately proud of it."

"Gold. Was he handsome?"

"He seemed to think so. When he sought a female to ground himself, he'd boast that she just had to see his hair to fall into his arms." He gave her a light squeeze, seeming to recall himself. "Unlike my darkness, which I have to compensate for with my charm."

"I am glad to tell you your darkness is most handsome, my lord." She threaded her fingers through the wet raven strands. "And it's a good thing, for your charm is rough around the edges."

"You wound me, little one."

She smiled as more of the tension eased from his shoulders. "Are the others all like you? Handsome and intolerably arrogant?"

Something glimmered in those ebony eyes. "No, they are worse. And ugly. You would not like them at all."

His upper body was beaded with the falling rain. Impulsively, she placed her lips on a drop high on his chest, rising to her toes, and she tasted it, his skin with the rainwater. The absence of salt in the water, the taste of salt from the skin. The way the ocean and the earth came together, sharing the salt. The same way the two of them came together, an angel and a mermaid.

His hand came up, cupped the back of her head. He held her like that, the rest of his body so still, restrained power. She didn't even think he was breathing as she let her own hands glide like birds down the slope of his back, that shallow indentation, over convex sets of muscles to the rise of his buttocks. She rested there, feeling the smaller feathers on the undersides of his wings touch her.

"I miss them. So fiercely I want to hurt someone when I think of them." Jonah felt it within him, the violence simmering, and hated that it rose up in him now, when he held a creature in his arms who was the antithesis of it all. He pressed his forehead to hers, wishing he could just absorb her calmness, the tranquility he felt in her young soul.

Earlier, he'd taken her body with passion and strength. She'd bitten him, clawed, responded in kind. But this, this bare brush of contact was somehow even more powerful, standing out here in the rain, just the two of them.

Had the battlefield, painted in blood, become his true home? Had his enemies, as much as those fighting with him, become his family, if only for those moments of utter violence, when there was room for nothing else? The thought was abhorrent, but here, where he finally, after so many years, felt a quiet connection, it reminded him of how disconnected he'd felt for so long. Purposeless, except when he was killing.

"Goddess, I've told no one I missed them. What magic is in your arms, little one? Your touch? You shouldn't be anywhere near me."

"I can sing you to sleep, my lord." She seemed unconcerned by that warning. Instead, she looked out toward the sea and Jonah knew, whether or not the house was protected by the power of Neptune, she was worried about the Dark Ones finding him as they exposed themselves to the forces of the storm.

"Will I sleep for days?" He could think of nothing else to say when she looked up at him with her large violet eyes.

"No." Her small pink mouth curved. "The destructive power of my ancestor is different in me. But I can weave dreams. As I sing you to sleep, I can bring you whatever you wish, in your dreams. If you tell me of their faces, their voices, I can give them back to you. Ronin, all of them. For a night."

His thumb moved across the full bottom lip, collecting rainwater. "And do you ever sing yourself to sleep, Anna? Give yourself someone in your dreams?"

She shook her head. "No, but the Lady had pity on me. She brought me an angel instead."

He stared at her. She'd revealed herself to him earlier. Maybe that was the key that had unlocked his trust, his willingness to give to her parts of himself he'd given to no one else. She was innocent and far removed from what he was supposed to be to others, but she did understand what evil was.

"I'll go with you, Anna. We'll go see the shaman. Perhaps there will be answers on this journey for both of us."

Anna swallowed, disbelieving for a moment that he'd agreed. But when she leaned into him and saw desire rising in his eyes, her pleased surprise was replaced by a different anticipation. She knew he would have her again this night.

"I am glad to hear it, my lord. But at least for this evening, I think all the answers we need are here."

Nine

SHE'D woken before him, just before sunrise. So when she'd slipped from the bed and watched the sky become gray, then shades of pink laced with the traces of gold heralding the sun, she also watched his wings slowly disintegrate and then vanish, leaving a handful of feathers scattered across the bed and her floor. Though his torso altered somewhat, she was still captivated by the long, bare length of leg, his sex at rest, his testicles a dark shadow curved on his inner thigh.

He had been inside of her. She'd felt the shift of his biceps against her flesh as he held her, the line of his jaw pass over her cheek as his lips feathered over her skin, teeth taking an unexpected, fierce nip, rousing an equally fierce response from her.

All silent wonder, she knelt next to his hand, lying loose and open on the covers. Those long fingers had touched every inch of her flesh, teasing, caressing, gripping . . . Now she placed her own hand into the cup of his palm, carefully straightening her fingers, one by one, holding her breath so she didn't wake him. She wanted to see again how delicate her hand was against the elegant power of his.

Tilting her head to gaze at his face, she found his eyes had opened. Dark, dark brown, the human whites so odd to her even though she'd been used to his true appearance such a short time. She liked figuring out his emotions from the tone of his voice, the shift of his body. Watching the fire flash through the solidly dark eyes from desire.

"Good morning," she said softly, and then wondered if he'd consider it good, considering he was waking to it in this form.

———————

HER hair had fallen forward, brushing his forearm. That's what had woken him. That, and a very strange sensation. He knew the ways of humans, had moved silent and unseen among them for a long time. But seeing human appetite and hearing it rumbling in his belly were entirely different. It sounded alarming, as if an animal were in there and would soon rip its way out if he did not appease it.

The second thing that confronted him was a cat. Sitting on the footrail just beyond her, peering at him with half-closed yellow eyes that opened a tad wider when he raised his gaze. He contemplated the two things—cat, empty stomach—and didn't feel any particular pull toward consuming the feline, so it apparently wasn't what his stomach craved.

He turned his attention back to Anna, for his reaction to her was much easier to understand. Under the guise of sleep, for the past few moments he'd just watched her playing with his hand, like a newborn discovering a fresh revelation with everything touched and seen. Her guilty flush and the way she drew back told him she was embarrassed.

"Can you change on land? To a mermaid?"

Her brow puckered, but she nodded. "Not for long. I need the water to move of course, and to keep my gills and scales wet." She arched a brow. "Why, my lord?"

Because he wanted a visual reassurance that neither of them was truly human. He didn't have the words to explain that. But then, why did he have to?

"Is that why you have the pool up here?" He gestured.

The loft bedroom contained only two objects. Last night the only thing that could claim his attention was the bed. This morning he noted the walled pool, a lotus-shaped creation with sandstone block walls to form a seating area around it. It explained the extra reinforcement beams under the balcony. Several baskets were placed on the edge of the sandstone wall, and they contained soap shavings shaped and scented like rose petals. There were floating candles in the pool, apparently lit by her in the night, for they were still burning in this dawn hour, casting a gentle light over the dim room.

"I don't like to be too far from the water, my lord."

"Change for me," he murmured. "I want to see."

Anna seemed to consider that. Then she withdrew from his side, her eyes lowering so her thick lashes swept her cheeks. She'd donned one of the human garments, the gauzy skirt from yesterday, but she'd put on the black T-shirt he'd been wearing. It pleased him to see her wearing close to her skin what he'd had close to his. She dropped the skirt first, then slowly drew the shirt over her head. Not for the first time, he thought how beautiful her breasts were. Small and firm, tipped with delicate pink nipples that made his mouth suddenly moist. As he swallowed, she stepped over to the pool, taking a seat on the edge.

Jonah sat up, watching her. "Anna, why can't you look at me? You liked looking at me a moment ago." He injected a teasing note in his voice and was rewarded with a slight smile, but she kept her eyes down.

"It's an intimate thing, my lord. I . . . I've done it in front of Mina, but we both do it, so it doesn't seem as significant to shift before one another."

"Well, for the time being, I'm a shapeshifter, too, you know."

Her silence told him it was different, that his change was forced, involuntary and unwelcome. And temporary. It tightened his mouth to even think of it, though he tried to soften his expression as he noticed her hands tensing, wringing the fingers together nervously.

"Anna."

She raised her gaze, a fraction at a time.

"I command you to shift," he said quietly. "Now."

Her eyes went to half-mast again, like the cat, who'd moved to the doorway and lay on his side, lazily watching them both.

Her toes curled. Uncurled. Small pearls of flesh, so pale, and then suddenly his eye was drawn to a purple and blue streak spreading across her legs, like ink marking all the veins beneath, only the iridescent color was widening, the texture of the skin changing beneath it. Flashes of silver sparkled over it then, replacing the flesh in a blink, scales overlapping, her lower body shuddering, elongating when she leaned back on her arms. She arched in sensuous display as her lower body twisted, writhed and altered. The blue and purple lines snaked up her upper body, over her rib cage, their delicate tendrils tattooing her abdomen, following the outsides of her breasts and ending in elaborate curls over the roundness of her shoulders.

The overlapped scales gave the womanly shape of her hips an even more lush outline, now that he could compare the difference between her human and mermaid forms with more accuracy. His attention traveled back down the length of her tail, where the scales became smaller and smaller until they were like jewels in a delicate maid's shield of armor. The fronds of her caudal fins unfurled like feathers, the various shades of purple and blue highlighted with tempting glitters of pink and silver.

When Jonah rose from the bed, he could tell the part of her that was instinct, bound to the sea and its laws, immediately became apprehensive, knowing how vulnerable she was in this form with no ocean to provide her grace and speed. He would not have her suffer a moment's fear.

"*Sshh . . .* " he said, coming to one knee beside her. As petite as she was, it put them nearly eye to eye. He curved his hand beneath the weight of her hair, traced the sensitive crescent of gills that hid along her throat, a different type of beauty. Just like his current form. A different way of surviving. He needed to think of it that way.

Lifting her, he stepped into the pond, lowered himself and her into the clasp of the water, the familiar touch of an element they both knew. Her hair floated around them as he settled in, finding out it was roomy enough he could put his back to the side and hold her between his thighs, pressing his attentive cock comfortably against her lower back as she slid down into his embrace.

Turning her in his lap, he rested his arm over the bend of her tail and perused her at his leisure. "So"—he let his gaze travel down her body, lingering with particular pleasure over her breasts, his fingers passing over the ornamentation embellishing them, feeling the slight raised texture of the intertwined colors, registering her tremor—"where do I find your . . . ?"

The inflection, the trailed-off sentence, told Anna what he meant. She flushed. Would she ever stop doing that? He'd had his mouth on her, his body fully inside hers, and yet, when his gaze pinned her like this, she felt warm and hot, and was so conscious of the way the water moved over her . . . in her.

Lifting his right hand from her breast, he extended it, held it before her. "Take me there. I want to touch you like this. You're beautiful, Anna."

It gratified her to hear it. She'd worried that, because he had legs, he might find her mermaid form unappealing. But she'd been born a mermaid. The human form was just a disguise. Although she used it often enough it had become more comfortable to her, there were physical limitations she had that could not be overlooked. Hence, Mina's sharp warning that she needed to head back to the sea at a certain point.

Which turned her mind to other worries. She had to get Jonah to Nevada. Into the middle of the desert, and they could only "travel by Fate." They couldn't drive a car or pay to take a bus, but had to be carried there by the kindness and motives of others. Why had Mina been so specific on that, so vague on other details? Damn it.

But right now there was this. She'd figure out the rest later. He was waiting, those dark eyes riveted on her face, so still, in a way that suggested his true otherworldly nature even in this mortal form. And he wanted her *as a mermaid*.

She took his hand in one of hers. Reaching out, she curved her other hand on his shoulder, at the corded juncture with his throat. Her slender thumb pressed at the base, feeling his quickened pulse as she shifted to one hip on his muscular thigh. The movement told her he was aroused, and his casual attitude about that combined with the focus in his eyes made her short of breath. She had to remind herself to use her lungs, not gasp through the useless gills.

She guided his hand around her hips, back, back. As she did, it arched her upper body up and his attention settled on the breast now tilted invitingly toward his mouth.

She rested his hand on the indentation just below the skirt of her feathery anal fin. The blue and purple silk of it rippled over him, brushing his knuckles. Her lower body quivered as he kept his gaze locked on her breast, but felt his way beneath her with his fingers, exploring that indentation, seeming to know intuitively how to move with the overlap of her scales, onto the smooth, tender dip at the crevice below the fin. He found the opening waiting there, hidden but giving way at the presence of his fingers, like the furled petals of a flower.

Jonah knew the moment his easing fingers penetrated. For one thing, Anna's lips parted, her tongue tasting them in a quick, nervous sweep. For another, the fluid, cool feel of the water in the pool gave way to the warm, viscous fluid of an aroused woman. He explored with gentle fingers, not only to feel that opening, but the tighter anal opening just above it, tucked in closer beneath the fin. Caressing them with his thumb and forefinger, he made her eyes widen at the unexpected dual sensation.

Though he was inflamed by her breathy moan, he took his time. If there was one thing an angel knew, it was that it was a sin to rush a female's pleasure.

Particularly when the exploration itself was such a pleasure. If she'd been in a human form, it would have been like laying her over a chair or table to touch her soft, wet cunt from behind, her anal entry within reach, as it was here. However, the warm, wet opening he was currently investigating was more narrow than the one in her human form. To get the same effect, he suspected he would have to have her cross her legs at the ankles, holding her thighs tightly together while he plunged into the excruciatingly snug opening.

"Holy Mother," he breathed, his cock rising hard and hungry at the thought. He'd never been like this, so carnal and demanding at once, so quickly. While he didn't want to think about what limitations his human body would force upon him, apparently one thing it managed well enough was lust. He would focus on that, rather than the unfamiliar, unbalanced feeling he'd had when he rose to cross the room to her, so that for a moment he'd been afraid he was going to pitch at her feet.

Keeping his gaze on hers as long as he could, he turned her away from him, so he could settle her more squarely between his thighs. Her head dropped back, resting on the wall, her body in a lithe crescent as he lowered her slowly onto his upright sex, taking himself into the grip of that narrow but blessedly slick opening. As he stretched her, she cried out, soft moans, making him ache even harder to take her down on him, to the hilt.

When he finally did, every glorious inch, her hips were

nestled into the cradle of his, his forearm wrapped over her breasts, his other at her waist, holding her securely on him, his thighs holding her still on either side. She'd gripped his forearm in tight hands, and he could see her nipples were now sharp points, her breath floundering.

"Breathe, Anna. Breathe. Tighten on me. Ah, gods," he groaned as the very command made her contract involuntarily.

He liked having her this way, knowing it was possible to Join with her in the form closest to who she was. Knowing once again he was the first to do it.

Her nails dug into him, and he watched her tail undulate involuntarily, which in turn brought her down on him in an incredible sensation of motion, stroking him almost like the movement of water. Pressing his face into her neck, he put his lips beneath her ear and over her gill, that elegant slit. The inner side looked like mother-of-pearl, but was a delicate membrane he teased with his mouth, experimenting, and earned a gasp of reaction. As well as an intimate clamp on his length that made him wonder if he had the strength to move her along it. He did, and she helped with the movement of her tail, her upper body quivering, flushing, a sparkle of silver flashing across her skin, energy collecting, collecting . . .

Was she conscious of it? Had she thought that was why he was doing this, another healing session of Joining Magic, getting Mina's daily prescription out of the way? It didn't sit well with him for her to think that, but as the energy closed in around them, he couldn't stop it. It stimulated the senses, pouring into his muscles, increasing the rapid pounding of his heart, enhancing his vision and strength, healing things that were not present in this body but waiting just beyond sunset.

The flood of magic surged through him as he held her against him, realizing he might very well be using her fragile body as an anchor against the poisons drawn up in a vortex inside him at the incursion of energy.

He didn't want the magic to remind him of who he was, even as he cursed being human. He only wanted to embrace her. She was the only thing that made sense.

"Stop, Anna," he muttered, thrusting into her hard, feeling her shudders. Reaching up to grasp her throat, he held her head alongside his, her hair brushing his lips. "Give me your cries. That's all I want. Let me hear your pleasure."

He didn't know if she heard him or not, for almost as the words came from his mouth, she shattered, surging out of the water, her scales glistening the way he knew her folds would be if he could see them instead of having only the aching glory of fucking her, rising, falling, stroking, demanding, until . . .

His body spasmed, gripped in two opposing forces, the physical realm of his body and the surge of heat energy that crashed around him, through him, rippling like electrical current. He didn't want the magic, only her, and so he threw up a block, a magical ability that apparently his human form hadn't taken from him, though it was a clumsy, cumbersome effort.

Too late, he realized what a shield recklessly thrown up to reject a surge of healing energy so far along might do.

Anna's cry of pleasure escalated into a scream, and her body thrashed, only no longer in pleasure. Clouds of steam billowed from the water as fire licked over his skin and hers.

No. He shoved her beneath the water, dislodging himself from her, holding her under as the fire roared over his skin. Though he knew how to conduct energy, he had no idea what power this mortal form had to absorb or channel it, but he made a fierce effort now to seize it back, bring the crush of the thwarted purpose back on himself, swallow the detonation of it.

He forced himself to reverse his reaction, accept the magic he didn't want, ameliorate the negative effect of his initial rejection. As he did, the human skin blackened on his forearms and began to fall away. Now he cried out at the pain, even as new skin began to regenerate at once, for he was still immortal when all was said and done. He struggled through the agony to keep his focus on the woman bucking beneath his hands.

Though she could breathe beneath the surface, he felt her panic, so he pulled her up though the air stank of blackened flesh and steam still rose from the water. Mercifully it occluded her expression. He was sure it reflected her confusion and fear, things he'd caused. He cursed his cowardice, but even feeling those emotions from her was more than he could bear.

With an oath, he erupted from the pool, stumbling out of it

to stand, dripping and gasping for air, several feet away, turned away from her. If he'd hurt her . . . Gods, how long had he known how to manipulate energy? Easy as breathing, but he'd panicked over an attempted healing, let it take him over so he reacted like a youngster in need of a mentor to protect him. Or protect others from him.

She'd shifted back to human form and was sitting on the edge of the wall, her hair draped forward but her eyes on him, worried. Worried for him. But she was also trembling, in pain.

In two steps he was to her, kneeling and tunneling his fingers through her hair. Searching her face, the front of her body. Pale, unmarred. Either he'd done better than he anticipated, or . . .

Tightening her muscles when he tried to turn her, she attempted a smile. "I'm fine, my lord."

He rose and looked over the top of her head. Her back was scorched, the skin already a deep red, with several seeping welts.

It could have been worse. He told himself that even as he felt impotent fury at her pain. In his usual form, he could incinerate her with no more than a thought. Only his ineptitude and this limited human shell had saved her life, or at least protected her from more damage.

"I can heal you . . . tonight." He'd retained a substantial arsenal of his magical ability, and yet his healing power was denied to his human form. A cruel joke. Sunset was hours away, hours while she'd suffer. "You won't have any scars." It sounded pathetic.

He turned away, unable to bear it any longer. "Why didn't you just let me die?" he snarled. She flinched as if he'd struck her. Snatching up the jeans, he left the room, afraid of what he might do, enraged by what he couldn't do, enraged by all of it. If she'd left well enough alone . . . He'd been buried so deeply in her, and that was all he needed, wanted. To stay in that moment.

Had he given her pleasure? He frowned. He couldn't remember. He couldn't remember if he'd given her release. Perfect. He couldn't heal her, couldn't do anything for her like this, in this . . . mutation. That cursed seawitch.

Jonah found himself back out on the deck, staring out at a

turbulent ocean. The day had become overcast, with a promise of more rain. In fact, a soft patter of drops had already started to speckle the sand rolling away to the beach from the front of the cottage. It drew his eye to a flash of red among the beach grass. One of the hardy wildflowers that could make it in a dune environment. Red petals, large brown center. The petals soft, the inside bristling.

Slowly, his fists unclenched. *Why didn't you just let me die?* The seawitch, Anna. Both of them were blamed in these irrational bursts of anger he couldn't seem to control, like a child.

The Lady had once said that flowers contained all the wisdom that She could ever offer, Her very favorite creation. Like many things, She hadn't elaborated on why, but the wisdom was there, waiting for him to push past his self-pity and see it.

He *wasn't* a child. If he'd reacted like one, the answer was not to continue doing so now. He fought back the feelings of anger, treating them as any other enemy. Repel; contain if you can't destroy. Then see to the wounded.

He removed the flower, scooping out the root ball. Finding a cup in her small kitchen, he put the flower in there and carried the mug back up the stairs. She didn't hear him come in. She was standing at her closet, clutching a dress of light fabric in her hands, her head tilted down as if thinking.

Though he winced anew at the sight of her back, he put down the mug and went to her. Her head lifted as she sensed his approach, but before she could turn, he laid his hands on an unmarked expanse of skin at the top of her shoulders, stilling her.

He used one hand to gather her hair, lift it away from her back where she'd hastily shaken it when she did note his presence. He twisted it into a tail, laid it over one shoulder. The froth of curls, like the unfurling of an ocean wave, tumbled over one breast, the tips tickling the soft vee of her mons.

"You won't hide your pain from me," he said. "Give me the dress."

It was a worn, soft cotton he knew would still feel like sandpaper. But he recognized easily enough that she was feeling vulnerable, flayed by his anger, and was seeking shielding.

"What happened?" She said the words almost as two separate sentences, as if the energy to form one was too much.

He laid the dress to the side, turned her. She was studying the center of his chest so hard he was sure she could drill a hole there. Was there anything that made a male feel so chastised as a female's refusal to look at him?

Tilting her chin up, he lightly, lightly brushed his lips over hers. Then her eyes. Her nose. The set of her chin. "I was being a complete bastard. How can I give you comfort? Tell me how I can ease your pain until nightfall, when I get my healing ability back."

"I'm fine. I—"

"Anna." His grip increased. "I didn't ask. I've been a commander for a very long time. My men will tell you my mouth does not open unless I am about to issue an order."

She pressed her lips together, revealing her own streak of stubbornness. "I am not part of your army, my lord."

He arched a brow. "I am bigger, stronger and determined to have my way. And I will spank you if you don't listen to me."

Her gaze flew up to him then. But he couldn't hold out against the emotions surging in her eyes. "By the Lady, let me help, Anna. I can't bear your pain any more than you can bear mine, though I hope by now you realize mine is far more deserved."

Amazingly, again without having done the slightest bit to earn it, he won a small curve of her lips, despite the tremor of her hands which told him the pain she was suffering.

"That's the second time you have threatened to spank me, my lord. Your threats are going to lack weight if you continue to issue them without following through."

"Very well, then." He made as if to turn her over his knee, gently, and she pulled away, emitting a short giggle. She put her hand over her mouth, shifted. He gave her a level look and she sighed.

"Cool fresh water, my lord. That is likely the best thing."

He nodded, squeezed her hand and went to her bathroom, which also had a large tub. Bending over, he turned the spigots, getting the water started. He turned, seeing her watching him with a bemused look on her face. She looked away, coloring, and he came back to her, took her hand. It made him curse himself anew, for close to her like this it was enhanced, how much bigger and stronger he really was. At least physically. As she tilted her head up, the clearness of her gaze so pure, he felt she could decimate him with nothing more than a tear or frown. "I can carry you," he said.

Her eyes sparkled, a quick trace of humor. "I am sure my legs are functioning properly, my lord. Let's test them out."

Helping her to the tub, he let her sit on the edge until it finished filling. He leaned in the doorway and watched her bend forward now, the ends of her hair dipping in. Her hand drifted on the water's surface. He could imagine her sitting on a rock in the sun, sailors happily dashing themselves on that rock to get close to her.

When she was ready, he held her hand as she stepped into the tub, steadied her as she sat down. Before she could reach for the sponge, he took it, saturated it in the water and then began to squeeze it over the top of her back, watching her shiver as the water made first contact, the skin sensitive enough to feel the drops as a much heavier impact. He brought the sponge closer so the drops fell more gently and then started to do that in a continuous motion to make it more of a flow than a rainfall. The slight flinching ceased, and she closed her eyes.

Smooth curve of spine, her bottom a heart, the curves flattened where they pressed into the porcelain. It reminded him of the give of the flesh under his fingers when he squeezed them. Pale, soft. As opposed to the red, blistered skin above, his doing.

"I'm sorry, Anna. For all of it."

He had his other hand on the edge of the tub and she covered it without even opening her eyes. "Already forgiven, my lord." Her fingers tightened as her mouth firmed and he could tell she needed to say more. Things he didn't want to hear.

"The Joining Magic, my lord. You need—"

His stomach made that terrible gurgling noise again, only far more pronounced this time. Her eyes opened, going to the affected area, then up to his face. "You're . . . hungry."

"Apparently. Though I've no idea what exactly a human eats. I've never paid much attention."

Her eyes were dancing with that irrepressible amusement again. She really wasn't angry with him, wasn't holding a grudge at all. It was amazing, how it diluted some of the heaviness in his own chest, made him want to smile with her.

"I know just the place. It's on our way."

"On our way to what?"

The humor banked somewhat, but she continued on in a light note, as if she didn't realize he could read every slight shift, every nuance of her expressions. "To begin our journey, my lord."

Ten

DESPITE his attempt to delay the inevitable, citing the pain in her back, Anna wouldn't let herself be dissuaded. Fortunately, he chose not to be too stubborn about it. She put two changes of clothes for each of them and a few other essentials in a backpack, while he prowled around.

It would be too easy to give in, stay in the protective comfort of her cottage, where she didn't know for a fact that every step they took toward Nevada and the shaman was a step closer to Jonah healing, leaving. If she was successful.

He wasn't hers. Not remotely, not ever. And if she hadn't known something was terribly wrong earlier, she'd have known it after his violent rejection of the Joining Magic that morning. When it had happened, she had felt something more than Jonah shove her offering away. Something dark and frightening, which disturbed her to consider even now.

So instead she watched him out of the corner of her gaze as she got them ready to go. The way he moved around her cottage, picking up things and examining them. Interested in her life but seemingly so detached from his own. While his distaste of his human form and its physical limitations had been clear, he didn't seem to embrace himself as an angel except in terms of what was essential. The ready ability to block her attempt to heal him, for example.

But he was a creature of the sky—that much was obvious. After coming in from the rain, he'd left the glass doors open, and even now he returned to them every few minutes, stepping out under the now clear sky as if to confirm it was still there.

She had traveled before, but always where salt water was in reach. Physically, in human form, she didn't have to have the proximity every day, but some part of her needed the reassurance of it, often. So she understood what he was doing. Empathized. And tried once again not to worry about how far they would be leaving the ocean behind, or the promise Mina had tried to extract from her.

Despite the weight, she put a gallon of seawater and a few of her shells in the pack. She might need all of it before it was done, even rationing carefully. After making sure the stray cat who'd attached himself to her was left enough food and water to supplement his own hunts while she was gone, she felt ready to go.

The diner was in walking distance. Though he took the backpack from her to carry, she noticed he was having to focus on his gait, clumsily compensating for the unfamiliar absence of his wings, the different weight distribution when he turned to look at this or that feature of the landscape. It made her heart hurt, but she knew what was done was done.

He wore the jeans she'd given him yesterday and the T-shirt. They should probably stop and get him one that fit his broad shoulders better, but of course she knew the clothes were spelled to fit the wearer. Or perhaps they simply reflected the pleasure of the daughter of Arianne who offered them. A flutter of humor moved through her mind at the thought, and she wished she could share the observation with Mina. Which sobered her again.

"How long will it take to get to the shaman?" Jonah asked.

"I'm not sure. I suspect no more than a week under the worst circumstances; otherwise, Mina would have cast her transformation spell for a longer duration." Actually, Anna didn't know that for sure, but she was hoping that Mina's mind had been working far more quickly than her own during their narrow escape. "She said we can only travel by Fate, and only during the day. The daylight travel is so we don't attract the notice of people, or Dark Ones, when you return to your actual appearance at night. She warned us to stay on guard even during daylight hours, however."

"I think she just wanted me to experience blisters." As he glanced down at his feet, she could imagine his toes curling resentfully in the confinement of the athletic shoes. "There's a spiteful streak in her. You cannot deny that, for all your championing of her."

Anna smiled. "I won't deny that any more than she would, my lord."

Jonah snorted. "I'm sure the Dark Ones will be looking for a human in ill-fitting clothes, walking along a roadside carrying a backpack embroidered with flowers and . . ." He turned it, peered at the design. "What is this?"

Anna cleared her throat and focused on the pack instead of his expression. "It's Prince Eric. From the Disney movie *The Little Mermaid*? And Flounder and Sebastian. Ariel's friends."

She added hastily, "A little girl gave it to me on the beach one day. I don't know why, but she was very earnest about wanting me to have it. Have you ever been to the Magic Kingdom, my lord? It's somewhat irresistible."

"I think your seawitch isn't the only one with a tormenting streak. It pervades the female species, starting from the highest upon high." He shouldered the pack and relented. "Ronin once did a flyby over the castle before the nightly fireworks show, just to make the children think they'd seen the real Tinkerbell. Of course it startled the acrobat set to slide down the wire from the castle spire half to death. The actual Tinkerbell performer. He made it his business to find her later that night and . . . soothe her feelings."

Anna suppressed a chuckle. At Jonah's narrow sidelong glance, she changed topics. "According to Mina's vision, the shaman lives in a place called Red Rock Schism, a magical fault line of sorts, in the Nevada desert. She has spelled the map into my head, so I can keep us on the right course."

"So he lives 'somewhere' in the desert," he echoed.

She nodded, studying the wildflower array as they followed the roadside. This section of road was built on a causeway, so the water of the ocean stretched off to one side, the marsh on the other. A great egret watched them pass with stately elegance, his gaze trained on Jonah. She noted flocks of seagulls that altered their courses just enough so they did not pass directly over his trajectory. He might think no one would recognize him in a human form, but she only had to watch the natural world around them to know differently. She resolved to follow Mina's instruction to the letter, despite the derision in his tone.

She didn't think even humans could mistake him for anything but an extraordinary being. Keeping things in terms they could understand, they might wonder if he was a well-known figure in a gladiator sport like football or wrestling. But each time those dark eyes settled on her, she was hit by the power behind them, just waiting for sunset. As distractions went, he was a perfect one to help keep her mind off her throbbing back, which in turn would hopefully ease the concern in the gaze he kept passing over her. She could get lost in those eyes and forget just about anything . . .

Until he knocked into her, tumbling them both down the embankment. They rolled and stopped just short of the marsh, thankfully, as the eighteen-wheeler semi roared past them. It had apparently emerged when she was in thought. Perhaps he'd been as deep in thought as she had been, but she knew the movement of ocean waters and wind tended to swallow human noise until it was right upon the unsuspecting person.

He scrambled to his feet even as the truck was passing, assuming a protective stance over her, which he held in rigid confusion as he registered what it was, what it wasn't. The utter stillness and battle readiness that existed in every line of his body, his concentrated expression, made her decide he didn't need Mina or her to warn him to be on guard. She suspected she was with a being who'd done nothing but be on guard, perhaps for centuries.

Biting her lip against her own discomfort, Anna slid from beneath his planted feet, touched his thigh, glancing up at the tense line to hip, to chest, to his face and all the things chasing across it.

"It's all right, my lord. It was just a truck."

It was an inane thing to say, of course, reflected in the irritation on his face, the clench of his jaw. "I know that." Shaking his head, he lifted her to her feet with a gentle and strong hand, but there was something wild in his eyes, like a stallion about to bolt. "I let my mind drift and it . . . startled me."

She placed a hand on his taut forearm. "We're almost there. We can walk along this bank here; it's fairly flat. All right?"

"I hate this," he said.

Jonah hated everything right now. Huge waves of red anger seemed capable of swamping him in unexpected moments, with no form or reason, no purpose. Like the angry red of her back he'd caused. "You should let me do this journey on my own," he said abruptly. "Stay here near the water. Just draw the map out for me."

She began picking her way along the bank. She tried to shoulder the backpack he'd dropped, seemed to think better of it and carried it in her hand, though it gave her an awkward gait. "They make fresh bread at this diner every morning, my lord. You can smell it, if the wind favors us and turns this way."

He stared after her. "Anna," he said in measured tones. "It's not a wise idea to patronize me."

"You'll feel better after you've eaten something," she said, her voice drifting over her shoulder like birdsong. "Most men do."

Whether she meant human males, or the male gender in general, he didn't know, but his mermaid had a clever tongue. He was finding that out. Which gave him thoughts of other uses for it. Those images made it impossible to retain his irritation with her, particularly with her up ahead, her hips moving with a graceful pendulum swing beneath the skirt, the movement unconscious physical evidence of her true form.

"Mothers say that kind of thing to cranky babies," he observed, stalking after her.

"Do they, my lord?" She glanced over her shoulder at him, her hair whispering across kissable lips. "It has the sound of wisdom, doesn't it? The simplest things make you feel on firm ground again. A good night's sleep, a good meal. A flower offered at just the right moment."

She'd not remarked on it at the time, but now he knew she'd noticed his earlier gesture, given it more credit than it deserved. Than he deserved. Again.

She was humming, and the sound of her voice reminded him of how she had sung him to sleep during the rainstorm. He'd drifted off remembering Ronin's laughter, the way it could transform Alexander's dry sarcasm into wit and make Diego smile that slow smile as he tested his sword blade on the edge of one of his crimson and gold feathers. In between the ghosts, he'd remembered the first time he taught David how to recover his balance if he was knocked a hard blow in the air, how to pull up before he crashed to earth . . . Why had it been so long since he'd remembered that stunt of Ronin's at Disney? He'd taken him to task over it, even as he'd done his best not to laugh. Why could he only dream of his laughter now, and only with the help of a mermaid's sweet voice?

———————

THE diner was full of noise, but the kind that was like the rushing of surf, with a rhythm to it that could be anticipated. Clinking silverware, murmuring voices, occasional snips of laughter or a raised word to call out to the waitress. The aroma of cooking food was a warm blanket over it all, making it a good space. Wrapped in windows, the building provided a view of the ocean and marsh for the locals and early rising vacationers, so there was no sense of being closed in. And those smells . . . His stomach responded vociferously, so that when they slid into a booth, he eyed the platters of food on neighboring tables.

He'd taken the backpack from her again of course, but set it next to her on her side of the booth, having somewhat of a male distaste of being associated with the pretty pink and purple flowered carrying case. Anna ordered the "Hungry Man Platter" for him, which apparently would come stocked with enough food to maintain him for the rest of the day. When he got his wings back at nightfall, he suspected he wouldn't be able to get off the ground even if his newly mended wing did cooperate.

He'd had the hostess direct them to a booth in a far corner where he could watch all angles of approach. The automatic decision comforted him, for it told him his training was not affected by his human form. He had a limited ability to defend and protect, even if he did not have an angel's extraordinary strength and maneuverability.

He also discovered he could still read a human soul at a glance. The family that had come in behind them had a grim, gray aura which made the occupants of the tables nearest them glance up uneasily. While they wouldn't recognize the aura, it wasn't too difficult to pick up on the situation.

The man's soul was well compromised, for he was beating his wife. Hers was dangerously teetering, because she knew it wouldn't be long before his fist would find their child, now just a toddler. She moved stiffly, telling Jonah the man was one of those who left his marks where they weren't obvious. Nothing could conceal the wariness of her body language, however, the way she kept her body between him and the toddler, a mother's protective instinct not beaten out of her—yet.

When the waitress brought Jonah's plate, sliding it before him, he shifted his attention away from that table to examine his meal. He'd studied human behavior, so eating like one of them was not difficult, but he wondered if this meal would be rejected if not fully digested when he resumed his angel form. If so, he might just need to accustom himself to his stomach growling during the daylight hours. However, for now, maybe because some part of him was hoping there was an element of truth to Anna's words about the comfort of a full stomach, he dug in. Eventually he coaxed a bite of the apple pie she'd ordered with her own breakfast, enjoying it enough she had the waitress add a second piece to their ticket.

When at last he came up for air, amazed at how satisfying it was to fill a hungry stomach, she'd finished her breakfast and was studying the family herself.

"Looks like they're tourists, here for the week." She said it quietly, as the toddler started fussing and the woman hastily worked on quieting him.

Jonah nodded. Anna brought her attention back to him. "Look at all of us. We look away. We all know what's going on, but we don't feel like it's our place to interfere. Humans have such a strange, isolating culture. In the sea, it would be brought to Neptune's ears immediately, and he and some of the other merpeople would bring the male before them and tell him his behavior would change, or he would be expelled, forced to leave his family behind."

"And yet, he does nothing about their ostracism of one of their own. Two, if you count the seawitch."

"Oh, I think he would . . ." Anna shook her head. "It's different. No one is physically hurting me, or threatening me. It's just . . . I don't want merpeople to be forced to accept me. In that type of situation, people accept when they're ready to accept. If you force them, it may work out in the end, but it's always best for them to get to know you and then accept you, if you can do it that way."

She switched direction, obviously having no desire to speak about her own situation. "What would you do about that man? I mean, as an angel, if you could. Well, I mean, of course you could . . ."

"I know what you meant." He paused, studying the trio of humans. The man was detached, drinking his coffee, but it didn't affect the wary alertness of the wife's gaze, the tension in her shoulders. "Kill the child," Jonah said at last.

Anna's head whipped around. "What?"

Jonah shrugged, added more of the sweet-smelling stuff called syrup to his last pancake. "Earth is the karmic field for humans, Anna. So the man must stay here and be punished to learn from his brutality. Even if he was removed, the woman's soul is weak. She would simply hook up with another abuser. The child is innocent. His soul is not that of a former abuser, so he's most deserving of returning to a Hall of Souls for reincarnation to a better situation."

Something shifted behind Anna's eyes, something raw and unreadable. "I'll take care of the check and wait outside," she said, rising and leaving a few dollars on the table for the tip before proceeding with her awkward gait to the cash register by the door.

Of course she had money. Neptune would have seen to that. But he didn't like the feeling of her providing for him any more than he liked seeing the stiffness in her walk, the obvious comparison it drew for him to the gait of the beaten woman. There didn't seem to be much he could do about either right now, however. Jonah swallowed the last bites, which went down like sawdust.

Maybe that's why he did what he did next, interfering in something he knew was like taking one raindrop out of a flood.

As he passed the table, he stopped when he was aligned with the man, laid a hand on his shoulder. Shot a full measure of light energy into him as he glanced at the toddler, forced a smile that made the child gurgle and gave the mother a startled moment, a passing ease to the fear in her features.

The man stopped eating, placed his hand over his mouth and erupted from the table, dashing for the bathroom. Once he'd retched out the darkness, Jonah knew, he might have half a chance of seeing things in a different light.

He could do something like that, but he couldn't heal Anna until he had wings. Stifling an oath and leaving the diner, he found Anna following the sand on the ocean side. She'd apparently known he'd catch up to her painful walk in no time, if he'd a mind to follow.

When he reached her, he tried to take the weight of the backpack from her. She stubbornly held on to it. "I'll manage."

"Tell me what's wrong. I thought you'd be glad to think of the child out of harm's way."

She whirled on him. "Is that what my mother was thinking, when she said, 'I don't have the courage to kill you'?"

As understanding dawned, he cursed his carelessness. "Anna—"

"I have the right to try to overcome the challenges in my own life," she continued fiercely. "Who's to say that's not what makes us strong and decent? How much character and strength do you think someone who's never had any sorrow or loss or hardship possesses, my lord? Everyone should be able to command his own destiny. You don't get to make that decision for me, or for that child." She poked a finger in his chest, startling him. "If I'd had that taken away from me, I wouldn't know Mina, have flowers . . ."

I wouldn't have met you.

He knew she wouldn't immediately realize he'd caught that direct thought, but he grabbed her hand and refused to let go. She pulled against him hard enough she sat down on her backside in the sand so that he followed her down, dropping to one knee between her splayed feet. The wind whipped her hair across her angry eyes.

He sought for something to say, and could only come up with what was at the forefront of his mind. "I'm sorry. I wasn't thinking about it the way you were."

She blew out a breath through her nose, shook her head. "Why would you say something like that?"

"I don't know." Jonah shrugged, examined her fingers in the grip of his. "An abuser like that feels helpless, angry about something outside his control. He lets darkness close in around his soul. Striking out at something weaker makes him feel more in control, more powerful."

While it had a bitter taste, he made himself face the simple truth, say it aloud. "I hurt you in the pool because I was feeling out of my element, out of control."

Shock coursed over her features, replacing the anger in a blink. "No, my lord. You are nothing like that man. You had no intention of harming me. There is pain in your soul and you were protecting it, until it's ready to heal."

The simple words, the touch of her hand, balanced him, even as the sense of shame didn't abate. Regardless, he wouldn't add to his crime by making her expend energy to assuage his guilt. "You would pull a thorn from a lion's paw, Anna," he said with forced lightness.

Anna gave him a disparaging look, then let him help her to her feet, take the backpack. They resumed their walking silently, and when they left the causeway, they crossed over to the main beach, a wider stretch where the road disappeared behind a dune ridge.

As Anna thought about what he'd said, she realized it wasn't his assessment of the family's situation as much as the dispassionate way he'd said it that bothered her. Of course he'd have a different perspective on such matters, for he saw a far wider picture of such things, whereas she had demonstrated quite embarrassingly that she saw things in perspective to herself and her own experiences. But there'd been something . . . unsettling about his analysis. The more they walked, the more the question burned into her brain, until she had to ask it.

"Why do you hate the humans so much, my lord?"

"I don't hate them," he said. Turning away, he sat down on the sand to pull off his shoes as she had already done for herself. He added them to the backpack.

Almost an automatic response, she noted. As if he'd had to answer it before. "But you hate this human form," she persisted.

"Of course," he said with a derisive snort. "No wings, no healing power . . . Then there's these wretched shoes."

"You haven't lost your most important powers. You did something to him in there. I saw it through the window."

"So you weren't merely fuming at me," he observed. Anna gave him a pointed look and he sighed impatiently. "I took him back a few years, to where he could remember wanting to be better, wanting to love her, wanting a child. The choice to walk the same path or not is his. And he'll also remember what he became. If nothing else, it will give her a breather for a little while."

Her gaze softened. "So you do care."

"No," he said shortly. "Don't think well of me on this, Anna. I don't care about them."

"So while all of us were helplessly restrained by our embarrassment and standards of public behavior, you were just apathetic? I don't believe that."

He lifted a brow. "Why should angels help them? Humans harm each other every day."

"Because angels are like the police." She squatted by him, her skirt pooling around her ankles, even as she registered his growing irritation with the topic. "Humans are supposed to be able to trust them, count on them. The police aren't supposed to be apathetic."

"That's just idealism."

"Yes," she agreed. "Something to hope for, like Heaven. Maybe the Goddess has angels to protect humans because it gives humans the time to overcome their weaknesses to discover . . . enlightenment. She's exercising compassion, helping them find their right path, like a parent to a child."

"They're definitely like children," he snorted. "But you're right about one thing. They have an abundance of the Lady's compassion. Though only She knows why."

"You have compassion, my lord. It's just spoiled with contempt. I'm not trying to make you angry. I'm just trying to understand why."

He muttered an oath and got to his feet. "Some topics are best left alone, Anna. But since I can tell you're not that sensible, let's talk about spoiled. Do you know where Dark Ones come from?"

She shook her head, rising as well. Something ugly took over his handsome features. Something close to hate, like what she'd felt from him this morning when the magic had rebounded on her. He was toe-to-toe with her, so she had to tilt her head. Goddess, but he was intimidating when he was like this. But he wouldn't hurt her intentionally. He *wouldn't*. She was sure of it. So sure her fingers itched to lay a hand along his face, stroke a soothing hand across his temple, even if he kept that forbidding expression and the hard line of his mouth.

"They come through rifts in time and space, caused by human evil," he continued. "*Human* darkness. Whenever there's a massacre, a war, enough women struck by their husbands' fists, there can be a tear, a puncture. The stars are the holes angels have sealed. The vast darkness left is the possibility of rifts to come.

"Given any opportunity to do so, humans will destroy Creation," he said decisively, his mouth taut. "They lack the necessary respect or understanding. And yet, they embrace their ignorance *and* they have free will, Goddess only knows why."

The frustrated resentment in his expression was another puzzle piece falling into place, but any foolish idea she might have harbored to pursue it further was interrupted.

The sound of grinding gears and the knocking cacophony of an overworked engine coming over the dunes heralded the ironically timed arrival of a school bus full of laughing, excited children, glimpsed through the opening for the nearest public access.

Twenty children of mixed races poured out, herded by their chaperones, who apparently gave them the freedom to make an abrupt dash for the water. They exploded with energy, pounding across the narrow channel of sand between the dunes to charge down to the beach just below where Anna and Jonah were.

Seeing the two of them at the last moment on this otherwise deserted stretch of beach, one of the chaperones called out, but it was like calling back an infantry charge. Jonah drew Anna to his side, putting his arm around her to hold her in place as the class ran past them, shouting, taking little notice of the two of them against the excitement of seeing the vast ocean.

Anna turned to watch them, bodies formed of the various colors of the earth flashing past, arms pumping, white teeth flashing. There were screams as they plunged in and registered the first cold. Some hung back, coming to a halt and venturing forward far more slowly, getting used to the temperature. Some of the chaperoning parents had brought younger children, two or three little ones they settled in one of the tidal pools with buckets and plastic shovels, as well as a tiny red float that looked like a lobster. The claws were armrests, the whimsical face forming a headrest.

As she watched him register the creature the float was supposed to represent, she felt some of her own tension ease when his lips twitched. "Now, my lord," she managed with a straight face, "a species that can come up with something as useful as that can't be all bad."

The inner-city schools sometimes had field trips out here, she knew, bringing kids who'd never seen anything but the bleak vista of their gang-torn neighborhoods to a different view. She loved watching the children, their exuberance, their discovery of a place she knew as well as her own beating heart. While she also knew she and Jonah should keep moving, in a day's time they would be out of reach of the ocean.

So she cast off her dress, carefully pulling it over her head to reveal the swimsuit beneath it she'd decided to put on after her cool bath, before they'd left. She always wore it beneath her clothes in case the pull of the water got too strong when she was in her human form, and despite the discomfort the straps caused to her back, today was no exception.

"Let's go swim with them, my lord. The adults can use our help to keep an eye on all of them."

As Jonah dragged his gaze from the float and registered her intentions, he wondered if it was possible to hold on to anger around such a creature. He was already sick of his rudderless anger. Her fingers whispered along his arm, her eyes acknowledging the seriousness of what lay beneath their argument even as she left it floating behind like foam in the water. She splashed in, catching up with one of the teachers and introducing herself as an off-duty lifeguard before being accepted in a matter of moments by a short staff, grateful for the help.

"Your woman is fine."

Jonah looked around, then down, at a young boy who didn't quite reach his waist. The boy's cocky assertion had Jonah's lips twitching again. "Thank you," he said gravely, then incited a shriek of alarm which quickly turned to laughter as he caught the boy up under his arm and turned him upside down to toss him into the surf with the ease of a football.

————————

THAT was all the invitation the boys needed to accept Jonah. Anna had anticipated the teachers' wariness, particularly of a man with Jonah's intimidating size and presence. However, she'd underestimated the underlying, instinctual recognition of what he was, and so except for the occasional careful sweep to ensure he was staying close with the boys, the teachers accepted him.

When they saw him wrestle their fellow into the waves, the children needed no other encouragement to hurl themselves on him, en masse. He went under, taking six or seven with him, their arms and legs tangling with his. While it was mostly boys, there was at least one girl.

Anna couldn't blame her. She wouldn't mind tackling him herself, though she'd have far less tomboylike motives. Unlike her, he wasn't wearing a swimsuit beneath his clothes, so he'd simply stripped off his wet shirt and tossed it onto the beach, where some maternal parent had laid it out over some dune vegetation to dry and dislodge the sand.

When he wrestled in the shallows, the water and sunlight glinted on the muscles of his upper body, the wet jeans clinging to his hips and legs. She couldn't help herself. She salivated. It was ridiculous. Of course he was beautiful. But lust alone shouldn't make her heart hurt like this. She told herself it was fine to dwell on the physical, but not if it mired her in more dangerous emotional waters. Damn Mina for planting the idea of a daily prescription of Joining Magic. Damn him for choosing it in the first place. She could hardly finish getting mad at him for one thing before she wanted him touching her again. She must be losing her mind.

When he emerged onto the beach a while later to wipe his face with a borrowed towel, he shook his dark hair like a dog, amusing the parents. Anna was holding the hands of two of the more timid children, having coaxed them into the water. Out of the corner of her eye, she watched him sit down in the sand near the toddlers in the tidal pool.

Drawing his knees up, he linked his hands over them. There were two little girls, both with tiny, sausage-shaped bodies, arms held carefully at their sides for balance when they walked. One waddled over, falling against his legs. The other took a fistful of his hair to climb up his chest. They were like puppies nestling on the alpha of the wolf pack when he was in a benevolent mood.

Daylight, human form and bad temper—he was still an angel. No one sensed that better than children. It radiated from him. Forcing her attention to her charges again, she immersed herself in their simple joy, rather than the confusing complexity of her own emotions and apprehensions.

———

TINY warm body, soft breath at his throat. Jonah held the toddler easily in one arm as the other planted herself on the sand between his splayed legs to pick up fistfuls of sand and create a mud pie on top of his bare foot. A group of young girls a little farther away were busily creating a more complex sand castle, looking around for shells to decorate it. The boys came and offered to bury him fully in the sand, an offer he declined with mock threats if they tried, and of course they were soon quickly back in the waves, giving him the pleasure of focusing on Anna again. Sunshine, water, an innocent child falling asleep against him, foot flexing and unflexing against his abdomen. When the mother offered to take her, he noted the weariness in her eyes and told her he didn't mind watching over the two a few minutes more while she sat down nearby with a couple of the other adults.

She studied him, hand on hips. "She doesn't take well to strangers. You bribe her with something? Candy?"

He shook his head.

"She does seem to know when someone's okay. If she's wrong, I'll hunt you to the end of the earth and cut out your heart, you hear?"

Jonah blinked. "Understood."

Satisfied, the mother moved about ten feet away and sat with the other parents, giving in to what he heard was a pair of swollen ankles, which didn't dilute her threat a bit.

"You're not to get so much as a scrape," he muttered to the drowsy child. "Else I expect I'll be held responsible."

Goddess willing, the baby in his arms would grow to be a young girl like those near him, then into a woman, the childish, oblong body elongating into curves, slim legs . . .

His gaze drifted out to the water, where Anna had a bevy of children around her, teaching them about swimming safely in the waves, if her gestures and quick smiles were any indication. Though of course her more diminutive size and gender would discourage roughhousing, it moved him oddly, seeing the children demonstrate an unusual sensitivity, being careful of her back.

He wondered if her father had held her like he was holding this toddler, then remembered it was likely she hadn't known him. As he also remembered their argument and how Anna's mother had taken her own life, he wondered at the weight of carrying that in her mind, the reflection it cast upon her sense of value. And yet there she was. Beautiful, perfect, full of love, hope and healing. If he'd ever doubted the existence of miracles, she was one.

He did understand what she'd been trying to tell him, when her anger had been turned on him. But he also thought the idea of someone like Anna being made to suffer the type of loneliness and pain she'd been forced to endure was pointless. At one time, had he understood the cycles of sorrow and pain better? Why did she seem to grasp it so easily, when it only roused fury in him, particularly where it concerned her?

The children were coming out of the water, being called to collect their things and head out, field trip over, disrupting his thoughts.

But Jonah kept his eye on Anna as he turned over the little girls to their parents and bid them good-bye. She stayed in the water, in profile, apparently watching the noon sun sparkle on the water. Her palm moved just over the surface, sharing her aura with the sea's.

Rising, he went to the water's edge. As he did, the boy's words came back to him. *Your woman is fine.*

His woman. Angels could take lifemates, but he'd never thought of himself as a candidate for it. He liked the way it sounded, though. Which just proved without a doubt he'd lost his mind. His and Anna's lives . . . He had no idea how they would mesh. It was absurd to think they could. She deserved stability, children of her own. He was so steeped in blood . . .

He was able to give these children happiness with the simplest effort, but he couldn't give it to himself or offer it permanently to anyone else. But as she turned, he saw in her eyes she didn't want to fight anymore, and he didn't, either. Not with her or with himself.

Moving through the water to her, he felt the cool touch of the waves through the denim on his skin. Her hands stilled, her head tilting as he approached, though she wasn't facing him any longer. The swimsuit she wore was a modest bikini, but he could still see the curves of her bottom, the sweet hint of cleft and, from the side, the ripe weight of her breasts, hint of nipples, the slim line of her neck.

He slipped his arms around her, as natural a gesture as the waves moving around them, the blue sky overhead, the sand dusting his skin and hers above the waterline.

"I'm sorry," she said, surprising him. She continued to look out at the waves. "I guess it proved your point, that family. You see that, and you see the potential for an invasion of Dark Ones. A battle and blood. I've never looked at it your way. Maybe I'm afraid to."

He thought of the way she'd splashed in with the children, laughing, her joy as unfettered as a bird's outstretched wings, and the dark history he'd seen in the pictures on her wall. A stone statue staring into shore at one fixed point, never seeing anything else. A black square locked within a gray-walled prison.

"It's been a long time since I've been able to look at it the way you do." Bending his head to her temple, he laid his jaw there and held her closer, feeling the soft give of her body. He wouldn't want her to look at it his way, wouldn't want her to become that statue. "I liked the pie."

"The apple pie?" She tilted her head so she could glance up at him. "It's impossible not to like apple pie." Her gaze drifted then to his shoulder, and the smile in her eyes deepened, a pleasure he could sink into like soft, fragrant grass. Turning in his arms, she reached up and brushed a wet hand over his shoulder, at the curve where it met his neck. She dipped her hand in the water and did it again, dousing the skin with a shivery trickle of water as she massaged the muscle there with her fingers. "Baby drool," she informed him.

The way she turned toward him, leaned into his body, made him instantly aware of every curve. His reaction didn't surprise him. What surprised him was her desire.

"My lord. I . . . I want you again." She adjusted so she was standing on his feet in a most charming way to get closer to his wet lips. However, she paused a breath from them, such that he developed a terrible thirst. That light, playful look came into her eyes, for she was certainly aware of the hardening in his groin, which grew noticeably at her words, at the press of her body. "If I'm not taking advantage of you."

A glance toward shore showed him the children were gone and the beach was theirs again. A part of him wanted to simply hold on to this moment, but it was impossible to deny his body's reaction to the mounds of her breasts as she pressed up against him, the slide of her thigh against his leg.

"I'm like a rutting beast," he muttered, trying to back away, but she moved with him, holding him and stilling him at once.

"I want you, too," she reminded him softly.

What an understatement that was. Anna was still sore from their first time in the caves, but it hadn't stopped the ache that seemed to begin the moment he wasn't Joined with her, and built until all her thoughts became about this. If he was near, but out of touching distance, it was even more excruciating. Watching him in the waves, wrestling with the boys, his broad back flexing, haunches tightening as he tossed them into the waves, the dark hair stranded across his tan shoulders. Or on the shore, sitting with his legs bent up, somewhat splayed, feet dug into the sand so she could drink in the curve of testicles beneath the denim, the long line of thigh. Then holding the little girls, the different expressions on his face. He watched them with the wisdom of the ages carved in the depths of his eyes. But he had never tried pie.

Even now, he looked at her as if he hadn't ever had the pleasure of sinking into a woman's body on a wave of pure, uncalculated desire. He was the miracle, not she.

He was here, and within touching distance. She couldn't think beyond wanting him with the same hunger for which he was admonishing himself. Tentatively, she lifted onto her toes. At the moment he was unyielding. She was laughably sure he thought himself taking advantage. Taking, period. She wanted him taking advantage, for she certainly was going to. She was his. She never wanted to suffer the delay of him thinking he had to ask for this.

Catching her fingers in the wet strands of his hair, she tugged hard to bring him down to her and yet still climbed halfway up his body, catching her legs around his hips.

With an oath, he let go of his restraint. She whimpered a relieved gasp into his mouth. Reaching behind her, he released the clasp of the suit against her abraded flesh, guided the top down her arms, leaving her upper body bare, the water deep enough it lapped at her tight nipples. When he lifted her beneath the arms to bring her up higher, her legs automatically locked around his waist as he brought one taut peak to his mouth, sucking it into wet heat. His other hand slid inside the back waistband of the bikini bottom, squeezing. He so easily took command of her body, as if he knew everything about how it would respond to him.

When he laid her back in the water, letting it cushion and soothe her skin, she floated, her arms out to either side. She tightened her legs, rubbed herself in slow, dragging strokes over the hardness beneath his jeans. She'd not done anything that forward before, but she was aching. He'd awakened her body, and watching him on the beach, knowing it was all temporal, how could she not take her fill of him as often as possible?

Jonah's jaw tightened, a muscle flexing there. He opened the jeans. Wet and constricting, the denim was stubborn, but before he tore them trying to get them off, she anticipated. Anna surged up, her stomach muscles contracting, and found his sex, filled her hands with the steel bar of it. He caught his hand under her bottom, pulling the bikini fabric out of the way, his other hand at her neck, and let her position herself over him, their eyes locked, inches away from one another, all of her resting in his hands.

She guided his broad head to her opening, the slickness of her flesh below the waterline, ready to accept him, take him deep.

"No magic, Anna. I forbid it."

Darkness coursed through her gaze, but Jonah brought her up to him for another rough kiss, plundering the softness of her mouth, and increased his grip on her buttock to sheathe himself in her welcoming heat. "Just us," he muttered, even as he knew part of it was a flatterer's lie to avoid the truth of why he didn't want her to use the magic.

She moaned against his mouth, her body spasming against him. Goddess, he couldn't bear it. He drove into her, harder, harder, knowing she was delicate but needing to lose himself, needing to just shatter into flecks of foam on the waves. Reduce his life to the simple, uncomplicated pleasure of sliding along the sides of her body as she passed his way, caressing and teasing the pink tips of her breasts, getting trapped in the salty, wet crevice of her sex, playing with those lips as she rolled beneath the ocean's surface.

From the clutch of her hands on his forearms, he could tell she was close. He kept that rhythm and bent his head to her breast again, taking the nipple in, sucking on it hard, and was rewarded. Her hands seized his hair, tugged ruthlessly and she came, her legs clamped over his hips, heels digging into his buttocks.

When she cried out, he moved up to her throat, bit down like a possessive animal and let himself go, wishing the darkness of his thoughts wouldn't follow him over the edge. But as she held on to him with her fists, like the little girl who had held on to his hair, he wondered if the fiercest gestures were desperate ones. The hope that something solid wouldn't slip away, leaving them yearning. Girls learned early there were no guarantees.

As his climax ebbed, the vision of the broken woman in the diner came again, as well as the black desolation her husband's soul had become. One night, that woman had turned over and found the face of her lover had become that of a stranger.

Her angel had become a monster.

Eleven

DAVID paused, hovering. The Abyss yawned below, murky and forbidding, as he was sure it was intended to be. Lord Lucifer took pains to discourage sea creatures from stumbling into the graphic realities of redemption, which could certainly sear a memory forever.

However, there *was* something here. Close by. Watching. It wasn't the careful but benign curiosity of a sea creature. Not exactly. He waited, listening.

He'd kept returning to this yawning crater, for it was the most likely place for Jonah to have sought refuge from a pressing enemy. But the maze of caverns was limitless, also making it impossible to find Jonah. And if he'd been strong enough to make it into the caverns, why wouldn't he keep going until he reached Luc's realm where he'd be protected, his wounds treated?

But still, David knew he wasn't off base. Even Luc, before other responsibilities called him away, had sensed there was something to the theory and left David to pursue it.

There. A shadow. He would have missed it if he hadn't been looking in that direction at a lucky moment. He didn't twitch a muscle, his whole energy and concentration tuning him in to the exact position of . . . there. He had it.

Angels of Jonah and Lucifer's caliber could move beyond the speed of light if they chose, circumnavigating the world in a blink if it was needed. David couldn't achieve that speed and remain in control yet. He'd hurtle out of orbit and bounce off an asteroid. They'd teased him about the bumps and bruises before. That was all right. The teasing of the angels never bothered him, because their love and protection of him and each other was absolute. They were connected in a way that kept him from feeling lonely. Many times he needed to draw from that energy to forget his mortal life and what he'd had to leave behind, unprotected. But he wondered when was the last time Jonah had drawn on that energy. David had an uneasy feeling that at some point Jonah had cut himself off from it and lost the vital reassurance.

Now was not the time for distracting thoughts like that, however. He *could* move faster across a few hundred yards than any mortal creature, and he used that now. He flipped back, his wings arcing over him in the water for balance and propulsion and shot toward where he'd seen the motion. He arrived directly before the creature, intercepting its retreat into the recesses of a cave to seize a bundle of rags that exploded in his face, striking at him with sharp nails, shrieks and . . .

He sucked in a breath. *Dark One*. It was a Dark One . . . wasn't it?

As he took the precious second to process the confusing signals, a serpentine tail coiled around his thigh, spinning him into a nasty bed of fire coral. Leaving him cursing and holding the rags, the creature hurtled away from him.

Dropping the garment, David pursued his quarry into the cave and caught it again, slamming it up against the wall. It earned him a shocking, feminine cry of pain.

There were no Dark Ones with female energy. But their energy was pulsing off her, making it hard to fight down his automatic reaction to kill.

Focus. If she was connected to the Dark Ones, she might have knowledge about Jonah. By the Goddess, if she did, she would tell him, even if he had to cause more of those terrible shrieks to tear out of her throat.

He had one of his daggers out and against her neck, holding it close enough the creature could not move forward without decapitating herself. All he could see was a dark swirl of hair, a pale chin, a bare shoulder. Without the bundle of rags, the creature wore nothing but raven black hair that almost hid her features as she leaned against the shadowed rocks of the wall. But her Dark One energy outlined her to him like the illumination of a nightmarish sunrise.

"Show your face."

"Kill me and be done with it. I do nothing at your command."

David grasped a handful of hair, pulling it from her face, and yanked her head back.

A girl. Younger than him. One side of her face was severely scarred and embedded with one red eye, the crimson signature of a Dark One. Which only enhanced painfully how beautiful the other side was, so much so it stunned him for a key moment.

What he now recognized as a tentacle lashed around both of his ankles, slammed them together. She struck him across the face with a piece of pipe she'd had hidden on a ledge in the shadows, likely scavenged from a shipwreck.

Yes, Jonah would say he deserved that. David managed to hold on to her, fought past the throbbing pain and flipped her, breaking free of the hold of her unusual appendages with the flex of his legs. She scrabbled for the dagger he'd dropped, which had fallen on a lower outcropping. It got kicked off and disappeared in the murky waters as he yanked her back against him, arms pinned to her sides. Sleek as an eel, she slipped out of his grasp again, tangling his arms in her hair of all things, a more effective net than expected, leaving him holding a handful of strands and nothing else.

It might be a holdover from his days as a human, but he knew he would *not* live it down with the others if he had his ass whipped by a girl. Catching the slender whip of one tentacle around his wrist—Christ, she had stingers—he yanked hard, jerking her off balance and making her flail. As she tried to recover, he propelled himself out the cave entrance and up, jolting her body back into his arms as he did so, spinning up, up, up, knowing her mortal equilibrium couldn't handle it the way his could. Churning through the water like a rising tornado, he heard her garbled cry as she realized what he was doing, where they were going.

Time to take this one out of her element. It was an acknowledgment he grudgingly gave her—she was a hell of a fighter.

Emerging into a world domed beneath a night sky, he shot up in an arc over the sea as she snarled and shrieked, raked him with her nails, taking a stripe of skin off his neck. When he dropped her at that height, she howled in surprised fear, cut off a second later as he caught her in his arms, floating them down onto a narrow sandspit that existed only at low tide, about a mile out from the nearest substantial landmass. She scrabbled back toward the water, and he caught her again, flipped her to her back.

"Stop," he commanded. Then any sense of indulgence disappeared as he registered what was caught in her hair. A pure white feather, limned with silver.

Jonah. Every angel had a unique color pattern to his wings upon reaching maturity. David's wings still had the cream color and brown tips of a fledgling, as all angels had in their first fifty years.

Rightly sensing his change of mood, she made another attempt at the water. David drew a second dagger from the strap across his chest and speared flesh and muscle, pinning one tentacle to the sand and rock beneath.

Her scream ricocheted over the water, startling a moored flock of pelicans. It wrenched something inside David. But how many times had Jonah, Luc and other veterans told him? *You're young; you still feel compassion for Dark Ones.*

But she wasn't a Dark One. Dark Ones didn't have the tail or fins of a mermaid, though hers wasn't a typical tail. More like a cross between the powerful, sensitive tentacles of an octopus and the whip style of a sea serpent.

"If you bite me, you'll be sorry," he promised. Still, he cupped her face warily, using pressure to turn her toward him, to verify the remarkable thing he'd seen below the water. One half of her face was destroyed, as if the flesh had been gnawed away and never healed. The other . . . He'd never seen anything, short of the Goddess Herself, so beautiful. It was heartbreaking. Long black hair, a blue eye with dark, sooty lashes, the iris as vibrant as a jewel. She wore an earring. A pretty bauble fixed in the unscarred ear, something a young girl would wear. A little silver dolphin with a turquoise stone, likely found in the same wreck where she found the pipe that would have broken a mortal's jaw.

"You're Dark Spawn, aren't you?" They were a terrible and rare thing, something he'd never seen. For one thing, females of any species raped by Dark Ones didn't typically live. And if they survived, the children were either born as evil as their sires and angels dispatched them in the same manner they did Dark Ones, or the hapless creatures were so mutated coming out of the womb they couldn't survive.

He plucked at her hair and earned a hiss, a swipe of those sharp teeth. It was a near thing, but he sensed the energy a blink before it detonated. Throwing himself over her, he pressed down on her struggling body and snapped the counterspell. The explosion that would have flung him from her became scraps of electrified air, drifting around them like confetti. The other tentacle whipped up, struck his back with the fierce fire of a scourge. She howled as he spun out another dagger and pinned that tentacle as well. Christ, he hated this.

"Enough, witch." He snarled the Inert command, which should neutralize anything she could throw at him, and watched her brow furrow and her desperation increase as she realized he'd rendered her helpless. Her tentacles were bleeding from where his blades pierced them. She was trembling with pain, and her fear of him.

Steeling himself against that, he raised the feather. "Where did you get this, Dark Spawn? You know you can't lie to me, so don't try."

He would detect a lie, but he couldn't necessarily wrest the truth from her, unless he wanted to resort to greater torture. He'd forced Dark Ones to reveal information before, and in similar circumstances, he'd have reached down and twisted the dagger. But this wasn't normal. She wasn't . . . He didn't know what he was dealing with. Dark Ones were not young, not mermaid-looking . . . not girls.

This time he swept her hair from her in one decisive moment and looked upon her form fully, trying to school his face to impassivity and ignore how her trembling increased.

But the scarring ran so deep and wide down her left side that she didn't have a left breast. She was missing two fingers on the left hand, and the rib cage on that side was marked, like the side of her face, as if she'd been dragged over oysters. In contrast, the right breast was perfectly formed, the curve heavy enough to attract his eye. Elegant fingers, slim hand and arm, a beautiful arch of rib cage and flare of hip.

While the mermaids he'd seen had the typical tail, she had a split at the juncture of her sex like humans, only instead of legs she had those two dangerous tentacles, each one nearly six feet long and very capable—as supple and as flexible as hands. Perhaps more so.

There were tight black and blue scales over her hips, matching the one blue eye. The scales themselves had a silken gloss like sleek skin. The undersides of the tentacles were coated with feelers, which he knew explained her ability to find her way around in such a dark place as the caves she must inhabit.

"I won't tell you where he is," Mina spat. "You may destroy me if you wish, my lord. He's in good hands and seems in no hurry to leave their embrace."

David's gaze shifted back to her face. "You think you are protecting him."

"I don't know you or your intentions."

"But he is being hunted . . ."

"He is beyond where the Dark Ones can find him. For a short time at least."

David straightened, though he kept a close eye on her as he passed the back of his hand over his mouth and came back with blood on his fingers. She wasn't lying—he could tell that. Jonah was in no danger from her.

"I'm going to remove the Inert command and pull the daggers out now," he said. "If you can find it in you to trust me that far, I will heal the wounds so they will trouble you no further."

She watched him with that disconcerting dual-colored gaze. "Why would you bother?"

"Child of a Dark One." His gaze drifted down. "Daughter of a mermaid. I sense no pure evil in you. Dark Spawn are rare. Those without pure evil even rarer."

"Not as rare as you think," she said enigmatically. "Just set me free. I'll tend to myself."

"Sit still until I tell you otherwise," he said shortly. "I've proven I'm faster and stronger, and you cannot use your magic against me. Don't try my patience with another attempt."

She sat sullenly while he removed the spell and then the first dagger. He did it with quick precision, knowing it was better to do that than to make it slow. She made a quiet noise, but her jaw was clenched. When he laid his hand over the wound, the wet blood seeping between his fingers, she tensed. Damn it, he wanted to remove them both to ease her pain, but she'd bolt.

"Do you know why he doesn't want us to find him?" He asked it in a low voice as he concentrated, reaching for a sense of her physiology before he activated the healing. He didn't really expect an answer unless it was a taunt, but she was the closest link to Jonah he'd yet found. He had to try.

"No. And yes. I know the symptoms, not the cure, angel. And the answer is the cure."

The wound wasn't responding as it should. Taking up the dagger, he slit his palm for a fresh, free flow of blood and squeezed it over the wound, pleased at last when he saw the edges begin to come together, to knit.

When she cried out, writhed, his gaze snapped up. She'd laid a hand on her face. The left side showed a patch of healed skin where scarring had been just a moment before.

An angel as young as himself could heal only fresh wounds. Someone like Jonah could heal ones still festering after a month or more. Only Raphael and his Legion could cure afflictions years old like this.

"No. No!" She snatched the other dagger out herself, at an angle that tore the flesh and caused another, even more desolate cry.

When she dove at him, only his quickness saved him from having the metal tip plunged into his throat, but in hindsight he wondered if she'd just wanted him out of her way. She scuttled away from him, her breath laboring, the cry still bubbling in her throat, making her sound like a rasping crow. He'd taken her up on the sand to a point where she had to drag herself down to the water. She thrust the knife away to help her increase her painstaking speed along the sand, leaving a trail of blood.

David rose and watched her. He should kill her. The darkness obviously had a tight grip on her, and for that reason Dark Spawn were usually treated no differently than Dark Ones themselves. But watching her determination to get away from him . . . for *healing* her, he couldn't. He didn't understand what she'd said about Jonah; he didn't understand *her*. But he knew he needed to understand before he acted.

He caught up with her in several strides, bent and lifted her. He held on, reestablishing the Inert command since her draping tentacles could wrap around him like a python. The ferocity of her inventive curses impressed him, though. *"Sshh,"* he ordered. "I'm taking you back to the water. Be still. What's your name?"

Fire burned in the depths of her unsettling eyes. So did fear, and a rage strong enough to consume her, he expected. She was a strange mixture of both the nightmarish monster waiting in the closet and the child shivering in the bed, knowing it was only a matter of time before it emerged.

"You already know. I am Dark Spawn."

"I asked your name."

"Mina." The answer was slow in coming, but as he stopped a few feet from the water, waiting as she gazed at it longingly, it came at last.

"Good." He took another step closer. "Pretty. Mina, I've given you my blood. If you call to me at any time, anywhere, and focus on it as I'm sure you know how to do as a magic user, I will hear you. Use it if harm threatens him. Will you do that?"

"How do I know you would trust me if I said yes?"

"I likely won't. Unless you call me if he is indeed in need." He set her down at the water's edge but kept a firm hand on her arm, cupping her chin to make her look at him fully, both eyes, which seemed as difficult for her as looking directly into the sun. "If you don't, you will be very sorry."

She stared at him. "You reveal too much to one you shouldn't trust."

"Perhaps. I'm told I'm young and foolish. But it is no secret angels look after each other." He also knew the shared blood would let him locate her if he or Luc wanted to question her again. He released her from the Inert command, more reluctantly than he'd expected. Impulsively, he brushed his fingers over the meeting point of scarred and fair skin, skimming his fingers down her nose, almost in benediction. She stilled in shock, her eyes widening.

"You may do the same," he said.

As he backed up, prepared to launch, her brow furrowed. "Do what?" she asked.

"Call me if harm threatens you."

Nodding to her, he went aloft, leaving her with Jonah's feather and that astonished look on her macabre, tragic face.

Twelve

JONAH and Anna caught a ride with a migrant worker headed toward Nevada. He explained in Spanish that he could take them to the state line. While he had no room in the cab of his small pickup because of his wife and two children, he'd thrown a mattress down in the open bed of the truck and offered them that to sit upon as they traveled.

Jonah studied the man only briefly before nodding and giving Anna a hand up onto the tailgate. When he stepped up to follow, however, he misjudged and would have toppled except Anna leaned forward and caught his arm. The worker steadied him on the other side.

"Gracias," Jonah muttered, feeling anything but gracious. But Anna smiled at the man's kindness, and tried to hide her amusement as the worker made a discreet tippling gesture to his wife, suggesting he thought one of their passengers was soused.

"You're laughing at me." Jonah settled across from her, bracing his feet on the wheel well. Her feet didn't reach that far, so she had them drawn up, her knees bent, her back resting gingerly against the truck's side.

"Just at the suggestion you're drunk, my lord. Can angels drink to excess?"

"I don't think so," he said, pinching her toes. "You're being entirely too disrespectful of my exalted status."

"Does anyone ever treat you as an equal? I mean, have you

always been . . . a commander?" At his look, she hurried on. Anna had no illusions about his "exalted status," though the affection and passion he showed her in such sudden, intense bursts would have made it easy to forget what she couldn't forget in other circumstances. "Mina said you're known as a Prime Legion Commander. Second only to Full Submission angels."

He shrugged, looked around as the landscape started to move, the pickup truck grinding to life. A young boy looked out the open back window, grinned and handed them each a soda.

Anna smiled and thanked him as she turned her attention back to Jonah. "Were you born that?" She watched for shadows, knowing she could be getting into areas he didn't want to visit. But at least for right now, Jonah seemed to have left his tension on the beach. He seemed relaxed, almost amicable.

"Sometimes it feels that way," he said wryly. "But no. Angels are like other creatures. We have a time of youth and inexperience. Even those few who are made from human souls. We must apply ourselves to determine where we will be placed. Then we mentor others, bring them along, help them find their calling."

"And your calling . . . You fight Dark Ones."

"I fight the enemies Michael commands me to fight. But yes, these past few centuries, it has been mostly Dark Ones. The ancient evils, the things that humans called demons, have been contained or placated for the most part. Though ironically, at one time anything otherworldly, including angels, was called demon."

His hair was blowing around his face, whipping the sculpted cheekbones and the distracting mouth as the truck gained speed on the highway. It seemed unreal, studying him like this, a man in jeans only, the T-shirt tied to one of the hooks in the bed to dry out further. His long legs stretched across the bed, one arm along the side of the truck, the other hand balancing a Dr Pepper on his thigh.

"When you were talking about . . ." She made a face as they accelerated to the point that the furor of the wind forced her to raise her voice. Which meant the driver and his family might hear her.

Tucking the soda between his thigh and the truck bed, Jonah grasped one of her hands just under her knee. His fingers caressed the skin beneath the skirt as he pulled her across and tumbled her into his now mostly dry lap with one easy move. It allowed her to be balanced and upright without the uncomfortable pressure on her back the metal lip of the truck bed caused. He snugged her hips down between his thighs, legs draped over his calves.

"What?" he said, his lips close to her ear.

"Do you touch each other this easily?" she asked first. His dark eyes were warm, the warmth of darkest chocolate. Anna often touched the animals of the sea and the land, the flowers and trees. She needed to touch life, connect with it. But she touched her own kind so rarely, mermaid or human, and had never been invited to do so. She would have welcomed it from the homeliest, shyest example of either race, but this . . . Jonah not only welcomed her touch; he was willing to touch *her*. He almost seemed to demand it. And he was a far cry from shy or homely.

"Not like this." That glint of humor again. She liked it, wondered if it was a glimpse of the younger, more carefree angel he might have once been. "There are angels who enjoy men more than women, but I am not one of them." His brows drew down. "Now, what were you really going to ask?"

She wondered that she was bold enough to ask, but she was curious. And maybe, since he was male, it would help keep his mind away from less pleasant things.

"It was just, the other night, the way you described how you all sought pleasure for grounding. Is there a place you go? Or does each seek his own . . . source?"

She got distracted by the sensual set of his lips, particularly when he brushed hers with them, parted them, teased her with a fleeting touch of his tongue. "What are you looking for, Anna?"

"Are there—I don't know—brothels for angels? Houses of pleasure? I mean, if you need this so often . . ."

He chuckled then, and the sound shot warmth straight down to her core, which pooled into heat as his voice lowered to a husky murmur. "Am I too demanding? Would you prefer me to spread my attentions out?"

"No," she said instantly, then flushed to the roots at her unsophisticated vehemence. "I mean, that's not for me to say. If I don't, if you need more—"

"It's curiosity," he realized, studying her. "What I said the other night made you curious, didn't it?" Gathering her hair in one hand, he tucked it into a twisted bun to keep it out of her face, but he left his hand at her nape. It restrained her in proximity to his mouth, allowing him those occasional maddening tastes at unexpected moments to keep her befuddled. "Tell me what you've imagined. It's going to be a long drive." He shifted, let her feel the pressure of him against her hip. "See if you can torture me with nothing more than your mind."

"It's not that. I just imagined . . ."

"Tell me, Anna."

She shook her head, smiled. "I tend to be fanciful."

"That's all right. Tell it like a story."

"Okay." She raised her attention to his forehead, finding his direct gaze a little disconcerting. "I'm imagining all of you in a secluded lagoon . . . with water nymphs. The trees are hanging low over the water; the banks, lush and green. Like one of those Romantic period paintings. In fact, I think it's likely some of those paintings came from an artist stumbling upon you." She stole a quick glance at him, then continued. "You made him think he was seeing men, not angels, so that's what he painted. Six or seven of you, entwined in the nymphs' arms and legs. You took the nymphs on the banks; their legs wrapped around you like slim white flower petals." She moistened her lips, encouraged by the growing heat in his gaze, the reflected heat in her own body. "Later, you went back into the water together. The nymph's hair was spilling down the front of your body, her back against your front . . . as you would take me in my mermaid form. As you entered the nymph's body, your hands clasped hers and they skimmed the top of the water in front of you both."

Just touching. The marvel of it to her being all the contact. Flesh, bone, muscle within one's grasp, living. The nymph's body pressed so generously against the angel's, so he could hear her heartbeat and she could hear his . . .

Jonah's hand, still tangled in her hair, loosened enough that he eased her head down beneath his jaw, her ear against his chest. *Thump, thump, thump*. Strong and steady, even over the rush of wind and roar of engine.

"Like that," she whispered. She closed her eyes as his arm tightened high around her shoulders to enclose her completely without hurting her. "Do angels always make everyone feel so safe?"

His lips pressed against her forehead. "When my wings are healed, I'll enclose you in them when you sleep. There's nowhere safer I could put you."

Smiling, she lifted her body to look at him. Reaching up, she gathered his windblown hair, pulling it from his face as he'd done for her. She tied it back with the wire bracelet she'd worn today, keeping the strands from flailing against his strong features. "So is it like that? As I described it?"

"Sometimes. When we desire Joining pleasure for grounding, we often go alone. However, I don't deny there have been times we've gone in groups to places we are welcomed. Once, when I was much younger"—he slanted her a smile that was astonishingly almost a grin—"a nunnery."

"No—you didn't."

"Well, it *was* during a time when it was mostly women escaping hard circumstances or who'd been confined there by husbands or fathers who wanted to be rid of them, so it wasn't as if their vows were a calling. And of course, we *were* servants of God. In a sense. Ronin was the one who came up with the idea." He said it with amused defensiveness and then she saw his eyes darken at the memory. When she pressed her fingers into his skin, he looked down at her hand, the shadows clearing somewhat.

"By the Goddess, they were so hungry for a man's touch . . ." He focused on where her hand clutched the front of his shirt. "As women who are not permitted physical contact often are."

When she would have drawn away, he simply held her closer.

"You loved him very much," she said into his chest. "When did he . . ."

"About two years ago." At her surprised look, he shook his head. "Time doesn't mean much to an angel. And yet it can be more interminable to us than those with less."

"Yet you remember so many things, so many details."

"Not as many as I expected. I'd forgotten how delicate the inside of a shell is, how sweet a flower lying against a woman's flesh smells." Bending his head, he inhaled beneath her ear, making her shiver, her body feeling so warm in the embrace of his.

His proximity helped her keep her mind off of her back, but the damage and the swimming with the children had sapped her energy, nonetheless. As she listened to his human heartbeat, noting it sounded not much different than an angel's, she let the rock of the truck, the rhythmic sound of the breaks in the asphalt bumping under the wheels, relax her. Enjoying his touch, she imagined she was one of the water nymphs, surrounded by a laughing group of angels, tall, beautiful men including Jonah, their hands gentle, their desire fierce. The energy was so strong it became a large pair of wings in her mind, enfolding her in the scene of that painting forever. It was easy to doze, turn it into a dream where she was still close to the water, not getting farther from it.

"Great Goddess, that's frightening."

She opened her eyes in time to see a passing battered-looking van garishly covered with painted flowers. It was speeding along like a fugitive from the 1960s, trying to stay ahead of the grasp of time that might yank it back into its proper decade.

"It's very colorful." She smiled against his chest.

"Do you ever say anything negative about anything?"

"Not about things like that." She yawned. "They liked it enough to do it. If they see me making fun of it, it's like I'm somehow destroying what makes them feel good, chipping away at it. Their joy in it becomes a little less."

When she tilted up her chin to look at him with sleepy eyes, she found him gazing quizzically at her. "My lord?"

"It has been a while since I've been properly chastised. I'm adjusting to the shock of you being right."

She grinned into his shirt, succumbing to sleep with his chuckle tucked warmly around her mind.

Jonah held her over the next hour, watching her fitful rest. He could tell her back was making her uncomfortable, but she'd made not one complaint. The wife of the migrant worker occasionally glanced back at him, her arm around her son, and she smiled, apparently moved by the picture they made.

He didn't like to think how good it felt, to simply hold her. How he wanted to just keep rolling along this highway forever with no destination. He wondered what it would be like to pick fruit or do whatever job the migrant worker was headed toward.

It was astounding, watching the world go by like this. Vehicles passing in different directions, a group of deer grazing on the side of the road, flirting dangerously near traffic. Endless numbers of cell towers, exit signs tempting motorists with fast food, gas. A group of girls in a sports car went by and gave him an open appraisal, casting flirtatious looks that turned harmlessly envious when they registered the sleeping woman in his arms.

The silky head of a smaller boy now emerged up front, large dark eyes blinking at Jonah. Like his mermaid, he'd apparently been sleeping.

"Mano!" The mother's sharp admonishment came too late, for the small boy had already wriggled halfway out the cab's back window, tumbling onto the mattress and sprawling across Anna and Jonah's legs with an unrepentant grin.

"*Está bien.*" Nodding to the mother, Jonah hauled the boy up on his other thigh to keep a firm hand around the small body, making it clear he'd be fine until he was ready to return to his exasperated mother.

Anna opened her eyes at the jostling, blinked at the boy. He reached out, touched her face and laughed. He had a marker in the other hand, and while she sat docilely, he drew a tiny, somewhat crooked smiley face on her cheek. Then he considered Jonah.

"I am not a wall for graffiti," he informed the dark-eyed child, who smiled and began to draw on him anyway.

"You don't dislike human children." Her voice was a quiet murmur into his chest.

"Of course not. The young are new . . . no matter what they might become, what soul they're carrying. Until they discover self-awareness, they're pure, unsullied." He glanced down, studied her face. "Are you all right?"

Anna nodded. She'd started awake from a bad dream. Jonah, in a dark, tumultuous sky, his red studded battle skirt matched the red of the blood dripping over his shoulders, streaming across his skin from the bodies he'd vanquished. His eyes fierce, deadly . . . empty. He'd been magnificent, fearsome . . . disconnected from her, from everything but that turmoil. She'd been afraid that he would not recognize her when his sword turned in her direction.

It was an abrupt but welcome transition to wake from that to an innocent child drawing. Leaning forward, she touched the image Mano had drawn high on Jonah's chest. A stick figure with wings and a halo. "*Ángel,*" the boy pronounced in Spanish.

She'd never noticed the Spanish pronunciation made the last syllable into "Hell." She shivered, recalling Jonah's words, that the earliest references to angels called them demons.

Sitting up, she sought his face, needing to see him. She even reached out with her fingertips to touch his lips, see the response to her in his eyes. Jonah. Angel. Servant of the Goddess.

"Bad dream, little one?"

He saw far too much, of course. But when she nodded, he brought her closer, putting his lips over hers as the little boy was held between them. Then Jonah deepened the kiss, tasting her mouth, teasing her until the dream began to melt into something different.

"You've had a brush with the Dark Ones," he murmured. "Don't let them chase you in your dreams. I'll chase them out for you."

She wanted that to be true, but she was also afraid for him. Despite his bumping along in an old pickup truck in such mundane surroundings, he looked as if there should be voices raised in heavenly song limning his every movement. Wouldn't he laugh at that thought?

But not songs composed with gentle harps. Instead, fierce battle songs beaten out on Celtic drums, foretelling the forces of good triumphing over evil. She held on to that thought, even as the darkness of the dream made her shiver, made his eyes turn back to her in concern and his arms tighten around her again.

Thirteen

T HE Hispanic father dropped them in a small town just over the Nevada border. After purchasing some food and making an inquiry, Anna took Jonah to a large park that closed at sundown. However, without a car, they slipped in during the late afternoon without notice, losing themselves in the woods and looking for the creek she'd been told would be there.

It was approaching twilight. Nevertheless, Jonah muttered a vile curse as he stumbled over a root, and Anna reached out to steady him.

"We were in the truck a long while," she observed. "It's hard to get your land legs back. Particularly when you didn't quite have them to begin with."

"I'm a clumsy oaf without my wings and you're trying to be kind. How did you do it?"

"Do what, my lord?"

"Learn to be graceful, switching so often between fins and feet."

"Oh." She was amused at the description. "Dancing. I saw a couple dancing on the beach and it looked like swimming, how you can get lost in the rhythm of it and start doing it unconsciously once you have the way of it."

"Hmm."

Anna barely muffled a sigh of relief at the sound of the creek. A moment later, they were there. The meadow leading to it was populated with wildflowers, and behind the creek was a backdrop of one of Nevada's many mountain ranges. Trees hung over the gurgling ribbon of water, and she spied several soft places that would make a good bed for the night.

First things first, though. She was already moving toward the water, kicking off her shoes. Wading in, she breathed another sigh as the water swirled around her calves. Her skin craved the wash of salt-flecked foam, the rolling advance of a tide, but this would do. It was a natural body that flowed into something bigger, which she could pretend eventually would reach the ocean. Later tonight, she would use a sparing amount of her seawater to bathe her hands and feet, spread some of the vital moisture thinly over her torso. If nothing else, Jonah might get some pleasure out of watching her do that.

Another snarl, the sound of stumbling, and she broke out of the arousing image to see Jonah staring balefully at his now bare feet as if he were considering the biblical suggestion of lopping off offensive appendages.

"Are all angels so surly, my lord?"

She quelled the urge to chuckle as he sent a narrow glance her way. Then she thought of what had led them to this moment, and what might still be following them, and her amusement fled.

"Here, my lord." Emerging from the water, she came to him, affected a curtsy. "Can I interest you in a dance?"

Before he could decide, Anna put her hands on the hem of his T-shirt and lifted it. First, because she wanted to take his mind off things she saw weighing heavily behind his eyes. Second, because she knew it was getting near sundown. Third, because he'd be more comfortable that way. And finally, because it pleased her. She stretched the cotton over his upper body and he raised his arms, let her take it over his head, helping when it exceeded her height. Putting it off to the side, she traced the child's drawing of an angel, the lines of which had blurred somewhat in the heat.

Then she looked up at his serious, troubled eyes and moved into his armspan, putting one hand on his shoulder, her wrist resting on the angel drawing, and placed her hand in his other.

"A waltz is three beats, my lord. Once you get them, you can start twirling like you're flying, and you'll realize they aren't so different. Well, they are"—she dimpled—"but the spirit of the movement is similar. You can swim, fly or dance in your mind and it all feels the same, in a way."

She walked him through the steps slowly, engaged by his concentration, the way his hair fell over his forehead, such that she had to reach up, finger the silk of it and throw them off step. Even as she laughed and got them back on course, she was amazed that only a couple of days ago she would have trembled at the idea of being within ten steps of an angel, let alone touching one, dancing with one, teasing one.

He made her think of all the things she wanted. She couldn't accuse him of doing it deliberately, but it didn't make her any less helpless before the power of it, any more than when he commanded her sensual submission to him.

She noted her touch seemed to distract him as well, so she kept doing it, matching steps with him, stumbling and laughing a little at them both until he was smiling, too, because her determination to tease his hair, his lips, was causing the majority of the missteps. Then he was kissing her, his lips coming down on hers as they moved. It was no surprise that was the moment he got it perfectly, the dance steps flowing like the water behind them. She was the one holding on to his upper arm as he increased their pace, shifting his balance back and forth, foot to foot, swirling. Turning while he touched her mouth, drew her in closer, feeling the way of it while he felt his way inside of her mind, invaded her to the tips of her toes with that long, drawn-out kiss.

"We need music, Anna," he murmured. "Sing to me."

She found her voice with effort, modulating it so instead of sending him into dreams as she'd done the other night, she kept this waking dream alive and active, weaving its way around them like mist, keeping them in its grasp. She infused it with reassurance and joy, things she knew he needed and which did her no harm to feel as well. The words spun a silly tale of a foolish mermaid who fancied herself a shepherd and tried to herd a school of flounder home to her mother. An old, old children's song about the joy of being that innocent, of believing one could do anything. A child could believe that he or she was a fearless hero or a shrewd villain. Whichever was more fun, no harm done.

"You're getting it," she said, trying not to turn into a complete idiot because his hand was on her waist. The frown line between his eyebrows as he concentrated made him so . . . irresistible.

As they moved through the glade, he became confident enough to twirl her under his arm and then bring her back to him again. She locked both hands around his neck, feeling the tickle of feathers as the wings began to materialize with the sunset.

Abruptly her toes were barely brushing the ground. She gave a pleased cry as he made the turn with an extra lift . . . and a grimace. Anna brought them to a halt. Jonah tested the wing again, stretching it. She could tell by how swiftly her feet came back to earth the second time that it was too tender to bear their combined weights.

If they did the Joining Magic, it would help. Mina had said they needed to do it daily. But he'd refused to let her do that, twice now. Her lips thinned. Stubborn male. Obstinate angel. Well, she'd just have to figure a way around that, wouldn't she? Mina had suggested . . . well, it was best not to think about what Mina suggested. Maybe there was another way she could try first.

"Can you fly with it, my lord?"

"We've got more important things to do first." He guided her to a rock. "We're going to heal your back."

Which would drain his energy. Even if they did Joining Magic, he would not get the full benefit of it, because some of it would be to refill the well of energy he was about to use.

"I've a simpler way, my lord." She stopped and faced him. "I have another form I can assume. It will make the healing easier." Before he could question her, she shrugged off her clothes and the swimsuit beneath, leaving her completely naked. Blissfully, for the cooling night air soothed skin that had been raw and burning all day long, though she'd managed fairly successfully not to make too much of it. She hadn't wanted him to berate himself further. Faith, but the male ego was a fragile thing.

"You're smiling. I suspect you're up to mischief. How many shapes can my shapeshifter take?"

"No mischief, my lord. And I have four. Mermaid, human and this one." She gave him a quick smile. "The fourth is a surprise. I will tell you that one another day."

As her body began to shimmer, she stepped onto the rock, using his shoulder to get there, so she stood tall above him, which was disconcerting as she realized she'd just displayed the most private parts of herself right before his eyes.

"I've no objection to this so far." But he watched her closely as the shimmering increased and her form began to waver. Just like when she made the transformation to mermaid, she was self-conscious, but for a different reason this time. Transforming with the burns was painful. If she could just get the process started . . . There.

Oh, Goddess. It was as if she were being scalded anew, only this time she'd known it was coming, had to sit still and mark it as it grew larger and larger. While, perversely, her size went in just the opposite direction.

Her hands closed into fists and Jonah stepped forward. "Anna, stop."

"Can't . . ." she gasped, and her form dissolved before him, folding in on itself, her hair whipping around her as if weaving into a cocoon. Pinpoints of light sparkled over her skin, giving it a sheen before her body disappeared into a flame-infused shower that flew out in different directions, a whirling spiral of sparks shaped like water drops, which funneled down to the surface of the stump in a vortex of misty smoke that had the unexpected aroma of seawater.

The mist began to float away. Jonah reached out his fingers to it, suddenly fearful. "Anna?" Was he holding the essence of her? What—

"I am here, my lord." She stepped out of the mist, and while he heard a strained note in her voice, he was riveted by this newest side of his little mermaid. His *very* little mermaid.

Who was no longer a mermaid, but a pixie fairy, no taller than the length of his hand.

Her wings were translucent and had the wavering texture of water-streaked glass, as if they were made of water in truth, with touches of pink and blue glimmerings, the colors the early rising sun often gave ocean waves. Her body was slim, much like her human body, only more elongated. Long and curling hair still the same, her eyes just as violet, so large in her delicate, pointed, almost foxlike features.

"I can fly with you like this and not overburden your wing," she pointed out. "I can't fly as high as you can, but I can keep you company for a time. And in this form, the area for you to heal is much less. If I stay this way for a couple of hours, when I shift back to human or mermaid, the full area will be fixed."

Her voice was a soft whisper of sound like the wind, swirling and coming together around the syllables as they emitted from her throat, embossing them for his ears to detect.

"Then turn around, *little* one."

Though she smiled at the irony in his voice, she obeyed. Jonah studied each step of her tiny feet, the way she gathered her hair and brought it all forward, her wings quivering as she increased their spread so they pressed to the outside of her arms and displayed his earlier handiwork, no less shameful to him now that it had been reduced so significantly in size.

He put that aside and focused on the skin, opened himself to feel the heat from the injury, the throbbing nerve endings. Reaching out toward her with two aligned fingers, he pointed them just below her nape. Not touching her, but so close the heat of his skin and the heat of the inflamed flesh touched, a cool blue aura meeting red.

He'd used his ability to heal frequently after battle, to shore up wounds sustained by his Legion, until they could get to Raphael's corps for more in-depth work. He was relieved he'd not hurt her beyond what he could handle on his own, though he quickly realized there were some murky layers to that statement. Uneasy things that had nothing to do with the wound she bore, but having to do with things he could inflict upon her later. He was a walking nightmare right now, and anyone in proximity was likely to get more than burned. She was a simple, pure soul that had absolutely no idea the level of power he was capable of wielding.

He should heal her, take her for a flight and then send her sternly back home. He'd travel on to this shaman or not . . . Whatever happened, she would not be part of his destiny or downfall.

"My lord . . ." That soft whisper of sound rippled over him, made him have the conflicting and yet equally fierce sudden desire to scoop her up, keep her close to him. He would let her travel in the soft nest where his wings met between his shoulders and never let her come to any harm. Devote himself to her care.

But he couldn't protect her from himself. That much was obvious, right before his eyes.

She probably thought she was helping a lost soul, her woman's heart turning the wounded lion into an injured house cat in her mind. As he recalled what he'd said about her ability to remove a thorn from a lion's paw, the terrifying thought occurred to him that maybe she *did* know she faced a lion. Yet stayed within range anyway, as if daring him to do his worst.

Focus, damn it. A fledgling could handle something like this. What was the matter with him? Closing his eyes, Jonah called forth the source of light in his soul, built it with brutal force, feeling like a human using a knife to scrape at the last bit of mustard in a glass jar. *Clatter, clatter, clatter*, like he'd seen one of the humans do in the diner.

There. A pathetic trickle, but it was there. The light came from his fingertips, a healing balm that spread out on her skin, sinking down to the nerves, cooling, numbing, repairing. As he saw it happen, the light strengthened within him, gained power, even as his mind castigated him for what was initially a weak flow. *Thanks to her magic, you have less area to heal. Otherwise you might not have been able to do a damn thing for her.*

For a while now, he'd turned more and more of the post-battle triage over to his lieutenants and wing-soldiers, using the time to assess the next strategy. To clean and sharpen his weapons, until the slightest pass over his skin would draw blood, mesmerize him with how it ran down the blade . . .

You need the Joining Magic. To heal you. He could almost see the words in the set of her shoulders, the underlying admonishment that raised his hackles.

No. I don't. Though he couldn't deny something was broken within him. Every time he thought of trying the healing rituals, making their lovemaking into that, he turned away from it, sickened by the idea of letting that pure white light fill him. He'd stood in the Lady's presence before, and oh, by all the gods, what a feeling that was. So . . . complete. And yet, it seemed to escape him now. If She summoned him to Her presence, he wasn't sure he could stand before that white light without screaming in agony.

Like a Dark One.

It wasn't just that he didn't want the Joining Magic. He didn't deserve it.

"My lord?"

Opening his eyes at a brush of wind on his face, he found Anna was at eye level with him, hovering before his face. An iridescent, magical butterfly, one small hand brushing his nose like the passing touch of a spider's web. Though her eyes were far too knowing, and worried, he saw her offer him that shy smile. For some inexplicable reason, he took it as a gift, the small tendril of reassurance it unfurled in his belly. "I'm good as new," she said. "Better, in fact. Will you fly with me now?"

Anna was fairly sure for an angel of his standing, what he'd just done should have been as easy as a child's trick. But he was sweating and trembling. She wanted to demand he perform the Joining Magic right then and there with her for his well-being, but she'd boxed herself in with the shift to her pixie form. If his healing was going to transfer to her larger form, it had to have time to sink into her core. Besides that, he had that obstinate look that told her he would still resist. So she would try something else. Be creative, as Mina might suggest.

Before he could answer, she floated backward several feet, did an elegant somersault. "You see? I'll bet I can even outfly you. Old bird."

Jonah blinked. "I know you did not just call me that."

"Positively ancient." Her violet eyes danced. "You might not want to go above the tree line, in case you dodder right out of the sky."

"Anna, you are trying my patience."

Her eyes widened, all innocence. "Patience? You have patience?"

When he made a playful grab for her, she slipped out of range. However, instead of starting the chase that Jonah expected, she floated down into a bed of purple wildflowers and rolled there, partially disappearing as she delighted in them.

A smile tugged at his lips as he looked at her, lolling about in the flowers, still demonstrating her ever-present grace as a mermaid with her sinuous movements. Then she was airborne again. When she twirled, she made a very fetching display of gossamer wings with the pink and blue markings on them. Her body had some of the same markings like the tattoos of her mermaid form. And not a bit of red, angry skin.

When he made another mock grab for her, she spun away deftly. In this tiny form, he was too worried about hurting her, and he knew it gave her the maneuvering advantage. So did she.

As she ascended so she was quickly above his reach, she was joined by several butterflies, a couple of pale gray moths. A dragonfly.

"They tend to come when I transform," she explained, dancing among them, rubbing playfully against a butterfly, somersaulting over it as it flitted back. "I don't know why."

He knew why. She drew life in its lightest, most fragile forms to her, with the matching lightness of her heart. He stretched out his wings, testing, getting ready to join her.

Seeing his intent, happiness shone from her face, a sense of triumph that felt shared.

As he launched, he balanced the weakness of the left wing with the right while still giving the left the opportunity to move, stretch, work the muscles. Wind ruffled through his wing tips, sparking along the nerve endings where the feathers joined to his flesh, his bone and muscle. He saw her look back, turn and rest in the grip of the air, displaying her open amazement at the unfurling of his wings, stretching out so far to either side of him. He liked her pleasure. Liked pleasing her. So he took off after her.

She spun in her cloud of butterflies, sending the dragonfly darting off in a mad zigzag pattern she followed, turning and twisting. While she had to move quite fast to stay ahead of Jonah, he kept to an easy pace, following her maneuvers, even duplicating some to amuse her, spiraling up in the air with her, diving down, dropping a few feet, then catching himself. He felt the strain on the injured wing when he hovered or held the weight of the air beneath it, but he managed it without much pain, just a cursed weakness.

She didn't let him linger long with his darkness. Darting

beneath him, she tweaked one of his chest hairs, yanking it out with sharp, pinching fingers.

"Ouch—" He flipped backward and managed to come up beneath her in a flash of movement.

She altered course and skimmed down his leg, using one of his toes to swing around in an arc and shoot upward again, tickling the bottom of his foot with her wingspan.

He was laughing now as he gave chase. He could have caught her several times, but chose not to, enjoying the wild, spiraling, tangled dance they did in the air, until a much larger group of butterflies was with them, a flock that made it feel as if they were in a multicolored cloud. Their many colors in the twilight sky blended with the wildflowers in the meadow below, even in the fading day's light, like a watercolor tapestry. At times she blended with them all so he had to find her laughing face, look for the paleness of bare skin.

With some sense of embarrassment, he realized she was no less alluring to him in this form. When she dove down, skimmed across the creek and came back up to join him, water ran down her breasts, her stomach and thighs, the ends of her hair silken points against her skin. The tiny, round breasts were high, the nipples tight from the water. He was fascinated by the curved perfection of her bottom. The way the creamy white cheeks shifted with her maneuvers was only enhanced by the silver and pink markings that scrolled along them, etching the delectable shape. Her breasts wobbled with her efforts. Perhaps he couldn't have caught her as easily as he thought, for not only was she quick, she was damned distracting.

And intuitive. She paused briefly in the air, considering the direction of his heated glance. That mischievous look came into her face again. "These poor humans, thinking angels have all these virtues. Chaste, sexless, patient, tranquil . . ."

"Why would chastity be considered a virtue? The Lady wants us to enjoy one another."

"I believe it's the idea of doing without something we want, denying ourselves for spiritual clarity," she said primly.

"You're baiting me."

Spinning up in the air above his head again, she soared

higher, but as they passed the top of a bristlecone pine, at about sixty-five feet, he could tell she was reaching the limit of her flight altitude. The butterflies veered off and she was soaring straight up, up, up."

"Anna, what are you . . ."

She floundered, fluttered and then turned in an abrupt dive, tumbling, the wings plastered against her.

He shot up, curving his wings tight against his body, the pain forgotten. Coming up beneath her, he twisted so he caught her with precision in that soft nest of down feathers at the joining point between his wings, where his hair mingled with it. He felt her hands grip two fistfuls of strands as she righted and oriented herself, her wings beating a gentle tattoo against the arch of one of his as she made her way onto his neck, tangled in his hair.

"That's as high as I can go, my lord," she said breathlessly.

"You shouldn't have pushed it like that."

"I knew you would catch me. That's why I tried. I've never been that high."

The simple faith in her voice tore at him. "Let's go higher."

"Oh. Should you do that, with—"

"Hush," he said, and spread his wings to soar. "Hold on."

He took her above the pine trees and more. Higher, higher, into a night sky where the stars were beginning to shine, the evidence of victory over darkness. Their light could not warm him, but perversely, her touch could, the tiny fingers against his jaw, her cheek against his ear as she wondered at the vastness of the sky, the way the world looked below, quiet and getting ready for bed. A bat moving erratically around them. An owl, who gave Anna a considering look but veered off when Jonah shifted, altering course to ensure that side of his body was between her and the predator.

"I want to . . ." He missed the last part of her sentence in the movement of the wind, but then she'd loosened her hold and was drifting from his shoulder. He dropped so he wouldn't hit her with his wingspan and turned, hovering protectively as she held her own in the thinner air, her eyes glowing like sapphires. Her wings trembled with effort as she looked at it all, did a full, slow 360-degree turn.

"How utterly marvelous," she whispered. "Look, my lord.

The lights of that town, like a cluster of fireflies. And the trees, dark soldiers guarding the world. The space and room . . ." She spun, over and over, so that when she came to a halt, she was swaying in an alarming fashion, though her face was beaming. "It's the ocean, only it's the sky. The same, but gloriously different." Something soft entered his eyes. *Like the two of us.*

He didn't know if the thought came from him or her, but it was there, the strength of it suggesting a truth he'd once known but had lost. Like so many things, so many truths that no longer felt true to him anymore, leaving him in the dark, mocking him as he blundered about. This moment alone felt clear. Strong.

She'd drifted back to him and now her small hand touched his mouth, tracing his lips. When he parted them, she tapped a tooth, let out a startled yelp as he caught her arm between his teeth, holding it in a gentle clamp, teasing the skin beneath her forearm with his tongue. She giggled. "It's like a dog licking me."

He snorted with mock affront, let her go and pushed her back with a finger to her abdomen, a flick she allowed to take her back in a series of easy floating somersaults until she was hovering, looking at him out of serious eyes. When he put out a hand, she stepped onto his palm and sat, the roundness of her bottom pressed into it as she drew her legs up and held them with her fingers looped over her knees.

"Do you sleep in the clouds, my lord?"

"Yes. Usually."

She nodded. "I can only imagine what it's like to watch you fly when you are fully healed. It must be like watching Creation itself."

He didn't know what to say to that, for all angels took fierce joy in flight. It was as necessary to them as the need of a wolf pack to run, a flower to feel the sun. . . . The muscles in his wings were burning now, and the weight of his thoughts was making it difficult to stay at this elevation.

As he took them back to earth reluctantly, she didn't comment on the sudden decision to descend, simply looking all about them as they dropped.

When his feet touched the ground, she fluttered back into

the air. He lowered himself beneath a tree, arranging his wings to cup his body though he shifted to one hip to ease the pressure on the joint of the one wing. Anna settled at the top of his thigh, stretching out with him. Then she put her hand out, a light feather touch . . . on his semierect cock beneath the jeans.

"Anna, what are you doing?"

"Touching. It's so amazing, like this." She flushed a bit but looked up his body to his bemused face. "Does it bother you?"

That wasn't the right word, but he gave a slight shake of his head.

His mouth was unsmiling, gaze intent upon her. It made Anna shiver, but she couldn't help herself. Watching him soar through the air as he had . . . Well, it had stirred her. "Would you . . . take these off?" She tugged at the button of the jeans, finding she could do little with it.

"You're going to destroy me." But he obliged, sending her back into the air as he opened the jeans, took them completely off so he lay back down, long and lean, bare and beautiful beneath her, his dark eyes living fire, his mouth so tastable, even if she'd be forced to take many, many tiny bites.

Desire consumed her. The lust she would experience in her human or mermaid-sized form all dangerously compressed into the smaller shape of her now. Descending beneath his penetrating regard, she landed on his upper thigh again, right above his hardening response. As she stretched out next to it, she ran her hand from the thick base, as far along the tall column as she could reach. And jumped when it leaped in response, for it was like confronting a large predator.

She chuckled at herself, tilted her head. "It's different when it does that at close range."

A strained smile twisted his face, his gaze glittering. "Do it again."

Though he might have intended to be teasing, she heard the underlying command. It made her mouth dry, her heart pound a little harder. She obliged, doing it again. And again, watching his abdomen muscles tighten and ripple, feeling thigh muscles bunch beneath her as he tensed his buttocks at the light, barely there caress. At least, she thought of it that way in her mind. His reaction suggested it had the effect of a strong electrical current.

Fluid gathered at the tip, like dew on a flower, fascinating her. She scooted up, touched it. It transferred to her hand, a gift from his body she could bring to her lips, taste its musky salt. Running her hand down her throat, she spread the slippery substance across her breasts, making them slick in a way that made the nerves beneath the skin hunger for . . . friction.

"Anna." His voice was throaty, dangerous. And he was far, far bigger than her now. She was delighted by it, even as the place between her legs felt so empty and needy. "Rub yourself on me. Ride me, Anna. Put me between your thighs and let me feel the tiny stickiness of you."

She needed no urging. She'd had the desire since she'd fluttered back down, seen that growing ridge beneath his jeans as he'd looked at her with want in his eyes, even in this form. Even to her proportionate human or mermaid form, he'd been an impressively equipped male. Now it was like stepping over a fallen tree of massive diameter. She slid her leg over the base, brushing her foot against a firm, round testicle, and bent, purely on impulse, to press her lips against the taut, hot—oh, so hot—skin. The steel of him was between her legs then as she settled astride his length, stretched out her body, bringing her breasts and aching nipples against him, rubbed their slickness along his shaft, working it between their bodies. She was already soaked herself, so dragging herself smoothly up the length of him was not difficult. She had to put her hands along the ridge of his broad head to slow her forward passage. And then she did take a tiny bite, making him groan.

But, Goddess. When she'd touched him in her human or mermaid form, the pulse from his cock against the pounding between her legs had been proportionately pleasurable. Lying on him like this, sliding her body against this one powerful organ of flesh, she felt that pulse like the thud of drums reverberating through the cavern of her body, her throat, the insides of her thighs, vibrating against her bottom. Moving. Blood rushing, pumping. So alive, a needy beast she wanted to feed with every crevice of her body. While she cursed having to stay in this form until the healing was complete, there was a pleasure in the anticipation as well.

For even if she brought him to a pinnacle this way, he would plow deeply into her when she shifted. She'd already seen that side of him. When she teased him, he would accept it but retaliate by claiming her, taking the upper hand again. She looked forward to it with a shuddering heat that almost compelled her to shift, damn the consequences.

But she wouldn't let him draw on energy he needed for himself. She rose now, sitting upright, her hand braced on the ridged head of his straight, hard cock, and began to rock on the balls of her feet against his lower abdomen, dragging her slickness on him, feeling the friction against her clit that made her gasp, her womb clenched on emptiness. Bending forward, she sucked the moisture off his tip with her mouth this time, shuddered as he groaned and thrust up in reaction, nearly unseating her. She took a tighter grip with her legs, rocking, riding him in truth, her hair swinging forward. He gently pushed it back, fingers trembling at the effort to restrain his movements, not hurt her. His gaze was riveted on the sight of her straddling him like this. Then he increased her fever by reaching over his shoulder and bringing back one long feather. A wing feather.

He started it at the meeting point between her body and his, brushing over her clit so she moaned again and increased her undulating movements, clamping onto him, the wetness of her body moving her hips up and down, a scant inch or two only. But the look in his eyes, the laboring breath, said he was far from unresponsive to the small area of stimulus.

Up, up, the tip of the feather trailed up her stomach, under her breasts, then over them, teasing her nipples.

"Ah . . ." She arched as it brushed her throat as well, made her whole body beg. She turned her face into the fingers holding back her hair, bit him hard, small teeth marking his flesh as her body bucked, wanting him.

Could she give him Joining Magic this way? He wouldn't hurt her again; she knew it. Even if he didn't want her to, the only thing that would stop her was stopping this, and she knew with the instinct of females from the beginning of time he wouldn't stop now. While logic told her she should respect his wishes, intuition also told her to obey the mindless, primitive urging driving her. Offering him magic was as elemental a knowledge at this moment as the response of her body. No thought or analysis required.

It spread out from her, a hazy heat. Her clit convulsed, her tissues rippling, that heat growing as she rubbed herself against him, arched against the strands of the feather, tasted his blood in her mouth as she bit down harder.

"Anna . . . Goddess."

She cried out, long and low, her body bucking, working furiously against the thick column between her legs, slick with her juices and his, the steady trickle that didn't cool the incredible heat of his cock. She reached behind her now, arching, giving her body to it further, to the orgasmic sensation between her legs, her hair brushing his testicles.

The climax took her, creaming her against his flesh, creating an even more slippery slope on his enormous length to rock against fiercely. It wasn't enough to send Jonah over, but enough to leave him hard and aching as he watched her work herself on his cock, her body flushed with the orgasm, breasts quivering with her movements, her legs spread wide to clamp around all of him.

The magic filled him, swept into his stomach, his groin, spread out like heat. Jonah wanted to curse her, but he couldn't. He cursed himself for his weakness instead, and so spoke the words harshly.

"Change, Anna. Change now."

Pain. She would feel pain. It was too soon. He remembered, and at the same moment remembered she would refuse him nothing, despite the risk to herself.

"No." He closed his hand around her, so quickly she squeaked in alarm, though it was the only thing he could think to do to stop it. "Don't. You need to stay like this awhile longer, don't you? To be fully healed."

The shivering light of transformation starting to enclose her shut off like a lightbulb with a short. She was blinking at him, her body still trembling, shuddering from her aftermath. He could feel the tiny pulse of her pussy against his hard cock and hell, he was so close, so in need. The Joining Magic could be done one-way as she'd done it, but it left a raging desire in the recipient above and beyond the raging desire he'd be feeling anyway. A desire he was not willing to answer with his hand. He wanted Anna. The slick lips between her legs. He wanted to plunder there, stretch her.

"When you can safely return to your human form," he informed her, "you best be ready for my cock to be hard and deep in you for a good, long while."

That increased her trembling. Her wings hovered over his curled fingers, quivering. Since her fluids were running down her thighs, he lifted her, used just the tip of his tongue to take it away, clean her, flick over the sensitive, engorged tissues so she squirmed against his hold, gasping. Testing, he took his smallest finger, which was still oversized, and pressed it on her wet folds. Without hesitation, she widened her legs, his name fluttering on her lips. He eased forward, slowly, slowly, and such was her trust, she kept still, now barely breathing. The heat of her narrow channel could just accommodate the rounded tip before he forced himself to stop, knowing he was stretching her hard but wanting so badly to go further, only using a different appendage.

Withdrawing slowly, he stretched out on the ground and positioned his cupped hand on his abdomen, providing her shelter to rest. Where he could see her, know she was safe. Angels didn't have to sleep, but he was feeling weary. A side effect of their flight he should resent, but because it did take some of the edge off his torturous lust stoked by the Joining Magic, he was grudgingly accepting of it.

He let his eyes droop closed as she settled down on her hip in his hand, small hands wrapping around the finger he'd had inside her, her cheek nestled against her scent and him. Her legs folded one over the other, one knee forward so the point of her hip was rocked forward. When he passed his finger over it, the bare buttock, she smiled sleepily. Since he could see her bite mark on his hand, he went to sleep with that lingering image, a comfortable curl of healing magic and simmering lust pervading his dreams and nothing else.

Which was the way he wanted it. As far as he was concerned, the seething, twisting doubt and despair could stay firmly locked down in the underbelly of his subconscious.

Fourteen

*D*ARK *Ones!*
He woke in an instant, orienting himself. Shifting, muttering . . . red eyes in the dark, their aura of filth and disease preceding them. Despair and violence.

It was an hour or so before dawn, so the night was still cloaked in darkness. Anna was sitting up, her gaze meeting his, small wings pressed in close to her body. His gaze shifted about and he gestured to her to seek camouflage in the tree branches just above. After all, it was him they were seeking.

Instead, she crept up his arm, using the spread of her wings to steady herself until she ducked under the curtain of his hair at his throat and shoulder, camouflaging herself there.

He was intent on plucking her out by her wings and using her hair to tie her to a branch, but there was no time. They were closing in, fast, and he had no weapon.

Launching himself from the ground, he cursed the stiffness of the wing, but still managed to hit the lowest branch of the desired size with his shoulder at a speed that snapped it off like a twig and sent it spinning. He snatched it out of the air, muttering his apology to the tree spirit before he rocketed forward and up, trying to get some height, as much height as possible.

"Hang on, little one."

There were three that he could see immediately, though it was a small group for a tracking party. He'd hoped for two, counted himself lucky it wasn't four. The first one descended upon him with the screeching that could rupture human eardrums and told him there were others in the area that had just been signaled. The dull gray metal of its axe slashed through the air at him. He ducked it, jammed the jagged end of his weapon in the lower torso, hard enough to punch through, and charged it with energy. He cut short the resulting scream by flipping his cudgel and knocking it into the creature's skull, pivoting to bring the other end into play, connecting with the face of the one closing in behind.

The third caught the edge of his wing, ripped, and he felt the glancing blow of a dagger as he let the movement swing him around, rather than resisting it. The powerful muscles in his other wing knocked the creature end-over-end through the air.

"Kara se vot!" A tiny but powerful whisper in his ear, and then there was a bright, blinding light behind him that startled one of the returning attackers enough that it hesitated, long enough for Jonah to flip. His miniature spellcaster launched herself and darted in and around the form of the Dark One she'd stopped with her simple flash spell. While she was moving swiftly, it made Jonah's heart stop in icy fear, for the thing's curved blade was coming perilously close to her. She twisted and slid down the blunt end of the blade, using it to escape the swing of the Dark One's fist, which landed cleverly on the more lethal end of the weapon, eliciting a howl as it cut off one or two of its fingers. As her enchanted light failed, Jonah lost sight of her, not because he couldn't see in the dark but because he couldn't spare a moment for her. *Damn it.*

Teeth sank into his shoulder, hands wrapped around his throat, talons piercing his skin. Legs, slimy with the afterbirth of the rift the creature had passed through, locked around his waist. Two more launched themselves on his front, hissing. He spun, somersaulted, using the one strong wing to knock one Dark One off, his fists to dislodge the second, but he was plummeting, his balance and strength not what they should be.

Anna had helped him, so if they caught her, if she refused to run . . . He'd not allowed her to do the Joining Magic on him, not participated. How much stronger would he have been now if he'd let her do that?

Fleeting thoughts only, useless for this moment. *You are invincible. You are unstoppable. You are a soldier for the Goddess, and there is none stronger than you.* Isn't that what he told his angels, that this was the only thought that should be in their minds in a battle? Even if it was the last thought they had when they were struck from the sky?

With a roar, he righted himself and struck upward on sheer force of will, wresting the dagger from one and driving it into the soft tissue of its face, shouting out the proper chant to infuse the blood, rewarded when the creature burst into flames even as it seared Jonah's skin. The one clinging to his back tore into his smoking flesh with those damnable teeth and talons.

Holy Goddess, another pair of them. They came at him from the left, knocked him and their fellow into the spreading network of branches of the large tree under which he and Anna had been sleeping. Jonah fought, but the branches slowed him. It did the same to them, but it didn't change the fact they'd taken his wings out of his arsenal, and that was a significant loss, for his reach was far wider than theirs.

They had him pinned. Savagely, he fought them, teeth, hands, all the power in his body. He had no idea where Anna was, so he wouldn't risk a lightning strike. He wasn't going to make his last conscious act that of killing her, foolish child though she was.

As if in defiance of that, thunder roared. A lightning shard, precise as a spear, lanced the Dark One farthest from him, exploding it in a burst of foul blood and tissue. The others whipped around, and Jonah took the opportunity to slam his head into the skull of the one still on his back, hard enough to stun it. He grasped one of its limbs, the one around his throat, twisted and bent it back as David came in on the left, long daggers flashing in both hands to decapitate. Seizing the body, the younger angel tossed it free as Lucifer incinerated it in the air before its foul blood could poison the earth.

Jonah turned on the next one with a snarl. It attempted to scrabble away but he caught it, twisted its neck, heard the snap and ran it into a jutting tree limb, impaling it before he, too, muttered the words and watched it sear to ash without burning the tree further.

There'd been seven, and he'd taken out four on his own.

With fierce satisfaction, he saw David execute a flawless upside-down twist in the air, dodging a pike, and cleave the creature wielding it in half. The young angel fired his blades with blue flame so they incinerated on the way through, a flood of heated topaz consuming and evaporating the Dark One.

Lucifer used a dagger in combination with the crescent swing of his deadly scythe. He'd hooked one with it, slung it out of the tree, half severing its head with just that maneuver before meeting the creature chest to chest, one of the few angels who could fight hand to hand with the Dark Ones, able to shield himself from the poison that slicked their skin. Jonah had the ability, but since he'd fallen victim to it when he was laid open by the axe, he couldn't claim the same shielding. Right now, at least.

A last whistling hiss, like a fire roaring away, and the forest was silent.

Jonah erupted from the branches, nearly taking a tumble to the ground when his wing didn't initially support him as he expected, and in too much of a hurry to care. Blood ran down his back, telling him the juncture point was torn again. The wing had taken a beating, both from how he had pushed it and the fact the Dark Ones had seemed to know to target it specifically. It didn't matter. Only one thing mattered.

"Anna." He called out her name even before he landed, filled with a sudden cold desperation. *"Anna."*

"I'm here, my lord." She emerged from the foliage, human once again and working the skirt of the light dress down around her bare hips. "I'm here." She came right to him, her vibrant eyes seeking his face, trying to see if he was hurt. Whereas all he could focus on was the trickle of blood at her temple where she'd come too close to the Dark One's blade in her game of cat and mouse that had been anything but a game.

She put her hands in his before he even realized he'd reached out, and gave him a quiet smile. "Angels are not dull traveling companions, my lord. I will say that."

There was a tremor in her fingers, and her face was pale, but serene. She was calm. Whereas he felt as if he needed to rip open more Dark Ones. Or throw up.

"What in the name of all Heaven and Hell were you

doing?" he demanded. "I told you to take cover. I did not mean on my person."

"You needed my help." Her lips firmed. "I wasn't going to cower in the bushes while you fought alone."

"You will do what I tell you to do," he snarled.

"She acquitted herself well, even as a firefly," David commented, landing next to Jonah and giving her a bow. "David. At your service."

"Anna." She was going to extend her hand in greeting, but since they were still held by one ominous-looking angel, she settled for a shy nod.

Quirking a brow at Jonah, David gave a semblance of a teasing smile that seemed to Anna a bit out of place on his serious features. "I can see why you've been out of touch."

Jonah's gaze shot to him. "You're not him," he said flatly. "Don't try."

A flash of hurt crossed David's face, but another voice cut across his response, impatient. "What we need to talk about is what you're doing here and why you haven't summoned us. Now that we've found you, we can take you back up to the clouds, get you a proper healer."

Anna turned as the dark-winged angel landed a few feet away. From the respectful way David turned to him and Jonah's stiffening, she had to concede this angel might be even more highly ranked than her powerful angel. Michael, perhaps? But he wasn't what she'd imagined Michael looking like.

The dark silk of his feathers swept out in an impressive mantle on either side of him, giving him the look of a landing hawk with his aquiline features and dark, expressionless eyes unexpectedly tinged with red. Power vibrated so strongly from him it made her dizzy, after all the stress of the past few moments. She swayed.

"Tone it down, Luc," Jonah said shortly. "She's been through enough."

Luc . . . Lucifer? Anna wasn't sure if knowing his identity wasn't as overpowering as the energy emanating from him, but she struggled to steady herself, sensing she was going to need all her wits about her.

"Indeed." Whatever he did, the heated weight of the air lifted considerably, and she was able to draw a clean if a bit unsteady breath. "You didn't answer my question. You're lucky your young friend has an ally. David got a summons from the Dark Spawn that you were in danger."

"Mina." Anna's gaze darted to David. "She is well?"

"Except for a nearly terminal case of bad temperament, yes." This time a glint of true humor passed through David's somber eyes.

"Jonah." Luc's tone indicated he would not tolerate being evaded much longer. "Why haven't you called us?"

"Do I appear lost to you?"

Luc gave him an even look. "Do you truly seek an answer to that question?"

Jonah had the grace to flush, but his face otherwise remained hard, resolute. "I'm where I wish to be, for the moment."

"You're where you wish to be," Lucifer repeated. "Where the Dark Ones are tracking you like hounds after a fugitive, and if they capture you, you can serve their purpose?"

"And how is that different from what I was doing?"

David drew in a breath. Luc seemed to go so still that everything about him was caught in frozen reaction. Anna's gaze shifted between the two angels, cold fear rising in her. Something was wrong here. She'd know it from the hair rising on her nape even if the dark angel's silence wasn't a warning to any creature with a trace of survival instinct. Jonah's face had shuttered closed, except for a simmering energy in his eyes that did not bode well.

"Our enemies are gathering. They're bolstered by your absence and the possibility of your capture. They'll be launching a strong attack soon. We feel it. Even if you are injured, you can help plan, organize, strategize. You are our commander. We need you—"

"For what?" Jonah snarled. Despite herself, Anna flinched, and even David retreated a step. Lucifer took a step forward. Jonah's anger flashed through the glade, ratcheting up the residual heat lingering from their battle. Anna's gaze shifted to the sky at an ominous rumble. "There is no final victory, because they're not going to stop coming. Not until they get what they want."

The darkness she'd sensed in him was perilously close to

the surface now, almost crawling over his skin. David had gripped his daggers unconsciously.

Lucifer's gaze narrowed. "Jonah, don't."

"I've been buried in their blood, in ours, for nearly a millennium." Jonah's voice was all sibilant menace, his eyes gone flat and cold, chillingly like her dream. "When I fight them, I don't know where I begin or end, or if there's even a difference anymore. What does it matter whose blood bathes my blade? It's all death. We fight and we fight, Luc. Because we're supposed to. Because we can't tolerate the presence of Dark Ones near us. As if it's in our very cells, making us do exactly what She created us to do."

"You're being a naïve child, wishing the world could be different. You're too old for petulance or running away."

Unholy flame shot through Jonah's eyes. When David began to move forward, Anna put a hand on his arm, stopping him. Whatever was between these two, they were far more powerful than this young angel, and he shouldn't be between them, any more than she should. She sensed it, even as she had to quell a similarly powerful desire to go to Jonah.

"*Petulance?* Century after century, human bloodshed and cruel ignorance, their greed . . . It all calls to the Dark Ones," Jonah continued in that terrible voice. "We fight for Her, but is She ever going to fight for *us*?"

She'd seen Jonah move with extraordinary speed. But it was nothing next to how Lucifer moved. She didn't even have a chance to scream before he knocked into Jonah and the two of them were snarling, twisting in the air like eagles fighting . . .

Lightning struck. Lucifer and Jonah landed, squaring off as David pulled Anna back. Before her toes, the earth became scorched, a black stain spreading from the strike of the fiery spear from the sky. Another fork came down on either side just behind Jonah, severing two tree limbs. He didn't even register the strike as the branches fell within inches of him.

Lucifer stepped forward again, his face gone terrible and cold. Heat swept over the glade, the fires of Hell threatening, hot enough that it prickled over her skin. Her attention shot to Jonah, the grim expression of anticipation on his face.

No, this is what he wants.

"No!" She cried it out. David made a grab for her, but she flung herself at Jonah. Not at his upper body, which she knew he'd react to instinctively as an attack, but at his legs. Dropping to her knees on the burning earth, she hugged them hard to her, her hair blowing wildly around his thighs from the wind the two angels were generating.

"Jonah, please. Stop. This isn't you. Come back to me."

Jonah blinked, angled his chin, his movements slow, ponderous. Deadly. The anger died out of his gaze as he registered her touch.

Anna. Anna was in the middle of this. In danger. That wasn't acceptable.

The sky, while overcast and grumbling, lightened, and the storm flashes died, drifting away with the thunder. David felt a wave of relief, though his gaze stayed fastened to Jonah and the woman at his feet. Lucifer had not powered down one iota. His heat still surrounded them all, threatening, keeping Jonah's hackles up, his stance combative. Only now instead of an aggressive pissing contest, David noted with great interest Jonah's manner was protective. From the speculative flicker in Lucifer's gaze, he knew the Lord of the Underworld had noted it as well.

"The poison of the Dark Ones has infected you, Jonah. But you are accepting it, which means you will not heal. It will only grow."

"I am tired and wish to be left alone," Jonah said, his syllables precise, clipped, his eyes still dark and flat, though the red flames had died back. "That is all. If it is my will to return, I shall. Until then, let the Lady find whatever sacrificial lambs She can for Her precious human pets. I'm done being Her shepherd."

In the aftermath of that momentous announcement, the light of dawn broke on the horizon.

The first and second times, he'd been asleep. Now, bleeding, his body still vibrating with battle rage, it hit him like a convulsion. With a strangled cry, Jonah was knocked to his knees, pushing Anna backward, the rippling of his body trying to accommodate the mortal form. The wings disintegrated in a spray of ash that vortexed around him, taunting before dispelling, leaving him balanced on one hand, breathing hard. Anna reached for him.

"No." Jonah snapped it out almost at the same time as Lucifer. The two angels met gazes again, telling Anna that no matter what else was going on in this moment, this black-winged angel knew Jonah well enough to know he would scorn help. And Jonah's expression said he resented that familiarity. Deeply. He made it to his feet with effort and squared off with Lucifer.

"As you can see, I'm a bit encumbered by a spell. If you take me aloft, I'll tumble out of the sky."

"That's an excuse." Lucifer snorted. "We can remove the spell, if you'd only ask."

"I wouldn't be too sure of that," David murmured. "It was a strong casting. Though temporary," he added at Luc's searing look. "To protect him."

"It did an admirable job." Luc hefted his scythe, stained with Dark Ones' blood. "We were entirely unnecessary."

Anna felt a little sick at the fluid flowing down to the hand-guard; then Luc blinked, and it was gone, the lethal blade clean, glittering. For some reason, the sight of it that way disturbed her even more.

"I thank you for your aid," Jonah said stiffly.

"Good. For it will be a cold day in Hell before I aid you again. How long will she be safe with you, hmm?" Luc glanced at Anna, took a second, slower look. She saw him notice how the breeze flattened the bodice of the dress against her unbound breasts, how her thighs were outlined.

Jonah shifted in front of her, breaking the contact. "She's not your concern. In any way."

"Will she be your concern, when she is dead?" Luc was merciless, his tone impassive. "You must come with us."

"He can't." Anna moved out from behind Jonah, though her voice quavered a bit as those dark, coal-fired eyes turned to her. "He's going to a healer. He must go to him. Mina said so, in order for him to be . . . well again."

Luc blinked. "The Dark Spawn is sending you to a human healer. And you're going?"

"I am not going back with you. That is all I will say."

"For now," Anna put in placatingly, though Jonah gave her a black look.

Luc's gaze shifted between them. For a moment, Anna thought David had bitten back a surprised chuckle, but then he coughed and she couldn't be sure.

"Jonah." Lucifer's voice changed, and though it was still stern, unyielding, she heard a note in it that suggested she and David were not the only ones personally concerned about Jonah. "We can help you."

She turned to see something vital shift in Jonah's expression. When he shook his head, for the first time, he broke contact with Lucifer's gaze. "I can't be with you now, Luc. I have no desire to return to it."

From the raw sound of the words, Anna thought something was tearing inside of him, leaving holes only fit to be filled with the battle rage he'd just demonstrated, as if he could bear no other emotion. Uneasily, it made her recall his description of Dark Ones, the way they tore rifts in the universe and charged through, seemingly propelled by fury alone.

A shudder went through him. Pressing a distracted kiss to her hand, he turned and left the three of them. As she watched him walk toward the copse of trees by the creek, she felt the passion and anger that had driven him evaporating, his desire to fight back replaced by something far worse.

While every part of her yearned to go to him, she made herself turn around and face both angels. Face Lucifer. Summoning her courage, she met his gaze and managed it for about a blink before she had to shift her own to the line of his shoulder.

"My lord . . . I wish . . . Is there anything you know that can help me?"

He cocked his head, studying her for a long, unbearable moment. It was all she could do not to retreat. "If I did," he said at last, "perhaps I would know the way to unlock this shield he's erected against us all. My Lady says give him some time, but She is patience. I am simply fire."

When he glanced at Jonah, kept his gaze there in reflective silence, she tried again. "Perhaps . . . could Ronin somehow be . . . Did his death change something for Jonah?"

That brought both angels' attention back to her. She saw

the answer in David's face, but it was Lucifer who spoke. "Yes. We began to notice differences in his manner when he lost Ronin."

"He doesn't seem to like talking about him."

"No, he wouldn't." Lucifer's countenance was terrifyingly impassive, but Anna paid close attention regardless, sensing he would not be speaking unless he felt his words had significance to her. And the flicker in David's eyes told her she was on the right track. "Jonah has had many sons, though none came from his loins. He has lost many of those sons. Ronin was his lieutenant for over two hundred years."

Anna swallowed. To have someone he loved as a son for so long, and then lose him . . . "How old is Jonah?"

"Over a thousand, at least," David said quietly, and Anna tried to mask her shock.

"Time can sit heavily on an angel's shoulders," Lucifer continued. "Ronin alone could tease Jonah, mock him. At times he goaded Jonah's patience, for Ronin went his own way, never growing out of his impetuousness."

Lucifer blinked, once, a brief respite from the intensity of his gaze. "Yes, Ronin is important to what has happened. David is, too. He'd started to love David the same way, just when he lost Ronin. I suspect Jonah feels he can bear to lose no more sons."

David's head whipped around, his startled eyes finding Luc. Luc glanced at him. "You should not be hurt by what he said to you before. He was right. You can't ease his heart by pretending to be Ronin. Look beyond what he said to what he meant. He cherishes your seriousness, David. And not just because he believes it will keep you alive longer."

As Lucifer shifted his attention back to Anna, he bit off an impatient sigh. "I understand my Lady's words. The answer is almost always simple. But the journey is not. For it to be his own truth, he must find it." His lips twitched. "While I find it ironic as well as frustrating that he is walking to his destination as a human, it is a reminder of that. This witch may have more of my Lady's wisdom than expected."

The dark gaze hardened and Anna took a step back, swallowing. "However, the unfortunate thing is we need Jonah now. If he isn't with us, preparations to do without him must take precedence over his state of mind. For good or ill, you seem to be the only one able to reach him at the moment. You should be terrified by that, Anna. It does not bode well for any of us, and we could sorely use him. I wish you the blessings of the Lady and as much luck as She can spare you."

Then in a blink, he was aloft, leaving them with a last look of frustration and disgust. He went into the sky so far and fast, the backwash from his launch blasted the leaves up into a brief, spiraling whirlwind around them and ruffled David's feathers.

Anna let out a breath. Okay, so she really hadn't lost her fear and awe of angels. Lucifer was terrifying. Magnificent, yes, but he seemed even more formidable and frightening in his quiet reserve than Jonah in a temper, such that she was glad they had not come to blows.

"They're a lot alike, the two of them. Things never go well when they disagree," David remarked, as if reading her mind.

"Is that why we have tsunamis and hurricanes?" she asked.

David almost smiled. "No, but they certainly could whip those up, if they didn't have the control they have. They can push Earth off her axis, completely alter the tides and destroy life as we know it. They just can't seem to figure out how to agree on certain points. They have some of your witch's stubbornness, come to think of it."

"You didn't hurt Mina, did you?" Her question took him off guard. Something flashed across his face. Apprehension and anger flared in her. "My lord, you didn't—"

"She is well, as I have said," he said firmly. "I thought she was an enemy. Now I know better." There was an inflection to his voice that caused Anna some curiosity, but he continued. "Anna, do you think taking him to the healer will help him?"

Anna found herself a bit flustered to be asked her opinion. "I hope so. He's not allowing me to help him heal in other ways. At least not as much as I'd like." Mortified at his shrewd glance, she blushed.

David chuckled, a pleasant male sound despite the dark worry in his eyes. "Then he *is* insane." He gave her an appreciative but inoffensive look before he sobered. "The lives of angels are determined by Fate and the Lady's will. We accept this. It's part of who we are, as much as breathing. I know that acceptance is still inside him, no matter what he says. Would you agree?"

She nodded. "At the core of him, he still serves the Goddess. He just seems . . . angry at Her?" Biting her lip, she added, "No offense to Her intended."

While a disturbed look flashed across his face, David nodded. "I suspected as much, but it's a hard thing for angels to discuss, let alone contemplate. So while it hurts me to leave him like this, it's obvious our presence will not help. Luc is right. We must go prepare for both the best and the worst that may happen."

The things that crossed his gaze made Anna uneasy, confirming that Jonah's defection was having more far-reaching implications than she could know in the limited scope of her world. "Can you tell me—"

"I need to go," he said, albeit gently. "Mina knows how to find me if he has immediate need of us. Remember that. Don't hesitate to use your link with her. Focus on him, Anna, and let us worry about the rest. He's very important to us. To all of us."

"I'll remember." She hadn't even known she had a link to Mina, one of many things she didn't know, but she didn't feel it necessary to share her ignorance of that with the worried-looking lieutenant. "He'll be okay. He just needs time."

She wanted to believe that, so she did.

"Let's hope Fate will provide it," David responded. "Goodbye, Anna."

Fifteen

THE darkness is growing in you, Jonah. Lucifer's words, her dream, David's worried look . . . She couldn't stop the shiver from running over her skin as she looked at her now human angel, squatting naked by the creek, tossing in pebbles, the line of his muscled back taut with the things fighting within him.

Though she'd shrugged off Mina's concern at the time, she *had* wondered why he hadn't contacted other angels to come to his aid. It had also surprised her, as it had Mina, that the vision pointed them to a human shaman, rather than back toward the heavens. Now two angels had come to their immediate physical aid, but both believed whatever ailed Jonah was not within their power to fix.

Of a sudden, she felt very alone. She'd been going forward only on feelings . . . Goddess help her, nothing but optimism. It had never occurred to her what larger things might be at stake.

The unfortunate thing is we need Jonah now . . .

He just needs time . . . Let's hope Fate will provide it.

Lucifer and David's warnings made it clear that an angel of Jonah's power wasn't supposed to be traipsing the countryside aimlessly. Lucifer had called Jonah a petulant child.

But Anna wasn't in the habit of letting others do her thinking, even if it was a creature as old and terrifying as the Lord of the Underworld. She studied the man crouched by the stream. His face was tilted up toward the touch of the wind; his eyes were closed. With features as perfectly sculpted as the Lady could make them, it was no wonder the wind kissed his face, caressed him. But there was no easing to his brow, no sense it brought him any comfort.

She had the sudden and disturbing realization that he had looked more at peace fighting a losing battle against the Dark Ones amid the forest of tree limbs.

He bowed his head now, an arm bending along the side of his skull, one fist clenched on the back of his neck.

When she stepped forward, he made a noise of warning.

"I'm a stranger to myself, Anna. Lost. Don't come near me."

The sound of his voice, so determined and yet so broken at once, wrenched her heart. What could she possibly know that could ease the heart of an angel like Jonah? Nothing. But then, neither Lucifer nor David knew the answer any more than she did.

She bent, started picking flowers. There was a variety of small white ones all through their little glade. Taking her time, thanking the plants for their sacrifice, she collected the petals, working her way closer. She could sense his attention drifting over her, while the rest of his thoughts dwelled in much darker realms.

When she was next to him, she hesitated, then opened her hand over the crown of his head. The petals floated down, landing on his clenched fist, in his hair, tumbling down his shoulders and back. Despite his warning, she followed their descent with her own fingers, stroking his blood-stiffened hair. There were crimson and brown streaks down his back, oblong patches of clean skin where his wings had been. She bent, placed her lips against his body there.

She'd always simply been who she was, a shapeshifter with no real place, no requirement to be anything except what she herself demanded. She'd not had anything to define her but herself. She could even reinvent herself if she wished. In contrast, she sensed Jonah struggling with the very core of who he was, and that battle was happening in such markedly fetid waters she wondered how he could see his sure path anymore. How anyone could.

She knelt, stroking his hair, still following the curve of his ear. "My lord?"

It was little more than a whisper, but his head snapped up as if she'd shouted. His eyes were unfocused, wild. The blood on his face made him look like a primitive savage. "What can I do to help you?" she asked.

Jonah stared at her. He could make no sense of his thoughts, but there was a part of him that knew she shouldn't be this close to him. His blood was charged from the battle, his body pulsing with the latent rage from it. He was angry at Luc for disrupting the numb mind-set he'd been in before it all happened. And David . . .

Ah, Goddess. He wanted to split out of his skin, leave everything he was behind, and knew he couldn't do it. The memories would follow him, haunt him still.

To escape those ghosts, he reached out and curled a hand in Anna's hair, winding it over his knuckles, watching the overlap of the thick, lustrous curls. The Goddess could create such a marvelous thing. Anna's shining mane of hair, her fragile face, those violet eyes and soft breasts . . . So perfect, it fueled the fire within him, the unreasoning anger.

He was filthy. He stank of Dark One, and he knew he had no business touching her, but her arms were winding around his neck . . .

"Goddess help you," he said.

He took her flat onto the ground, his hand on her throat, holding her still, staring down at her. *You could snap it with barely a thought.*

But she had no fear, not of him. She was quivering, yes, but she lay docile under his hold, trusting he would not harm her. *Will she be your concern, when she's dead?*

With a near sob of despair for the conflict of his thoughts, he yanked the skirt of the dress out of his way and shoved into her with the precision and violence with which he'd skewered a Dark One.

And Goddess help him, some part of him was delighting in his brutality, even as another voice raged at him to stop.

There was nothing more despicable than a man who hurt a woman for no other reason than the demons within himself. But those demons were hard upon him right now, and Anna was willing to give him shelter in that storm, as well as be the rocks he dashed himself against.

When his cock was gripped by her tightness, he belonged . . . somewhere. He dropped over her, burying his face in her neck, lips finding the pounding artery. Tried not to snap his teeth into it like a rabid creature.

No. He was a lord of the sky, always in control. He wanted her insane, as insane as he felt. He withdrew and pulled her legs over his shoulders, lifting her up to put his mouth between her legs. He banded his arms around her upper thighs as she lost the ability to hold on to anything, suckled her clit in his mouth, plunged his tongue deep inside her, tasting himself and her sweetness, feeling her shudders, hearing her mewling cries.

He worked her ruthlessly until she flooded against his mouth. But then he kept going as she cried out at the stimulation of her oversensitized skin, squirmed. He could hold her effortlessly, while her struggle fired his blood. She was his. His. He didn't release her until she stopped struggling, and when she did, he saw she was weak, her eyes glazed, and her throat bared to him. Good.

He rammed into her again, no finesse or rhythm. He was pumping, pumping, impossibly hard now. But no release came. Sweat gathered on his shoulders, fury built like a storm, but it was a fever that wouldn't break, a battle rage that could only find release in blood. Bending, he sank his teeth into the top of her breast and heard her gasp, the cry she bit back. As he worked down to her nipple she tried to hold on to his arms, but he caught her hands and pinned them to the ground.

"Mine," he said fiercely.

"My lord, let me—"

"No." He snarled it. "Lie there. Take me. That's all."

"Stop."

She said it softly, so softly that it shouldn't have registered at all. But it was like the slight whisper of an unexpected gentle breeze during the fury of his storm. Jonah paused, panting, his hands gripping her wrists with bruising force, his body pressed down hard on her as if he was pounding on his tormented soul. As if he'd somehow given it to her and it was staring at him out of those eyes. Only not with the accusation he expected, but something harder to face.

Anna's heart was racing, her mind in shock at the vicious assault. He'd brought her to an intense climax with his mouth that had swept her away like a riptide. But then he'd bitten her so savagely, gripped her as he might an opponent. For just a flash, in his dark eyes, there'd been . . . evil. Hatred.

No. She refused to believe that of him.

While Mina had never said how old Jonah was, Anna had no doubt he'd been fighting Dark Ones for centuries. And now she knew he'd been around over a thousand years. The battles he'd waged had probably taken place in areas decimated by plague, in the clouds of smoke rising above the gas chambers of concentration camps, over slaughterhouses and mass graves dug by dictators and conquerors, over bare ground stripped of forests and the homes of all the creatures there . . . wherever human beings created such evil as couldn't be imagined. Not only did he have to see it below him, he'd faced the creatures that tore holes in the firmament and that were called by evil. The angels who followed him into those battles, those he trained, whom he came to care for like his own sons, often died.

While angels apparently took longer to reach a breaking point, they did have one. Physically immortal didn't mean emotionally immune.

She was out of her depth. No question. But the Goddess had made her as well as great and mighty angels, so there had to be a connecting thread between them.

"Ssshhh." She lifted her head from the ground. While she was sure he wouldn't release her hands, she brushed her mouth, then her temple against his heaving chest, her ear to his heart. "My breast. It hurts, my lord. Will you put your mouth on it?"

A quiet request, and when she laid her head back down, Jonah's gaze moved to that area where he'd bitten her. The imprint of his teeth was visible.

Staring at it a long moment while she held her breath, at

last he bent, his grip easing without conscious thought, and pressed his lips there.

Light, gentle, the amazing quiver of flesh. As he relented to her need, Jonah found the soft silkiness of woman that he hadn't registered or savored in the haze of his fury. And as he gave to her, he remembered it was a much better form of pleasure than taking.

Her fingers turned to twine with his, held as she slipped the other hand free and threaded it up into his hair.

"Don't move, my lord. Simply . . . be."

When she lifted her hips, he slid deeper, into the wet, welcoming heat of her rippling over his organ. Tightening her muscles on him, she began to move. As he watched, curved over her, he stayed utterly still, mesmerized. Passion gathered energy with the slow glide of her hips, up and down, her lower body rippling like her mermaid form.

Now, instead of the relentless barrage of an electric shock, where no release from torture was forthcoming, the pleasure was building like a slow tide. The joy of feeling cool water running over his hellfire-scalded body, the slow approach to the promise of a waterfall.

"Little one . . ."

"Easy," she whispered. "Let me just feel you. Ride inside me, my lord."

Something was quaking in his lower belly, a remarkable reaction. She was so young, so much younger than he, but at this moment, the way her fingers passed over his face, it was as if that didn't matter. As if the blood didn't matter, as if she could see beyond it to something he couldn't see himself. The climax was intensifying to a level he'd never experienced before, and yet his grip was no longer bruising. He'd drifted down onto her, had his elbows on either side of her head, their foreheads touching, pressing together. His buttocks were clenching as he moved now, as unconscious and natural as breathing. Sliding in deep, withdrawing, thrusting in again, feeling her excruciatingly tight muscles holding him, stroking him. Her legs rose, clasped around him, and they were moving in one sinuous roll, perfectly synchronized like the sway of the tree branches above, the movement of wind, rhythm of the earth.

"Let me in, my lord," she said softly. "Don't deny me. I love you."

The words were simple, true and sweet. He had no defense against them. Her energy flooded into him, and while he could not bring himself to match it, create the synergy of healing that he knew she and her seawitch would find optimal, he could do this one thing for her. Passively and yet wondrously experience her energy moving through his body, clean and innocent, healing where it could. It even surrounded the deep blackness squatting balefully on top of his soul. Though it couldn't permeate it, the Joining Magic settled over it like a cloak offered to a shivering vagrant, a touch of kindness toward something lost and desolate, even as the creature spat and hissed halfheartedly at the offering.

His release came then, quiet, overwhelming. His body shuddering against hers, fingers digging into her fragile shoulders and slim upper arms. Pressing his face into her hair, he emitted the groan of a soul-deep release.

They lay silently that way for a while, his jaw pressed against her wet cheek, so that the tears on her face transferred to his skin.

When he rose to his knees at last, pulled out of her, his gaze drifted down to her thighs. Mixed with her fluids, he saw the smears of blood where he'd thrust into her. The tremble of her thighs where he'd pushed the muscles relentlessly.

He swallowed. He couldn't ask forgiveness for yet another unforgivable act. But he could offer her this. Bending forward from his knees, as if genuflecting before her, he kissed her inner thigh. One side, then the other, taking away the blood, soothing her flesh in between with his tongue while her muscles left impressions like butterfly wings against his jawline as she quivered, held her breath.

"I'm all yours, my lord," Anna whispered.

To destroy with my darkness. Bowing his head and closing his eyes, a shudder rippled over his skin beneath her touch. "I should have David take you home," he said, his voice harsh. "You're not safe with me."

"I'm where I belong, my lord." Anna raised her chin as he lifted his head, met her gaze. "That is not a decision you can make for me."

Jonah gave her an ironic look, which indicated he was more than physically capable of making that decision for her. Her lips tightened. "It is not a decision you *should* make for me."

"Well, as you may have noticed, I am not necessarily making the decisions I *should* make these days."

The wry observation drained some of her tension, though she remained wary as he turned with a muffled grunt to lie down next to her. Gathering her close, he let her lie across his chest. "Did Lucifer and David tell you how best to handle me?"

"They respect you too much to do that, my lord. And I am yours to command."

"Oh, really?" The incredulity in his voice, the underlying humor, clear now, brought with it an overwhelming rush of relief to her. The worst had passed, for the moment. "Perhaps you'll tell me one command of mine you've obeyed thus far. Unless memory escapes me, you've ignored anything I've told you to do."

"I suspect you should be getting sleepy now, my lord," she evaded. "The human male form does tend to require sleep . . . after."

He squeezed her in light reproof. "You seem to have lost your terror of angels, little one. Standing up to Lucifer himself."

"You all are not so fearsome. A lot of grumbling and bluster for the most part. Much like blowfish."

That of course was a lie, on many different levels. Lucifer aside, Jonah had been fearsome during the battle with the Dark Ones. The way he'd taken their lives with such fierce, single-minded precision. It had been awesome and terrible to watch how he fought even as he got overwhelmed. It was obviously what he knew best. He was at home in battle, more comfortable than anywhere she'd seen him yet. Even in her arms.

But she hadn't truly feared him until he sank his teeth into her breast and she saw that trace of malicious light in his gaze. For that second, she'd wished Lucifer and David hadn't left.

No. She couldn't think that way. It wasn't Jonah. It was the darkness she feared, the emanations a cold echo of what she'd sensed from those terrible creatures tonight. That Jonah could succumb, become one of them . . . Was that what Lucifer had hinted the poison could do to him? No. She would get him to the shaman, and everything would be all right.

Winding her arms more closely about him, she buried her fingers in his hair, held his face to her throat, felt his breath there. She did love him. She didn't know if she simply loved the amazing idea of him, or the man himself, but it didn't matter. The man and the idea were the same. She believed in that, believed in him. She had to help restore him to that if she had any meager ability to do so. The two angels seemed to think that was the case. Even Mina had intimated it.

Okay, so Lucifer had said she was the only one who could do anything with Jonah, which was a little different. But she was going to take it as a bolstering thought.

He'd fallen asleep while Anna held him in her arms. She propped herself on an elbow, studied his face, traced the strong bone structure, the sensual fierceness of it. If David and Lucifer had stayed, traveled with them, the next time Jonah wanted her, would he have taken her this way before them, the way he implied that angels often did, sharing women together?

She remembered Jonah's possessive reaction when Lucifer had looked at her. But could what she'd interpreted as a protective, singular attitude been simply part of the poison gripping him?

"Mine," he'd said just now, as if she were a slave, his property.

For a moment she felt swamped by doubts again, terribly alone. But with him in her arms like this, how could she feel lonely? When she held him against her heart, a childish fantasy it might be, but she felt the clasp of the other half of herself.

Settling down next to him again, she held him as he muttered, called out in his sleep. Holding him in her arms and stroking him as needed, both for his comfort and her pleasure, her fingertips lingered on his broad shoulders. She followed the line of his chest down to his hard abdomen and remembered its weight pushing her own legs open. His cock, even in its replete state, still looked able to fill her. Perhaps angels weren't the only ones who craved this for grounding, for nourishment of the soul. She couldn't imagine what she was going to do without it when it was gone, but that would come whether she tried to prepare for it or not. Her task was before her.

It was time to rouse him and continue their journey. She had to get him to the shaman.

Sixteen

THE day's heat had long since passed oppressive. When Anna glanced at Jonah, she saw that, despite his human form, his core was still angel, for his skin barely gleamed with sweat. He seemed relaxed, walking and taking in the landscape around them, whereas she was certain every cell along her skin's surface was gasping for air.

As they moved deeper into the state, the occasional sign told them they were headed into the Mojave Desert, moving toward the Black Rock wilderness area. Even without the signs, their surroundings reflected the change in topography.

As if he'd picked up that she was having some difficulty adapting to their decidedly nonoceanic environment, Jonah was goading her natural curiosity about new things by pointing out features of interest. She was surprised to find that, while she didn't know the names of her own wildflowers, Jonah was a rich resource on the vegetation of the area, patiently telling her the names and histories of the different bizarre-looking plants. Joshua trees with their upraised limbs like a supplicant prophet, which had given them their name. Saltbush with tiny clusters of shell-like leaves and crusty surface. Thorny, tall greasewoods whose leaves had a salty taste. Yucca with their thick white blooms.

In the distance, smooth gray formations of what she thought of as mountains were the remnants of volcanic craters. Jonah noted they would find no vegetation in those areas. But he told her mammoths and saber-toothed tigers once roamed there.

"You were alive when . . ."

Jonah chuckled. "No, sweet mermaid. Their time was far before mine. But angels do have very regimented occasions to move through time doors, and it was a period I was allowed a brief glimpse of."

She stopped, stared at him. "You've gotten to see and do so much. How . . ." She bit it off, realizing at once the error of going down that road, but he'd already sensed what the question was. He looked out at the volcanic formations, the remnants of volatile things.

"Because I *have* seen numerous wonders. Experienced and learned every philosophy, seen the way they cycle into one another. And yet the nature of evil is never changed or healed by any of it. Never wishes to do anything but destroy the wonders of the universe. Believe me"—his lip curled in a bitter sneer—"blissful ignorance is the closest friend of faith."

She cursed herself for bringing the shadows back into his face. He'd seemed better today, the despair that had gripped him after their encounter with Lucifer and David going dormant behind his apparent enjoyment of her insatiable curiosity, her excitement over things that were so commonplace to him.

Resolutely, she turned her gaze back to the landscape. "It's like we're about to walk on the moon, isn't it?"

"Astronauts have trained in this area for just that reason."

Fortunately for her gasping skin, it was also the type of area where the sparse population and fierce conditions meant that the infrequent passing drivers automatically stopped to ask if they needed a ride. Jonah had therefore offered most of his explanations to her as they bounced along in the backs of the pickups or other off-road vehicles that were the predominant transportation for this remote area.

Anna was quietly relieved, for the area was also rife with breathtaking mountain ranges that would have made for difficult travels. Every step she took on the hot asphalt, even with the sunscreen and hat she now wore, and the ample supply of drinking water they carried, seemed to be dragging down her limbs. She had no desire to show Jonah how the heat was affecting her. Just a little farther . . . Another day's travel at this pace, with these many helping hands, and they'd be there.

She saw the gas station as a paradise when their latest hitch dropped them there. The two surveyors turned off on a highway toward California, away from where she and Jonah were going. Anna went inside to buy something else cold and wet for both of them while Jonah stayed outside, still preferring open spaces.

As she went up the stairs of the wooden porch of the trading post, Anna noticed an old man sitting on a straight-backed chair at the end of it. There was a rocker next to him, but he'd chosen the chair that didn't move, which she thought was odd, when she would take any opportunity to increase the air movement around her. She couldn't tell if he was sleeping or just staring out at the desert landscape, but he was so motionless, she at first guessed the former. Then she realized his head was not touching the back of the chair, nor was it bowed forward.

Then Jonah passed her, his fingertips grazing her lower back, distracting her with his absent smile before he headed in that direction, apparently planning to take a seat in the rocking chair.

She wondered if he'd ever sat in one and if she should warn him about the unexpected motion. Suppressing a smile, she decided to let him make that discovery himself. Despite the heat, she couldn't help but take an extra moment to watch him. The way he walked, the invisible sense of those wings, though he was much steadier in his human form now. Shaking her head at her foolish crush, she made herself open the screen door to enter the store.

A middle-aged woman with tired eyes and a lined face but a pleasant smile was running the place. She introduced herself as Pat, offered Anna any help, then continued working on receipts. Anna wandered, finding some ironic merchandise options, including a T-shirt with the familiar saying, "Never drive faster than your guardian angel can fly." She utilized the restroom to change into it, as well as a pair of light cotton shorts and sneakers that she knew would be better for the area than her dress and sandals. There was also a bobble-headed angel she couldn't resist. She tied it to the top of the backpack, which she'd brought in with her to pack whatever supplies she bought.

"The world is obsessed with angels, aren't they?" the woman asked, a note of amusement in her weary voice.

"Well, it is nice to think someone's looking out for us," Anna offered as she brought two fountain drinks and an ICEE to the counter. She wondered if Jonah could get a brain freeze by drinking one too quickly. She was going to find out. "After all, it seems like a lot for one deity to do."

"Tell me about it. I can't keep track of one teenager." The woman sent a glance to where the teenager in question was sullenly stocking shelves, a boy rapidly approaching Jonah's height but who'd not yet grown into the lanky limbs.

"Maybe God keeps hoping we'll look out for ourselves," he commented. "Unlike Grandpa there, sitting on his butt, letting the world take care of him."

"John," his mother snapped. "That's enough."

"Yeah, yeah." He gestured to the shelves. "He used to do this. Now I'm stuck here doing it because he's just a lump on a log. Not a thing wrong with him. Maybe I'll go fight in some stupid war a hundred years ago, so I can cop out whenever there's something I don't want to deal with." He stomped off toward the back for another box.

Pat pressed her lips together hard, and Anna noticed a tremor in her hands as she took her money for her purchases. "I'm sorry," she murmured. "That's been building up for the last hour. I think you just came in at the right time for him to blow."

"It's okay," Anna said, but the woman shook her head.

"I know he seems horrid, but he's not. He wanted to be with his friends today, maybe needed to be, but I really needed the help and . . ."

Anna, remembering the way they all looked away from the abused woman in the diner, reached across the counter and gripped her hand. "It's all right."

Pat swallowed, her eyes filling abruptly with tears. She latched onto Anna's hand as if desperate for the touch. "Alan . . . that's John's dad. He died a couple months ago in a car crash. You know teenagers. They strike out when they hurt. And unfortunately, it hasn't helped that Alan's death sent Gabe back off into his own world. I really could have used his help with John, to help him get through this."

"And you," Anna observed.

Pat dashed away the tears with the back of her hand. "It's not Gabe's fault. He's done a lot better these past few years, but he's not ever . . . Well, he's never been who he was before the war, according to Alan. Came back to this store when Alan was ten, and he's been just pottering here like a ghost for all these years. Alan's mother had to go and do everything that happened off the property . . ." She stopped, mortification gripping her features. "God, listen to me. I'm so sorry. I can't believe I'm telling you this. I don't even know you."

"It's all right," Anna repeated. "I guess you don't have a lot of people to talk to about it out here."

"No." Pat shook her head with a slight smile. "There's a group of us that get together, but sometimes it just gets so quiet, I think I might go mad. Alan and I loved it here, the isolation and landscape, but that was because we had each other . . ."

Abruptly, she gave herself a shake. Giving Anna her change, she nodded. "I can't afford to break down like this. I thank you for your kindness, though. Have a good day. I should go check on my son."

"Hope everything will be all right," Anna said softly to the woman's back as she stepped behind the curtain between the main store and what she supposed was the supply or living area for the family. Anna drew another couple of bills out of her wallet and put them by the cash register, hoping it would help.

When she stepped out on the porch, she found Jonah sitting at the end of the porch next to the man she now knew was Gabe, the boy's grandfather. Instead of the rocker, Jonah was sitting on the top step of the side access stairs to the porch, his head propped back on the rail. Oddly, he was gazing at the same view as the old man, both quiet, no conversation apparently needed. But there was an unusual sense of . . . togetherness in their posture toward one another.

Anna stopped, holding the screen door so it wouldn't slam and attract attention, studying the two of them for long moments, as the seed of something grew in her mind. Could it be so simple? As simple as the apparent mystery of a human shaman?

Her heart pounding in her ears, she stepped back into the store. There was something else she wanted to ask Pat.

IF their next hitched ride thought it unusual for Anna to ask him to drop them off at a point of the highway where there was nothing but desert on either side, he didn't remark on it. The park ranger headed to his post on the Black Rock Wilderness Reserve was apparently used to hikers and researchers in the area, though he verified they had the type of supplies that would care for them in the survivalist conditions, probably to save him having to rescue them later. Jonah covered what they didn't have by showing enough familiarity with the terrain that the ranger was satisfied they knew what they were doing.

If he only knew, Anna reflected grimly. The mindmap Mina had given her told her this was where they had to strike out across the desert, off the known roads. They would be walking in a northwest direction to get in the vicinity of the Schism, and from the guarded questions she'd asked the ranger, she now knew she'd been mistaken in her time estimates. It could be as much as another day and a half until they stumbled on it. Then, once they found the energy signature of the Schism, it would be entirely up to it as to when it would decide if they were worth opening its gateway and giving them access to Desert Crossroads, the shaman's home. Anna deliberately didn't watch the Jeep leave them behind, facing instead the desert landscape stretching out before them.

Neither she nor Jonah had lived the majority of their lives in man-made environments, so the lack of roads shouldn't have been daunting. Regardless, it took an act of courage to make that step off the pavement, and for the first time she understood human attachment to signs of civilization.

I can do this. I must do this. Jonah will not do this without me. This is my purpose.

"Are you worried about getting lost?" Jonah's voice spoke just above her, to her left, and she felt the brush of his body against her arm, a reassurance.

"No. I have Mina's mindmap," she reminded him, with a grimace. "I think somehow that spell is also how she's tracking us. How she knew where we were and that we were in danger last night, so she could send David and the other angel to us."

He slanted a glance at her as they started to walk. "Why won't you say Lucifer's name?"

Leave it to him to assume the truth rather than accept the absurd but courteous idea that she had forgotten his name.

"He's a little daunting."

Jonah snorted. "More annoying than anything."

"Maybe to an angel that can stand toe-to-toe with him, but to the rest of everything breathing, he's a little scary. You know, *you're* a little scary."

"And yet, you're not scared of me. Nowhere near as much as you should be. I think that ICEE did freeze my brain. It still hurts." He stopped, his eyes closing so they almost disappeared as his brow furrowed. "You're trying to kill me."

She made a face at him, but a moment later his hand closed over her elbow, guiding her to the right before she put her foot square into the middle of a low-lying shrub with spiny branches. She hid a smile, knowing he'd just proven why she wasn't as afraid of him as he thought she should be.

"Maybe if I understood Lucifer better, I would feel less intimidated. I'm not saying I understand you, really," she added hastily. "But sometimes knowing a little bit about why someone acts the way he does helps. Like that man back there on the porch, Gabe. He's that way from fighting in the Vietnam War." She glanced over at Jonah. "I talked to his daughter-in-law. She said he's gone through all sorts of counseling, and she has literature on ways to help him deal with it."

"Like what?" Jonah's voice was neutral. He squatted to take a look at a rock, turn it over and examine the bug life there before resettling it. He might not even be listening to her words, just the companionship of her voice. He'd done that occasionally on their journey, and she hadn't been offended by it. But she hoped he was really listening now.

"She said the counselors taught him how to visualize. You know, have a picture of something ready in his mind to call forward when he remembers the bad things and it becomes overwhelming. They've also told his family to try and get him to talk about what happened, how he wants to change how he feels, how to improve things. You know. Coping skills. Get him to face that he's carrying blame and guilt for things that aren't his fault."

Jonah pressed his hand on the flat rock, staring down at the shape of his fingers on it. Tilting his head, he looked up at her, squinting. He was wearing one of the bill caps they'd bought to shade their eyes and faces from the sun, but it didn't make his dark eyes any less intense, able to reach inside of her with their ancient knowledge, the things he'd seen and knew.

She knew she should feel incredibly foolish for thinking, even for a moment, that human psychological ploys could apply to him. But when she'd seen the two of them out there, she'd heard the click in her mind, the sense that she'd been given a clue and had to follow it.

"Do you think that truly helps?" he murmured. "It's all games of the mind. It doesn't change the truth, the reality. The why." He rose. Reaching out, he slid his knuckles along the curve of her face, a distracted gesture, like the way he'd placed his hand on the rock, feeling the texture as if it were something alien, distant to wherever he was in his mind. "That's what Gabe can't find. He's used the things you described. Coping skills, just as you said. Then he loses his son in what appears to be a senseless accident, another body on the pile stacked up in his mind. His coping shields got blown into shrapnel, taking him back to the ultimate question. If there's no *why* that makes sense to him, that makes it worth it, then the rest of it has no meaning to him. He can't fully recover until he has that. And in the face of evil, there is no *why.*"

His expression darkened. It reminded her of her earlier thought, of how he could be almost as intimidating as Lucifer. She had to suppress the instinct to take a step back. "It's even worse when you've always thought you did understand the why, but then that gets taken away," he said. "That's when the answer strays into the realm of gods. Men like Gabe, they've stood inside that realm and screamed for answers, for accountability, and met only silence. Even the Dark Ones couldn't have conjured a Hell as diabolically ironic as that."

He turned, dropping his hand, and continued walking.

Perhaps, she reflected despondently, it was best for her not to trust her intuition quite so implicitly when it came to dealing with an angel.

Then he stopped, came back just as she started to trudge along with him, and lifted the backpack away from her.

"You *will* stop carrying this," he admonished her gently. For the first time, he seemed to notice she'd changed clothes, and a corner of his mouth twitched. "No danger of you outrunning this guardian angel. Would you like to ride for a bit?" He indicated his back.

As much as she wanted to say yes, she feared it wouldn't be long before it wasn't a choice. So for now she demurred, indicating her desire to walk. He had her follow behind him, instructing her to follow in his footsteps so he could keep her from stepping into softer places where the volcanic sand would go down deeper than expected, or places where the ground cover would scratch her legs. There was also the occasional poisonous snake or bug to avoid. In return, she spoke up if they strayed off the direction they needed to follow.

While he'd encouraged her several times at the beginning of their journey to turn back, Anna now knew he hadn't ever really wanted her to leave. Whether that was an unhealthy dependence on her or something more played in her imagination, giving her alternately worried and warm thoughts.

She should just count it a blessing he'd stopped trying, for she sensed he could be implacable in his purpose when his mind was set. She wasn't so sure at this juncture if he couldn't tempt her to capitulate.

They discovered a hikers' road of sorts, which of course contained the inevitable evidence of human travelers—trash. To pass the time, she coaxed him into a game of kick the can as they made their way down the dusty track. They worked the soup can back and forth between them at an ambling pace. For a time the clanking was the only sound breaking their companionable silence. That and the desert creatures, insects and birds making their harsh calls and chirps, warbles and hiccups. Most they did not see, but then he pointed out a large gold and black lizard.

"Gila monster."

Anna squatted to look at the large snakelike lizard burrowed under one of the shrubs, but when she leaned forward, Jonah's hand came down on her shoulder, keeping her still. "They aren't necessarily friendly. They only eat about four or five times a year, but when they do, they consume about 50 percent of their body weight. That would make you an appealing meal."

She made a face at him, then she saw him studying her face, his eyes sharp on what she knew was a pale complexion. Adjusting her hat, she rose and returned to the road and their game.

"So what did Lord Lucifer mean, that you could have called him whenever you wished?"

Fortunately the question broke his scrutiny. "Angels are linked, telepathically, for lack of a better word. To each other and somewhat to the Lady Herself."

"So you're in each other's heads all the time?"

"Goddess, no." He chuckled. "What a racket that would be. There's a skill to it you have to learn. Which is good, because otherwise a young angel, still inexperienced at shielding his thoughts, would be popping in and out of the mind of everyone he thought about. It's like a very heavy door, and you have to learn to hold it open. It takes effort, so it shuts on its own when you're not focused on it."

He eyed the can, gave it a deft kick that took it in the air and cleared a desert tortoise crossing their path. The creature plodded onward, unconcerned. Jonah guided Anna in a wide berth around the creature.

"Surely he's not a danger."

"It's not that." He shook his head. "If you startle them, it can make them void their bladders. They store fluid in their bodies to last them for months out here without a water source. If you scare them, they can die."

"Do you know everything?"

He flashed her one of those devastating grins that could make her toes curl. "When it comes to the Lady's creations, I have access to a universal library. As soon as I see something, I can bring information about it into my head. But after so many years, I've retained a great deal of it. Angels have vast levels of memory, so I rarely have to access that library anymore unless it's something new I haven't seen before."

"So is accessing the Lady like that?"

He slanted her a glance. "Not exactly. You know some of the different stories, like the Tree of Knowledge?"

She nodded. It relieved her, how comfortable he appeared with the discussion. But then she realized this would be familiar territory. Patiently teaching her what he likely had taught many young angels before, like David. "There's a veil over the world, over every world inhabited by Her creations. She won't delve into thoughts or intent below that veil. When you pray, it can pierce that veil, and reach Her. It's like a radio signal. If you pray with pure intent and focus, She hears it better. If you pray for a pretty dress"—he slanted a humorous look at her—"it never makes it past the static."

"I'll keep that in mind," she said dryly.

"When She gets prayers, it's not like Santa going through a laundry list. She sees cycles, knows how things are supposed to fit and work for each life and how they all connect. She therefore knows whether it's a good wish to grant or not. She understands every ripple in the pond. At least that's what most believe."

"Does She ever walk the Earth among us?" Anna interjected quickly, before he could follow that line of thought into darker territory.

"She's in everything." Reaching out, he touched the small fuchsia-colored cactus flower he'd put in the band of her hat earlier in the day. She tried not to lean into his touch like a lovesick girl, but she couldn't help brushing her lips against his hand as he pulled it away. His lips curved, his eyes warming on her. "Especially in spontaneous acts of love."

"Can She read your mind if you're above that veil?"

"Yes and no. If you're in Her presence, She can, but She won't unless asked. If you ask, you feel Her there, but just like mist. If She focuses too hard, She can destroy your mind."

Anna came to a stop. "You've been in Her presence? I mean, like a real audience?"

Jonah turned to face her. "Of course. Though it's been a long while. Perhaps fifty years. Not like Lucifer or Michael."

"Well, of course," Anna said with forced casualness.

"Michael is a Full Submission angel. And Lucifer may be, but he's closemouthed about his status. A Full Submission angel is permanently, completely mind-open to Her, their will Hers to direct. You're giving Her everything of yourself, holding up a mirror to your own soul. Michael, Gabriel, Raphael—they're all Full Submissions. Lucifer's in charge of what humans call Hell, but it's about redemption and justice, not eternal damnation, unless someone is just stubborn, too stubborn to learn."

At her sidelong glance, his lips twisted. "He always said if I were human, I'd be the one too stubborn to learn."

She laughed then. But after a moment, she drew closer to him, touched his arm, looked up into his face searchingly. "You stood before Her. With Her. What was it like?"

"Beyond words, little one," he said after a long moment. His hand rose, massaged his chest, then a little harder. "It . . . was the answer to everything. You just want to stay there . . . but you know you can't." He winced as if he'd hit an old wound and kicked the can again, she supposed to cover it, but she'd already seen.

"You're the second in command of the armies, right? Have you ever considered it, the Full Submission thing?"

"Once or twice. I'm sure there's an appealing peace to it, having your will belong to another. But I'm not ready to relinquish that."

"Why?" At his quizzical look, she shrugged. "I mean, if She's the Mother, She takes care of all of us."

A wry smile touched his mouth. "My job is to take care of Her. Perhaps I'm not entirely sure She's the best judge of how to do that all the time."

"You suspect your wisdom is greater? Why don't I find that surprising, my lord?"

His eyes glinted at her teasing, but he responded with a shrug. "I'm not sure it's that my wisdom is greater. It's just She created us with minds and wills of our own, and there was a wisdom to that as well, one not lightly abandoned."

"So when you were hurt and fell into the ocean, you could have called to them for aid. But you didn't."

"I didn't. Perhaps I should have, if for no other reason than to keep a mermaid out of trouble." He flicked at her clipped-back hair, and she pulled it out of his reach, frowning at him.

"I, too, prefer to make my own choices regarding you, my lord. As I've said before, and maybe for the same reasons. I'm not entirely sure you're best suited to determine what's in your best interest."

"Oh, really?"

She gave a shriek as he lunged for her. While he managed to snag an elbow, she darted under his arm so he was forced to let go. Summoning a guise of energy she didn't feel, she jumped on his back, wrapping her legs around his waist and locking her arms around his neck and shoulders. Oh, Goddess. His flesh was blessedly *cool*.

"I have you well and truly pinned, my lord," she managed. "You must concede."

"If I throw myself backward, I can crush you like a bug." But instead of doing that, he put his arms around her calves, holding her in place. "Stay there." He freed a hand to pass it over the tips of the greasewood shrub that brushed her head. Above, white clouds floated lazily against the blue sky.

"What might you be doing on a day like today?" She made her voice a quiet whisper against his temple. "If you were in the sky."

"Planning the next battle. Training."

She tugged his hair. "For leisure. Other than seeking out angel bordellos."

He smiled. "What better leisure activity is there?" He spun on his heel, turning her in circles, and she tightened her arms around his neck. It was a blissful relief to be carried. The weariness had been closing in and she wasn't sure how much longer she could keep it from him. Or maybe that's why he was carrying her. She knew he was far more sharp-sighted than was comfortable. She didn't put it past him to have teased her into getting onto his back.

"Studying," he said at last. "When we're not planning for battle or engaged in it, we do help with other areas. Some of the angels I command are healers, watchers. Messengers, couriers. Magic creators, through music or voice."

"What do you do?"

"A variety of things. Actually, not much other than the fighting anymore," he admitted. "The planning and doing, training, recovery and planning again became more of a full-time job as I was assigned more and more angels. My Legion has over ten thousand, with a generous handful of captains for the different battalions, but I personally oversee the training of each and every angel, testing them frequently, drilling them. To make sure they're ready as they can be."

So they would live for another battle, another risk. But rather than voice that sobering thought, she tugged on his hair. "Ten thousand angels. Do they salute you? Call you *sir*?"

"At the moment I suspect my captains are calling me a variety of names, none of them respectful." A shadow crossed his gaze. Then he pinched her leg. "But you're being impudent now."

"I like to see you smile, and that seems to make you smile. Maybe I should suggest that to your men."

"I don't think that would be wise."

"Look." She pointed. "Is that . . . a cabin?"

Jonah squinted. In the distance, one of the craggy rock formations with its colorful layers of sandstone did in fact seem to include a rock cabin built into the side. As they drew closer, Anna was amazed to see that was what it was, with a small door to a cellar to the right of the cabin, possibly a way to keep things cooler by putting them in a storeroom belowground.

"An old miner's cabin," Jonah mused, examining it as he let her down. "Could be well over a hundred years old. We've probably passed by other ones that look just like part of the rock face, because all that's left of them are ruins. There are whole ghost towns in Nevada, from the mining days."

The door to the cabin was gone, though some stray threads suggested it had been used recently by someone who'd employed a blanket curtain against the nighttime desert chill. Anna glanced in and saw a dirty floor, the remains of campers who'd not observed the expected courtesy of "without a trace." The room was also hot, facing into the late afternoon sun, and she found herself drawn to exploring the cellar room. Besides which, based on their previous night's experience, going somewhere they could not be seen seemed a welcome idea.

"Should we stay here for the night?" Jonah asked, apparently reading her thoughts.

She nodded, turning to find him sitting on the slope outside and removing his shoes. He curled his toes, wiggled them, bemused. "Strange. I suppose it makes sense, the way people wear shoes, but I've never done it."

"Some human women have dozens. Three- and four-inch heels that make their legs look like egrets', all sleek and graceful." She lifted one foot by example in her hot pink sneaker, and humor flashed through his gaze as she rotated her foot. "It's good that the spell on those clothes make them fit the wearer, though. Otherwise your new shoes, walking this long in them, would have caused you blisters."

"These pants and shirts could be somewhat looser."

"They aren't too tight. You're just used to your battle skirt being open and . . ." Her cheeks pinkened and she looked away, though she had the suspicion he muffled a chuckle, as if he'd been teasing her all along.

Jonah reflected that she had no sense of how innocently charming she was. When she wasn't worrying about him, taking his mind places it didn't want to go, being with her was like a breath of a world Jonah hadn't experienced in so long. He wasn't sure if it wasn't even altogether new, a place he'd never visited. Watching her take such simple pleasure in life, wonder at everything around her, ask him questions, drink in every bit of knowledge, it was ironic she didn't realize she was providing a similar experience for him.

Plus, she knew what tragedy and isolation were, so her innocence wasn't naïve and wearing upon his soul. If anything, he felt as if she held the key to a secret he couldn't fathom. While he suspected he was long past having the state of mind to accept the knowledge if he ever learned it, as long as she was carrying it, he thought just being around her would let him draw some sense of peace from it. And that, more than a pointless quest, was likely what had kept him with her.

Squatting by the front of the cellar where she was in a square of shade provided by the cabin, she pulled out the gallon jug with the seawater, arranged her shells and then carefully baptized her feet, her hands. He noticed her deep sigh of relief as she leaned against the cellar door, closed her eyes and sat very still beneath the touch of the sea's blood. He also noticed the circles under her eyes seemed to get a little less shadowed. Perhaps his mermaid needed more sleep. He might be having her travel too much, too quickly.

The sun was starting to melt on the horizon. He removed the shirt just in time as his back arched, and he made the sudden lurch forward to his feet as the wings came back through.

Anna watched him out of the corner of her eye. She remembered the previous night, their exultant flight in the air, which had been one of the most amazing experiences of her life. But it also recalled the battle. Lucifer's frustrations, David's worry. While watching his wings return every night was a miraculous thing to witness, it was also the clear reminder that he didn't belong here, with her.

"Anna." He squatted outside the cellar door, close to her side. "What's the matter?"

"Nothing. I'm fine. I was just thinking about how different we are from one another."

"We're both lonely." His observation, the steady look from his dark eyes and the way he stretched out his wings now to provide her additional shade despite the sun's descent, almost pulled her composure from her like the mask it was.

"But you've seen so much I haven't seen," she said quickly. "Tell me something I don't know, something I can't possibly imagine ever having existed. I can imagine this cabin, because it would make sense. Tell me something totally unexpected, something that will make me smile, but will amaze me."

Stroke my mind, she thought. *Soothe me.*

"Hmm . . ." He stood and stepped behind her. As she looked up at him, he adjusted her so her back was against his denim-clad legs and he was looking down at her. "In medieval Europe, there used to be men in long black cloaks." He spread his arms, taking his wings out to a half span, giving her the impression of a cloak. "They wandered the city streets carrying a chamber pot."

"Oh, no. I'm not sure I'm going to like this story."

"*Sshh,*" he admonished. "If you needed to relieve yourself when you were out doing your shopping, you could pay him a certain amount and he would set the pot on the ground, open up his cloak"—he spread his wings out further and then started to draw them around her—"and curtain it around you while you sat on the chamber pot, doing what you needed to do."

She'd wanted a story of something she couldn't ever have imagined, something that would touch and amaze her, and he'd done both. It didn't surprise her that he'd pulled the perfect thing out of his millennium of knowledge, but she was quietly delighted all the same. She stroked her hands over the feathers closed around her, thinking about it. A stranger who provided a service for a crude bodily function, yes. But it was also one person, intimately close to another, to provide an act of care . . . like this. As he tightened the enclosure around her, she rose, turned inside the folds, shivering when his hands found her upper arms. She simply couldn't think when he kissed her as he did now, deep and thorough, holding her close to him, those wings protecting her on all sides, bringing her coolness from the sun and reassurance.

"I'm sure the Privy Man didn't do much of that," she managed in a thick voice when Jonah raised his head. He smiled.

"Unless he was very clever. And handsome, like me."

"Modesty so becomes you, my lord." She chuckled and ducked out of his wingspan, trying to mask the stagger she decided to assume his dizzying kiss had caused. "Let's go look at the cellar. It might be the perfect place to spend the night."

She tugged on the cellar door, whose padlock had long ago broken, leaving a rattling, rusty chain. Jonah helped her pull it open. The creak of the hinges was like the groan of an old man's bones, and the odor that drifted up was of trapped air, damp cement . . . and something else.

He studied the dark interior. "Something's down there."

"Unfriendly?" She turned serious eyes on him.

"Not dangerous," he responded cryptically. Putting out a hand so he could precede her, he took the top two steps down.

Jonah studied the shape of the darkness. It was not a large area, though roomy enough for two people to spend the night. Or more. And it was cooler, being belowground.

"We mean no harm if you cause us none," he said firmly. "May we share your cellar?"

There was a shifting, then the darkness moved. Anna drew in a breath, at his shoulder now.

"An earth spirit. A cellar dweller. I didn't know they still exist."

He was surprised she knew what he was seeing, but then his little mermaid was constantly surprising him.

"They do, but it's unusual to see them close to active human habitation anymore."

There was a chitter, and then the shadow became still again, as if there was nothing there at all and they'd imagined it. But now that Anna was looking where Jonah was, she saw it, the brief gleam of eyes. "Oh," she breathed softly, and the tiny slits of light became defined small orbs. The shadow moved forward a few inches.

"I've never met a cellar dweller," she admitted.

Another chitter. "They prefer cellar inhabitants. They feel the rhyming is undignified," Jonah said dryly.

Anna cocked her head. "You understand him?"

"Of course."

She smiled. "Do you understand all languages, my lord?"

He considered that. "In a sense. Angels don't hear the words, exactly, just the meaning. It's why you can't deceive an angel for long. We hear the lie in the tone. It's like listening to a piano concerto, and hearing how all the individual notes make the whole have meaning. So whether you speak or he speaks, I understand what you're saying."

"So that's how you speak any language."

He nodded. "I can communicate through the method of speech of whoever is speaking."

"So what you just said to him, he heard in his language, even as I heard it in mine? Then it's not necessarily that you know a million languages; you just hear everything's meaning, not the words." She gave him an impish smile as she slid around him. "You're not as clever as I thought you were."

He caught her arm, keeping her close, and gave her a mock admonishing look. "I can also block your understanding of what I'm saying to him and his of what I'm saying to you. So I can tell him you're likely to be trouble and he should chase you away."

"Of the two of us, I think he seems more concerned about you."

"I think he particularly likes your voice," Jonah agreed

with some amusement, watching the creature come out farther as she spoke.

"Should I sing to him to calm him?"

"Well, if I do it, he'll die of fright." He loosened his grip, albeit reluctantly. "He doesn't necessarily mean us harm, but he's unsure of us yet. Take it slow."

Nodding, she began to hum. The creature studied her, eyes bright, then rose on hind legs, swaying to the tune. It gave her a sense of his form, which reminded her somewhat of a hairless, slender bear or an oversized ferret. His skin appeared to have a soft, rubbery appearance. She sang to him of reassurance, that they meant no harm, and infused it with calming magic. When she was done, he was settled back comfortably in his shadowy corner, watching them, but now with more curiosity than anything else.

As she sang, Jonah prowled around the cellar. There was ample room for his wings, which he liked, but there wasn't much in the way of a comfortable bed for Anna. Anna assumed they would just make the best of it, but he wanted her to have a deep sleep.

There was an old bookcase in the corner, suggesting this cabin had been a more permanent habitation for someone in the last twenty years, perhaps a researcher studying the volcanic history, and he'd brought out the bookcase to hold tools or water stores.

Lifting out the shelves, Jonah laid the piece of furniture on its back on the floor, blowing out the dust with a puff of enhanced breath. He lifted his head and sent another puff her way, making her giggle as it rippled through her hair and across the front of her T-shirt, making the angel cartoon on it shimmer comically, its wings fluttering.

"Tired?" he asked. Anna shrugged.

"A little." She *was* fatigued, but now that night was descending, she needed his closeness more than sleep. It was something she couldn't explain, but there was no way she was going to give in to her weariness before she could grasp that closeness, pull it into her, pull him into her. The physical proof that she wasn't alone, that he was here and that she was doing what she was meant to do. Moistening her lips, she drew his gaze there. As he registered her desire, flame flashed in his eyes, kindling the same heat in her lower belly as well. The fact she was getting weaker and wouldn't be able to hide it from him much longer hit her anew, increasing the yearning as well as the heat.

"Come here, then."

When she got to him, he lifted her T-shirt over her head. Slowly, making her feel the heavy weight of her arms as she lifted them over her head and then let them drop, her palms on his broad, bare shoulders. Staying there, she kept her fingertips in his feathers as he slid the loose cotton shorts and panties down her legs, worked off her sneakers and socks, letting her hold on to him. She watched as he put the pair of shoes off to the side, lined up next to each other. One long finger whispered over them in a way that made her toes curl into the ground as if he'd touched them instead.

"Such small feet."

A quiet chitter, and one seven-toed, clawed foot extended out of the shadows and drew a shoe into the darkness. "Do *not* eat that," Jonah admonished. "She has to wear those tomorrow."

He looked back up at her, him on one knee as she stood, and she ran her fingers along the strong planes of his face, through his hair. "Goddess, you are so beautiful," she murmured.

His eyes, already so dark, deepened into obsidian as he turned his head to kiss her wrist, nuzzle her hand. When he rose and lifted her by the waist to touch her breast with his lips, it made her breath leave her. He held her that way, with effortless strength, showing that his wings might not be capable of bearing her additional weight, but his arms were another matter. Her toes curled again as he put his mouth over her nipple, including some of the tender breast flesh in the moist heat. Suckling her deep, he sent liquid tendrils spreading out from her belly through the rest of her vital organs as if a living creature were unfurling inside of her, primal and needy, and perhaps it was.

With some effort she brought her legs up and around his hips, which brought her in closer. Obliging, he cupped his hands under her bottom, moving them toward their makeshift bed. He stepped in it, sure-footed. Heat shimmered through him and then . . .

Her eyes opened wide when his wings tucked in close to him, and all his feathers released at once, dropping as a heavy, pillowy mass into the frame of the bookcase.

Anna gasped, watching the smaller feathers float back up from the impact, landing in her hair or lightly tickling against her skin.

"Oh," she said, amazed. "You did mean to do that, right?"

Jonah smiled, mysterious and sensual, his mind apparently on things that didn't encourage conversation, increasing the longing within her exponentially. Lowering them into the bed he'd created for her, he put her beneath him. Arching his denuded wings over them like the sleek branches of a black tree of bone, he displayed the intricate, delicate network capable of carrying him powerfully through the air when layered with feathers.

She lifted her chin as his fists curled into her hair and he took command of her throat with his mouth. The touch of his lips on that sensitive area was enough to arch her up into him as if she'd been shocked by a delicious burst of heat lightning. It was the perfect angle for him to slide into her body.

His charged silence, everything conveyed through the heat of his wholly dark eyes, the passionate grip of his hands, the urgent movement of his body between her thighs, spreading her open wider, had more impact than a stream of seductive words. She didn't feel like some nymph or woman he'd seduced in the past. He considered her his, someone who meshed with his body so easily and completely, it was bringing together two halves that already fit, no adjustment or conversation necessary.

At least that was the way she wanted to think about it right now.

For all his strength, his hands were gentle, curving into her hair, his weight on one arm so he didn't crush her. Then a puff of breath, a slight squeaking, and Anna was startled to see their cellar inhabitant peering over the edge of the bookcase at them. With a tentative glance at Jonah, it went over the wall and into the bed, tunneling thoughtfully under her head, giving her a pillow even as she sensed its desire was to be closer to the magic they were creating between them. Anna closed her eyes, turning her face into the creature's smooth and hairless skin, so soft it reminded her of a manta ray. She heard his small heart beat as Jonah surged deep inside of her. She raised her legs, opening wider, clinging to him as she began to cry out, her flesh rippling against him.

Of course she gave him the Joining Magic she could raise on her own, and tried not to let it pall the moment for her when, once again, he didn't make the same effort. He kept it all about the lust and passion he could offer her, which should be more than any female could ask.

Their cellar inhabitant helped her balance that disappointment, for remarkably she felt him expanding beneath them, the feathers, the soft body becoming more rubbery and flexible, until . . . Yes, it expanded until it reached all sides of the bookcase, making their bed into a downy water bed that moved like . . . the ocean, the rock of the sea, giving her comfort, soothing her.

Oh, Goddess. If they only knew how much she craved it . . .

"Thank you both," she whispered.

"It was his idea." Jonah smiled, though his eyes burned deep into her heart. "Come for me again, little mermaid. Move your body against mine like you do in the waves. Carry me to the ocean with you."

Seventeen

ANOTHER day. Maybe. Anna knew it was a bad sign that she was counting the minutes of every hour as a way of blocking out the fact that the final stage of the "mindmap" was entirely unclear on where Red Rock Schism would open to them.

All the specific instructions Mina had given seemed pointless torment. Or just plain torment. Travel by "Fate." Only travel by day, not by night, though traveling on foot in the desert during daylight had all the earmarks of idiocy.

Jonah, perhaps picking up on her growing agitation, mentioned what she already knew rationally. That this was the way magic worked. The Schism would open itself when they'd proven the sincerity of their intent. Following the odd instructions was part of honoring that intent.

When they passed the noon hour of the next day, they at last saw proof they were in close proximity to the Schism's energy signature. Though at first Anna privately worried that they might be seeing nothing more than heat mirages.

As they walked, in the shimmer of the sun on the horizon, they saw wavering illusions of unicorns, galloping through the dust. Dragons tipping their wings, giants moving ponderously. Perhaps even mammoths. She and Jonah made a game of what they might see next in the rolling clouds and heavy air currents. Then Mina's map confronted them with a steep formation of rock, and Anna's resolve flagged. Jonah helped her over the worst of it, telling her the view would be incomparable from the flat top, pointing out how the striation of this particular rock made it look as if a rainbow were etched into its side. When he stopped several times and let her rest in the shadows, his expression getting more and more worried, she rallied enough to manage a wan smile and told him that walking was just far more strenuous than swimming, was all. Different muscles. And of course she was used to the water. She was fine. They were nearly there.

She hoped, by the Goddess. And she dreaded it, as well.

As the sun started to drop on the horizon, they came over the mountain and looked down into a dry river basin where it appeared a compass had been drawn out, a deep, wide circle of road bisected north to south and east and west. A man-made impression, but no sign of the men who'd made it. It had a good feeling to it, however, and Jonah decided they would rest beneath the stars in the center of it since unfortunately there was no real cover to be found.

As the cool desert air set in and his mermaid again did her short ritual with her seawater, Jonah sat nearby, watching her closely. She'd trudged along today, usually ten or twenty paces behind him, her head bowed beneath her floppy straw hat with her wilted cactus flower.

She'd said she wasn't used to the climate, walking this way mile after mile, and his human body felt some of the strain of that as well. While he'd indicated he could hear a lie just in the cadence of a person's voice, he couldn't hear one in hers, even though he'd asked after her well-being in several ways today. But something was off. It occurred to him for the first time that perhaps there was something in her unusual repertoire of magical abilities that might keep him from fathoming when she was possibly hiding things from him.

He wasn't going to push it right now. Not when she looked so exhausted. She hadn't lain down immediately, however. She'd eaten a light dinner of one of the sandwiches bought at the trading post, giving him half. He'd found he really didn't need food. His human self got hungry, but apparently the transition to angel at night fortified his system amply enough to carry him through the twelve hours as a human. He didn't mind sampling the different tastes, however, particularly the cookies she offered him. Or answering the bottomless well of her questions, which increased at night, like a favorite bedtime story that readied her for sleep.

"Lucifer's wings were black, and David's were light brown. Do all of you have different wing colors?" She was sitting cross-legged next to him now as he stretched out to gaze up at the stars. Jonah noted she'd snagged some of his down feathers that had fallen out as part of his transition back to angel tonight. She was wearing several of them in her hat and working others among the branches of a scrub bush.

"Not all different colors, but different patterns." He studied the movement of the constellations, his fingers locked behind his head, amused as she tucked several feather tips under his buttock to hold them in place against the nighttime breeze while she decorated the bush. "Certain functions or groups have things in common. You can identify an angel's position, rank, age, all by the colors, pattern and shape of his wings."

"Why do humans think they're white, then?"

"Messenger and guardian angels, the ones most likely to be seen by humans, typically project what they're comfortable seeing."

"So they do pure white, not like yours, with the silver tips?"

"No. That pattern is unique to me." He ran a finger along the edge of the feather she was holding, the diagonal line of the silver. "What are you doing now?"

"I thought I might decorate this shrub with some of your feathers, and then, just like the compass, or whatever it is, it will be something for the next traveler to marvel at."

He knew most of the feathers would disintegrate at dawn, but he liked watching her doing it. But within a few moments, she lay down on his chest, and watched the ones she hadn't used tumble with the night breeze across the compass etched in the dense sand, paving the road with flecks of white and silver, like a reflection of the stars above.

It occurred to him they would also be leaving a trail, but they were so far from where they'd been. Still . . .

Gently moving her aside, Jonah got up, searching the night. Turning, he caught it again. A flash of light. Narrowing his gaze, he focused, then relaxed. Somewhat. Man-made.

Anna had come to stand beside him, looking. "It looks like a radio tower."

"Want to go see what it is? It might have a building."

She looked alert and interested, so he was pleased to offer her something to perk her up. She nodded.

"Want a lift?" He spread his wings invitingly.

"I guess we won't attract too much attention if we stay close to the ground. Do you think you can . . ." She hedged, apparently trying to be mindful of his wing injury, but he could tell she was delighted at the thought. He lifted himself a few feet off the ground.

"I think we can. Put your arms around my chest, your foot on my foot. Short, horizontal lift only."

He felt a bit of strain in the one wing on liftoff, but that was all. Once the air got under him, it felt almost as effortless as normal, giving him a lift in spirits as well.

"Can you fly into outer space?" she asked against his skin, her body warmly pressed against his groin and thighs. "I don't mean right now, but usually."

"Yes. Among asteroids and planets. Circle the moon and come back. I'll bring you a moon rock if you want."

She smiled, and tilted her head back to meet his gaze, her hair streaming out, swirling around them with the air currents. Jonah reached down and touched her face, traced her lips with his thumb, and thought how he'd like to take her that high, to places that fired her imagination.

They had to gain some height to get over the next rock formation. It was too small to be called a mountain, but a little more substantial in width and breadth than what they'd crossed earlier. But he managed it, and heard her indrawn breath at the stunning landscape of volcanic craters and rock formations that expanded for miles around them, like the surface of a different planet, in truth. He could see it as if it were daylight. Full of smoky grays, deep reds, rose hues now giving way to the brilliant, deep midnight blue of the night sky, the jeweled stars and a heavy moon sitting low over it all, the embodiment of the Great Mother.

Despite himself, he hovered there a few minutes, letting himself look as much as Anna, feeling a tightness in his chest, a whisper of the things he'd always known, never doubted. Things he was doubting now, isolating himself from them.

Slowly, he descended, and a few minutes later landed them about a hundred yards away from what was indeed a radio station. A four-wheel drive was parked out front, battered but tough-looking, like a tank, weathered and proven in this environment.

Standing out back, smoking a cigarette, was a man in his fifties, startling them both.

"I didn't suspect it would be manned," Anna whispered. "I assumed it would just be a relay tower or something. What should we do?"

Jonah kept a protective step in front of her. Oddly, the man didn't look at all surprised to find an angel landing on his back doorstep.

For a moment, they just studied one another. The man had tidy dark hair, a white cotton shirt and brown slacks. He wore comfortable loafers and seated next to them was a pair of small dogs. At the sight of Jonah's wings drawing in to his sides, they backed up into the open door, but did not bark.

"That was some stunt," the man said at last. "But I already have my guest lineup for the *Are There Really Angels?* segment. Don't see why you can't come in and listen to the show for a while, though. Desert hospitality and all. I can at least applaud the effort with some air-conditioning and a beer. I've also got an excess of food if you'd like some."

He crushed out the cigarette and pocketed it. Unconcerned by their lack of response, he shouldered in the door, then turned his attention back to Jonah. "You didn't fly that rig all the way from L.A. or one of those other places where people have more ideas than sense, did you?"

Anna covered her mouth to hide her chuckle. "He thinks you're trying to get on his talk show," she murmured to Jonah. "He's a radio host. Do you want to go now?"

"No." Jonah studied the radio towers. "Let's get you a safe place to rest a bit. There are few coincidences that strong. I think we should go in and meet him."

Travel by Fate . . . He was gaining a grudging respect for the witch and wondered at the true scope of her power. Or if Mina herself even knew what it was.

While he kept all his senses honed as they approached, it was quite obviously just the man and his two dogs inhabiting the radio station, which, while small, had an impressive garden of antennae and satellite dishes.

Jonah put a reassuring hand against Anna's back and followed her in, folding his wings in a tight overlap to manage the door. It was an automatic gesture for him, like folding his arms, but he was glad to feel a lesser twinge from the one wing than he'd expected. It was definitely getting stronger.

The talk show host had stopped to watch him, and his brow creased. "You're well practiced—I'll give you that. You're welcome to leave them outside, though."

"I'll keep them with me," Jonah said, unperturbed, while Anna hid another smile.

"Suit yourself, but be warned, it's a bit cramped in here. Come on in to the studio. I'm running a pretaped show on extraterrestrial sightings right now. Won't be starting up the angel segment until past midnight."

Jonah noted the art on the walls ran to numerous photos, news clippings and articles pinned up randomly, covering all manner of nonmundane topics, from aliens to global warming theories, to angels and the origins and geographical location of Hell.

One of the articles had a photo of their host, probably from five years earlier. Randall Myers. It indicated he'd left a popular station management position to be a talk show host on an independent airwave, a show which focused on the inexplicable, theories that were mostly scoffed at. The boogeyman in the closet, the existence of dragons . . .

"What would you like? Out here, it's usually water that's preferred. And I've got some day-old pasta my wife made."

"Give it to her." Jonah nodded to Anna. "I'm fine. And you eat it," he added before Anna protested. "You're looking pale, and you know I don't need it."

When she subsided without further argument, that concerned Jonah more. Here where the light was fluorescent, for the first time he noticed the things the glaring sun, the artful shadow of her hat, or the nighttime darkness could hide from him. Her skin was looking damn near transparent, the blue veins close to the surface. Her lips were cracked, the inner membranes of her eyes red. He could tell the shape of her skull, the hollow slope of cheekbones in a way that was alarming.

Randall's face creased in concern as he apparently noted the same things Jonah did. "You shouldn't be bringing someone in a fragile condition out here, just to get your ten minutes of fame."

"He's not—"

"I know that," Jonah interrupted her, giving her a quelling look. "I take responsibility for her well-being. We're not here for your show, Mr. Myers." Having made his assessment of the man, not just from the articles and evidence of his personality scattered about the studio, which was obviously the center of his existence, Jonah had no concern about speaking frankly to him. "We're traveling along the Schism, looking for a gateway into it. Do you know how close we are?"

"Why do you think I know about the Schism?"

"It's here." Jonah indicated the wallpaper of clippings.

"There's no article about the Schism up there."

"Exactly." Jonah showed his teeth. "You study the theories of all things outside the known world, air them, talk to a mixture of the wishful thinkers and the true thinkers, but you don't expose the sacred in your own backyard. You cut a very careful, close circle around it, and it leaves an outline."

"You're a hell of a speed reader." When Randall took a seat in his chair, his dogs hopped onto the sofa beside Anna and eyed the food she was eating. He laced his fingers across his stomach and leaned the wheeled chair back on its stem. Lights winked behind him on the control board. "The Schism is important. I've never seen it, but I know that much. You're still a good fifteen miles from where it's reported to have opened in the past. Not that that means much. You doing it on foot?"

"Possibly. We're required to travel by Fate . . . by chance."

Randall grunted. "Like most sacred places, can't be reached the easiest way."

"Dumb rule," Anna muttered with a tired sigh. Jonah watched, momentarily fascinated as she sucked a stray noodle into her mouth and self-consciously reached for a napkin when she saw him looking.

You're the first purported 'nonhuman' I've entertained out

here." Randall's face creased into a wry smile. "Though I could have sworn a couple of my past guests had done enough recreational drugs to have mutated into alien life-forms."

"Who said we aren't human?" Anna chuckled. She rose, swaying a little, and gave the dogs the remains of the bowl. "That's much better. Thank you. We should leave you to your show."

"Stay a little while." Randall waved. "You can nap on the couch and your silent companion here can snort with derision at my call-in questions on angels. Stay," he repeated. His attention shifted to Jonah. "The girl needs some rest."

"I am right here," she mentioned to them both.

Jonah held Randall's gaze. "We'll stay," he said.

DESPITE the exasperated face she made, Anna did not seem unhappy with the decision. Jonah put her further at ease by taking a seat on the couch and getting her to settle her head on his thigh. Her body curled inside the curve of his arm and wing while he listened to Randall whittle down the long hours of the night with angel theory. At one point, when he shifted, he found the two dogs had arranged their small bodies inside the curve of his wing as well, weighing down the tip end, an act which caused a bemused expression on Randall's face.

"Angels. Stories of rescues, attacks . . . seduction. Folks, it seems that there's a tremendous desire to believe they are here among us. Maybe to kindle hope, but hope for what? Proof of an afterlife that has a recognizable order, a legion of staff, so to speak? Or just a sense of higher meaning and purpose, proven by the existence of beings more advanced than ourselves? Perhaps, dear listeners"—Randall's deep, melodious voice reached out through the night—"hope and faith ultimately reside in yourself. We are the cells. If we fail, perhaps whatever we wish to call God also fails. Perhaps we're more of an interdependent relationship than we know, and that's why angels might walk among us, trying to keep the cells healthy, eradicate the cancer before it becomes fatal and destroys the whole body . . . that which we call God."

Jonah's brow creased as Randall got on the conference line with a philosopher and a biblical scholar, let them debate the symbolic versus the religious overtones of angels. Then he took calls from people who were sure angels had been active in their lives.

Rescues . . . A person who'd been caught in a flood. When she couldn't hold on to a tree branch another moment, she'd felt hands, strong hands, helping her hold on to the tree and to her toddler a little longer. Just long enough.

Seductions . . . Those who felt it was possible, despite the lore that angels were sexless, they'd been sensually awakened, lifted to a plane of spiritual ecstasy and physical fulfillment that would never be matched again by a mortal lover. Jonah raised a cryptic brow at Randall's quizzical look.

Then came a call by a man who claimed he was attacked by an angel when he tried to mug a woman in New York. He bore the burn scars of the angel's fingerprints on his chest, but considered it the most fortunate thing in his life, for he'd turned his back on crime, struggled through his hardship by honest means and come out the better for it, realizing there were consequences to his actions beyond this life.

Subtle details told Jonah which stories had probably involved his brethren and which ones were rationalizations of extraordinary luck or resources the person involved hadn't known he or she possessed. There was the usual cadre of attention seekers with no real knowledge or belief. Impressed, Jonah noticed Randall weeded almost all of them out of the panel he put on the air. The radio talk show host knew his business well, had learned to judge people by voice quality, intonation, what they did or didn't say. And he did it with quiet ease.

That impression was further reinforced by how Randall looked toward him after each story. Not to seek a confirmation, just studying Jonah's face, his body language. Though Jonah made no indication one way or another, a slight smile appeared on the commentator's face at different times, as if he'd received a response. Jonah found himself wondering if his expression was as unreadable as he'd always assumed it was. Or perhaps Randall Myers was just that good.

But there was also a fragility to his unflappable demeanor. Jonah narrowed his eyes, remembering the articles. The mention of a wife. A wife struggling with cancer, perhaps explaining the cancer metaphor, though he suspected it was the last thing Randall wanted to think about. But he loved her enough that it pervaded everything. Her suffering, her impending loss. They'd likely hoped the proximity of the Schism would slow it down, and it probably had, for a while.

"Rescues, attacks, seductions . . ." Randall repeated, bringing the show to a close. "Maybe they are what so many think they are. But sometimes, folks, I wonder if angels are another level of life, like ourselves. Maybe they're searching for meaning, too, as they interact with us in their mysterious ways we don't understand. Is the Great Beyond any more forthcoming with them than It is with us?

"Again, I go back to it. What if the birth, life and death of hope and meaning are inside ourselves? That whether God lives or dies is up to us and our actions?" Randall took a drag on a new cigarette, seemingly unconcerned with the moment of radio dead air as he pondered. "Gives a whole new meaning to taking responsibility for your own deeds, doesn't it?" His rich voice paused for a chuckle, and as if he knew Jonah's attention had lifted and fixed on him, he glanced toward him and nodded. "This is Randall Myers, and I'm going to call it a night. I'll be back tomorrow, same dead-of-night time. Good night."

Laying down the headphones, he switched the station to a classical program, shutting down the microphone before he turned. "Despite my earlier comments, it's obvious you're very protective of that young woman," he noted, his gaze passing over Anna's sleeping form.

"She's risked her life for me. Several times. Despite that utter foolishness, she's worth protecting."

Randall's eyes glinted and Jonah bent over her. "Little one . . . Anna. Wake up. It's getting near daylight. We need to go."

"They say radio frequencies can carry the energy of spirits," Randall observed. "There was a good energy to the calls tonight, as though they could all feel it, sense it."

The idea at first struck harmlessly off Jonah's mind, but then abruptly he was standing, lifting Anna on her feet though she was only half awake. "Wh–what?"

"We need to go." He could be wrong, but he hadn't

thought . . . Fifteen miles to go, and an unpopulated desert, where they'd stick out like a sore thumb.

"Wait." Randall rose, pulled out two more bottles of water. "I'd drive you, but I can't leave the station until . . ."

"That's fine. We'll get where we need to be."

"All right then." With obvious reluctance, Randall cleared his throat and led them to the station door, held it open.

When she stumbled, Jonah bent and lifted Anna in his arms, despite her sleepy protest. Now he turned to look at the man and the small building, antennae thrust into the sky like reaching, yearning fingers. "Thank you."

Randall nodded, then paused. "Can you . . ." His voice got thick, which he immediately covered with an embarrassed shrug. "Ah, hell. I don't know who you are. But sometimes your gut tells you things. I don't need to know exactly what comes after. I just need to know . . . Well, death just seems too damn ugly for there to be anything merciful afterward . . . Will she . . ." He swallowed. "Damn it, I can't bear thinking there won't be an end to her suffering, a place where she can be happy and well."

Anna, waking to the broken tone of a man she'd sensed was otherwise as stalwart as the silent rocks of this desert, wondered if there was anything more heartbreaking than a man who refused to cry when the thing he loved most was being taken away from him, one torturous inch at a time.

Though Jonah hadn't yet answered, she stretched out a hand from her position in his arms and Randall, still looking self-conscious but determined, tentatively closed his fingers on it. She squeezed, making him meet her eyes.

"I've always thought that death is so ugly so that we don't give the gifts of mortal life short shrift. If getting to Heaven and a life of no cares was as easy as wishing it to be so, no one would value what we have here." Glancing up at Jonah, she put a pleading desire in her expression. *Say something. Be compassionate.*

Her angel bit back a sigh. "If your wife has lived a good life, then her soul will be reborn. She will not come to harm in the afterlife. Of all the species in all the universe, you are most protected by the Lady. That in itself should bring hope."

Anna could tell it was an effort, but he kept the derision

from his tone, so he didn't sound as if he were delivering a message of doom. Randall's expression eased at the same time hers did.

"He's very cynical," she said quietly, summoning the shadow of a smile. "But he's not himself lately. There is hope. There always is." She got Jonah to let her slide down and stand on her own feet. As she reached out a hand to Randall again, she noted that Jonah grudgingly softened when the radio man enclosed it gently in both of his this time. "Good-bye, and thank you for letting us spend the evening with you."

"Wait a minute." Randall brightened. "I just thought of something."

Retaining her hand, he pulled her toward a storage shed next to the station, Jonah following them both. Randall opened the door, gestured to two bikes with thick tread wheels. "The sand is packed enough in places they'll save you some time, and there's a basket on this one for the pack. If nothing else, it will give you something to lean on. I'd give you the four-wheeler, I swear, but my wife, she's undergoing chemo treatments and I have to have emergency transport for her if she has a seizure. We don't have any close neighbors, and—"

"This is fine," Anna said, laying her hand on his forearm. "We wouldn't want to endanger your wife. We're not far from where we need to go." Eyeing the bikes, she wondered if Jonah knew how to ride one. "This is the way it's meant to be. Don't worry."

As the ray of morning sunlight speared down into the valley where Randall's station rested, Jonah's wings began to dissolve and disappear, the feathers sizzling into ash in the air.

She heard Randall's breath draw in and turned to see the handful of feathers blow past his legs. A couple caught on his pants leg, compelling the dogs to dance behind him to avoid contact.

"See, you were right," she said with tired amusement. "Just paste and glue."

Eighteen

"WHY did his question bother you?"

"It didn't." Jonah imitated Anna, putting his leg over the bike when they were out of sight of the station.

"It's like the dancing," she encouraged. "Just find your center balance. And now you're lying to me."

He gave her a warning glance, but sighed. "When angels die, we experience a form of oblivion, out of reach of the memories of those we loved and lived with. We become part of the cosmos, of the Lady's energy, adding to Her strength. Humans have the choice of being reborn. While they have no conscious memory when they're reborn, they tend to reconnect with the souls that meant the most to them, again and again. And then those that reach enlightenment are able to at last reunite with their loved ones, with full knowledge of who they are. It . . . pisses me off."

She bit back a smile. "You're becoming somewhat more human yourself, my lord."

Jonah narrowed his gaze at her, but fitted his foot to the pedal. While he wobbled, in a relatively quick time he steadied.

The sun hit the horizon as they made the crest of the first hill, and Anna paused, taking a deep breath. "We'll make it there today," she said.

Jonah put a hand on her arm. "Anna, why are you getting weaker? It's time for you to stop lying to me as well."

She glanced up at him, the shadows under her eyes making

them look more sunken. "I'll be all right, my lord, once I get you there. It's the ocean. The salt water. I just get a little bit weak when I'm a certain distance from it. What I have left in the pack should get me the rest of the way."

Of course. It was as simple as the glare of sunlight on the sand that would soon become blinding. He'd taken a creature of the sea farther and farther from her home. From the first he'd known Anna's truest form was the mermaid. He was a self-centered idiot.

"Don't, my lord." Her chin was suddenly quite resolute, her eyes flashing at him. "It has always been my choice. You compelled me to do nothing." A teasing smile tugged at her mouth. "You didn't even want to come, remember? I've had to haul you grumbling the whole way."

"You are a constant thorn in my side," he said with a lightness he didn't feel. "I only went to spare myself the nagging until my wing healed and I could fly away from your shrewishness. Anna—"

"I thought as much." She nodded. Then she pushed off and went coasting down the next hill before he could argue with her further.

As he followed, he thought of what she'd said about dancing, swimming, flying—how finding a balance for each of them was the same. Maybe she'd meant something more than that, that the *source* of balance was the same, physically *or* emotionally. He wished and wondered if it could be as easy to find his own center, so he could make her suffering worth this. He needed to send her home.

Free will. There was one of the more ridiculous codes of the Lady. But he still had a hard time shaking it, even as everything inside him was starting to shout that it was time to override Anna's wishes and put her well-being first. She thought she was fated to die at twenty-one. He sure as Hades didn't want to be the next link in the curse, any more than she wanted to die without purpose, as her mother had. Damn it.

As the sun rose higher, they were able to balance the increasing heat with the occasional breeze from a downhill slope. The bicycle did make it easier, for there were flat rocky areas they were able to traverse, after Jonah got the hang of riding. Even so, Anna was more confident and practiced, and should have been able to stay ahead of him. Instead, she kept dropping back, until he was slowing to ensure he didn't lose her on the rise of a hill. He also took frequent breaks, until it was late afternoon and they'd only covered about eight miles.

Jonah tried not to outdistance her too much, but he found pleasure in taking the hills downward at a good speed, feeling the wind through his hair, against his face, watching the sun descend. When he got to the bottom of one and estimated their distance at five more miles—if Randall was right and the Schism was cooperative—he turned, waiting for Anna to crest the hill to give her the good news.

He anticipated her coming down, her hair streaming, face lifted to the blessed touch of the wind, blowing the thin T-shirt flat against her soft but firm breasts, the hint of nipples. It made him think of the night before, in the cellar, her body lifting to his. He hadn't had that pleasure last night because of their time with Randall, which was fine, because Anna had gotten to rest in a cool place, but he felt his loins tighten now with the anticipation of the evening.

She still hadn't crested the hill.

He waited thirty seconds before he was off the bike and running up the slope, reaching the crest to find her bicycle on its side, probably no more than a couple of pedal strokes from making the top. Her body was crumpled on the ground next to it.

"Anna." He skidded onto his knees beside her and lifted her upper body. He pulled off the hat and discovered her pallor was gray, her lips bleeding. Her violet eyes were glassy, almost pale, as if the color was leeching away with her life force.

"Keep going, my lord," she rasped. "You're almost there."

"You know far less of me than you think you do, if you think I would leave you here to die."

She shook her head, coughed, and he saw blood fleck her saliva. "I'm going to die anyway, my lord. This is important . . . and you have to go. They're coming. We've somehow . . . I'm sorry, my lord, but I think we were on the fault line, but now we're not. It was protecting us somehow, and now we've strayed off. The directions Mina gave me . . . They're coming. I can't feel where it is anymore. You need to keep moving."

He lifted her in his arms and jogged back down the hill, to the bottom of the slope where there were several clusters of rock, a formation of fluted erosion that provided some shade.

"There's a road, there. Look."

He saw the faint impression of one winding away to the west and nodded. "Another track for the people who live out in this wasteland, I'm sure."

"You have to go on, Jonah," she insisted. "That's it. Take that road a few more miles, and you'll be there."

"Anna. Tell me the full truth. This is more than what you're telling me."

"The sea," she said wearily. "I can't get too far from the sea. But I thought, with the water and shells, I'd make it further than two days, no matter what Mina said. I had to get you here. That was most important."

"Like hell." Easing her down to the sand, he rummaged quickly through her pack. One third of the seawater left, her bag of sand and shells. "Can you use this, no matter what form you're in?"

"Yes, the mermaid is the core of me . . ."

"Stop talking. You answered the question." He stood, scanned the scattering of rocks around them. There. A rock about four feet tall and three feet across, which had a concave top likely accomplished over the years by dew dropped from the spines of the yucca overshadowing it. "Anna, can you shift? To the pixie?"

When she blinked, he recognized the disorienting effect of dehydration. He cursed himself for being an idiot, for relying on his powers of intuition instead of his own damned eyes. "Anna. Shift. To a fairy. Right now." And God help him if she misunderstood and shifted to a mermaid.

"But it'll take me . . . long time to turn back. Not strong."

"It's okay." He gentled his tone, touched her face, felt something twist hard in his heart at the immediate gratification in her face, her pleasure at his spontaneous touch. Why didn't he do it more often, all the time, so that she'd know how much he thought of her?

"Want you to touch me. Be inside me before you go. Can't if change."

"Anna." He crouched, took her shoulders, and gave her a look that would have made even one of his most battle-hardened captains piss himself. *"Do it now."*

Giving him a grumpy but fairly vacant look, her body shuddered, rippled. The lights started gathering over her, but they were weak, faint. Almost transparent.

"It hurts." It tore him apart to hear her cry out, his always stoic little mermaid. He wanted to hold her, touch her, but of course he couldn't while she was shifting. Despite himself, he thought of what Luc had said. *Will she be your concern, when she is dead?*

Then it was complete, and she was sprawled at the base of the rock, so disconcertingly like a dead butterfly, her wilted wings covering her shoulders.

Lifting her gently to the surface of the rock, he removed the remainder of the seawater and pulled out the shallow bowl she'd been using. Pouring the water into it carefully, he tried not to spill any in his haste. Then the shells, arranged on the side, a bit of the sand thrown into the basin. He propped the pack up where it would shade the whole area. At the smell of the seawater, she'd started to move painstakingly toward the pond he'd created, but he gently nudged her onto his hand with a finger and lifted her, lowering her into the water. She hooked her arms onto his forefinger to hold on, so he was able to watch her expression ease as the salt apparently penetrated through the outer physical form of the fairy and found the waiting mermaid soul within. With his other hand, he gently stirred the water so it lapped upon her in a credible imitation of the ocean.

He shook his head. "We'll travel after nightfall."

"But Mina said not to travel at night. To get under cover."

"Stop arguing with me." Sliding a thumb gently beneath her face as well, he frowned as she leaned her head against it. "You're so determined to follow everything that witch says, except when it applies to yourself."

"If anything should happen to me—"

"Nothing is going to happen to you. Perhaps this shaman can help. If he can't, or if we don't find this place tonight, I'll summon David and he'll have you back to the sea and your cottage in ten minutes."

"Like a supersonic jet," she murmured. His lips twitched, but he nodded.

"Faster, I'll warrant. I should summon him now." He put a finger on her mouth, part of it on her throat, since the pad of his finger could almost cover her face. "But I won't. Don't distress yourself. I understand how important this is to you, Anna."

But not to you, Anna thought, trying to ignore the sinking of her heart. All the times she had seen passion in him, it had always been on her behalf. He was very angry with her now, but because she'd risked herself. Protecting her, lying with her, arousing her, all those motivated his desire, but he had none for himself. For life.

No, she wouldn't let her thoughts go in that direction. She'd *had* to break her never-made but implied promise to Mina. The inexplicable magic that had allowed a simple mermaid to draw one of the universe's most powerful angels out of his element, convince him to accept being turned into a human and drag him through nearly a week's worth of Western human culture, would help her survive long enough to get him there. And once she got him there, the shaman *would* be able to heal his soul so it would be important to *him.* She refused to let herself believe anything different. There had to be some kind of sense in the universe. Someone had to have a happy ending, in a situation where a happy ending truly mattered to the balance of the rest of the universe.

"I would prefer to stay with you until you return to your own kind, my lord."

"I would prefer you to be well."

Her eyes opened. "The same goes. I never . . . felt lonely with you. Only safe. Warm. With wings wrapped around me." Her gaze drifted over his wings, which had appeared with sundown, which oddly she couldn't remember happening. Had she drifted off? He'd also shed the jeans for the cooler battle skirt. "Couldn't figure out why my aunt Jude felt afraid . . . but it's you. The way I feel about you."

"I don't want you to be afraid."

"I'm not." She smiled then. "I was loved by an angel. How could I feel a moment of fear?"

Jonah didn't like the serene acceptance in her features, as if they were already down a road where Fate had removed the choice of turning back. *Travel by Fate* . . .

"You *are* loved by an angel. You are also the most exasperating female. You have no sense of when not to argue with me."

"My time may be short."

"It is not," he said with sudden, frightening fierceness. Sliding her more deeply into the water, he kept his hand near in case she was too weak to stay above the surface herself in her non-water-breathing form. "Damn it, Anna, I—"

"I meant, if you're going to send me away." She smiled, actually almost laughed at him with her sweet mouth and gentle, all-too-knowing eyes. "Besides," she said sleepily. "If you let David rush me back to the ocean, such an intense and long trip would require him to ground himself, and you've said the easiest way to do so, the most pleasurable way . . ."

He tapped her forehead, managed to catch a strand of hair and tug on it like a group of threads. "I am going to drown you," he promised. "As for David, I'd advise the safest way for him to ground would be a nice, cleansing meditation."

She closed her eyes again, though the smile stayed, fading only as she relaxed against his hand. "Do angels know any songs, my lord? Do you sing?"

"We are trained to do so, yes. The Music Master worked diligently with me for nigh twenty years before he recommended that my tongue be removed so I couldn't cause the next apocalypse with my singing voice."

"Oh, no . . ." Her laughter was a quiet whisper, weak. It made Jonah's vitals tighten with an emotion he'd rarely felt in himself: fear. "No wonder you said your singing would frighten the cellar dweller half to death. But it can't be that bad, truly. Sing something to me. A lullaby. There's one about a sea horse, who twirls himself in a bed of seaweed and swings, back and forth, back and forth, while he watches the light of the moon thread down through the water to him . . . closer and closer, until he swings in the moonbeams."

She sang it for him, soft and easy. Though she spun no magic in her voice, the notes were clear and pure, the magic contained in their sheer simplicity. She ran out of breath, several times, but finished it. "You try."

For her, he did. He rumbled through it while her head came to rest on his knuckle again. She tapped out the time against him. Jonah wanted to kiss her, hug her to him fiercely. He was going to fly her back to the sea himself, to hell with it.

When he was done, her eyes opened to slits, a twinkle in the violet blue depths. "I think the apocalypse *has* started. I sense great chasms rending the earth."

"You were warned," he reminded her. "Little firefly. You know, it's believed by some that fairies are fallen angels who weren't bad enough for Hell."

"I've heard there are angels as big as giants. One that could whack you with one hand, like a fly."

"While you would be one of those tiny, irritating biting bugs he can't see."

A smile touched her mouth, then died away again. "We're supposed to love all of the Lady's creation, but I admit, my lord, I miss the ocean so much I am beginning to lose an appreciation for what is beautiful about the desert."

"You're in it," he said. When her gaze flickered up to him, her small hand came to rest in the crevice between two of his fingers.

"No matter what happens, my lord, this is not your doing. It was my choice. Even the men you command, it is their choice. Do you know that? They don't expect you to be infallible. They expect you to be a man worth following, even into death or worse."

He swallowed, his hand tightening on her small body. Suddenly he wished she were larger, as large as the Goddess Herself, and he could bury himself in her arms, in her, and escape the feelings those words unexpectedly prodded to life in an aching chest. "How can a man deserve such loyalty, except when he keeps them from being slaughtered?"

"It isn't about keeping them from harm, my lord." She shook her head. "It's about doing what's right and true, not shirking from that. I was frightened of helping you. Did I tell you that? That I thought about swimming away with the others? But that wasn't right. I knew it, when I saw you for the first time."

"You could have been killed."

"Yes, I could. But it would have been worse to make the

world a little less bright, because of my cowardice. Such things add up in the subconscious of the world, my lord. Become part of its blood."

"You're too young to understand that."

"No, I'm not. Truth is truth. It's just difficult to accept when you lose the people you love."

She looked up at him as a tear splashed on her abdomen, proportionate to a cup of warm water hitting her skin and splitting into a dozen other drops, warm and salty. Jonah looked away, ashamed of his weakness, but her words made him close his eyes to fight more tears he couldn't afford. "Love adds up in the subconscious of the world as well," she whispered.

He brought his attention back down to her then. When she pressed her forehead against his fingers, the contact resonated throughout his whole body. The way the slight weight of her rested in the cradle of his palm with such trust. The fragile impressions of her curves, the edges of the diaphanous wings. "We're not far now," he repeated, though he was swept by a sudden uncertainty as to what the destination of this journey truly was. What it would mean to both of them. From the first, she'd been leading him, and he'd been shamelessly content to follow.

She nodded, apparently too tired to speak anymore.

The approaching night wind whispered over the desert. Jonah lifted his head, turning in its general direction. Anna stiffened in his grasp as his muscles tightened and the confusion of his thoughts cleared in an instant. The quality of the wind changed, the whispering becoming a sibilant hiss.

Holy Goddess.

"Evil, persistent beasts," he muttered.

Nineteen

IN a flash, Jonah leaped up on the rock, balancing over the bowl and its precious contents. Staring into the dark, he shifted his attention between the multiple approach points, cognizant that they could even come over the rock formation he'd placed at his back.

When he heard something below him, he glanced down to find Anna gazing bemusedly up into the folds of the battle skirt he'd donned just before sundown while she dozed in the water, for he'd felt more comfortable in it.

"If I'm going to die right now, my lord, this will be quite a view to have in my mind. They'll be sure I deserve Purgatory, right from the off."

"I can think of far more justifiable reasons to send you to Purgatory for some discipline," he said, torn between exasperation and amusement.

Even as he teased her, he kept his guard up, searching. If he had to, he'd call Luc and David to him. He wouldn't risk her life any longer for pride, and she was bound to him now. The Dark Ones wouldn't ignore her. He could feel them shifting out in the darkness, drawing closer, seeking. He and Anna were hidden in the shadows of the rock. Once the Dark Ones found them, they'd announce their discovery with their usual deadly shrieking, diving upon them like unnatural birds of prey. With his energy signature as an angel, it was only a matter of a few moments.

He tensed, crouched down over her. *David* . . .

With his senses so tuned to the impending threat, he first took the sound for a muted growl. But it was too constant, too . . . mechanical. It was drawing closer as well, getting louder.

Light. Twin lights, piercing the night. A vehicle coming. Coming fast.

Jonah cursed. If the occupants got too close, the Dark Ones would push traces of sadness to full-blown despair, stoke anger over a minor offense to psychotic violence. They'd enlist human help to try to take Jonah down.

There'd been numerous cases of Dark Ones possessing human bodies, making the human's actions indistinguishable from that of a serial killer or the most dangerous of schizophrenics, until a savvy priest—or at least one slapped awake by an angel—would assist in tearing the wretch out of the human body. Now he had more than Anna to protect.

But before he could reinitiate his summons to David, he felt a hesitation among the oncoming Dark Ones. They were . . . milling. Confused by the energy or intent of the vehicle. A strong intent, so strong that when Jonah adjusted his stance to see its approach, the aura blasting before the large red Dodge Ram pickup appeared like a rolling ball of fire.

The truck skidded up, jumping off the hint of road and coming to a sliding stop, a barricade between Jonah, Anna and the darkness bearing down on them.

A slim waif of a woman with blonde hair and vivid blue eyes, shoved open the passenger door. "Get in. Hurry!"

Jonah seized the pack and Anna, with only a blink to regret not being able to salvage the water.

"Take the wheel, Maggie." A hand reached from within, dragged the woman back into the cab. "Drive like you've got the hounds of Hell behind you. Just like I taught you."

A man as tall and broad as Jonah emerged from the driver's side. When Jonah leaped into the back bed, knowing his wings wouldn't fit in the cab, the man put a foot on the wheel well to swing a long leg in, taking a stance beside him. "You better give her to Maggie. We're going to have a hell of a fight to get home. I haven't seen them this bad since the last drought."

He was smart enough not to reach for the tiny, precious

bundle Jonah held against his chest, but Maggie leaned out the back window, her two hands cupped together like she was about to receive a priceless treasure. Jonah took the important, vital second to stare into her wide blue eyes, so gentle and kind, so determined despite the undercurrent of fear.

"Matt's right. You better let me take care of her."

"She's a little weak."

"I'm better now. I can help—"

"No. You go with her." Jonah transferred Anna into Maggie's hands, noting his one almost dwarfed her two. She had pretty fingers, unadorned except for a simple gold wedding set.

A cold breeze skittered up his spine, like a ship passing, but infinitely more unnatural.

"Drive, Maggie," Matt bellowed. Jonah noted him hefting two shotguns. He tossed one toward Jonah as Maggie disappeared into the cab, holding Anna. "Can you shoot, angel?"

"Bullets won't—"

A shriek and Matt cocked the gun with one hand, rotated it up smoothly and blasted the air at a forty-five degree angle in front of them. The flash illuminated the skeletal, red-eyed visage of the winged Dark One bearing down on him, less than twenty feet away. The double cartridges somersaulted it back, causing it to explode in a shower of flame that flashed light across Matt's firmly held jaw, his cool hazel eyes.

"Brace on the floor." Matt jerked his head down, gesturing toward triangular rubber grips spaced across the truck bed. He had a boot solidly against one as the truck jumped forward with a horrible jerk, hesitated, then leaped forward again with a roar.

"Bless her sweet heart. Still has trouble with the clutch." Matt took another shot in the dark. "Ah, Hell's bells. Closing in."

Jonah took the gun to his shoulder and fired off the four rounds, watching as the charges ignited the air. He spread out his wings to balance himself, and as he did, Matt dropped to a knee to give him the room and use the cover, firing another shot. "Here!" He held another sawed-off shotgun to Jonah. "Keep firing. I'll keep loading and shooting from down here."

There wasn't a weapon Jonah didn't know how to handle instinctively, but he was wondering what in all of Hades was firing out of these guns that could destroy Dark Ones. Two swooped in together.

"Arggh . . ." Matt got struck by one and Jonah fired into it. It dropped Matt onto the roof, sending him rolling down the front windshield while the other tackled Jonah. Striking it with his left wing, he knocked it off himself and the truck and took a shot at its body as it rolled. Cursing when he missed, he went up and aloft, flipping the necessary few feet to grab Matt by the collar, pluck him off the windshield. He caught a glimpse of Maggie's horrified eyes and a tiny fairy on her shoulder, gripping her hair.

Matt rolled into the bed and was back up with a loaded gun before the two Dark Ones could circle back. The two men went shoulder to shoulder, the cab at their back, and fired simultaneously. Matt racked in another round as fast as an angel could fly, and took out a third.

Silence. A great, vibrating silence. Jonah searched the sky. So many stars out, no blot of darkness heralding their enemy's presence. He knew where all the constellations were supposed to be in a clear sky. But he was too wary to relax his guard. They'd been all around, thick as a cloud, though he now realized there'd only been six or seven. But they'd descended with that ferocious, confident aggression he'd rarely seen in such smaller numbers. Damn it all, Luc was right. They were getting ready for something.

He glanced over at his new comrade. Matt had a bloody gash on his head, and his eyes and the set of his mouth were still warrior fierce.

"Goddamn it. I lost my hat. I'll have to go back in the morning and see if I can't find it." But despite the casually irritable comment, Jonah noticed he didn't release his gun or relax his stance, either.

The men stayed pressed shoulder to shoulder, studying the night from all angles.

"Everyone all right in there?" Matt yelled, and the horn honked in reply. "Keep it going as fast as you can, Maggie."

"Matt," he called out over the wind and engine noise, glancing at Jonah. "As you may have guessed. Carpenter."

"Jonah. Angel. As you may have guessed."

Matt glanced at the wing that was brushing his shoulder. "You don't say?"

The grin that creased his face loosened something in Jonah's gut. He'd missed the camaraderie of soldiers. It took him by surprise, because, until now, he hadn't allowed himself to identify that empty space inside of him. It had been just one of many empty spaces. Perhaps that one tear Anna's words had wrested from him had opened up some other things.

Jonah hefted the gun. "These aren't bullets."

"Bet your lily-white ass they are. Wal-Mart special, less than twenty bucks for a hundred rounds. But they've been blessed by Sam the Shaman, and it makes 'em lethal to the likes of them." He nodded at the empty sky. "He said you were coming, for several days now. We've been keeping watch. We're his neighbors, the last house on the track before the Schism."

He cocked a brow at Jonah. "It's hell giving the UPS guy directions when Maggie orders her sundries from the catalogs. 'Take the last house on the left before you hit the magical fault line, where you might be sucked into an alternate reality. Careful, the streets aren't really well marked.'" He chanced a quick look over his other shoulder. "Here we are now. We should be okay as soon as we get in through the gate."

Jonah glanced back to see the silhouette of a two-story wooden house, caught briefly in the headlights as they wound up the road toward it. The wood fence around the property was split rail, but a mixture of polished, carved white oak and rowan, burned with protection symbols. "They can't go past the gate," Matt said. "Sam says so."

The truck stopped in front of the gate and the driver's door opened. Maggie stepped out on the running board, her hand gripping the top of the door.

Matt whipped around. "Maggie, damn it, use the remote—"

"It's the woman; she's—"

Before Maggie could finish the sentence, she screamed. Her chin hit the driver's door as she went down. Her body landed in the dirt and was jerked out of sight beneath the truck.

"Under the truck, one of them was—" Jonah leaped out of

one side with a weapon, Matt off the other, shouting his wife's name.

Catching the back of the truck in one hand, Jonah lifted it, bringing it up on its forward wheels. He had a brief, horrific flash of a Dark One completely blanketing the struggling Maggie. She screamed, her hands clawing, trying to push it off. Younger angels had difficulty dealing with prolonged physical contact with Dark Ones. For humans, it could be lethal, if the Dark One was in attack mode.

It would already be in her mind, her body, taking all of her pleasurable thoughts or happy memories and turning them into twisted nightmares, violating every part of her with its foul stench. Matt seized it before Jonah could roar at him not to touch it, and his arms went into the blackness up to the elbows.

"Matt, pull free!"

The gun was tooled by a human and its timing and sight could be off. Jonah took the shot anyway. After so many battles, he knew hesitation was more fatal. He blasted the beast's head apart inches over Maggie, clipping Matt's shoulder. The man didn't even flinch, grasping Maggie and rolling away with her. Dropping the truck, Jonah caught the creature's leg and pulled it out, sending its body sliding ten feet away before it exploded from the magic of the charge, showering him with Dark One body parts.

"Get inside, inside," Matt panted, lifting Maggie in his arms. Leaving the driver's door open, he shoved Maggie in behind the wheel, stepped up on the running board and leaned over her struggling body to activate the gate's remote and put the vehicle in drive. Jonah followed it in, guarding their backs, probing to make sure the closing gate restored the magical protections on the circle the fence provided around the property.

As soon as the vehicle had cleared the gate, Matt reached to cut the engine. The weeping Maggie ducked under his arm, tumbling to the sand. When she fell, she didn't notice the impact, digging at her face and writhing, her cries escalating. The man leaped out, going to one knee next to her as Jonah surged forward.

"Maggie."

"Help her . . ."

Jonah's head snapped around, hearing Anna's weak voice from the front seat. She was fully morphed back into a mermaid. Her tail was over the gear shift, body canted at an uncomfortable angle against the window because of her length. Her beautiful purple and blue colors were a mottled, sickly gray, her face sunken, her breath wheezing. The seawater hadn't had time to take effect. "Jonah, help her . . ."

"Water," he called out desperately. "Matt, do you have a tub . . ." But of course Matt was focused on his wife, who was shrieking and trying to get away from him, for all she'd be seeing was darkness. Utter darkness.

Anna reached out to Jonah, scraped his chest urgently as he leaned over her in the open door of the truck. "Only the ocean can save me now, Jonah, and it's too late to get me there. Help her. Fix her. Help her now. You can't leave her like that."

With a curse, Jonah straightened and moved quickly to kneel by the two. Anna struggled to the driver's side so she could look down upon them.

"Stop it. *Stop it now.*" Maggie was wailing, trying to get away from Matt's helpless grip. "Kill me. Don't . . . I can't bear it . . ."

Jonah met Matt's gaze in warning. "I'd give this more time, but the poison will settle in too fast if we wait." By then, the damage to her mind would be irreparable.

"It's okay, Maggie." Matt used his strength to pull her out of her fetal curl, held her back against him despite her struggles. Adjusting so his legs were stretched out on either side of her, he formed a stalwart brace at her back. "You're the bravest girl I know. You're going to be fine."

"I'm never going to be fine again. I don't want to live like this. I can't bear it." When her wildly seeking eyes turned to her husband, seeking comfort from the source Anna was sure she'd always been able to depend upon, she could tell the woman hit a wall of desolation, standing in the way of all he had to offer. She began to scream again, and Anna didn't know what was worse, the sound of Maggie's pain or the reflection of it on Matt's face.

"If you're going to help her, goddamn it, do it. Anything's better than this."

Jonah laid his hands on the inside of Matt's, against Maggie's throat on either side.

The healing light was immediate, reassuring at least to the observers, but then the sickly black and bloodred charged poison rushed out and over her skin, as if Maggie's blood vessels had erupted all along her sternum, revealed by the open neck of her shirt. It ran away from her, though, and over Jonah's hands. When it met his skin, Anna had to bite back a cry as it burrowed in with the eagerness of leeches seeking blood. It stained his skin the same color, strengthening in his pigment as it started to fade from Maggie's. It was alive, writhing under his flesh like living snakes, moving rapidly up his arms to his chest.

"Jonah—" She leaned out, trying to take hold of him.

"Don't touch me." It was a sharp command, obviously done with attention he couldn't spare, so she pressed her lips together hard. His white and silver wings started to turn the same bloodred, the black of decay. He flinched as it injected itself into the base where they joined with muscle and cartilage to his shoulders. Something escaped from his lips, low and guttural, a growl that startled her, particularly when his gaze snapped up and the wholly dark irises had become red. Matt stared up at him, his expression obviously warring between holding on to his wife or reaching for the gun several feet away.

Anna wished she knew if it was usually this difficult for an angel as powerful as Jonah to absorb and transform Dark One poison. Somehow, she doubted it. He was already carrying some of that poison within him. Plus, they'd hit Maggie particularly hard, perhaps for this very reason, knowing it would take more of his energy to fight his own poison to save her. Despite their macabre, monstrous appearance and berserker methods of attack, they were sentient, thinking monsters. She'd thought they couldn't be more terrifying, but now she knew she was wrong.

Maggie slumped against Matt, her eyes rolling back as she went limp. Matt's grip on her tightened, holding her steady as Jonah stepped back at last. "Maggie . . ."

"She should be all right." Jonah's voice was low, hoarse. While his wings were white again and the poison had decreased from the size of snakes back to wriggling maggots, Anna still had to quell the urge to struggle out of the cab and clap her hand around his arm. As if such a weak tourniquet could prevent them from inching upward toward his chest, again, where so many vital organs rested, like his heart.

In truth she didn't know *what* was vital in an angel's body, since they were immortal. But since many of Jonah's soldiers had died fighting these things, she didn't have the comfort of believing that immortal meant invulnerable.

A glance toward Maggie showed her expression had eased, her fingers even in unconsciousness curling over her husband's arm. Jonah had succeeded. He'd repaired the rift torn in her soul by the Dark Ones, driven out the blackness they'd poured into it. Anna had the suspicion, however, that he'd trapped it in himself, given it a much more attractive host to inhabit. When she turned her attention back to him, disturbed by that thought, she found he'd gone.

She had no strength, but managed on will alone to drag herself out the driver's open door. She tumbled to the ground, feeling the thud through her body. It took a moment for the world to right itself again and the haze of pain to clear from her eyes. Then she started struggling after him on trembling arms, ignoring the painful rasp of sand and brush against her sensitive, brittle scales.

Fortunately, he hadn't gone far. He'd circled the truck, strode the few feet to the gate and gone over it, just outside of the boundaries of the property. As soon as he got there, he'd dropped to his knees and begun to retch, expelling wave after wave of dark, foul-smelling discharge with the disconcerting odor of blood. Blue traces of his own life fluid were in it, an ethereal light she didn't want to see mixed in that evil brew.

Since the fence was split rail, she managed to pull herself beneath it and came up on him quietly, praying she wouldn't pass out. He needed her. She held on to that thought, wielded it like a weapon against the fading light of her own body. While she had breath and a heartbeat, she'd give it to him. Though he'd told her not to touch him, she reached forward and gathered his hair on one side, where it had fallen forward on his face. Gently, she pulled it out of the way as he bent forward, obviously concentrating on the purging. She wished he could remove it from himself as he had from Maggie, but she suspected what she was seeing on the ground was from Maggie. The blue blood was the only thing that came from within him.

When he stopped, his head down, sides heaving, she tugged on his elbow. "Let's move you away from this."

"No. Need to bury it, burn the ground."

"Let me help."

"No—"

"I won't touch it, but you're not doing it alone."

While he dug the hole, she carefully pushed sand over the stinking mess, adding in a few dried sticks from the vegetation around the gates. All that was once living around the front of the gate was dead. She wondered if the Dark One's presence had done that instantly, or if it was just evidence of how often evil clustered outside the entrance to Matt and Maggie's property, testing the power of the circle.

He set fire to it with merely a glance, and the smell of it had her covering her mouth. Jonah glanced her way, and with a flicker of his fingertips, a breeze lifted, taking the stench downwind from her. But then he returned to staring at the insidious funeral pyre.

"You know it's growing in you, don't you?" she asked softly. "You know that's why you don't care about the shaman. It wants to win."

"It merely came at an opportune time," Jonah said, without shifting his gaze. "The poison had to have something to attach itself to. You understand?"

"I do." She used her fingers to wipe the moisture from the corners of his eyes, a result of his exertions, not sentiment. She doubted he'd ever taken the easy way out of anything. Perhaps the best way to defeat a warrior was to take away his belief that what he was fighting for meant something. How would a male like him ultimately deal with such a black despair? Fighting itself might become the only answer. That thought brought a shiver of apprehension with it, recalling that hideous brief moment when his eyes had been crimson.

"You have a great deal to live for," she managed. "Just think of the women, far and wide, who would line up to hold your hair out of your face while you throw up."

When he focused on her, pulling out of whatever horrors were battling within him, she attempted a smile, even as she felt something in her chest stutter, send a bolt of pain through her. *Hold on just a little longer,* she pleaded to whatever god might be listening. "It's a human joke."

"I'm familiar with it." Reaching down, he closed one hand on hers. "Anna."

With his hand on her, she was steady enough to cup his jaw, relieved when he didn't stop her. She traced the firm smoothness of his perfect skin, even if what roiled below the surface was far from perfect. Making her stiff lips move again was a vital effort. "The shaman will help. I know you don't care, that you don't know why all of us are bothering, but I have faith that you are meant to live, my lord, and what's more, to take joy in it again."

"Anna . . ." When her body swayed forward, Jonah moved his touch to her shoulders, holding her steady.

"Ronin made you laugh when you forgot how to do it on your own," she said, breath starting to labor. But this was important; she knew it. She clamped her hand over his on her arm, her nails digging in to hold his attention. "But his laughter is still out there. And there's your own laughter and passion inside you still. I've . . . seen it. You've given it to me, as a gift. I wanted to live long enough to see you reclaim it. You're a gift to all of us, a treasure beyond price. Please try. We all need that. We need to know you're there, protecting us. I need to know it. Promise me you'll go to the shaman."

Her head was so heavy, she needed to lay it down. So she did, sinking to the ground and laying her forehead on his knee. "You go on. Dawn's almost here. Be what you're meant to be."

The convulsion rippled over her, taking her words, seizing her internal organs, squeezing, making things blur, even the outline of his face, his pale wings like clouds. This is the way it would end, and that was fine. But, oh, she would have liked to have him a bit longer. She hadn't anticipated leaving him before he left her, and she'd wanted to remember him as happy, whole. That was okay. In a week, the Goddess had given her more than she'd ever expected.

"No. No." Seizing her shoulders, Jonah tried to lift her up, rouse her, feeling desperately for the faint flutter of a pulse. He would make his wings work, even if it destroyed his ability to use them ever again. He would get her back to her beloved sea. What had he been thinking? He could . . .

The rising sun hit his back and he snarled. "No!"

He tried to resist it, but the transformation shoved him over her body, made him press his chest down hard on her laboring one. The wings were gone in a blink, like mortal remains into dust, the small handful of feathers that always seemed to survive the process drifting across the ground. As he was held there, temporarily paralyzed by the transformation, he watched them tumble over the ground, under the truck, to Maggie on the other side. They stopped there, lying at various points against her body.

"Matt . . ." She was conscious, and now she was trying to struggle to a more upright position. When Matt tried to stop her, she batted at him, caught a lock of his brown hair and yanked, hard, to get him to pay attention. "Cellar. Take her there. Quickly. The spring."

Jonah snapped his attention to them. "The spring has magical healing properties." She coughed. "It might help." As Matt hesitated, her voice rose. "I'm in the circle now. I'm safe. She needs our help, Matt. She's dying. Go!"

He gave her a rough, desperate kiss, and then wrenched himself from her side to come to Jonah's. "I'll help you lift her. She's right. The spring might help."

Maggie was weak and helpless, lying on the ground a mere handful of feet and one gate away from the remains of the Dark One who'd almost taken her from Matt. As Jonah looked down at Anna, thought about how he felt about her, he made his decision.

"Tell me where to go," Jonah said. "Stay and care for your wife."

Twenty

It was the second cellar they'd visited this week, though their cellar dweller might have preferred this one to his current abode. Jonah opened the door in the kitchen floor with the key Matt had given him, and took Anna down the steps, into a world of red rock and the not-too-distant but unexpected smell of salt water.

He hated he had to carry her over his shoulder like this, knew it was uncomfortable, but the stairwell was too narrow and her body as a mermaid too long to carry cradled in his arms. He tried to keep his steps even. Her lack of response put a cold fear inside him. How many dead had he carried like this, knowing the feel of lifeless weight over his shoulder? He quickened his step.

Even the first, truly deep breath of saline couldn't give him reassurance. Just when he was sure he was going to have to put her down to make sure she was still with him, she stirred weakly, her fingers brushing the back of his thigh. "Ocean?"

"Something like that. You hang on, Anna. Hang on. You hear me?"

Relief flooded him when he heard the gurgle of water, the tumbling sound of the underground water source Matt had indicated was fed by the ocean in some mysterious manner, another of the Schism's secrets, a confluence of all the elements. What more powerful representation of water could there be than the ocean?

It'd been nearly a week since he'd met his mermaid, and of course Mina had said it would wear off in a week, this detested spell. Before he'd sent them toward the cellar, Matt had said he couldn't cross the Schism's threshold into the shaman's domain as an angel. He should go today, then, but he'd felt no haste to meet the shaman from the beginning, and he certainly wasn't going to leave Anna now. Somewhere deep in his lethargic consciousness, he knew she was right about the poison. But he just didn't seem to have the will for anything but to take care of her.

"Jonah . . ."

"Here we are." He didn't hesitate. It was broad, nearly a dozen feet across. As he maneuvered down the bank and walked directly into the flow of the water, he found it quickly went past his waist, lapping at his chest. Her tail was immersed first, and then he shifted her into his arms to lower the rest of her, holding on to her body as she dropped her head back. Following her impulse, he took her beneath, immersing her in the precious salt water, the smell reminding him of the aroma off the shores outside of her cottage. The echoes in the cavern caused by the flow of the water were even similar to the sound of the waves washing up on the sand.

The gills along her neck were working, soft ripples of movement. Her eyes were open and she was studying him, gazing upon him with that soft, wistful look that was so unfeigned, so scaldingly pure. Her hands held on to his biceps as the water soaked into his battle skirt.

Her color was getting better, the purple and blue shimmer of her tail becoming more luminescent, losing its brittle texture. Her cheeks filled out, their normal light pink blush returning, like the pearlescent interior of a shell. But as he watched her eyes he knew to keep her beneath the flow. She'd come far too close to the end. The strength of her body was not the only thing that had almost left her.

"You must go," she mouthed. He shook his head.

"I'll go tomorrow morning. I'm not going until I know you're all right. Besides, we need to care for our new friends."

He knew that would convince her where attending to her own welfare would not. And it wasn't a lie. Even with the healing, it would be good for him to have Maggie under observation one more night. Not for the first time, he wondered if angels were male because Dark Ones had such a devastating effect on female energy. Plundering their sacred balance, the well of strength that kept the Earth strong because it directly linked to the Goddess. Something shifted in his mind at the thought, a secret there he felt he should know, but didn't. He shook it off. He had no time for mysteries right now.

"You should have told me about the two days," he reproved. "I thought we agreed from the beginning that you were always supposed to tell me the truth."

Her lips curved in that smile, unapologetic but silent, for they both knew why she'd risked it.

The Dark Ones had seemed very determined that he not get here. This last attack had been the most aggressive yet. He had enough will in him to want to resist their desires, but because of hatred of his enemies, not for some higher good. He doubted the Schism would be interested in opening up for that purpose. And why should it?

As he saw the salt water restore some of Anna's strength, he couldn't ignore the stark image of her out there, a mermaid in the desert, helping him bury the vestiges of evil, willing to die for him, when he had done nothing to protect her from the beginning.

He deserved Randall's contempt.

Even as he had the despairing thought, she surfaced, holding on to him. Her expression wrenched something in him. He thought of the desolation in Maggie, created by the poison. All the Dark Ones had had to do to infect him was ride upon the despair he'd created in himself.

"Where does your joy come from, little one? Does it never flag?"

"It does, my lord. But there are always moments like this to take sadness away from me." When she smiled again, it took his breath, the way it seemed to place a balm on the aching pain in his chest.

"Every merman in that damn ocean should have been fighting for the right to love you, cherish you."

She looked startled, then that mischief he seemed unable to

dampen crept into her eyes. "And what would you have thought of that, my lord? Would you willingly turn me over to their hands? Their lips? Their . . ."

She was already nearing his mouth, but before she could say whatever unthinkable thing she was going to say, he closed the distance. *Oh, Goddess.* The sea had brought strength back to her physical body in a miraculous matter of minutes, though as he'd sensed, her spirit was still recuperating from its near separation. But the passion she gave him now overrode it, that mortal reaction when the body brushed too closely to death. The desire to connect. To live and create something more than itself.

It pulled an answering response from him, which shouldn't surprise him, because she'd roused desire from him the first time he'd touched her, sinking down into the Abyss. But now it surged forth on a wave of frustration and despair so strong he knew he couldn't inflict the violence of it upon her.

He forced it back to focus on her. Maybe he could make this moment even more than what she expected. Maybe he could use her pleasure as a powerful magic of its own, to create and convey to her a credible semblance of what he might have once been able to give to her. And if he did it right, maybe she wouldn't realize the magic all came from her. As it had from the beginning.

Goddess knew, she deserved something from him, with all he'd put her through.

Maneuvering them to the edge of the spring, their mouths still joined, he broke the contact only to lift her up onto a flat rock shelf. He kept most of her tail immersed, since his knowledge of mermaid biology told him her sensitive scales were the primary conductors of the healing effect of the ocean waters. He'd brought their pack and now searched through it as she watched curiously. He chose several of her shells, two small round ones and one oblong angel wing she'd had wrapped in tissue to protect its more fragile structure. Knowing her odd sense of humor now, he suspected she'd deliberately chosen it for the journey.

As he took them out, he placed them on the shallow platform of her belly to hold them, increasing her amusement.

"What are you doing, my lord?"

"Giving you something to think about other than mermen," he said.

While she quirked a brow at him, the shells dipped in a slight movement, revealing the quiver of response running under her skin. It made his own blood heat. But again he tamped it down.

"I've told you about the Privy Man," he said, moving the shells again, this time placing the two small round ones on her breasts, one fitting over each nipple snugly enough to stay there, letting her sensitive tips feel the texture of the shell inside. "Tell me something I might not know about."

She studied him, her eyes growing brighter with arousal. He wanted to watch it grow and consume her, confirm for him that not just her body but her soul had a firm hold on life again.

"You've lived so long, my lord. I can't imagine . . ."

"Try," he said quietly, picking up the angel wing, caressing her stomach with his fingers.

"There's an underwater cave near Mexico," she said at last. "It tunnels from the ocean beneath a riverbed. There are rock formations in that cave over a million years old. They crumble if you touch them, so you have to swim slowly. In places the water is a brilliant crystal blue."

As she remembered, her eyes seemed to become more vibrant as well. Jonah watched her face, studying it so hard, trying to find the secret of it, why it'd had the ability to hold him in such close proximity from the first, seeking something he didn't want to give, but still couldn't tear himself away from. "At one time, there were openings in the riverbed, to the surface. The tribes of Mayans that lived along the river area used to dive down and leave pottery, as gifts to the Goddess Ix Chel. I found them there, huge mounds of pots beneath the water. The stalactites and stalagmites are like columns in a temple."

She settled her head back on a rise of rock, careful not to dislodge the shells. As she did, her breasts tilted upward. When his gaze followed their movement, a flush of response heated her throat. He was grateful for the cooler water, helping keep his body motionless, bound by her voice.

"Deeper in, I found a statue of Her, as tall as two of you. She's sitting cross-legged, and when I went to Her base, I couldn't help but touch Her, just a tiny part of Her foot so I wouldn't do much damage. But She was solid, didn't crumble at all. As if being in the water all this time only enhanced Her strength. And so"—her breath drew in as his fingers glided up her stomach, between her breasts—"I curled up in Her lap, which was this perfect curve for my body, and I slept. Oddly, it felt like my gift to Her, keeping Her company that way. My lord . . ."

"Be still. You've traveled far in the sea, haven't you?" His finger traveled left, followed the curve of her breast, his eyes stilling on her face in that way that made Anna's tongue feel like it didn't work properly. "The first time we met, you told me your family was used to your absences. You've spent much time alone."

"No." She shook her head, her fingers curling at her sides, trying to obey his command to remain still even as feelings spiraled wildly inside her, all coiling in toward that single touch. "Even that day. Ix Chel was with me. Then there are whales . . . stingrays . . . fish and sea life of every description. Even the cranky blennies."

"But no one who can do this . . ." And the small shells were moving, a slight elevation, like the movement of a hidden creature beneath as her nipple tightened, lengthened, responding to him.

"If you were in your human form, I'd put this one"—he passed a hand over the angel wing shell still resting on her stomach—"over that sensitive flesh between your legs, just over the wet opening to your cunt. I'd watch the way you'd react to the barest of pressures there."

She could imagine it vividly. Like when on the shore of her own familiar ocean, how she placed the sole of her foot on the wet sand, waiting for that first tiny lick of foam . . . that barest of touches . . .

Like when he'd first placed her in this water. The soul holding the moment, overwhelming the body's base need for mere survival. Giving the mind a powerful lesson in the importance of stillness, of savoring the overwhelming flood of significance of what that one touch, one feeling, meant. Even if the next moment took it away.

"Can anyone else do that to you, Anna?"

"Well . . ."

He stopped, his gaze shifting to her, hot and possessive in a way that arrowed heat straight to her cleft, swelling her tissues such that it was as if the shell compressed her in fact. She let out a little moan.

"No, my lord. Definitely not." But when he looked at her like that, like he considered her exclusively his, it did such marvelous and terrible things to her soul, shredding it. Tearing open the thin membrane holding the joy of new life, but all her vital, fragile organs as well, a jumble of agony and pleasure at once, just as new life would face.

She slid back down into the water, beneath it, sending the shells floating. When Jonah bent, she reached for him. She let just her face come out of the water, the reach of her arms bringing him down enough he could taste her wet lips. Then she drew him down until he sank below the surface, lying upon her. Her mouth gave his human body air, as a mermaid could do, making it possible for him to breathe, even as his heart pounded up behind his ears and his cock got deliciously harder.

As she pressed her breasts against him, Jonah felt the smooth line of her stomach against his, the artful layering of scales in a vee down her lower abdomen, making him think of what was hidden there. But for the moment, there was just the incredibly intense pleasure of her mouth.

Maybe the battle had given him the same reminder of the fragility of life as the dehydration had to her, stimulating them both. Or maybe that magic he wanted her to conjure was affecting him as well. Regardless, he was hyperaware of her fingers pressing into his shoulders, flexing into the muscle. The arch of her body, the line of her ribs he now followed with his fingers, like ripples in the sand left by tides. It made him think of her pixie wings, which appeared shaped by the water, and he wondered if the sea, the spiral of Her, was within Anna, such that when she opened herself like this, all the sensual mystery of the ocean's turbulent waters engulfed him and that was why he couldn't seem to hold on to any cynical resolve. Selfish bastard that he was, had he started this for her pleasure, or his comfort?

Does it matter?

He didn't know if that soft whisper came from her mind,

unconsciously responding to his conflict, or something far larger he wasn't prepared to face.

They were surfacing. He trapped her between his body and one of the larger rocks that shaped the spring's banks. He briefly noted there were carvings on the rocks, more protections, but it also reminded him of the dragon fossilized in the first cave, where Anna had brought him to save his life. A life he'd cared little about saving.

While he didn't see much value in it still, with her teasing about the mermen, he found himself thinking about who would take care of her. Make sure all that beauty and gentle but miraculously enduring passion for life was never diminished. She was only twenty years old, and he was as ancient as history. Yet there was something so precious in her, something that almost gave his life meaning. And, with the wisdom he couldn't deny, he knew not just his own. Whatever it was, he could only equate it to the quality of the Goddess Herself. If Anna wasn't alive, existing, then life as a whole would be less, for everyone. And wasn't it the height of irony that she'd said almost the same thing about him?

Such things add up in the subconscious of the world, my lord.

You are a gift to all of us . . . We need to know you're there, protecting us.

He *did* remember Ronin's laughter. His heart had been struck from him when that was lost . . . But had he lost it, or let it go in the numbness of his grief?

Her body was trembling, pressing insistently to him. "Do you want me, Anna?"

She nodded, her cheeks flushed. "I don't know if I can . . . but I need you inside of me, my lo—"

"Jonah." Cupping her face, he passed a finger over her moist lips. "Call me by my name. I need to hear you say it, know you understand that it's just the two of us here in this moment. And know you understand that I'm the one on *my* knees, worshipping you. Needing you."

She swallowed, her emotions naked as the early emotions of the Earth, all lines etched out in perfect detail on her face, everything there for him to read.

"Jonah. My lord."

He closed his eyes and she said it again, her hand reaching up and passing over his hair. At that gentle touch on his head he remembered a haunting line from an Irish song David had struck out on a drum one night. After the battle where Ronin was killed.

And his sword will strike ne'er more.

Now he wondered if David had played it as a comfort rather than a dirge. To lay one's head down in the lap of a woman, and your sword need strike ne'er more. She was safe, and he was home.

"This one time, my lord. Please. Raise the magic with me, make it a part of what we do together, for both of us. Don't make me feel as if I'm alone in it, forcing it upon you, that it's a separate thing from the pleasure we can feel from each other."

It was a long moment, but then Anna felt it, a warm wave like the comfort of the water itself. More than the water. All of it. The sun, the sea, the earth and the wind . . . She closed her eyes, feeling it wash over her. Angel magic, even though he was in human form. Goddess, if this was a halfhearted attempt, his full strength might make her delirious with bliss, never to recover her wits again.

At last she understood, in a way she hadn't before, why doing the Joining Magic by herself had left her with such an empty ache in her heart. Bringing together their bodies brought together the elemental wish of every being, to be fully inside the heart and soul of someone else. It was divinity and mortality at once, the searing regret and joy that could hold a soul suspended in time.

She knew all beings feared change. Change meant nothing was guaranteed. But for some reason, this felt so still, so permanent. It would be hers, never changing, never altering, long after he was gone. After she was gone.

Finding the strength then, she could tell she surprised him by transforming to human and lifting her legs to close them over his hips. While she felt most like herself as a mermaid, she wanted to see his face, be breast to chest like this. Physical form no longer mattered when the soul was so close to the surface.

Jonah held her, knowing she wanted his body inside of

hers. Needed to see his face while he took her. But for a moment *he* needed, too. To hold her like this, her hand against his chest, her soft cleft pressed against his groin. He discarded the battle skirt and clutched her bare buttocks beneath his hands as he took her to the bank where he could lay her down on the wet earth, paint her with soft traces of silken clay, dark and gray and some red, over the lines of her breasts. She arched up into his touch, gasping, and desire surged, hot and pure. He bent, kissed an earthy nipple, and then pulled it, slow, into his mouth, tasting her and the earth, rolling the soft peak which became small and tight.

When her hands fell to either side, the unconscious surrender inflamed him, her instinctive submission to him. He had an unexpected, overwhelming need for it now, the surge of feeling that the evidence of her trust and acceptance of his possession brought.

Water and earth, air. She was all of those things, and since she raised a fire in his blood, it made them complete.

He hadn't realized how much he needed something to call his own. A sanctuary, a place that seemed created solely for his heart and soul to find rest there. For his eyes to find endless pleasure, his mind eternal stimulation. In Anna, he'd found all of those things, and while she met all those needs, he found an equal desire to know all of her, be that place for her. To be a home for each other.

He couldn't pursue such insane thoughts, and not just because the ability for rational thought was slipping away. He worked his way down her body, spreading the clay, molding her curves in his large hands, wondering at the fragile but resilient perfection of her. At length, goaded by the impatience of her arousal, she reached for him.

Not myth, but real, female, wanting him, the musk of her in his nostrils as he tortured her further, bending between her legs to nuzzle there with his mouth. He tasted her slick petals as she cried out and tugged at his hair, dug her fingers into his shoulders as an anchor as he tasted, penetrated her with his tongue, that narrow opening waiting for his cock to stretch her, to pull him in.

She was bowed toward his mouth like water held on the curve of a powerful waterfall, wanting to crash like creamy foam on the slick rocks below. He cupped her bottom and straightened, holding her where he could see her face as he slowly, slowly impaled her on him. Her legs clamped around his back, her body open to him as he put his hand between them and stroked the stretched lips, the swollen clit as she rippled, so close. But he wasn't letting her go just yet, because he was mesmerized by her response, even as his own body surged dangerously close to that precipice.

"Jonah . . . my lord . . . please . . ." She surprised him again by heaving herself upward. As he caught her to him by reflex, her hands dug into his arms, clawing up to his shoulders until she'd brought herself full against him. That angle took her down deep on him, such that she sucked in a breath and he saw the moment of pain at the adjustment turn to wild pleasure in her eyes.

Putting his palms flat on her back, beneath her heavy fall of hair, he curved his thumbs around her sides, feeling the hint of breast in their rhythmic movement against his chest, the hardened nipples dragging, teasing his own skin. He couldn't hold out anymore. As he pushed her down, brought her back up, she held on to him as if he were a boat she was riding through a storm, her head thrown back, wet hair trailing so he knew it was caressing the delicious shape of her backside. He had the fleeting thought that he wanted the time, years maybe, to lay her on her stomach so he could press light kisses on those quivering curves, see her smile, grow taut with desire again, overflow with it as she was doing now.

"Ahhh . . ." Her eyes, desperate, turned up to him.

"Hold on," he commanded without mercy, but his own muscles were quivering. He let the magic build, build, felt it surge forth in her, and knew she'd been right. Even if he didn't agree with her about the use of the Joining Magic, the intense pressure of it building within him, reaching eagerly for hers, told him he'd been wrong to deny her this, to make her feel as if her effort was solitary and unappreciated.

Spiraling, spiraling. The magic began to fit itself to hers, much as their bodies were interlocked, arms, legs, sex . . . and it was his turn to be amazed by the weight and shape of it, the pure scope as it built around them. Dazzling silver light mixed with the blue of his blood, joined by that rich purple that had been part of her tail color before she shifted and which still lingered in the faint markings along her arms. He'd noted the tattoo pattern changed every time she shifted, positing a wild array of creative tracings for his mouth, his fingers.

When his cock hardened further at the thought, he wanted nothing more than to release inside of her, feel her squeeze down on him as she was now. His sultry innocent who knew no restraint with him, had never been bruised by a lover such that she'd learned self-consciousness, and she never would, because he could never bear anyone else to touch her . . .

He lost the thread of that unlikely and unexpected thought as the climax roared over him, taking her with it. Their magic came together like the creation of a universe, exploding and pulling their bodies together, an irresistible gravitational force, his face buried in her neck, her hair streaming down his arm, her arms locked over his shoulders as she worked her hips on him, slamming down, taking him fully to the hilt, gasping out her release, a soft, whispered word he knew she thought he wouldn't hear.

Yours.

He didn't know if the word applied to him or her. It didn't matter. The magic washed over them both, and the poison cowered in his soul before the power of it, ducked beneath the hard rock of his fears and doubts as it swept by, swept through him, making him want nothing more than to be the person she most needed him to be.

He could do this for her, go see this shaman. Maybe, just maybe, everything would turn out all right. If it didn't, at least he would have tried. For her.

At last, they came down, in almost the same cyclical path, for he felt a sense of dizziness he saw reflected in her silly smile, a young girl's shyness. He couldn't help but smile back, but he also saw the weariness she'd kept at bay close in. The waters had restored her, but the healing process had been draining, as most healings were. On top of that, her demanding lover had seduced her into a mind-altering coupling that pushed her right back into the arms of exhaustion, whether she resisted it or not. So now he turned her in his own arms, wishing he could wrap his wings around her to hold her in her sleep. In a gratifying way, she seemed as comfortable as if he were doing just that. Snuggling back against him, she fit her body so tightly to his he knew he would likely wake with as raging a desire as that which he'd just released. He looked forward to it.

As he settled behind her, Anna wondered if her angel realized that, even without the physical presence of his wings, she could feel them. For he was right—she'd never felt so safe and content in all her life.

SHE slept for hours. He was content to stay there holding her, even dozed himself. But Jonah knew she wouldn't think of herself long once she woke, and so was already working up the strength to rise to his feet when she stirred.

Anna lifted her upper body onto an arm and looked down at him, her hair tumbling over one breast and tickling his abdomen, a tempting rope for his fingers to climb to her face, the delicate line of ear and jaw. Her fingers stroked along his feathers, the wing curved around his shoulder.

"It's night," she observed.

"It is."

She smiled, but there was something sorrowful in the back of her gaze he understood, but knew she didn't want him to probe, particularly when she added hastily, "We've been down here all day. We should—"

"Go check on Maggie." He nodded. "Let's go."

As they dressed, Jonah watched her closely. Though pale, Anna looked far more herself today than she had in a couple of days. He would make sure she was back to her ocean before that changed. Even if she had to be taken kicking and screaming.

For the time being, though, he kept that thought to himself and followed her out of their temporary haven from the world, taking a last look back at the enchanted area. It was ironic that in less than twelve hours he would be likely to find something as unpleasant awaiting him in the Schism as this had been pleasurable. Such was the nature of magical places. Unpredictable, turbulent, fraught with peril or joy.

When they emerged from the cellar into the kitchen, Anna saw a very comfortable cooking and sitting area, with carved benches by a handsome oak table. Maggie apparently had made them dinner, and it was waiting on the stove. Matt was against the counter with a cup of coffee in his hand, his other arm around his wife. Maggie lay against him, her head resting on his shoulder, body leaned into the formidable shadow of his.

She hadn't had much time to get an impression of their male rescuer, but Anna now saw Matt was as tall and broad as Jonah, no mean feat, and had that same resolute look to him. Confident, protective. Still more than a little shaken, but masking it well enough beneath the surface, probably to keep his wife calm. He had gold-flecked hazel eyes and brown hair, kept trimmed close beneath a bill cap with some type of contractor supply logo on it.

When Maggie straightened, Anna noticed she kept her backside firmly pressed against Matt's thigh, a reassurance, maintaining that connection. Jonah had healed her, but he couldn't take away the memory. Having had only a brush with the Dark Ones herself, Anna assumed Maggie would be peering in closets and under beds for the rest of her life.

Matt's hand stayed on her shoulder as he put down the coffee cup.

"I'm sorry," Maggie said. "I should have checked on you."

Two strangers, who had risked their lives for both of them. It was a gift that could never be repaid, and Anna found herself momentarily overwhelmed, as she often was, by unexpected kindnesses. "You're not yourself," she managed matter-of-factly. "I expect it's not every day you have to rescue an angel and a desiccated mermaid from the desert."

"You'd be surprised," Maggie said with a shaky smile. "We've seen some strange things out here. When Sam told us we had to go get you, I . . . Well, I guess last night was a new experience for us. Let's eat. I'm actually starving, and though Matt's too nice to say, I know he's always hungry." She gave his tall frame a fond look. "It's hard to keep a man that size full, especially when he works outdoors all day."

She glanced toward Jonah. "I didn't know if you'd eat, but if there's something special you prefer . . ."

"This is fine," Jonah assured her. "I don't need to eat, but I enjoy a bite or two, and it smells . . . comforting." His gaze searched the room, and Anna had to suppress a smile.

"Baking," Maggie explained. "I bake to settle my nerves. Thought you two might like an apple pie."

Anna took Jonah's hand and looked up at him, her eyes sparkling. "I don't think there's any food he likes better. That's perfect, Maggie."

During dinner, Anna found out Maggie and Matt had come from the South some years before. They worked together on carpentry projects across the region, explaining the beautiful woodwork in the house, complete with curving staircases, handmade furniture and picture frames, arched windows and a variety of detailed moldings that Anna admired freely when Maggie gave her a tour later. By that time, Matt and Jonah had gone onto the back porch to sit, Matt with his after-dinner coffee and Jonah with another slice of pie. Their male conversation was a comfortable rumble drifting through the open windows along with the cool desert air, as the two women explored the house.

When they went to see the upstairs bedrooms, they could see the men from the master bedroom window. As Maggie smiled down at her husband, who appeared unaware of her regard, her eyes filled with sudden tears. Anna immediately stepped close, her hand closing on Maggie's arm, but the woman shook her head.

"I'm sorry. I'm fine, really. Your angel's healing skills are formidable. It was short, so it seems ridiculous—"

"It doesn't," Anna said emphatically. "I've seen them. Felt them." *I have a friend who is haunted by their blood.* And now she wondered if every day was like that for Mina. Did she always fight that despair and darkness?

Maggie nodded. "It was like being imprisoned for ten years in the most horrible place you could imagine. But please don't think I'm complaining. Memories shouldn't be forgotten, good or bad. They make us who we are."

She gazed down at her husband for a long moment. "He'll tease me when you're gone, because I've always called him my angel, and here one came, wings and all. You know that country song, about a woman who just knows that her man's a real angel, and so she just smiles when he insists he's from Houston? I was saved by Matt from terrible circumstances, but I fell in love with him beyond that, too. I was blessed with his love as well. We give to each other. Just as he's done for me today, I can make it better for him, too, when *he's* hurt or mad or lonely, in a way no one else can . . ."

She shook herself, gave a little laugh. "That's my Matt. I'm just silly about him, I guess. I do believe there are angels here on earth, though, and he's one of them. Maybe they don't have the wings because all their good deeds are done with feet solidly on the ground. It scared him so badly tonight," she added abruptly. "I think he's always assumed it'd be him attacked, because he's on the front line more often, and he's so protective of me. But Sam, that's the man your angel's come to see, he's always warning him the Dark Ones know the best way to defeat an enemy is not to take his life, but to take his heart."

"He might mean that literally," Anna murmured, remembering Mina's words.

Jonah was sitting on the top step, one leg crooked, his back against a post, listening to something Matt was saying as he sat in the rocker, leaned forward, the cup in his large hand. She couldn't help smiling a bit, and Maggie squeezed her, seeing it.

"They're really big babies, aren't they? Males of every species, when all's said and done. I can't get him to pick a shirt off the floor, but he won't let me lift a single thing that weighs more than he thinks it should, and at night, he always curls around me, puts his arm over me. Not once in all the time we've been together have I woken without him that way. Doesn't turn away, even in his sleep."

She sighed. "Like I said, this scared him, and he doesn't scare easily. He's never liked being so close to the Schism. Not because of himself, of course. He has enough courage to turn my hair white. To see the things he's done and faced . . . They do tend to be overprotective, but think nothing of risking themselves."

"Why did you stay out here instead of going back down South?" Anna asked curiously.

"Is it that obvious we don't really fit here?" Maggie gave a wistful smile. "I do miss the South, something fierce. We came out here so he could build an overlook at the Grand Canyon. We were married on it. After that, we intended to head back, because Matt has a home in the North Carolina mountains, but then we met Sam, and he introduced us to the Schism. He said we'd be needed here, and so we've stayed. We've done a lot of things, seen a lot of things here, but I think rescuing the two of you was what he meant. He'd said a night would come where we'd be needed more than at any other time. That the future of everything else could hinge on that particular night."

Anna didn't want to think about all the meaning behind that statement. "Have you been together long?"

"About five or six years now. We met one snowy night in Charlotte, North Carolina. He was on his way to the job at the Grand Canyon. I was . . ." She took a breath, looked at Anna. "I was homeless, living out of my car, one step away from desperation. I ran into the back of his truck when I was trying to get a better look at him through my windshield. His mirror was angled, so I could see his forearm. Just his forearm. So strong and capable, tan . . ." She gave Anna a mischievous wink. "I found out the rest of him was just as fine, awfully quick. Matt has a tendency to go after what he wants . . . knows what that is right off."

Anna looked at the woman's perfect skin, light blonde hair, her willowy form. "I can't imagine you as . . ."

"Homeless? Bad things happen, no matter your looks, though they helped keep me out of some tough spots. In a good way," she added quickly. "I never got that desperate, but I was close when he found me. He offered to take me then and there with him to the Grand Canyon, teach me how to be a carpenter, give me a trade. And I trusted him from the beginning, big brute though he is. I knew he wouldn't hurt me. There's just . . . something, sometimes. It's like you're inside their head the second you meet. Not like you know everything about them, but you care so much about them immediately, you want to know it all, the little and the big."

Despite the fact there was an angel sitting on her front steps, his wings arched and trailing across the boards so Matt had accidentally trod on the tip at least once with his boot, Maggie only had eyes for the broad-shouldered man in the flannel shirt. It made Anna like her even more.

"He was so honorable. Almost too honorable." She slanted another mischievous look at Anna. "Despite him deciding we belonged together awfully quick, and using those looks of his shamelessly to convince me of it, I had a time getting him into bed with me. But when I did, holy God." She put a hand on her chest while Anna chuckled. "And since there's an angel of God in the house, I've no worries saying it that way, because I do mean it as divine praise. He was worth the effort. Much as I suspect that one is."

Anna nodded. "I'll miss him when he's gone."

Maggie got quiet beside her, but her fingers remained on Anna's shoulder, stroking as Anna felt it tremble through her, the first time she'd said it out loud.

"Sometimes things you don't expect can . . ."

"No." Anna said it with a strained smile. Kept her eyes on the two men below. "This is how it is. Be glad Matt's only a man, Maggie. You can't keep an angel."

Twenty-one

AFTER Matt and Maggie went to bed, Anna stayed up with Jonah as long as she could, watching the stars over the desert, the silhouettes of the rock formations in the distance, the play of moonlight on the cactus and tufts of sage dotting the landscape. She leaned against him, saying little, surrounded by the curve of his wing. They made love on the porch again, her fingers buried in his feathers, face pressed into his neck to muffle her cries.

But the closer dawn came, the heavier the weight on her heart grew. So much so she wondered that Jonah was able to carry her so easily up to the guest bedroom Maggie and Matt had given them. She opened up to him again there, feeling his body press her into the mattress, fiercely willing him to impale her deeper, fill every empty part of her, keep her from flying into a million desolate pieces.

The arrival of the faint sliver of sun on the horizon was a shining, sharp blade that could cut her wide-open. Between the weight of her heart and the pain of that sunlight, she could barely breathe, watching it come up.

She told herself she needed to be rational. She'd known this was coming. He'd been a part of her life for only a week, so the loss of him in her daily life was something that would ease in time, the vestiges of first love becoming a soft, pleasant memory.

It was a lie that she would make into truth, by saying it over and over. In a million years, she might believe it.

Now she turned and faced him, to find her angel's eyes were open, studying her. They'd drifted off a bit, that last time, and so she wondered how long he'd lain there awake. She knew angels didn't need much sleep, but she wondered if they really needed any. There were many things she hadn't asked him, that she'd just have to wonder.

His wings were gone. Because of that, when he reached between them and lifted a long wing feather he'd somehow managed to keep from disintegrating with the spell, she had to bite back tears. Memories didn't disintegrate, she told herself. She agreed with Maggie, that they were too rich and powerful to ever wish away. It was the only treasure of him she could have. This, and a feather.

The tears were coming, and she couldn't stop them. When she would have turned away, his hands settled on her shoulders to ease her up against his chest. He held her there, let her cry.

He didn't say anything, made no assurances or platitudes, simply kept her from breaking apart. This was not the first time life had seemed intolerable. It didn't often overwhelm her. She didn't let it take her over like this, so when it did, it hit hard. And for some reason, this time hit harder than anything she'd ever felt.

Reconciled since the beginning to the knowledge that she would die young, never have a family except in the most peripheral sense. She knew that her life had started bathed in her mother's blood . . . All that meant nothing compared to this. Oh, she might see him again, but it wouldn't be the same. He'd be an angel in the sky who might deign to stop and gaze upon her fondly, or say a kind word to her . . . and that would be almost worse than death.

Until now she'd never had a reason to be glad her life would be short.

"Sshh . . ." he said softly into her hair, not to silence her, she knew, but as a sound of comfort.

How will I bear it? How can *I bear it?* But she would, because if he was restored to himself, if the heavens shone brighter because Jonah was repairing rifts and fighting back the darkness without, the darkness within him purged, she could bear it.

Her life would mean something. It would not have been hopeless, and therefore whatever might come after that would be all right.

At length, she pressed her forehead to his chest, then her lips to the same spot. "We should feed you breakfast before you go."

"No." He sat up, drawing her with him, still holding her in his arms, across his lap now. "I have a feeling today's journey is better done on an empty stomach. I want you to go back to sleep. You're still drained from yesterday, and still too far from the ocean. Underground enchanted spring or not, you need to conserve your strength. I've sent a summons to David to come for you today."

"Not until nightfall," she said, gripping his arm. "Let me stay here for the day. I'd . . . I'd like to get to know Maggie better."

It was true, but such a small part of it that she couldn't meet his gaze. She looked down, worrying the covers inside his armspan until he gave her a squeeze, kissed the side of her neck, a soft brush of firm lips. "All right then, but don't push it. Whatever I'm meant to face today, I'll face easier knowing you're back safely in your ocean."

While she sensed he was curious about what that challenge might be, he didn't seem apprehensive or overly eager. Not that she'd expected him to be. He was going to see it through, if for no other reason than that was what she'd asked him to do, the mermaid who'd saved his life.

That was okay. She'd gotten him here. That was all she could do, right? She'd wanted to go on with him, even into the Schism, but not only had Jonah adamantly refused to let her go farther with him, Matt said Sam specifically had instructed Anna to stay behind.

"Sing yourself to sleep, Anna," Jonah said, laying her back down on the mattress, spreading her hair out on the pillow with caressing fingers, his dark brown eyes dwelling on her face, committing her to memory, she thought. Hoped.

"What? I've never done that before."

"I know. You told me that. But I want you to try now. Sing

to yourself of the dreams you have, the beauty of flowers, and butterflies . . ."

"Of angels," she whispered, reaching up to touch his face. "I love you, Jonah. You don't . . . I'm not asking you for anything, but will you remember that one thing about me, when you think of me now and again?"

He studied her, a frown appearing between his eyes. "Anna, I'll see you again."

Anna bit down on her trembling lip, because she knew he wouldn't be coming back. Even if he himself didn't know it. If the shaman was successful, coming back to her would just be awkward, and painful. The extraordinary magic that had brought them together would no longer be needed, and would therefore no longer exist. Her purpose would be over, and he would be needed in the skies. She wouldn't contemplate what would happen if the shaman was unsuccessful. "I know. It will just be different. But a good different. Strong and beautiful, restored in your heart and soul, so every heart and soul in the whole world will feel it and rejoice when you're healed . . ."

She began to sing of that before he could say anything else. A soft whisper of notes, about a land that was dark. It was the terrain of his soul, until light came, and it was good. That soul, looking around, was so pleased with its world it began to create. Landscape it with flowers, trees, lakes, streams, mountains and animals of all kinds, all things that inspired joy and imagination, all of it for love . . . He would remember it all, why life was worth living . . .

Jonah stayed leaning over her, his hand curled in her hair, watching her lips, occasionally brushing them with his own. Not enough to interrupt her, but as her eyes began to droop he moved to one eyelid, then the other, then back as she let them close. Her fingers curled on his chest, slowly relaxing, then relaxing some more, until the music died away and her even breath told him she'd fallen asleep again, taken away to dreams by her own enchanted voice.

He studied her a long time, then he picked up the knife she'd used to cut an apple right before bedtime. She'd had a desire for the raw fruit Maggie left in appetizing display on the kitchen table. Anna been amused when he'd tasted it and indicated he liked it better in the pie. Carefully, he severed a lock of her hair, long as his hand. He braided it with deft fingers and put it around his wrist, interweaving the ends to form a gleaming golden brown bracelet. When he passed his hand over it, he'd imagine tunneling his fingers through the silk of the thick strands.

But it would be nothing like bringing her close, touching her, dancing with her. She was better off without him, that was a given, but he disliked the idea that she thought he might not be coming back because she'd simply been an instrument and her part was done. At least that's what he supposed her thinking was. Her apparent acceptance of that, that he would be so superior, so arrogant, annoyed him further. But it didn't matter. Maybe taking the lock of hair and leaving her the feather would tell her differently. Because he knew whatever happened next, she was right about one thing. He couldn't come back to her. Not this way. For her well-being.

Rising with a stifled curse, he arranged the covers carefully over her, pressed one last kiss to her forehead. Inhaling the smell of her hair, the traces of the sea, he closed his eyes. Damn it all, things used to be so much clearer to him. If he loved her, he needed to leave her be. The simplest adages were always wisest. A fish and a bird didn't belong together, particularly if the bird had manic depressive tendencies which had managed to get the fish almost killed several times during their brief association. There was a darkness in his soul he knew did not bode well, not for a fragile creature like Anna.

He wanted her more than he seemed to want anything else these days, and yet she was the one thing he still had the presence of mind to know he shouldn't have.

While dressing in the human clothes that still felt odd, he reflected they at least did not feel so constricting any longer. According to Anna's explanation, this was because denim stretched.

When he headed for the darkened staircase, he forced himself not to look back. If he saw the shape of her body under the covers, the silk of her hair spread across her bare shoulders, the serenity of her delicate face, he'd never leave.

Despite the fact he and Anna had both strongly admonished Matt and Maggie there was no reason to get up and send him off, Matt was standing on the front porch.

"Do you ever not have a cup of coffee in your hand?" Jonah observed as he stepped out, shouldering the pack Matt had loaned him last night to carry a few essentials. Water to replenish his human form, the battle skirt for his angel form. The talismans he'd decided, with some manly embarrassment, to carry: the three shells from yesterday, a pressed purple flower from the field where she first became a pixie . . .

Matt considered the cup. "I put it down when I have to go save angels and mermaids in the desert."

"For which I count myself fortunate." When Jonah held out his hand, Matt clasped it. "I've fought so long on behalf of humans, I forgot there might be some worth saving. Though that may make little sense to you."

"It makes perfect sense to me." Matt flashed his teeth. "I've lived among humans all my life."

Jonah nodded. "She wants to stay until tonight. Another of my kind will come for her today. If she stays well, she can stay. If she starts to decline again, he must take her. She's willful, but you and he are bigger." A smile touched his lips. "Though I suspect any man would have to be deaf, dumb and blind not to be persuaded to do anything she asks. Take care of her. I would consider it yet another debt I can never repay you."

He'd never trusted a human before. Even now, he suspected what had tipped trust in their favor was the way Matt and Maggie loved each other. That made him certain Matt would understand the significance of what he was asking.

Matt nodded. No species barrier existed in that moment, just two males who understood what was most important. "I'll protect her. And, as far as the other . . . my wife will heal from what happened yesterday. That debt's paid, right there. We won't be here much longer. This was what we were here to do, and it's done. We dedicated five years to it. There comes a point when you've given enough to one thing, and it's time to move on to the next."

"What would the next be?" Jonah asked, turning at the bottom of the steps.

Matt gestured. "Probably taking Maggie back home. Having a baby. She wants to adopt two or three as well, but have at least one that looks like us. Hopefully more like her than me."

"Goddess willing," Jonah said gravely, and Matt laughed.

"I guess life then will be about teaching them how to give more than take. It's hard to say, all in all." He shrugged. "With our limited life spans, we mere mortals have to figure out what best to do with our time so that when it ends we aren't ashamed to put our name on it, call it our life."

Jonah considered that. "I think you and Maggie are doing very well in that regard. Yesterday, you saved something very much worth saving." He looked up toward the window of the bedroom where Anna slept, hopefully with dreams worth having, that would last.

"Jonah." Picking up one of the shotguns leaning against the wall, Matt came down to offer it. "I put a box of shells in your pack last night, as you may have noticed. Just in case."

He met Jonah's gaze. "I've never been the type of man to tell another man what he should do, let alone an angel, but I want to say this. You can be doing what you were born to do, and still get lost. Some men are born to be warriors. Doesn't matter where you find them. When the need comes for a fight that can't be solved any other way, they'll be the ones that step to the front line, protecting what's important. For everyone who wants to make that kind of sacrifice, there are powers that want to take it. And the two sides *are* different. Don't forget that."

Matt shifted. "I guess what I'm saying is that while you've got the high ground, there are those of us that are always fighting to hold the low ground, to give you one less thing to do. Good luck to you."

"As I said, I'd forgotten there are humans worth protecting. Thank you for the reminder." Jonah found the words were thick in his throat. Matt overlooked it, shook his hand once more. The silence that passed between them, heavy with words unspoken, was one Jonah recognized from fighting side by side with other males, in so many other times and circumstances.

As he looked up at the window again, he held the grip an extra moment. "Whatever happens to me, Matt, she's the most important thing. Take care of her. Please." When he realized how long it had been since he'd said that word, he wondered what that said about him. About who he'd become.

"No harm will come to her while she's in my care. I mean it. I'll watch over her the same way I watch over Maggie."

Jonah nodded. Despite the reassurance, he had to bite back the sudden feeling he was abandoning his responsibility to protect Anna. How many times had he told his men, those whose comrades had fallen next to them, that they could not be everywhere, protect everyone? That they must rely on others to help, in order to focus on the most important thing: defeating the enemy. He understood that, damn it. But he equally, fiercely felt that it wasn't a matter of an army here, but Anna. Anna was *his* to protect. Care for. Make smile . . . give her someone to tease, someone to kiss her body, make her undulate in those sensual moments of pleasure. Shelter her back while she slept.

Without another word, he turned on his heel and strode away. He'd wondered if it was possible to feel less comfortable with who or what he was, or more confused, than he had been these past few years. Now he found it was, and bleakly decided it was likely to get worse, the further away he got from Anna.

But she'd be better off. She'd be safe.

She'd be alone.

MATT had given him the landmarks, and Anna had described Mina's mindmap to him. It was therefore relatively easy to follow their directions in daylight with his senses now tuned to just the one thing. Or perhaps the energy of the Schism was just getting stronger.

According to Matt, the magical fault line, while ever shifting to a certain extent, ran for an unknown length. Despite that, they suspected its breadth was fairly narrow, no more than a few hundred yards. He'd also noted what Jonah already knew. It was impossible to open when it had no desire to be open, or when the seeker was not meant to find it. Matt had discussed the parameters with a certain resigned humor, but having been exposed to magic for his entire existence, Jonah recognized it as no more than the basic principles governing most magical energy.

In fact, in past, more lighthearted days, he'd made the dry observation that magical energy reflected a great many of the characteristics of the divine feminine energy likely responsible for its existence.

The remembrance gave him a faint smile as he walked.

The heat was not bothering him, but still he stopped to drink from the water bottle occasionally, since he was in human form. Matt and Maggie's house had disappeared after he crossed over the first rise and then turned to begin following the geographic markers for the fault line. Anna had done a good job keeping them aligned within its range of influence, but it was an ominous indication of how closely the Dark Ones were watching for his movements, that they'd attacked so swiftly when they wandered off course, outside where the Schism or Mina's mindmap had apparently been providing some extended umbrella of protection.

He shouldn't be leaving Anna. Not until he knew she was safely back in the ocean. What if . . . He stopped, clutching the straps of the pack. He'd lost his mind. What on earth had made him decide to leave her before he knew for certain she was safe?

"Is running back to her a retreat from me, or yourself?"

Jonah turned. Where there'd been nothing but a stretch of desert and scrub with a backdrop of clay and sandstone mountain rock formations on his last glance, now stood an old man.

Jonah blinked. If not for the colors of his clothing, the man might have been an engraving on the lines of red rock in the distance, the impression of an ancient Indian who'd once walked the desert alone in search of his own visions. The lines shimmered again, giving Jonah the sense that there was even more moving in the backdrop behind the man, but then it smoothed, like a curtain of camouflage falling down, restoring it to still scenery again.

Jonah swayed as the world began to spin around him, as if he'd stepped on a merry-go-round that was speeding up. The mountains were moving around him, behind him, back again, while the clouds raced above like stallions thundering across the sky. As the shaman chanted, a throaty singsong, Jonah stumbled to one knee, steadying himself as the shaman completed what he knew was a time and space distortion, a pocket cut off from everything else.

"The Schism has often cracked along your way." The shaman's voice resonated in his head. "That's why the landscape sometimes changed in ways you didn't expect. Some of what you experienced was of the human world; some of it wasn't.

The Dark Ones can't come directly into the Schism, at least not yet, but it's a power center, and there's always a small handful hovering around it at different points when they can escape the notice of the angels. And you attracted more of them to it, of course."

When Jonah blinked and opened his eyes, it was night, full dark. There was a moon in the sky as red as the hills it illuminated, so that they and everything else seemed stained in blood, including a hallucinatory ocean stretching away in front of it, the desert meeting the sea. Then he realized it wasn't the hills, the water or the moon, but his own vision that was tinged with red. His wings split from his back with more violent eagerness than he anticipated, almost taking him off his feet, wrenching the weakened joint so that he grunted.

"Just in the nick of time," the shaman observed. "The spell has worn off, angel. No more will you turn into a human. You must face who you are now."

"I thought I was facing you," Jonah retorted, getting to his feet. The shirt he'd donned was ripped, so he tugged it free, but he bundled it into the pack. It belonged to Anna and he was loath to discard it. Since she'd slept in it at least one night, sometimes he could still smell her scent upon it.

"You view me as an enemy," Sam observed.

"I'm not afraid of you, old man."

"You've never feared an enemy, so your defensiveness is unnecessary." He cocked his head. "Also, I am barely out of diapers compared to one of your age. So you seem confused already. You're not nearly as clever and intimidating as I expected. And here . . ." The shaman stepped forward, plucked at Jonah's right wing where one feather had become dislodged and was stuck up in the layers at an odd angle. "You're looking like a bird that hit someone's windshield and rolled off. I suspect the witch could have warned you the spell would wear off in such an abrupt and physical manner, but what dark pleasure would she have derived from that?"

"You obviously are familiar with Mina." When Jonah put up a hand, pushing the man's touch away, Sam stepped back, faced him. On closer study, he appeared to be a mix of Native American and Asian heritage, perhaps a descendant of the Asian railroad men and the women of the Sioux tribes.

"I am. She has invaded my dreams. A remarkable gift, being able to trace those who come to you in vision and communicate with them, actively. If only she weren't so . . ."

"Shrewish?" Jonah suggested. "Tongue like a viper?"

"I've met gentler vipers. But a gifted child, nonetheless." Sam allowed it with a smile. An impressive array of crow's-feet appeared at the corners of his eyes. He gestured. "Shall we get to it, then?"

"Get to what?"

"Why you're here. Which you know but still refuse to acknowledge, because of the poison that glimmers inside of you, and what lies beyond that poison."

Sam had started walking. There was no choice for Jonah but to stay behind or keep up, so he fell in step next to him.

"That was impressive shooting last night," the shaman noted.

"The bullets were somewhat helpful," Jonah responded.

Sam made a noncommittal noise. "The spiral grooves of a gun chamber allow a bullet to come out spinning, hold its aim, stay in a straight line."

"I know that."

"Yes, you would. It is one of the mysteries to me, that angels have knowledge of all weapons, even those not created by the Mother. But there are messages in all things. The Great Mother is the way of the spiral. And the striations in the metal mark the bullet, such that you can tell exactly what gun it came from. Again, like the Mother, who leaves Her mark on each of us, the impact of change, of ending, of pain. We know Her mark upon us, the promise and hope behind it."

While nothing else changed as they moved, one feature appeared as if they had in fact walked through a clear curtain into another room. A sweat lodge with a fire crackling out front. Steam escaped in a frugal flow from the top of the lodge. Jonah made only brief note of that, however, as he registered something far more unexpected.

His sword, the one knocked out of his hand in the battle that took his wing, was driven into the ground by the fire.

"She may have the temperament of a viper, but she does not lack courage. She risked much to find that blade. Found it and had it brought here. Another impressive spell. Her visions say you will have need of it. These are not my visions, but I do not doubt her word."

Jonah approached the sword, eyeing it. The blade sharp and glittering, the hilt simple, well crafted, two metals wrapped and melded together to form the shape of a pair of intertwined serpents with emerald and blue eyes. A gift from Lucifer years ago. Jonah put his hand out, let it hover over the hilt. He'd used it for decades, until it was something as commonplace to him as having an arm or leg. It wasn't an extension of his body. It was part of it.

Just as he was about to draw it from the ground, Sam stopped him, laying a hand on his wrist. "Come inside. You may want to strip off everything for the lodge. Whatever you wear will get soaked. Do not touch the blade yet."

"Why?"

"It is not time." At Jonah's deprecating look, the shaman shrugged. "Believe me or not. I abuse no man's will. But you came here believing you may find some answers. All I can tell you is how best to seek them."

But as Jonah stripped, he was surprised to see Sam himself take hold of the hilt, pull the blade from the ground and heft it. "You can feel the power singing off of this," Sam noted, his brow furrowed. "It has the power of the giver, his friendship. It has your power, that power that exists before all other power-givers in your life. And then it has the power of the blood it has shed."

"What is it I'm supposed to do here, old man?" Jonah cocked a brow. "And for your species, you *are* old, so do not lecture me again about our differences."

"I would no more consider doing that than a mother who has grown weary of counseling a grown son who should have better manners." But Sam shrugged before Jonah could retort to that. "I don't know what you will do, what will happen to you in there. That's not for me to say. My vision was that you would come, and I would have this prepared for you, and be ready to complete the task my vision set before me. You will enter the lodge and you will seek your answers. You have not sought answers before now. You have been wandering. A man may wander most of his life, but you know better than most that he finds his answers when he stops, becomes still. Here you can only sit, and wait."

As Jonah felt tension coil in his stomach, Sam nodded. "You believe the blood you have shed will drown you if you let your mind stay at a fixed point. But you must let it drown you. Much hinges on the crossroads you have reached now. You must seek your own visions and the truth in them, or give yourself up as a lost wanderer in the desert, a fate that serves no one, but could destroy many."

He gestured to the lodge. "The way to strong visions is through focus, and when focus is hard to find, great pain or physical stress can bring it. When the heat takes over your senses, robs you of consciousness, then you will catch up to your mind, find where it has been wandering inside the labyrinth of your soul."

Jonah glanced toward the tent, felt the heat coming from it. He spread his wings slightly, gestured toward them with a tilt of his head. "That's for your human victims, shaman. In this form, I'm not affected by heat. It will take much more than that for me to reach a state of great physical stress or pain."

Sam cocked his head. "Do you wish to find truth?"

Jonah knew the answer to that. The sullenness in his soul that made him care little for any of this was still there. But he could not push away his promise to Anna, the faith in her gaze, the sweet gentleness of her touch.

I cannot wait to see you well . . . flying . . . That will be your greatest gift to me . . . He'd heard her thoughts during her song, his mermaid likely unaware of how many things unsaid she'd sent from her mind to his.

Why he didn't resent her asking of him what he didn't want for himself, he didn't know, but his only sense of right and wrong, his only motivation, lay now in what she wanted.

"I'm willing."

Sam raised a brow, acknowledging that he hadn't received a direct answer to his question. Jonah stared at him, waiting. Sam spread his hands out. "So what will cause you enough suffering to send you into a vision state, if heat will not?"

It clicked then. His jaw clenching, Jonah moved his gaze to the sword.

"I'm really beginning to hate that witch," he muttered darkly, ignoring the flash of amusement in the shaman's otherwise somber face.

JONAH found the interior of the tent suffocatingly hot, but as he'd predicted, its impact on him was atmospheric only. Taking a seat cross-legged next to the hot rocks, he told the shaman what needed to be done. As he rolled his shoulders, laid his hands on his knees and adjusted his wings, he allowed Sam to lay lines of beads and shells over his shoulders that draped down to his stomach and knees. When the shaman began to chant, the lines became rigid, winding over his arms and holding them to his sides, immobilizing him. Jonah expected it, knew it was needed so the shaman's blow would be precise, striking him just below the heart to cause mind-altering pain, not death. However, he reflected it was the first time in his life he'd willingly put his life into a stranger's hands, let alone a human's. Whether that was intuition or loss of good sense, it was too late to change his mind now.

"If you're an agent of my enemies, shaman, then you're about to be in a position to take my life."

"I am not your enemy, angel," Sam replied. "But I am not your friend, either."

In the dim lodge, his dark eyes glittered, piercing. Jonah almost expected the shaman to spread wings of his own, glossy black and brown like the hawk he suddenly resembled. Shamans often traveled upon wings in their visions, leading some scholars throughout the ages to point to them as part of the mythology of angels. The ability to fly, to transcend.

"What do you mean, old man?"

But for the moment Sam had dropped into the hypnotic singsong chant used by wizards of this barren land for centuries, a rhythmic cadence that connected directly to the songs of the earth and the sky. Jonah turned his mind from the shaman's cryptic comment and focused on the chant instead, for he knew it was part of preparing himself. As he did, he modulated his breathing for the stifling atmosphere. His mind had almost started to drift off when he realized Sam was speaking directly to him again in the same hypnotic monotone.

"You paid attention to the lessons of the Dark Ones, to

their words. You believe they say only what they mean, and they do. But what they mean may not be what you understand. Their ways are not our ways. They are closest to human ways, and there is an answer for you there, but you must listen closely for it."

Sam hefted the blade, used it and his hand to waft the steam over his face, closing his eyes as he spoke. "In battle, the Dark Ones destroy the heart of the angel to inflict a mortal wound. This is a physical matter. But in the spiritual realm, where the power they seek lies, they know the best way to defeat an angel is to *take* his heart. And so that is what they seek from you."

Jonah made a noise. "I know that."

"No, you do not. You listen with your ears still."

Jonah stared at Sam across the flickering firelight, through the clouds of steam. When the shaman shifted, Jonah did in fact see the shadow of dark wings thrown by the flame against the wall, and those images blurred. Hawk. Man.

"It has been in my dreams, and in those of the seawitch, that a great and horrible chance must be taken. By taking your heart from you, the Dark Ones may actually help you find it again. The physical and spiritual will come together there, such that there is no difference between the two. It is what we all hope and must risk. For the alternative is much darkness and the Great Mother's voice being silent forever." Sam's tone sharpened. "There is much more than you at risk here. And yet your pain, your confusion, is a mirror of what the whole world suffers. Your quest is the quest of us all."

"My heart is within me, old man. And no Dark One will take it. I will skewer it myself first."

"You gave your heart away. You could not bear the pain of its weight, and so you gave it to another to hold."

Your heart. The physical, versus the spiritual . . .

Oh, Goddess. Anna. Anna was his heart. They were coming for Anna.

The meaning hit Jonah as if the shaman had rammed the sword through his chest right then, though he still stood across the lodge. He struggled, but the weight of the ritual pieces with which the shaman had bound his arms to his body held him.

David. Anna. A force of Dark Ones would come, great enough to take Anna. David would fight them to the death. And here he was, in a temporal shift, unable to communicate with anyone.

"Let me go. I can't do this now."

Sam raised the sword. His gaze was sad, but implacable. "You must."

With that last directive, he drove the sword into Jonah's chest, between the ribs that were several inches below the heart.

HE'D prepared the damn blade himself, charged it with enough of his own power to help Sam knock him out of his own reality and into this far different one. Jonah roared his fury, but he was on fire. No, *in* fire, a place of black rock and orange flame. He turned on his heel, hemmed in on all sides, nowhere to go. Then, out of that darkness, a familiar figure materialized, the fire licking at his ebony wings.

The Goddess didn't create the humans, Jonah. She created all of what you see in the world and universe, including us, but not humans. Have you not asked yourself over and over why they are so different from any other creature on Earth?

"Luc, I have to go." Jonah said it desperately, even knowing it was futile. He wasn't really talking to the Lord of the Underworld but to an illusion of his own mind. "I can't be here. Anna and David are in danger."

But She is connected to them anyway. Lucifer took more corporeal form, his eyes red as bloodshed. *That's important. Remember that.*

Jonah shook his head. "Why are you here, Luc? What is this? What—"

But then the vision was gone and instead of fire, he was in deep water. Deep as the Abyss and colder. He struggled, swimming against the weight of his wings, which felt ten times heavier, though angel wings were usually supple as fins in water.

There were millions of sea creatures around him, swarms of sleek sharks interspersed with silver schools of fish, the swiftly pumping tentacles of squid, as well as floating man-o'-wars with their ethereal forest of legs. Their arms caught him, burning, stinging, as if trying to keep him from ascending.

An angel did not cause harm to a creature of the Lady if it could be avoided, but only the discipline of a millennium kept him from sending out a blast of electrical energy that would have scattered them from his path.

They rolled him, over and over, until he wasn't sure if he was going the right direction, if he was even conscious.

Up, up. He had to get free. A whale struck him, hard enough that he heard bones creak inside his chest cavity as he tumbled along the creature's side. When he had the presence of mind to seize a fin, it dissolved in his hand. They could impede and touch him, but he could do nothing to them after all.

He thought of Anna in the waves. She seemed to get where she wanted to go by a curious mixture of not resisting and not losing sight of her destination. He tried it, letting the creatures carry him. Their drifting or turning at a key moment resulted in openings that let him be elevated upward in a slow spiral, rolling with them, feeling the silky passing of a dolphin's side, a blowfish's sudden startled expansion along his instep . . .

The increasing warmth of the water, its sensual caress on his exposed skin, reminded him of being buried deep in Anna's body, rediscovering that soft, warm wetness. Despite the stories he'd told her of couplings with women, those had been earlier times. He had been grounding himself with meditation for some time. When *was* the last time he'd taken a woman? Had it truly been over two years? No wonder he'd been such a rutting animal with her.

As the darkness in him grew wider and wider, he hadn't trusted himself with the fragile gift of female flesh. He couldn't obliterate the sense that his hands were covered with blood when he touched their soft skin.

Or maybe you had no desire to soil yourself in the filthy cunt of Creation. The Great Harlot . . . the Great Thief . . . Deceiver.

Darkness. The shark's teeth scored him as it passed and snapped down on a fish. The burst of blood and fluid misted before his eyes, a macabre cloud illuminated by some malevolent light source. Losing his bearings, he thrashed, shoving away, getting out of the feeding frenzy.

Stay with us; eat with us. Taste flesh and death.

It boiled up in him, an oil slick he could ignite, spreading fire and flood upon those around him. Send them to the bottom of the ocean and mire them all in a tar pit, those who would impede him, innocent natural creatures who were not so innocent and natural. Not if they were standing in his way.

No . . . He struggled for the thought of Anna again. Intimate, physical things, when the emotional eluded him. Of the stretch and give of her impossibly tight channel taking him, accepting him, Joining with him so they could both climb out of their darkness. Looking together at something that shone above these dark clouds, even if it was just the reflection of what they felt for each other. The axis of the world turning in that powerful moment of connection. Where meaning was found, though there was none to be found elsewhere. It was *the* divine feeling. The purpose. The way.

He was rising again, his lungs bursting, but his strokes were more sure as he turned and twisted in a symbiotic dance with the creatures, headed for the light spearing down in the water, seeking him.

When that first ray fell on his outstretched hand, its energy poured into him. Before he could draw a deep breath in reaction, a convulsion ricocheted inside his body like shrapnel. The poison was rejecting that light, trying to escape it, doubling him over, pulling him away. But he was disciplined, used to pain, tearing agony.

Anna. David.

The beams wrapped around his forearms, legs and his body like the shaman's shell ropes. Now he was turning again, only this time slowly, watching the sea creatures around him who were still free to move and turn, flirting with the light but then disappearing into the blue, cool waters again. In and out. The agony in his gut was going to tear him apart, even as the beams ruthlessly held him in the light. He screamed as the poison burned its way out of his soul, scrabbling to get away from that light, willing to tear him apart to do it. He tried to let the light do its work, purify him, even as the pain was so intense he shamed himself by crying out.

Then he was going up again, limp in the hold of the light, his body shuddering, too weak to straighten.

Wet sand. He was on a beach, the water lapping at his feet,

tide rushing over his bare buttocks and genitals. Just for a moment, he was disoriented enough to look for Anna's cottage, but that was too much to hope for. She was beyond his reach now, and likely safer. No, she was in danger. Wasn't she?

He made it to a knee, clutching his stomach, tried to rise and stumbled. Working his way up the beach on his hands and knees, he used his wings for balance. Though he couldn't yet stand, he stayed at least that far off the ground, taking shuddering breaths.

He couldn't collapse in the presence of the Lady.

The body of water he'd climbed out of was no longer an ocean, but a tranquil lake, just a piece of mirrored glass on which She stood, directly in the center. The Sea of Glass.

Though he still shook from having the poison extracted from him before he reached Her presence, the disorientation had settled. Nothing of the Dark Ones could bear any proximity to Her. Had he enlisted Raphael's help from the beginning to remove the poison, this was likely what the Full Submission angel would have done to ensure his healing was complete. Though Raphael might have chosen gentler methods to do the initial extraction. Well, Luc would say he deserved the pain. Bloody black-winged bastard.

Jonah finally managed to get to his feet, turn, and then purposefully drop to one knee. He stayed on the beach, though, while She still stood in the middle of the lake, facing away from him.

"Why do you not approach, Jonah?" Her voice was the breeze, the answer to so much inside of him, answers for the questions he couldn't ask.

"You might be part of a vision, my Lady."

"That's not an answer. Vision or not, you've always come and knelt at my feet, where I may place my hand upon you. Do you hate me so much now? Have I lost your love?"

The idea of it, voiced like that, in this place, did more than tear at his gut. It cracked his heart, twisted like the vicious bite of a sword in the empty place where the poison had been, leaving him an empty shell. It made him squeeze his eyes shut.

"No, my Lady. I . . . I must return. The shaman holds me here, but there . . . I must protect David and Anna."

"Do you fight so hard to protect them because you can't remember anymore why you fight for me? Has it been lost in the blood?"

She turned then. A woman. She'd chosen the simple form of an average mortal woman, and yet the energy that poured off of Her had him closing his eyes again, his heart breaking with all of it, everything. She was overwhelming as always, and whether he was seeing Her in the vision or in reality, She was here, inside of him, where he hadn't allowed Her to be for so long.

"Let me tell you a story, Jonah. A story of a young Goddess, who had to learn that compassion can have terrible consequences."

She moved over the water, and the scent of Her reached his nose, a mixture of several things. Deep earth, salty foam. The wind whispered as she moved. Fire was not a part of Her, but he often sensed it lingering upon Her person, one of Her many mysteries.

"I pondered whether to tell you this story before you found your own truth. May I touch you, Jonah?"

Never in over a thousand years had She had to ask. But he knew free will was both the blessing and curse of all species, except to those who delivered themselves for Full Submission.

"I'm unclean, Lady," he said, his voice choked. "I can't . . . I won't take the chance of tainting Your Spirit."

In all of those thousand years, he'd never lied to Her. Not until now. He couldn't bear Her touch, wouldn't bear Her looking at him, seeing all he was, had become. He understood now the stories of betrayers of gods, how they sought to hide from the face of their deity out of shame, revulsion. The darkness gnawed at the flesh of his soul, whispered evil, and it did so without the help of the poison.

The poison had to attach to something, Anna . . .

"Jonah." Her voice was the voice of love and compassion. Of justice. Of endings and beginnings. "You fear my answers to your questions. You fear it will further wall your heart against me, if the answers are wrong. But your fears have already built that wall, and that is what will keep you from your true self.

"The essence of everything I have created in the Universe is feeling. The male balance to that is structure. You have lost the feeling part of yourself. Rejected it. The branches of a tree spread far. Its leaves are magnificent colors. You can see the tree, touch it and smell it with your physical senses, but it is your soul that feels it, finds pleasure in it. Structure and feeling."

When She took a step forward, Jonah's muscles quivered. Just short of a flinch. She stopped. During the long moment that passed, he could hear a woman weeping somewhere.

"I shall tell you that story, after all," she said quietly.

"I am at Your service, my Lady."

Her robes rustled, like leaves in truth, but She didn't come closer. When Jonah lifted his head, he saw She was sitting on a rock that had materialized for Her. A mist drifted around Her, partially obscuring Her features from him.

"Back before the world was formed, I wandered between the worlds, dimensions, galaxies. Saw what had been created, what had potential, what was being formed . . . I found the Dark Ones, their dimension. All the utterly dark venom of it, a vat of hopeless despair. It was unfathomable to me, having no purpose I could understand except hatred and killing. At length, I wondered if I'd stumbled upon a well from which other worlds draw in measured amounts to balance and challenge good with the existence of evil. Perhaps that is their purpose. I did not know. Still do not.

"But something was about to change. They were at a pinnacle of evolution. The Dark Ones could not reproduce, and while immortal, their numbers could still be decimated. So they'd learned, with great effort, how to create children, only not through the sacred act we know and enjoy. They'd created bodies out of the clay of their world and infused them with breath and their darkness. There were nearly a thousand of them, preparing to be 'born.' As evil is not adept at creating life, the effort required of the Dark Ones to do just these thousand had apparently taken them thousands of years. As I moved among them, unnoticed, I could not bear it, all that potential life intended for evil. I thought, 'Perhaps the spawn of these evil creatures will have a chance at love and life if there is just one small spark inside each of them . . .'"

She put up a hand and blew, and a skitter of flame rolled across Her palm and disappeared. Jonah watched it vanish, even as he thought Her words were like Her breath upon that same precious spark within him, threatening to extinguish it.

"I dictate certain laws against interference, as you well know, and I make myself abide by them as well. But for that group of innocents, I forgot those rules. After I gave them each one small spark of my Light, I stole them away, through the skies, to Earth . . ." She looked around Herself. When Jonah blinked, he saw the desert and red rock formations in the distance, the sweat lodge.

"As you know, we have many worlds, but this one seemed best for them. A thousand children, left here to be given a chance." Her countenance darkened, and he felt it as a cold wind passing through his vitals, a shiver along his skin. "I underestimated the depth of the Dark Ones' obsession with their children, though of course that word has nothing to do with love. They have never stopped trying to reclaim them, only now there are billions of humans, far more than they ever imagined would happen. They didn't expect them to be able to reproduce, and perhaps it is my spark that made that happen. I do not know.

"To reclaim them, they have to get them to fully embrace their darkness again, and you've seen the many ways they attempt to do this. In some cases, they impregnate them, to see if the resulting spawn will be . . . sparkless, like them. But still able to procreate, unlike them. Dark Spawn."

"And that is why they hate female energy so much," Jonah said slowly, staring at the water, veering away when his gaze traveled to the tips of Her feet. "Because it was a female who stole their children."

She was silent for a long while. "They have no females among them. I do not know why. In the end, perhaps the humans will be reclaimed by their parents and it will all have been for nothing. But I took what was intended to be dark and evil and gave it something that could save itself, if a miracle happened. If we fought long enough to let that light grow . . ."

Jonah stared down at his knuckles. Time in a vision could be eternal, he knew, or simply seconds, but the silence that stretched out between them seemed to carry the weight of ages, before he found it in him to speak.

He raised his head, looked upon Her face, and the warmth and beauty pouring through him made him want to weep. Instead, as a soldier, he chose anger. "I thought I was fighting for You. Not them."

"It is the same."

"No. It's not. Else You would have told us, wouldn't You? Are Your 'mysterious ways' just an excuse for what You believed we couldn't accept?"

If Luc had been there, Jonah was sure the dark angel would have annihilated him for that comment, for the contempt he could not keep out of his voice. But the blood was there, on his hands. Spreading across Her Sea of Glass, staining the purity of it, and he thought he could see the bodies floating there beneath the water, under where She stepped, heedless of them.

"Jonah . . ."

"I must go and protect David and Anna as best I can. Unless You are going to tell me You are willing to protect them."

What had he told Anna about Gabe? *They've stood inside that realm and screamed for answers, for accountability, and met only silence.*

"Life is just moments, Jonah," the Lady said instead. He closed his eyes, something shattering inside him. "Each one has the chance to be Heaven or Hell. Think of it. How did you feel, watching Anna laugh and play in the waves? In that single moment, when there was no thought, simply seeing her that way, being with her . . ."

He'd always been honest, until that one moment when She'd wanted him to come to Her feet, and the darkness in him had recoiled. An angel wasn't supposed to know what lying was. Unlike his Creatress, apparently. But wasn't that just the nature of being female? He could be honest about this, though.

"It was everything."

"Exactly. Now, another moment . . ." A swirl of darkness. Ronin. His chest lay open, head arched back, a final scream, so at odds with his laughter . . .

Jonah was backing up, away, and yet She was there, staying with him. "What was this moment, Jonah? It was also everything, wasn't it?"

"No." He struck out at this vision and it was as if he were in a human coffin, trying to rip the planks away, his fingers bleeding, breaking, and it didn't matter. Pain was better than loss.

The Lady was there, but that wasn't what he wanted. He wanted Anna, but he was covered in blood, and he couldn't stain her with that. He had to run, but there was no running . . .

He howled, and the Sea of Glass exploded in a fountain of blood, wiping out the vision, tumbling him back through the sky, much like the night he'd lost his wing. Falling over and over. When he landed, he hit sand, not the sea, and found himself in the middle of the desert again. It was pouring rain, so he was lying on his back in a deepening pool of grit and bloodstained water. The rain would cause a flash flood and everything would be washed away. The turtle they'd seen. The lizard. The bristlecone pines would stand fast as they had for centuries, some of them. Others would fall . . .

Jonah, listen . . .

"No," he snarled, rolling. He was on his feet, running. The sword was in his hand, something he knew, could control. The enemy was waiting, and that was something else he could predict, their rage and bloodlust. Clean. Pure. Like his own.

There was no hesitation in his wings now. Powerful, sure, arrowing him through the sky toward the battlefield. They were ahead of him, a shifting horde, red eyes, claws, fetid breath. He was alone, but he was coming home.

Plunging into them with a battle roar that thundered throughout the heavens, he felt the surge of it. *This* was where he belonged. Hacking, snarling, drowning in violence, reveling in it, for it had no mind, no purpose. He was all alone, and that was what he wanted. Oblivion. Death. He wished he could have brought Gabe from the trading post with him, away from the draining demands of a daughter-in-law and grandson who didn't understand, who were better off without him. This was where soldiers belonged. Death was the friend, the companion, the answer to it all.

The skies blackened further as his rage grew. He let it loose, cared not if it incinerated the heavens. Nothing existed but the battlefield. Nothing mattered. Power surged through him. As long as he had something to kill, he wouldn't have to feel.

A devil's deal he was ready and willing to take.

Silence and darkness. His enemies and his sword disappeared. The roar of water closed over his head, a long, low cry of pain, perhaps his own, or perhaps a goddess's. Tears fell from the sky, battering his skin. His mind was numb.

The shaman sat in the corner of the sweat lodge, the door now open, the fire dead. It was daylight, and Jonah could see the desert stretching out beyond them, endless miles of wasteland, cluttered by only a few scrub bushes. The red rocks looked like infected sores in the distance, swelling in the ferocious heat.

Sam held Jonah's sword balanced across his knees. As Jonah opened his eyes, sat up from where he lay next to the fire, the ropes of beads and shells fell away from his bare shoulders with a tinny clattering noise. Sam offered the sword.

"You had no right to knowingly endanger her," Jonah said, his voice hoarse.

"You had no right to minimize your importance," Sam countered, just as harshly. "Second only to Michael in the heavenly armies, you protect all of us, the earth, the heavens. Her."

"I'm not protecting Her." Jonah snarled it, his voice thick with the venom of his dreams, and was not surprised to see the stoic shaman flinch back. "I'm protecting Her little human rats, swarming all over the earth, creating holes for the enemy to use. Stay out of my way, shaman. You mean nothing to me."

He stepped out into the open air, stretched his wings. The pain was gone, the connection strong, sure. Something pulsed within him, powerful, waiting. Not eager, just calm and ready. Dangerous and inevitable as violence.

David.

Silence. Then, faintly, through a haze of blood and pain, a message came.

They have her. Sorry . . . Jonah. I failed you.

No. Jonah knew David wasn't to blame. *He* had failed Anna.

Twenty-two

WELL over a thousand years he'd fought. During most of those, he'd been a leader of some sort. A captain, a lieutenant, a commander. Now he was the Prime Commander, head of all the Dark Legion, the angels who fought the Dark Ones, which made him second only to Michael, who commanded all the legions. Total focus, total discipline. Total commitment. The fury of the elements channeled through his body were capable of a power that could crack Earth like an egg and disperse the yolk as a mere cloud of gas throughout the universe. Very few angels had that power.

It would have been incomprehensible to the power-hungry human world, that kind of capability turned over by the Goddess to Her select group of angels, unfettered by anything but morals, a clear sense of right and wrong.

But that choice of right over wrong, ultimately, was vital. It kept the universe balanced, the only law needed in the angels' world. If chaos came, Jonah knew it was because it was meant to be.

He took to the skies, for he knew where he would find Anna. The Dark Ones were making no attempt to hide themselves—from him at least. As he reached the Grand Canyon and managed the air currents to dive straight down a narrow defile into shadows and darkness, it reminded him of an earthly form of the Abyss. But that was a passing thought. He did not think much about anything, for there was only one thing. He'd been trained for that focus, and he used it now for the only thing that seemed to matter anymore.

The one fleeting thought which got through was what they might have done to her. That they might have treated her like Maggie, only with a far greater amount of time to defile her, rape her soul. He knew if he found that, then he might just use that destructive power to completely obliterate this planet, eliminating both Her problem and his at the same time. And if She opposed him in that, then he would fight the Lady Herself.

The cave entrance was narrow, but within a quarter mile it widened into a cavern as large as a dimly lit king's hall, domed with tons of red rock. Jonah was able to navigate the narrow corridor swiftly, his feet barely brushing the ground, and he heard them well before he reached that hall.

It was crowded with Dark Ones. Not yet an army, but the advance guard to one. As he paused in the archway, he noted the broad incline of rock that started in the center of the cavern like the arm of a sundial, running in a narrowing point to the upper ledge, probably the result of a thousand years of cave-ins. The symbolism of that was not lost on him. That rocky incline was covered with the writhing, hissing bodies of hundreds of Dark Ones, a nest of unnatural snakes. At the top, one stood taller than the rest. Big and broad as a giant, the Dark One reminded Jonah of how Anna had spoken of angels as large as giants. And earlier, how he'd said that men had once called all divine beings by the name of demon.

At the feet of this giant Dark One, Anna was chained to the ground.

As he stepped fully into the hall, the closest Dark Ones went aloft like startled pigeons, but lost no time diving around him like malevolent bats, veering away before making contact, taunting. There were too many to allow him to simply fly up to her, so he began to walk, ascending the mountain on foot, much as he'd made his journey over the past week. Packed so close together, he had no choice—and didn't care anyway—but to proceed by stepping on a head, a shoulder, a skeletal arm, feeling the greedy whisper of their hands, their saliva mark him, their nails occasionally dare to scratch his leg, his bare foot. None touched the purity of his wings, however, the symbol of his rank with the Lady.

He was surrounded by hundreds of them, the largest group he'd ever seen assembled since the last Great War. It was true, then. The fall of an angel could tear a hole in the universe so great . . . This was because of him. The false confidence he'd created in them.

I've become a liability, Luc. You'll know what needs to be done.

As he approached the top, he could hear her. The clank of the chains as she struggled, the thin fear in her voice as she nevertheless implored him. "No. My lord, you can't . . ."

They'd hurt her; he saw that. Blood had dried at the corner of her mouth and on her chin. Her eyes were haunted by whatever they'd inflicted upon her, but they hadn't done to her what they'd done to Maggie, probably because it would risk her life. They'd apparently believed he wouldn't deal for a damaged or dead mermaid. Never realizing the fact that they'd touched her at all meant he would come, if only to annihilate them. He stopped. "Free her."

"You know what we want." The giant's voice was a death rattle. Another Dark One, tall but not as tall as the giant, stepped before him, to the left of Anna.

When Jonah put out his hand, the Dark Ones nearest shrank away, except for that one. The creature's lips split in a decayed grin. From somewhere in the shadows of his body, he produced the sharp, iron-bladed dagger.

Jonah closed his hand over it. The weight of it was as much from the evil infused in the weapon as the metal itself. It was cold. So cold even the fires of Hell wouldn't warm it.

"Jonah, for the love of the Goddess, don't—"

He plunged the dagger into his own chest, just below the beat of his heart. When Anna screamed, the tall one's talons dug into the pale flesh of her arm, puncturing. Jonah stopped, his eyes narrowing, lips pulling back to bare his own teeth.

"Stop, or I stop."

The tall one removed his hand, though he held Anna back with a grip on the chains. Jonah started carving again. Methodically, while he kept his gaze on the other creature's face. Jonah wondered if the burning in its eyes was a reflection of the agony in his own, a pain beyond the physical, one that would drive him to madness. They were so close, angels and Dark Ones. Why should that surprise him? How many battles brought together odd moments of communion between enemies, only moments before they did their best to kill one another? The killing didn't really have much to do with the connection. Or maybe that *was* the connection.

The glowing flow of blue blood splashed to the rock. Dark Ones scattered, hissing in revulsion. Reaching in, he lifted his heart, took it out of his own body, but did not yet sever the arteries. The world was darkening around him. Darkening. Narrowing.

"Free her."

"Heart."

Jonah's lips curled back in another snarl, his rage made sharper by the pain ricocheting through his body. He could cut out his own heart and go on standing, but that didn't mean it didn't hurt like a son of a bitch to do it. Immortality didn't come with a pain-free card. "Let her go now, or I'll crush it in my hand and laugh at you as I die."

The giant's eyes narrowed. When he nodded, the tall one shoved Anna forward, the chains dropping away in a shower of sparks. Anna stumbled and fell, but then she was up and at his side. Jonah caught her arm with his free hand before she could reach toward his chest. "Be still."

She stopped, trembling, her eyes filled with tears. All that they'd done to her, but it was for him she was crying. His mermaid. His miracle.

He glanced at her then, bidding her to remain still with the silent command of his expression. Letting her go, he dipped his hand into his open wound and painted the blue cross on her forehead so it gleamed there, his mark. Her protection.

"Go," he said, and it was the tone of a man who had commanded an army for over five hundred years, and fought as a soldier over a millennium.

"No," she replied, and it was the tone of a woman who would not be budged.

"Anna."

Her face crumpled. "No," she whispered, though with the intensity of a shout. "I *won't* leave you with them." Despite that, her trembling knees gave way, but when she fell to her knees, she wound her arms around his legs. "You can't have him. You can't."

"Anna, come up here."

He had to wait a bit, and the Dark Ones milled restlessly, but they would not come near the blue circle of blood in which she now rested and he stood.

Eventually she rose, wiping her nose gracelessly with a hand, almost making him smile. "You need to go, Anna."

"I can't leave you here."

"You can. You will."

As he stared down into her face, Anna thought her whole world could be destroyed by the intensity of such a look. "There are many angels," he reminded her. "There is only one of you."

"There's only one of you," she sobbed out. "To me." She put her arms around him, despite the awkwardness of doing so while he was holding his own heart, his chest cut open. She put her cheek against the unmarked side, her breath sobbing out, lips brushing his bloody fingers. "I love you, Jonah. I love you with all of my heart."

"I know that, little one. And never has there been such a great gap between the value of a gift and the worth of the recipient."

She snuffled against him. "You told a joke. Your timing is wretched."

"No," he said into her hair, his eyes closing. Suddenly, there was a quiet in this dark and evil place, a still space of just the two of them. "You're just too good of heart to understand the cruelest truths. I wish you to be always so blessed. Go now. That's the gift I need from you. The mark on your forehead will allow you to leave, but it will only last awhile. You must warn the others. A battle will be coming, and I am the enemy my angels will be facing."

He put her away from him at last, firmly. Still balancing the heart in one hand, he looked between her and it. "You know this has always belonged to you, from the beginning. I give them only the shell. You take the true marrow of it with you."

"Jonah—"

But then he focused on the cross on her forehead, those

dark, fathomless eyes sharpening. Anna found her feet leaving the ground, her body caught in the grip of bonds she could not shake, her body going cold from the expression in his eyes. Deadly. Still. Lifeless. "No, Jonah. Don't."

"Good-bye," he said.

He sent her soaring through the air as if from a catapult, high over the heads of the Dark Ones who would be unable to touch her with his protection, and out through the tunnels from which he'd come.

Somewhere deep inside, Jonah wished he could have warned her. He wouldn't want her to be frightened by how high and fast he took her in the sky, without his presence around her. But that didn't matter anymore. He pushed that away and focused on her destination, the deep well of the ocean, near where they had first met. When he was sure he had her on target, and that she would slow as much as needed before she hit the water, many miles away, he turned his attention back to the matter at hand.

Vicious triumph had swollen the ranks around him, the shrieks of the Dark Ones building until they were deafening, until they were like a chant in a dark forest of evil pressing in against him. Where heat poured sweat off the skin, and the bowels turned to water.

They'd been afraid when Anna held him, he knew. They feared her goodness and its power over him. But what they should fear was what was coming. He would go down with them, but that was all right. Anna would be safe. Luc would make sure of it.

With a feral grin, he severed the arteries that connected the heart to his body, and dropped the pulsing organ into the skeletal hand of the tall Dark One.

High above the ground, the sun turned its face away. The Earth hid beneath the gathering shadow of black clouds as the skies began to weep.

Twenty-three

And lend the eye a terrible aspect.
—*Henry V*, SHAKESPEARE

ANNA landed in the water with a splash, the last scream she'd made to dissuade Jonah barely out of her lips. *No, no, no.*

The speed with which she'd moved through the air had been blinding. At another time it would have scared the life out of her. But as she slowed in the descent and had time to focus on the ocean to know where he was dropping her, she'd confirmed he'd taken her so far away there was nothing she could do to aid him further.

Not alone at least.

She spun in the water now, getting her bearings, airsick from the speed of her trip and now the rock of the ocean, her fear and stress combining to give the nausea weight. But she didn't have anything to throw up, not after being in the hands of the Dark Ones for nearly twenty-four terrifying hours.

Her first fear, all those hours ago, had been for David. He'd gone down, fighting amid a horde of them, such that she'd lost sight of him after several of the winged Dark Ones caught her arms and legs, tearing at her clothes and flesh even as they ascended with her. She'd seen the flash of his face, a battle snarl on his features. Her name had been on his lips, calling out to her.

When they got her to the cavern, they hadn't tried to invade her body as they had Maggie's, but they had fed on her fear, devising ways of tormenting her. Delighting in her humiliation, frightening her into nausea and vomiting and voiding her body, such that she was glad for the cleansing touch of the water now. She fought through the panic and disorientation that she knew would likely translate into a lifetime of nightmares once the shock wore off. But that didn't matter. She found her center, focused. Hoped the connection David had implied she had with Mina did exist.

Mina. I need you. And David. If he was still alive, Goddess willing. *Please. Help.*

She didn't even bother to transform, treading water and crying, hoping the emotional venting would steady her and make her coherent before they arrived, but she'd forgotten how quickly angels could move.

Less than two minutes after she sent out her mental call, she received a response. At any other time she would have been mesmerized by the sight of over twenty angels winging through the sky to her, their wings a variety of colors and patterns, all with the unearthly beautiful features and bodies the seraphim seemed to share.

Like Jonah. He'd known he was beautiful, was so casually arrogant about it, about using it to get her to do things. She wanted to smile about that, but all it brought was more tears.

When the water boiled beneath her, Mina surfaced with the speed of an eruption. The source of her propulsion gave Anna a wave of relief as David let her go and exploded from the sea, his wings showering them both as he acknowledged the incoming squadron. His face was bruised and swollen, and he was favoring his left arm. She remembered it had been snapped during the fight. The skin stretched over his rib cage was a mass of black and blue welts, but he'd obviously had someone work on him, for he was flying, though nowhere near as easily as she'd seen him do the night he and Lucifer came to their rescue.

"What happened, Anna?" he asked urgently, turning back to her now. His expression was far more intimidating than she'd yet seen it, and she didn't think it was just the effect of the many lacerations. Even Mina looked a little unsettled by him, or perhaps it was his quick ascent to the surface with her in tow.

"His heart." Anna could barely get the words past the sobs,

and she struggled to get hold of herself. Mina moved close enough to prop her up with one tentacle wrapped around her waist and another beneath the soles of her feet to stand upon. "He told me to call you. There are hundreds of them, maybe thousands . . ." She swallowed, made herself meet his eyes. "He told me to tell you . . . he'll be leading them, because they have his heart. Because of me. He was rescuing me."

"Great Goddess," David murmured, and his eyes closed briefly. Then they opened and he nodded to Mina. "Hold on tight."

There was no time for the two women to ask his meaning, for in the time it apparently took him to transmit the thought, the sea heaved, and a legion of dark-winged angels split from the depths like a forest of geysers exploding across the ocean.

Lucifer was the spearhead, a dagger strapped across his chest, the wicked-looking reaper's scythe grasped in his hand. The handle of the weapon was wrapped in a red sash that rippled, snapping the water off itself with a sharp noise in the wind.

"Where, Anna?"

Anna had to shake off this amazing spectacle to focus on David again. "The Grand Canyon. We need to come. I need to come with you."

She had to shout it, because before the first words were out of her mouth, he was already departing with the others. David paused, looking down at her from thirty feet, a distance that would make it easy to keep flying and ignore her request. Lucifer already had, taking to the skies with his dark battalion, joining the other angels and heading out like a migrating flock so thick they blotted out the sun.

"Why?"

"I have to be there."

David's doubt on that score was obvious, but Anna turned desperate eyes to Mina. "Please, tell him. You said that first day that I was important. I'm still important, aren't I?"

"No," Mina said flatly. "Your part is done."

"Wait," Anna shouted. David completed a flip that apparently cost him, for pain jolted across his features before he controlled it and leveled a scowl at her.

"What? Anna, I have to go. There's more at stake here."

"I know that," she snapped. "Goddess, you think I don't? Mina is lying to protect me, because she doesn't realize how much *is* at stake." Anna turned a pleading gaze to them both, even as Mina's tentacles squeezed her uncharitably. "Mina, if Jonah defeats the angels, that will be the end of our world. You know that. You know more about this than any of us. I have to go to him. I'm the only one who might be able to get through to him, aren't I? *Aren't I?*"

When Mina refused to answer, Anna snarled. Lifting her hand from the water, she slapped Mina across the face.

Mina's head whipped around, eyes blazing with rage and shock.

"Don't do this." Anna spoke low, fury and resolve in her tone like she knew Mina had never heard from her before. "Don't take choices away from me. I would never take one from you. Deny whatever else you wish between us, you will not deny that simple truth."

Mina stared at her, then shifted her glance to David, who'd picked up enough of the undercurrent of what might be true that he was willing to sacrifice the extra few seconds. Anna had seen it in his face the day he came to their aid. She knew he loved Jonah as she did, and if anything could save him, *and* win the battle . . .

"My vision said she is the only one who can save him, if he can be saved at all," Mina said at last. "But if she goes, I go."

Now it was Anna's turn to look startled, not only by the bald admission of what Mina had only implied up to now but because she'd never known Mina to leave the ocean's embrace. But David was already speaking to two angels that hovered behind him, apparently part of his small command. They swooped down, one plucking Anna out of the water, quickly anchoring her to his waist so he could fly with wings spread and hold on to her.

"Anna, meet Orion. He'll get you there." David dropped, came back under Mina and lifted her up as her tentacles dissolved and she took the easier-to-carry human form that could also do without the water. Though that didn't seem much of a factor at the moment, since it had begun to rain. Heavy, fat drops that Anna realized were salty and warm, splashing down with a touch of silver against the churning sea.

"Tears of the Goddess," David said grimly. "Hang on."

———

WEATHERMEN across the globe, checking on area forecasts, quickly realized an astounding phenomenon. It was raining . . . well, everywhere. A cloud cover had gathered over Earth, surrounding it like a thick shroud. Without a sure sense of why, a soul-deep despair closed over hearts and minds. Humans began migrating to the churches, seeking hope, going to their knees to pray to whatever god they felt might be listening . . .

———

SHE'D known angels could travel fast, but experiencing it twice in such a short time was something entirely different. It was like a quick blink, coupled with an impression of great gravitational pull as Anna was rushed through the air beyond the speed of sound or senses. Then she was there, hovering over a battlefield the likes of which she was sure the world had never seen before.

They were over a wide, isolated chasm in the Grand Canyon. On the opposite side, Jonah stood in solitary splendor on a spear of rock sculpted by the irresistible forces of nature. On the lip of the canyon's edge, about fifty yards behind him, the Dark Ones created a mass of darkness so far back it was obvious her count had been correct. There were thousands of them.

Having just been their prisoner, the sight of so many ignited that same sense of fear and despair in her. However, apparently because of the presence of the angels, it didn't overwhelm her, drive her to her knees. But when she made herself look back toward Jonah, she faltered, despite herself.

She'd been with him when he was gentle, laughing, even seen a more dangerous side of him, but yet she'd never truly feared him.

The angel standing upon the tower of rock had a dark, expressionless countenance, his wings at half fold along his back. The silver and white feathers were stained crimson red, a wavering, sweeping pattern that kept shifting like clouds passing over the land in the desert. His dark hair fluttered over his bare shoulders, which were not tense, just set in calm battle readiness. One hand rested on the hilt of the sword where it was driven into the rock between his spread feet. The Dark Ones milling on the ledge were gaining in volume as the angels gathered on the opposite ledge. The din was overwhelming. It was obvious their confidence was great, and somewhere in that mass of evil, she knew Jonah's heart was being held. She looked hard, swept her gaze over the Dark Ones' army.

There. She caught a glimpse, in the third row of the melee. A blue light, a container of translucent material spelled to hold the treasure, the one that would give them dominion over Jonah's actions. His body . . . even his soul.

No, she couldn't believe that. He'd despaired, yes, but his despair didn't have the capacity to become true evil.

"David." She caught his attention. With several of his command, he hovered just above her and Mina on the lower ledge where they'd been deposited. There was a shallow hollow at the back, against the canyon wall, which provided some shelter from the rain as well as an underground water source, trickling out of a crevice in that concave surface.

The young angel's gaze narrowed as he followed the direction of her pointing finger. When he registered what he was seeing, he muttered an oath and pulled two daggers from his chest harness.

"No." Lucifer came in to his left, sweeping through the ranks, but pausing at David's shoulder, brushing it with a wing. "No, David. He would cut you down before you reached it." A faint, humorless smile coursed over the dark angel's face. Anna noted that, like all the angels, he appeared unfazed by the rain, not even blinking from the drops rolling down his face. His voice carried over the rushing noise with reverberating command. "This is not your Goliath to face. You and your command are to stay on this ledge, defend it. As for you, no hand to hand unless unavoidable. Use your formidable archery skills only. You are in no condition to fight."

"But—"

Lucifer gave him a searing look and David subsided, though with a flicker of frustrated anger in his gaze. As Lucifer left him, ascending to take the front of the field again, a flash of lightning illuminated the reaper's blade. At the same moment, Anna saw Jonah shift, almost imperceptibly, but squaring off with his mirror image across the field.

Oh, Goddess. It was suddenly so clear. Who else's strength could bring Jonah down?

We do not move on him until I give the order. Lucifer's command resounded inside every mind, even Anna's and somehow Mina's, if the startled look on the witch's face was any indication. *Jonah may still be fighting their hold. If we attack first, it will strengthen their command of him, because his instinct will be to defend against any show of aggression from us.*

His glance shifted down and remarkably, Anna found herself the focus of it. *I repeat. No* angel *should act until Jonah makes his first move.*

She only had to imagine blue blood running down that wicked scythe to propel her into motion. She spun around to Mina, who was still squatting like a dour omen on the ledge where the angel had deposited her. "Mina, I need to get to Jonah."

"Of course you do. Would you like me to defeat the army while we're at it, and let the angels go back to preening their feathers and admiring each other?"

Anna flinched as the two angels of David's command within earshot glanced down to give the witch a less than friendly look, but Anna had more important things to do than to smooth ruffled feathers. Literally.

Heavens, all the remarks she could tease Jonah with, if only she'd had a lifetime to do so, rather than one week.

"Mina." She took the witch's arm. "I need to get close to him. Can you get me to that ledge and help me spin enough protection to keep the Dark Ones from affecting me or trying to interfere? We have to try and stop this before it starts. Jonah won't be able to live with himself if he's harmed his own men. He couldn't bear knowing he'd taken their lives."

And knowing just a tenth of what she sensed was his full power, she knew that could be a lot of lives.

"You're assuming he's going to survive," Mina said dryly. "Besides which, it doesn't matter. I can't get you there by spell alone."

"No, not by spell alone." Anna gave her a steady, even look. Mina's face altered, her attention darting to David before coming back to Anna.

"No."

"Mina, please. You know I'm right. Fly, and I'll sing to protect you. As I sing, you can protect me. Drop me on the ledge and back off, holding the protection as long as you can."

Mina closed her eyes. "You're determined to die, aren't you?"

"No. I'm determined to give him back his heart." Anna dared, put gentle hands to either side of Mina's face, though outside the cowl of her cloak. "Mina, I trust you. We've only had each other, really, haven't we? And so I think of you as my friend, no matter what you think of me. Help me."

When Mina trembled in a curious way, Anna's throat grew thick. "I don't want to die like the others," she said quietly. "My mother, her mother . . . Arianne herself. Without hope, with no point. I always knew I would die young . . . That much I couldn't stop. But I get to choose how." Her chin rose and her resolute gaze flickered to David, who'd dropped down to the ledge, curiosity and wariness in his expression. She shifted her attention back to Mina. "I got to love an angel, Mina. And I may die saving him, which means he can go on protecting all of you, so you can find *your* meaning, your hope. It doesn't get better than that."

She glanced up. "Look around you. Do you think this is the way the world is supposed to look?"

The tears of the Goddess had continued to fall, so heavy that flooding had already begun in the canyon. The color of the drops had changed, red and black as well as warm, salty and clear, streaking and staining the angels so they looked like wild Scottish warriors. Forks of lightning crossed the sky without pause now, interspersed with fierce thunder. The lightning struck outcroppings of rock, sending them tumbling into the chasm, into the swollen river forming below. Still the Dark Ones bellowed, adding to the thunder with the stomping of their feet, the beating of their fists against the earth. The echoes could be felt in the chest, pounding at the base of the skull.

Anna shifted her attention to the gathering of angels above. He had said he'd trained many of them personally. They were arranged behind Lucifer now, and while she saw nothing in their posture but battle readiness, she noticed how their eyes rested on their Prime Commander. If they felt any of the same emotion she was feeling in her heart, she knew each was praying he wouldn't have to see him cut down. More than Jonah's soul could be lost in this fight.

"Mina," Anna pleaded. "Please."

"I hate you for this," Mina said darkly. With a yank, she sent her robes tumbling to her feet.

It was enough to catch David's attention, but his expression was only a momentary impression before Anna could tell that Mina shut them all out. Maybe so she wouldn't have to register any revulsion or disgust, or worse, macabre curiosity. It was always difficult to know what Mina was thinking. But now her body rippled, split and exploded in size. She made the transition rapid, perhaps due to time constraints and so that she couldn't change her mind. It also made Anna jump back with a curse, and startled the angels, which Anna was sure was a mild satisfaction to the prickly seawitch before the pain of the rapid transformation tore through Mina's body.

What began as a woman's cry of pain ended as a dragon's roar as she completed the conversion and stood over Anna on the tiny ledge, her wings keeping her balance, her nostrils smoking, red and blue eyes glowing, silver and sapphire scales glittering like polished steel.

"Holy Goddess . . ."

As Anna ignored David's reaction and put her foot on Mina's knee, over a talon curving out from it that was long as an elephant's tusk, David apparently recalled himself enough to lunge forward, catch her arm.

"What are you—"

"I'm going to try and get his heart back before the battle starts," Anna said. "When the call comes for your battle, you all do what you must do. But I can try this now."

David put his other hand on Mina's broad and muscular shoulder, ignoring her warning growl. "Anna. Jonah gave his heart to save you."

"Yes, he did. Because he knew you all would stop him. Lucifer can likely kill him." Her voice trembled as she glanced at the still form of the dark-winged angel. She could feel the energy pulsing off him like a solid wall, even at this distance. "*Will* kill him. Jonah knew that. But there's a bigger battle at stake. We both know it. He was willing to let the Dark Ones have him because he thinks he's no good to you all anymore. He thinks his soul is already lost. I can give that back to him."

She picked up Mina's discarded cloak to use as a saddle to protect her from the cut of the scales.

"How?"

"I don't know." She gave a half laugh that she realized came out sounding a little wild, because concern flickered over David's face. "I just know it has to be me, if anyone can do it. Mina knew it from the first."

"No." He repeated it. "Look at it out there. You're both mad. You won't get halfway across that field before their arrows cut you down."

Anna stopped, taking her foot from Mina's knee, and turned to face him. David should be dead. She remembered again, even more vividly now, how savagely he'd fought to keep her from the twenty or so Dark Ones that seized her out of the air. She'd underestimated him as a dangerous force and a fighter, probably because she'd seen him in the company of Lucifer and Jonah. But David had held on to her with one arm, fought with the other. What he lacked in experience had been compensated for with unflagging courage, determination and levelheadedness, where most would have lost their minds to terror. He would have been killed before relinquishing her, so she suspected a fortunate blow had knocked him senseless and dropped him into the sea. The Dark Ones had been more concerned about spiriting her away than making sure an angel was dead.

While there'd simply been too many, she knew he felt just as responsible for Jonah being on that rock as she did. For that reason she took the time now, despite the screaming impatience in her head to get to Jonah.

"David, I don't know if I can change anything, or gain you a valuable moment of distraction"—though her mind shied away from the thought she might give Lucifer and that horrible blade the opportune moment to cut Jonah down—"but Mina saw in her vision that I was the only one who could lead him back to himself. I thought that meant getting him to the shaman."

Her voice wavered. "To be honest, I was so relieved, getting him there, because I couldn't imagine what someone like me could do for someone as powerful as Jonah. But my heart tells me my task isn't done yet. And I love him so much . . ."

Despite herself, her eyes filled with tears, though she kept her back straight and voice firm, so he wouldn't think sentiment was driving her to foolishness. "If he doesn't leave this field alive, I won't be able to bear a world where he was struck down like this."

David held her gaze a long moment, and she saw a shimmer in the brown depths. Agreement. But he still didn't release her arm. She set her jaw, her control fraying.

"Jonah isn't evil. For a thousand years, he's protected us all," she snarled. "Now, damn it all, it's time to protect him. Fight for him."

The shrieking across the canyon swelled. Anna's gaze snapped in that direction, and David turned. The enemy shifted and the angels adjusted. Her heart nearly stopped beating, thinking her chance lost as the battle began. But apparently something else had happened, for the Dark Ones remained where they were.

"Christ, they're just posturing to wear on our nerves. Or Luc's temper."

With relief, she felt David's restraining hand leave her arm. Bending, he offered her a hand for a leg up as he cast her a wry glance. "I can tell you've been around Jonah. You sounded just like him there, for a second."

As she settled on the cloak, unsure how to respond to that, he turned his attention to Mina, whose great, serpentine blue eye blinked at him with her usual irascibleness. She showed him her teeth.

"A giant, temperamental predator," he observed. "Why am I not surprised? You couldn't shape-shift into a puppy? Something cuddly?"

Mina blew a stream of fire out of her nostrils. Anticipating her, he was already moving back, a graceful though shallow leap aided by his wings. The angels above him called out in alarm, which he quickly quelled with a waved hand.

"Good luck," he said. "Tell me your approach so I can communicate it to Luc."

"Mina and my own magic can protect me enough to get me

there"—she hoped—"and then I'll send her back here. At that point, it's up to me and Jonah. You'll stay safe and well." She directed that to the transformed seawitch. "No stupid heroics."

Mina's brow lowered. "Pot calling kettle . . ." she hissed, the words almost a rumble.

"I mean it. Promise—"

A sudden cacophony of shouts, and Anna spun to see the Dark Ones surging to the cliff edge. Jonah had hefted his sword, bringing it up so the flashing fire in the sky turned it molten gold.

"No, it's too late. That's a signal—"

"Go." Anna urged Mina. The dragon-witch launched herself.

David cursed, but didn't have his angels intercept, despite the apprehension that filled him, watching them wing across the open space toward that terrifying army, the horrible nightmare of who was leading them.

As the dragon flew up through the sky, headed for the column of rock holding a damned angel, he sent a message to Lucifer, telling their temporary commander what the mermaid was doing. Then he sought the magic that was most readily accessible to him. David prayed.

———

ANNA sung as she'd never sung before, weaving protection around them, feeling Mina's magic joining hers, propelling them through the air on her powerful wings, the shielding moving with them as a blue mist.

Arrows shot by Dark Ones speared through the air, seeking a weak point to stop the dragon's approach, but bounced off the shield. Jonah did not move, his gaze merely turning to them. The sword was still upright in his hand, but Anna was relieved to see he'd not made a move to launch himself or the army. Their surge had apparently been just another antic to keep the angels on edge. Or something else. Why were they waiting?

As they got closer, she realized he didn't wear the battle skirt which bore the red color of the Goddess's seraphim, but sleek black breeches made of some type of slippery hide, supple and formfitting such that she had a sudden sick feeling it was something's skin. If he'd grumbled over a little snugness in the seat of his jeans, she couldn't imagine what Jonah in his normal state of mind would have been saying now.

The solid dark eyes which had been at first so unsettling and then so much more expressive than she'd expected were now twin chasms of hellfire, crimson and gold, flickering like living flame. His upper body was bare, so that she could see the angry red but sealed wound where he'd taken out his own heart. The same black and crimson rain had painted him, giving him the fearsome mien of a barbaric warrior. The ends of his wet hair, tight and sleek on his skull as those pants were on his body, were dripping the stained water onto his broad shoulders, creating a mottled pattern.

He'd always been breathtaking, and he still was, in a horrible, fascinating way that called to her loins even as her heart beat faster, the rabbit recognizing the trap even as she was drawn closer to it. She saw nothing in his face that acknowledged or recognized her.

Anna knew beings could become what she never expected them to be, a betrayer or an unexpected friend, but no matter what came next, what she'd known of him had been true. So she clung fiercely to that.

And in truth, this form was not far from his other self. Jonah was not the soft and fuzzy angel of human lore, the sweet cherub flitting over the clouds, the feminine power come to lay a brow on the laboring woman's head. He was the warrior angel, the bringer of justice. The line between that and bringer of death and chaos had always been so close to his foot, just a step away. She knew what side of that line he belonged on, but suspected he no longer could see where the line was drawn.

At some point, he'd stopped wiping away the blood that kept hiding it from him, and no one else did it for him. The danger of becoming such a strong leader. Atlas did such a good job holding up the world, eventually no one believed he needed any help doing it.

She wondered if the journey to the Schism had been to arm and prepare her for this moment, even before Jonah had gone to the shaman. She didn't know what had transpired there, but she remembered what Gabe's daughter-in-law had said to her when Anna had gone back into the general store to talk to Pat.

*It's so hard for them to come back to what seems like the
trivia of daily life, to find meaning again after that dark place
of blood and death. Those images are so strong and powerful
and real. They have to find the reality in the quieter, gentler
things they were defending. But the longer they're in that dark
place, the harder it is to do that . . .*

While it might be ludicrous to imagine Jonah going to a
veteran's support meeting, she didn't see any difference between five years and a thousand years immersed in such a life
of bloodshed and horror. How could the soul embrace light
after seeing the dark side hiding just behind it?

That large, powerful hand gripping the sword had cupped
her in his palm when she was as easy to harm as a butterfly.
He'd kissed her with enough passion to consume her in flame.
What she'd said to David about her protecting him might seem
absurd, but somehow she knew protection in this case had
nothing to do with strength or battle skill.

Anna gasped, her hold on Mina's neck broken as they
slammed into a wave of collective power, the Dark Ones' energy force projected forward to keep them from their objective. She scrabbled for a purchase on the neck scales, cutting
her hands as Mina righted herself from the abrupt flip with a
growl of pain and rage.

Anna renewed her efforts, increasing the strength of her
voice, singing without words, just pure, clear notes. She heard
Mina's throaty roar as well, the dragon's voice sounding odd
over the words of the spell as a stream of flame shot from their
shielding and out over the cliff edge, driving the Dark Ones
back and disrupting their attempt enough that Mina was able
to bank and wheel toward the spear of rock.

The first line snarled, regrouping, fire erupting in skeletal
fingers, ready to be launched. Three hurled it toward them,
only to have the flame hit Mina's own, launched from her nostrils. It exploded back upon them, causing confusion in their
immediate ranks.

"Great Lady, Mina, how did you—"

"No time. Keep singing." The dragon roared it, and Anna
obeyed as she saw the Dark Ones renew their efforts, felt her
friend's dragon body tremble beneath her.

A quick glance behind her showed the angels were anticipating this drawing to a head. Their ranks had closed, flanks splitting off, positioning. They'd held back to see what would occur, but were probably quickly realizing that her and Mina's actions might spur things into battle whether or not Jonah gave whatever signal the Dark Ones were hoping for him to make.

Given the nature of Dark Ones, she was again surprised that hadn't yet happened. It *should* have happened. She realized a great deal of activity was going on around the sealed sphere with the heart. With desperate hope, she wondered if they'd figured out enough to hold his movements, but not enough yet to direct him into battle. Which suggested Lucifer's intuition, to hold back on taking the offense, might be wise. But their outcry when Jonah raised the sword said they were figuring it out. Any moment now, they could have full command of his actions, not just the ability to hold him passive. If Jonah hadn't gotten her free, sent her ahead with the warning that summoned the angels, they would have had much more time to prepare.

"Mina!"

Mina's wings flapped erratically as several of the arrows got through and one lodged under her front leg, in the vulnerable, unscaled skin. She dropped several yards and then recovered, careening down toward the rock, harrowingly off center so it appeared as if they might fly into the center of the teeming mass of Dark Ones. Blood came from one of her nostrils, and Anna could feel her great dragon's heart laboring like a sledgehammer against the ribs beneath her legs.

"Going to have to drop you next to him now . . . Will just have to tip you. They're eroding my protection . . . Be ready."

"Mina, you fly clear and don't worry about me further, you hear me? You've done what you can."

"Now," Mina rasped, and arced sharply to the inside, taking a spiraling dive down toward Jonah's position, a low swoop that put her close to the edge. Anna sprang from her back into space and Mina gave her an inadvertent boost with her wing, knocking into her as Jonah's attention turned and the sword came swinging around. Mina shrieked and surged forward, blocking Anna as she fell on the narrow platform and slid over the edge.

Anna cried out as the sword connected with the seawitch, a glittering blow that sheared off the tip of Mina's wing and raked her breast and back haunch, severing a major artery, if the spray of blood across them both was any indication. But then the dragon was fully turned, winging drunkenly out of range, back toward the angels.

As Anna clung to the edge of the rock, she had to brace herself. The wind was rising, pulling at her as it started to vortex around the spear of stone on which she now found herself. The sky had darkened even further, as if it were night. On top of that all of the Dark Ones were still screeching, of course. The angels were pounding on drums, the rhythmic, dangerous reverberation a counterpoint to the enemy's discordant cacophony. All of it was pounding inside Anna's heart, threatening to make it explode with fear as she recognized what she'd been dropped into the middle of.

How much longer would the stalemate go on? Was it crazy of her to think that Lucifer was giving her as much time as he could, to see if she could make a difference? However, unlike her own people, or humans, she didn't have to convince the host at her back that visions, prophecies and even irresistible gut compulsions could be vital to an outcome in a situation like this.

Anna glanced down beneath her scrambling feet. While open air would have been terrifying, it couldn't compare to the winged Dark Ones inhabiting the flooded chasm, ready to finish off any angel that fell. Even now several were speeding upward toward her location, likely thinking to pluck her off the side, dash her against the rocks.

During the hours they'd held her, she'd never been so afraid in her life. Their malevolence had been like the oppressive sides of a coffin, no escape from the inevitability of her fate. At times, she was sure she was going to go mad. If she hadn't been distracted by her argument with David, she wasn't sure she'd have had the courage to fly back toward them. But she was here for Jonah. He needed her.

As Jonah turned to look down at her, the thought steadied her, despite his fearsome mien. She couldn't think about what might be coming up beneath her, that she might be seconds away from hurtling through the sky. She struggled to get her elbows up, feeling his gaze like flame smoldering its way down her spine as she succeeded, dug into the flat surface of rock and somehow pulled herself up and forward, using her toes in the crevices on the steep sides. He wasn't helping, but then again, he wasn't stepping on her hands, either.

She could be thankful for small favors even as it wrenched her heart to remember his smallest acts of protection toward her, like lifting her into the pickup truck or making sure she had a soft bed in the cellar. Spreading out wings to give her a moment's shade.

The Dark Ones weren't firing arrows at her anymore, another boon. Probably because they didn't want to hit him. Also, that spiraling wind was rising, competing with the animal shrieking of the skeletal creatures.

She'd wondered if it would make more sense to transform into the pixie, a smaller, lighter target, quicker. Goddess knew, the wings would have been useful about now. But somehow she knew she would command Jonah's attention more readily as a woman proportionate to his size, who could meet him eye to eye, body to body. The Dark Ones couldn't change that he was male, and never had she known him not to be overwhelmingly virile in that regard. Perhaps pure and primitive physical instincts could offset or at least crack the most complex magics or emotional barriers. Plus, this wind would have buffeted her about like a leaf.

Wriggling up, she rolled to a sitting position to look up, up and up the body of a possessed, deadly angel. Holy Goddess, she'd forgotten how tall he was. Or perhaps he'd never looked quite so intimidating to her.

"Jonah." She made it to one knee. The wind shrieked, making her notice it had actually formed a funnel around the perimeter of the ledge as she'd rolled onto it. When her hand passed just over the edge, she realized they were in the still eye of a tornado and those Dark Ones that had speared up from below were being held back. Still harrowingly close, roaring their threat of death and pain at her, but on the other side of that wall of wind. Mina was still all right, then, for it felt like her magic. Then again, the stubborn witch might be using her last reserves to buy Anna time. The wound he'd inflicted on Mina had looked bad, a sword strike backed by angel fire.

"Jonah," she repeated.

He jerked at the sound of her voice. When she dared a glance at the Dark One army on the ledge fifty yards away, her heart faltered at the display of rage and dripping fangs.

"Kill her. Kill her." The strident mantra was being taken up and down the line. Their anticipation and bloodlust had an element of . . . glee.

Oh, Great Goddess. The angels hadn't fallen into their trap of instigating Jonah to fight, so she was Plan B. If he killed her before all the assembled, it would confirm where his loyalties now lay and the bloodlust would take him. Her blood would be the catalyst for the massacre they craved.

That paralyzed her, until she made herself think again what was at stake. If evil won this battle, there would be a whole world of humans to sweep through and claim. Matt and Maggie, Gabe and his family. The Dark Ones would take over their hearts and souls, banishing any good in them, destroying their souls so the Goddess would be alone in the universe . . . No angels, nothingness.

She would not give in to fear.

Anna looked toward them again, forced herself to meet the eyes of several on the front line, including the tall one who had chained her, the giant behind him.

You may take me, and yet you will get nothing. I will poison you with faith and love even as you tear the flesh from my bones. I belong to an angel. He said so from the beginning, and you can't poison that.

Then her focus was yanked away as a hand curled around her biceps. She drew in a painful breath as Jonah pulled her to her feet, the sword still lifted in one hand.

"Jonah," she sang it softly, but infused it with all the magic she could. It brought confusion to his face and protesting howls to the Dark Ones. A flash of light coursed through the heart sphere, just a flicker at the corner of her eye, but that was gone as he released her. Then pain exploded behind her eyes, as he hit her in the face with his fist.

It was a solid blow to the mouth that snapped her head back, such a solid-sounding *crack* that for a harrowing moment she feared he'd broken her neck. She skidded back on the platform of rock, her head going over the edge, and only fear of that drop galvanized her past the pain to roll, struggle back to her feet. She made it to her knees, her head spinning, and swayed there.

He was back in the center again, staring at her, impassive, those crimson eyes like raw wounds.

Taking a breath to steady herself, she crawled toward him, knowing that standing without help wasn't going to be possible. She made it just between his toes, which were covered in hard black boots, and sat back on her heels, trying to push down nausea. Tilting back her head, she held that unholy gaze, seeking Jonah. Laying her hand on his hip bone, she curled her fingers into the waistband of the black breeches and started to lift herself onto unsteady feet, leaning into him, bracing her elbow against his thigh.

She'd almost made it to her feet when he closed his hand on her wrist, turned it, yanking her sideways, and broke her arm. It dropped her to the ground again as she screamed. The Dark Ones roared their approval.

———

Back on the other side of the ledge, David was at Lucifer's side. "We have to help her."

"No," Lucifer said, his dark gaze transfixed on the terrible scenario. "Wait. See to the witch. Her protection is weakening. The wind is slackening around them."

David's gaze snapped downward, to the ledge where Mina had crash-landed. He had gone to her immediately, only to have her snarl and drive him and his angels back as she focused her energy on her primary task, which was apparently keeping as much protection around Anna as she could in the form of that tornado of wind. Hoping it was what Jonah was doing to Anna that was disrupting the witch's field, and not the injuries she'd sustained, he dove down to join her. But his heart caught in his throat as he descended, for he saw the witch was casting her faltering spell in an ever-widening pool of her own blood.

Twenty-four

Look well, for I am a form difficult to discern, I am a
new moon, I am an image in the heart. When an
image enters your heart and establishes itself, you flee in
vain. The image will remain within you, unless it is a
vain fancy without substance, sinking and vanishing like
a false dawn. But I am like the true dawn;
I am the light of your lord.
—RUMI

"JONAH." Anna managed to get his name past her bloody lips once again. Despite the din, the flashing light and horrible darkness, the oppressive weight of Dark Ones so terrifyingly close and Jonah's own overpowering energy. "My lord."

His head was tilted, as if listening to something beyond her, but now he slowly canted his head the other way, his gaze turning, click by click toward her, like the macabre hands of a ticking bomb. His hand gripped the sword, so easy and comfortable, and she thought of how many countless times that flared guard had caught blood running down the blade so it didn't make his grasp slippery as he wielded it. How often he'd been showered, bathed, drenched in the life fluids of others.

"Jonah," she repeated, just a whisper. The wind was dying, and a Dark One dove at their platform. Before she could try to evade its approach, it struck a wall of light that appeared several feet from her. The Dark One crashed into it, his body briefly illuminated by electrical current. Screaming, he fell into the chasm.

Was Mina still protecting her? Or channeling energy from the angels?

She was guessing the latter, for Jonah's gaze fired. That ominous sense of energy leaped, the energy she now knew was the power signature from an angel preparing for battle. Jonah lifted the sword, the tip moving in a harrowing arc over her. She thought for a moment it was over, braced herself for the blow, but then he stopped, head tilting, eyes studying the opposing army, who had not moved forward.

His instinct will be to defend against any show of aggression from us . . .

The blade's end came to rest in his opposite hand, a barrier between them. She got to her feet, took a shaky step forward.

"You remember when you held me in your hand, as a fairy?" She asked it in a voice laden with pain, sorrow. "So gentle. I wasn't the least bit afraid you'd hold me too tightly. When I tumbled from the air, I knew you'd catch me. You're an angel, Jonah. You protect. You love. You are love."

"I am death. Destruction. The end of everything. Despair. Darkness."

His voice sent chills down her spine, for it was not Jonah's voice. Sibilant, sonorous, it reverberated across the canyon and back, and ruptured her eardrums. Even as she cried out from the new torment, the voice sapped vital energy from her.

They had his heart, after all. There was no hope.

But he'd said it was the shell. That she had the true substance of it in herself, beating inside her own heart.

Anna was on her knees again, breathing heavily, her eyes streaming. It took four or five precious moments before she could get her body to do what she wanted it to do, but then she started to sing once more.

With her mouth bleeding, and her arm hanging uselessly at her side, the notes were plaintive, not rich and strong, but the magic was there, even though she could only hear it in her head. She wove it into the song, called out to him.

She remembered then how she'd used it with the grieving dolphin. The creature could not bear the higher, stronger notes of her magic, so she'd made them soft, soothing, healing, giving him visions of his brother and the many things that had given him joy.

Jonah had given her those images that first night in her cottage. Allowed her to make a lullaby of them . . .

Like Ronin's laughter . . . the bonding with his angels . . . fighting to protect the Lady, seeing with each sunrise and each passage of season that he'd been successful, that life had gone on . . .

Now she added in other things. Her love, which she would

never take away from him. She would always belong to him, be only his . . .

Anna could feel Mina still helping. Her life force was ebbing . . . *Mina, no* . . . but still, it was there. Friendship, love. Those were the constants. The simple truths, unclouded by motives . . .

Meaning and action. Jonah's heart had gotten lost somewhere between the two. At some point he'd continued to act, hoping the meaning would come back into it, somewhat like watching the wind arrange the clouds and hoping they'd take a shape he'd recognize.

That was it. It had niggled at the back of her mind from the beginning, what it was that had caused Jonah to go with her on their odd quest, the way his eyes would rivet on her and he actually made her believe he wanted her, cared for her.

By some strange twist of Fate that had elevated a simple mermaid into the key to the universe, in her was the embodiment of everything that gave his fight meaning.

In Gabe she had seen the despairing detachment, the way he could no longer feel anything. He'd been imprisoned inside his own soul, unable to escape the nightmare it had become. But in the way his eyes followed his daughter-in-law and grandson, he knew that somehow they were the key, if he could only get across the chasm his heart had become.

Sometimes a soldier couldn't fight for the world anymore. But he could fight for the one he loved. Countless mighty armies had fallen before people who, driven to the wall, with no larger principles, had won by fighting for the things that mattered most to them. Home and family.

Her voice strengthened as she made her way slowly to her feet, all the way this time, praying she wouldn't pass out. The music healed her ears so she could hear again. The vortex of wind strengthened once again as well, beginning to sing with her, a rushing backdrop, and it was just the two of them. Even if it all passed away, as everything must, it had existed, those joyous things she had shared with him. The amazing things he had seen and known. Some of them would exist forever. Other things would be replaced by new wonders, the gift of the ebb and flow of time.

It was no easy thing, processing all that when mired in a

nightmare world of fear and doubt, but she kept turning the wheel in her head desperately as he reached for her again, knowing her time was running out. It wasn't only one wheel; it was many wheels, many spokes, many details. All of them made a calliope so brilliant, a tapestry of threads that kept weaving on the looms of Fate, ever forward, backward, ever the same place. Hate and evil and death . . . Farewells would always exist because love, joy, pleasure, wishes would forever exist as well, unable to be destroyed.

Love could fall short and disappoint, but it would come back stronger for the lesson.

She put up her hands to try to stop him, but of course she couldn't. He hit her in the face again, and she only managed to duck it enough to save him from knocking her unconscious. When she fell this time, he kicked her, hard enough that he almost sent her over again, but she caught hold of the rock, pulled herself back onto the ledge, faced him from her back.

"I'm not afraid, Jonah. Neither were Ronin and all the rest. We love you. We will always love you, and you love us. That's what the Goddess is, the very essence of Her. Don't you understand, and remember? We aren't separate. Her compassion and justice are our compassion and justice. Love, and how we love each other, we're the heart, lungs, soul of Her, how we weave together, and only if we unravel, let that die, will all the good die."

Energy had started gathering around him. She remembered how it felt with Lucifer, how it had made her dizzy. This was going beyond that, into a pounding in her head, and the flame was growing in his eyes, the din of the Dark Ones exploding. It was no longer a simmering anger, but a surge of fiery triumph. The light in his eyes was their light. They had full control of him.

She wasn't ready to give up, even at the evidence of her failure. If it was her last act, whether it did any good or not, it was the one thing she wanted, needed, to do. And it was for herself as much as for any noble hope to save the world. She therefore asked forgiveness for her selfishness before she forced her failing body back to its feet.

She straightened, paying no attention to the blood that was now leaking from her nose, from her ears, making her hair itch on her neck. Tears were squeezing from her eyes from the huge pressure building around her, as if she'd sunk far down into the ocean, where a human could be crushed.

Ignoring the shuddering in her limbs, the throb of her broken arm, the fact that she could hear her organs pumping, desperately working as the weight grew upon them, she moved forward a step. Then another, struggling against that building energy, tears of effort mixing with the hemorrhaging to hold his gaze.

Oh, Goddess, it hurts. Help me. Help me reach him. Touch him just once more.

His fingers tightened on the blade, the angel fire surging blue and strong along it, though laced with that terrible blackness. But then she was there before him, looking up into his face, so temptingly close. That firm, sensuous mouth and sloping cheekbones, the hair like silk fluttering around his face. Her arms felt too heavy to lift, but she lifted the unbroken one anyway.

Perhaps the world around them had burst into flame, for now, this close to him, she seemed to be surrounded by conflagration. There were no details beyond the two of them, two beings trapped in a cyclone of Hell. When she touched his skin, it was like poison, black death rushing through her skin and into her veins, making her jerk, her fingers clutch.

"You *are* death and destruction," she said fiercely. "In order to bring mercy. To those who know only evil, you bring them oblivion. You keep things safe so that good can survive, so that evil can never fully take over. You protect me, and everyone like me.

"Put your hope and faith inside of my heart, and I'll make sure it's always there for you. After every fight it will be here, inside me, even if it's just inside the memory of me."

"No . . . heart. Not again."

She knew so little of him and yet so much. She knew he was in there, somewhere. "Just feel. Stop thinking and just feel . . ."

A flicker in his gaze and then she lifted onto her toes, leaned full against the sword barricading his body from her. The blade that was sharp enough to cleave hair cut into her just below her rib cage as she strained upward, brought herself to his mouth and kissed him, crying out as the fire invaded her body, the poison of the Dark Ones rushing down the blade and into the wound, coupling her to him, to the seething mass behind him.

She'd feared being among them again, but now she let it invade, let it do its worst, because all they could take was her body, her mind . . . perhaps even her soul, just as she had thought. *You may take me, and yet you will get nothing. I belong to an angel.*

She loved him more than anything else she'd ever been given in her life. She was no hopeless statue on a desolate shore, no mother choosing to end her life before she ever got to experience her daughter's. But she wasn't any more brave or special than anyone else, and that was the miracle of it. She simply chose to believe in her love for Jonah above everything else.

And there it went. At the end of a terrible journey that was minutes but seemed like hours, where she moaned in agony against his lips, the pain was dying away. Leaving just a spiral of thoughts now that seemed to come from the deepest part of her, the culmination of every experience, conscious or not. Her life. And she gave it all to him, mind to mind.

It all comes down to that still moment in time. It's all about that moment. If darkness completely takes over, those moments won't exist. Protect me. Protect all of us.

She kept her mouth on his, tangling the fingers of her unbroken arm into his hair. His body stood rigid, unresponsive, like a fortress of barely trembling stone, as she teased his lips, slowly pressed herself closer, closer, the blade biting into her stomach, into her flesh, into the vital organs behind. She wanted to be as close as she could to him.

"I love you, Jonah. My lord. Take my gift. Take it." She breathed into his mouth, finding the Joining energy, gathering it one last time, only this time she put something more into it, taking a page out of Mina's book from so long ago when she stood over an infant born under a curse. A gift freely given, an offering of a life to save a soul.

Her blood was running down the sword blade. It had now reached his hand, where he supported the wicked edge to hold the weapon between them.

Her hand dropped down from his neck to cover his fingers.

With the last strength she possessed, she squeezed, so the blade cut into his flesh and her blood mixed with his, running into his wound.

Light and darkness, a spiraling circle of it, one chasing the tail of the other, a spinning yin and yang. The speck of darkness and light in each were like eyes, whimsy meeting the secrets of the universe. The sky crackled with fierce energy, so fierce night became day briefly. She thought she saw faces up there, all different versions of divinity. Angels and demons, birds and clouds, perhaps even a whale or two soaring across the expanse of sky as everything turned upside down, the sea and sky coming together the way a mermaid and angel might, in the most unlikely of situations.

Jonah shuddered and the blade dropped to the ground between them. Anna fell to her knees as he staggered back. An explosion of light came from the ledge behind them. The heart detonated, the exploding shards of blue light spinning out like shrapnel. Jonah cried out, thrown to the ground, and she reached, straining until she could cover his hand with her own.

She tightened her fingers over his as the world erupted in chaos over them. Dark Ones surged off the ledge only to be met by a wall of angels who leaped forward, moving so fast across the sky they collided over the two of them in a deadly arc, engaging the battle.

Through the roar, Anna held on, and then cried out in tearful relief as she felt Jonah's fingers move . . . to interlace with hers. Through a haze of pain and weakness, the triumphant battle cries from the Dark Ones could only move her to pity. For she knew they'd just lost.

JONAH struggled to one knee, pulling her weak body up, cradling her in his arms. When Anna put her hand on his chest, a wave of relief, of peace, crossed her face as she apparently registered a thumping, sure and strong.

"Anna," he said, his voice thick and throaty to his own ears. But his voice, nonetheless.

"Good-bye, Jonah," she said. "I wish . . . I want to touch your face once more . . . but I can't feel my fingers."

He closed his hand over hers, brought it to his jaw and found her fingers ice-cold. "No. *No.*"

Her body was shifting in his arms, sluggishly returning to its mermaid form, all vestiges of energy for shapeshifter magic fading away, leaving just what she'd always been. A young mermaid.

"No . . . statues. No stone."

"Only flesh and blood," he said, and his voice broke.

"Go and protect me. All of us. Like . . . being wrapped in your wings." Her face turned, pressing her mouth to his feathers, now silver white again. "No place safer for me to sleep, just as you said."

Then, as inevitable and graceful as an ebbing shoreline, the life faded from her eyes. Her body went limp in his arms, the blood from the wound in her abdomen slowing as the heart that was pumping out her life fluids came to a halt.

He couldn't heal a self-inflicted wound. Nor one where the blood had been spilled for magical purpose. It was even beyond Raphael's powers.

Jonah stared into her face, his hand on her hair, thumb tracing her lips. He was aware of what was around him, of the dangerous pulse of energy all about, but for this second, he could not move.

All her words, all the thoughts moved through him, settling in, rotating slowly, a carousel. There had to be more than a reason to fight . . . there had to be someone to fight for. And that one heart was all that was needed.

The memory of me . . . I will hold it for you . . .

He put back his head and cried out. Somewhere in the middle, the cry of grief expanded, included not just her but all the rest. And then it became a roar of intent, a tidal wave of energy that rippled out through the air, causing the fault lines below the canyon to rumble in warning. His rage was fueled not only by him, but by those he'd lost. He stood with Alexander's fierce countenance on his left, Ronin's feral smile on his right, Diego giving him a sure nod from the head of his battalion, as if they and all the others were somewhere inside of him, drawing their swords, at his back and prepared to charge into battle with him once more. He could almost hear Ronin. *You about ready to do this?*

Get back.

It had the power of thunder, the command he sent out and

into the sky above him. His angels obeyed instantly, disengaging, falling back from the Dark Ones. Their unquestioning loyalty and trust took him beyond words or even thoughts, overwhelmed him like a flood, gave even more power to what he could unleash.

They'd always been connected to him. It was he who had turned from them. But now he could give them that love back, along with his own loyalty, not only to those in the sky but to the reason they fought.

It was the Goddess and more than the Goddess. It was in everything each one of them chose to love. They each fought for themselves, as well as for Her. Hadn't Anna as much as said it? Ronin and Alexander had followed him, but they had their own reasons for believing.

Feeling and structure, Jonah. Let the feeling back in and the balance is restored.

The second of confusion from their enemies was all he needed. Jonah spun into the air, charging his sword. There was a heartbeat, a blink, and the lightning forked from a hundred places in the sky, arrowing down into the point of his weapon, blinding the Dark Ones but not masking the danger they were in. The front lines were already scrambling back, but he could circle Earth in the time it took them to have a malevolent thought.

While he could incinerate the world in a thought, wielding power over a certain level was too dangerous, because of the control it required and the impact of the aftershocks. Nature had limits, always.

Today, however, he had no qualms. The wall of flame roared up and out like a wave of water, chasing them down as they scrambled back screaming, trying to scrabble over each other. His retribution engulfed nearly a third of them, incinerating the first ten rows of their army in a firestorm of flesh and shrieks. The sky darkened with the smoke, and the angels were on the move again, darting here and there to obliterate the ash so it didn't fall and defile the earth.

He was on the wrong side of this battlefield. But as the fire of his light ebbed, Jonah knew he couldn't leave her here, where any Dark One could lay his filth upon her. Scooping her body up in one arm, holding her against his side, his wings took him into the air. Some of the Dark Ones from beneath had moved to intercept in a foolish attempt to stop him. He cleaved the first that threw itself at him with a deft upward slice of the sword and felt his heart twist at the shower of vile blood that spattered her hair.

He fought his way through several more, until he was where other angels could surround him, protect the vulnerable side where he held her. How delighted she'd have been to fly like this, to see the amazing spectacle of the angels sweeping and darting, like a magnificent phalanx of chimney swifts, eliminating the ash of the Dark Ones.

Now, though, they were moving back, regrouping. Unfortunately, the Dark Ones still had overwhelming numbers and too much invested to retreat. They were re-forming ranks, leaving the angels more to fight.

The angels also were re-forming ranks. While his place was with them, first he found a wounded Mina, lying upon a ledge, watched over by several angels of David's division. The battered lieutenant was there himself, on point with bows and arrows. Lucifer's doing, he was sure, as certain as he was that his quiet yet determined lieutenant had not agreed to it easily. Having the seawitch to protect was the only thing that ensured David would obey Lucifer once the battle started. Another reason that it was a boon the witch had joined them.

Jonah would put Anna down there. While he didn't want to upset Mina with the body of her friend, he knew the witch would protect even Anna's lifeless form with her last breath. That would give David another reason to stay put, which his Prime Commander was about to reinforce, with threats if need be.

As Jonah dropped toward that ledge, his heart leaped in his throat. The body in his arms moved, the skin beginning to heat beneath his palms, rapidly.

Damn it all. He cursed as another small group of Dark Ones from below swarmed upon him. He swung the sword through them like a battle-axe, snarling, even as he felt the energy from Anna's body shifting, burning.

David's men were trying to get a bead on the ones closing in on him, but they didn't want to hit him with their arrows. In his mind, he heard David calling Lucifer for backup and hand-to-hand fighters.

Light erupted in his arms, flame gleaming with the purity of gold. Rays shot out in all directions, as though he held a sun in his arms. The Dark Ones in the way of its blast were consumed, and the angels in the cross fire cried out in surprise, but the fire was purity and they were not harmed. In fact, their faces, as they swooped in around him to help get him to the ledge, were momentarily etched in all their perfection, both the planes of bone and expressions. The physical and the spiritual. It was dazzling, like a painting on the walls of a cathedral, depicting the heavenly host, dauntless in the defense of their Creator.

Then flame became blue, cleansing smoke, rushing over his skin with the fluidity and speed of water. In its rush, he felt the sun begin to shimmer, disintegrate.

No.

A moment ago, he'd known she was dead, but that eruption of energy gave him a hope that was shattered like a knife unnecessarily twisted in a fatal wound as her body dissolved into particles of gold flame. There were thousands of them, like stardust shimmering through the air, a whirling vortex that swirled around Jonah, coated his blade, sank into the few wounds he'd sustained, and charged his body with his purpose, gave it one single focus.

End this. Be who you know you are meant to be.

The deepest wish of her heart, the last message from her soul. His mermaid who, if given any wish, might have wished Ariel to win the love of the prince, or her own mother to find hope in the love of her child. Or an angel to find himself and return to the skies to do what he was created to do.

The shimmering pieces drifted away on the air.

Jonah.

It was Lucifer. Also Michael, who'd brought the western flank of their army. He'd apparently given Lucifer the center, since that contingent would have met Jonah first, if the Dark Ones had been successful.

Jonah knew Anna would say he couldn't linger, but he could not keep himself from watching some of the gold flecks drift across his skin, the rest moving down the cliff side, carried by the wind in a thick, spiraling arc toward Mina.

Great Lady, the blood. He was close enough now to realize the wound he'd dealt the witch had been mortal. While he couldn't say he still fully understood Mina's motives, for this battle Anna's faith in her friend had been justified. And the strike of his blade was rapidly taking her life from her.

Pushing the weight of guilt and grief to the back of his mind, knowing he would have to face both later, he winged up, sparing a nod to a grim-looking David.

Lucifer's ebony wings were outstretched in an intimidating display as he hovered, reaper's blade in one hand, a foot-long dagger in the other. Jonah's men were arrayed behind him in a streamer of silver weaponry, wings holding them in formation, ready to launch forward.

At his approach, a wave of triumphant calls erupted all along their ranks, a shouting welcome that moved him enough he could only manage another short nod to them, a lifted hand.

As he came to Lucifer's side, he cleared his throat. "I thought you said it would be a cold day in your Hell before you would come to my aid again."

"Well, you'll note I came to kill you, not to aid you." Luc shrugged. The wind fluttering through the sash around the reaper's blade drew Jonah's attention, a moment before the scarf raised its head and became the venomous form of a crimson snake. It hissed, its fangs baring.

"That would have distracted me."

"That was the plan. I'm glad I can now use it on someone who, while not less deserving, is far less pretty."

Don't let him fool you. He missed you.

David's voice was clear in his mind. Jonah glanced down at the ledge. His lieutenant shot him a strained smile before returning to the preparation of his arrows, looking like a fierce Cupid, checking his array of daggers as well. Apparently determined to protect the witch as long as life remained in her.

I need to threaten you far more often, fledgling. Lucifer's thought.

I'll try to control my trembling enough to shoot straight.

Jonah closed his eyes as the banter continued, comments put in from his captains, as well as a couple of daring snippets from the unranked soldiers. The normal prebattle banter of men who might be dead in the next hour. During his vision quest, he'd thought the immersion in blood was an escape from the overwhelming agony of facing the darkness that had taken over his soul. It had not been an escape, but rather an embracing of that darkness.

But this time, this battle *was* the escape he needed, with those angels who chose to fight at his side. When this day was over, if he survived, he would have to face that he was responsible for Anna's death, and that of her friend. As well as the fact that he would never again feel Anna's touch, hear her teasing, see her smile fall upon him. See the absolute love in her eyes that somehow a week had created between them. Whatever else he had to resolve with the Lady, he did not deny that kind of love was one of Her miracles.

This would help him deal with it. He could do what he knew best, for the right reasons, and then maybe, when it was over, the cleansing power of fighting without the darkness in his soul would help him face the loss. The sense of loneliness tearing at the edges of him even now.

He focused as Lucifer turned his head toward him. As he said nothing, Jonah knew somehow that Lucifer understood all that was going through him, even the thoughts Jonah was choosing not to share. It was a surprising feeling, comforting and disturbing at once.

There also was another note of power to it, one he'd never detected before . . . stronger. One he realized Lucifer was deliberately letting him feel. Lucifer cocked his head, and his dark eyes held Jonah's.

"You know now," he said quietly. "Where the humans come from."

Jonah nodded.

Lucifer glanced back across the chasm. "Every time She sends Her angels out to fight them, She suffers. Sometimes, She gets an insane notion to join the battle Herself, but you and I both know the effect of Dark Ones on female energy. If the Dark Ones' energy overwhelms the human soul, drowns that spark . . . In Her mind, you're fighting for the humans. But I tell you here and now, you have always been fighting for Her. You understand?"

Jonah studied him, trying to wrap his mind around not only what Lucifer was saying, but why it was *Lucifer* saying it.

Lucifer knew. Had always known. Just as She had.

"In one moment of compassion," the Lord of the Underworld continued, "you can do the right thing and create tragedy. Or you can compromise your soul and life goes on. Have you ever thought of what the consequences are of compromising a Goddess's soul?

"She knows much we do not, but it doesn't mean She doesn't feel pain, loss or anger. She is all love, Jonah. And like your little mermaid, love is a tapestry against which pain can imprint itself again and again, giving it scars as well as richness."

As Lucifer's gaze locked with Jonah's, he was captured in the moment with the Dark Lord of the Underworld, even as the captains commanded the angels to draw weapons, to ready for the charge that would come in moments.

Everything is a balance . . . Female energy is feeling; male is structure . . .

What would be the balance to the Lady? Why would She have faith in love above all things? Why had Lucifer always championed Her so fiercely . . . Why had Jonah always sensed the lingering touch of fire upon Her?

Because Lucifer was Her Champion.

It hit Jonah so powerfully, it was like he'd opened his mouth and taken a gulp of water too fast. He drew in a painful breath. The warrior arm of the Lady, Her protection, Her balance. The Lord and the Lady, something that was almost a legend among the angels. Never doubted, but the Lord was illusory, such that the angels had not really thought to question His identity any more than they had the fact of His existence.

He was facing the Lord. Her Consort.

Lucifer gave a slight nod, his dark gaze flickering. Then, as if nothing momentous had happened, he glanced over at the still smoking ledge across the canyon. "Don't suppose you could do that again, about twice as strong, and save us all some trouble?"

"It . . . I've never had the ability to control that level of power so accurately before." Nor had he ever felt as he did when he did it. Not hatred. He'd had the fierce adrenaline he always felt during a fight, but he hadn't felt the dragging weight of hatred or despair he'd been feeling for so long. If one Dark One had asked him for mercy, a choice, he would have given it. Justice with compassion . . .

He was Jonah, Prime Legion Commander, and he would help keep the Goddess's earth safe for purple flowers, laughing mermaids, surly witches, children with pink backpacks, husbands and wives trying to find their way to the true path of love and light, migrant workers offering soda to stray hitchhikers . . .

He was an angel, soldier of the Lady, and he knew his cause was just, not just because of what he knew, but what he felt . . . how he loved.

Because he did it for Anna, he could do it for the world.

"Let's finish this," he said. Lucifer nodded and deliberately adjusted to his right, meeting Jonah's eye. Drawing his sword, Jonah took his proper position at the front of the army that was ready to follow its Prime Legion Commander wherever he would lead them.

Twenty-five

IT was the largest battle David had yet witnessed. Though they'd failed to gain a captive angel, the Dark Ones foolishly believed, despite his burst of fiery energy, that Jonah might be weakened and they still had a chance. Courage was something the Dark Ones didn't lack, though David preferred to call it mindless bloodlust. Once they had it in their nose, they did not typically back off, even when things were against them, as they were now.

Watching Michael, Jonah and Lucifer fight as a unit was like watching an ethereal, fierce ballet, the most perfect inner workings of a living body. The interweaving of drops, turns, spins and twists as they struck and dove within inches of each other, one scything through an opponent as another cut off the attack of someone else, was so mesmerizing that for once David was glad he wasn't in the thick of it. Instead he was afforded the occasional awe-inspiring glimpse as he notched another flying arrow and shot a Dark One out of the sky.

Whether she'd acknowledge it or not at this point, the sea-witch was too weak to participate further, not that he was so sure she would have. When Anna had died and Jonah had surged off the rock with her, she'd collapsed, her magic spent and purpose done. Even knowing she was mortally wounded, David had sent an urgent call for Raphael, though it wasn't likely the healing angel would put a Dark Spawn and the request of a junior lieutenant over other higher-ranking calls on this blood-soaked day.

Then Anna's ashes had fallen to the ledge and the seawitch had cried out in protest. He'd turned to see her trying to stave off the glittering shower that seemed to be . . . Yes, they were settling onto the cuts, healing them, sinking into her skin, limning her lips where they liquefied, forcing themselves down her throat. Mina had been caught somewhere half between dragon and human forms, too weak to complete the change in either direction. However, now, as the last dragon vestiges disappeared, her mercreature form reappeared, the long black tentacles and harlequin-scarred body. The gold ash melted into her skin, over the scars. The ones she'd gotten from this battle disappeared while the gold remained, forming swirling patterns on older scars and in the sleek black flesh of her tentacles, imprinting itself in protection symbols. Her struggles had increased.

"No, Anna . . ." Astonished, David saw tears coming out of Mina's eyes, running with the gold, giving her a macabre mask. It was oddly beautiful, like a temple goddess cast in bronze where the bronze was breaking away, showing the living woman beneath.

Following instinct, he'd dropped to one knee, caught her up to still her struggles. Of course, being Mina, her violence increased at his touch so he had to release her to calm her. He did manage to pull her inside the shelter of the shallow hollow, now that she was in a more diminutive form. While she didn't seem to be suffering from lack of water, the rain had stopped, so he put her next to the trickle of underground water, her tentacles receiving a constant flow of moisture, the only thing he could do for her.

"Liar," Mina had muttered. "She's such a liar. Never take any choices away from each other . . ."

A battle cry from above, a thunder of drums, and he'd had to shove aside his worry for her in the face of the more immediate task of protecting their ledge from attack as the battle engaged. His men had held well. Though they didn't like the duty of protecting a Dark Spawn, none shirked it, and every Dark One they smote was one less to engage their fellows above.

When next he could spare a glance back, he was somewhat relieved to see Mina had at last settled. She held two fistfuls of Anna's remains in her hands, the glitter of the gold faded so she was simply left with metallic ash that stained her hands with dust. At some point, perhaps she'd buried her face in her hands, for her face was marked with gold fingerprints.

He had the unexpected wish to offer her comfort, though he couldn't imagine what type she'd welcome.

"David!"

The urgent call from Orion brought him back, and he pulled both his daggers in time to meet a frontal assault of Dark Ones who'd managed to rush the archers, break the line and swoop down upon the ledge.

A quick glance told him the Dark Ones were losing all over the field, dropping out of the sky, fleeing, being incinerated in the air. But apparently they'd decided the one objective still within their grasp was killing the Dark Spawn who had fought against them.

David sent out the call, and Jonah and his front line responded personally, diving into their ranks to even out the odds. Even so, it was bitter hand-to-hand fighting, the kind where David lost sense of time and space. There was only the next Dark One before him, sometimes two, the flutter of lost feathers from an angel who'd had a narrow miss, the shower of dark blood as a Dark One was vanquished. The give of the body as he plunged his daggers in and yanked them out before his hand could get sucked into the dark abyss of poison that existed inside the bodies.

At one point, he was surrounded, going down among four of them, because he was the one closest to her. They pressed in upon him so hard he somehow felt their intent. They were going to tear her to pieces. No, they would take her back, torture her for eons . . . make her suffer in their dark world, where she would survive in a half life . . .

No. They wouldn't. He'd failed to protect Anna. He wouldn't fail Jonah again. Or Mina.

"David. *David.*" Jonah's sharp, authoritative bark brought him back.

He was slashing at air. Or, more correctly, at Jonah and Orion's faces, as they grabbed at his arms, hauled him back to his feet, held him while he swayed and got his bearings, blinked at the bodies lying around him.

"Most are yours," Orion observed dryly, his lips curving. "But the commander and I pulled a couple off of you before they could skin you alive."

David nodded, getting his breath back. Jonah's shrewd gaze was assessing him from head to toe, making sure he hadn't sustained any wounds. It was the first time he'd had more than a moment with his commander, and now everything about the past few moments disappeared for David. Jonah was assessing *him* for injury, when David could see the grief in his commander's eyes, waiting like a sword for him to fall upon when this day's battle was won.

"I'm sorry," David said. "My lord, I'm so sorry."

He always called him Jonah. Command hierarchy was understood among angels as necessity, but personally they were all on equal footing. But in this moment, the title felt necessary. Plus, David didn't think he could say his name without his voice breaking.

He dropped to one knee, startling Orion, he could tell, but he bowed his head, his daggers still clutched in his fists. "I wish I could have done better for you."

Jonah's hands were on his shoulders immediately, pulling him up. "Up with you, you young idiot." His voice was gruff. Cupping David's face, he turned it so he could see the bruises, tightening his hold and making a noise in his throat when David would have pulled away. "Look at me."

When David was able to obey the command, Jonah met his gaze squarely. "Victory isn't always in winning," he said. "Anna knew that."

As his commander said her name, David saw it in Jonah's eyes, behind the impassive battle expression. Saw the pain waiting to take him with the same fierce inevitability as the fire he'd unleashed on the Dark Ones.

"Jonah—"

Jonah shook his head. "Damn you and those basset hound eyes of yours. She never expected to live long. She told me . . . daughters of Arianne don't live past twenty-one . . ."

His voice broke, such a startling thing that the angels around them looked as if a new army of Dark Ones had appeared to face them, and maybe they would have preferred that. Jonah pulled it back in with a visible effort and a muttered oath, clapped David hard on the shoulder. "Never mind. Now's not the time anyway."

"Anna has lived under the shadow of an early death all her life. She never feared death."

Jonah and David's attention turned as one to Mina, who still had her back resting against the wall next to the trickle of water. She had her shoulder beneath it. At their sudden regard, she looked as if she'd regretted her words. Nevertheless, her jaw tightened.

"The night I called Lucifer and David to your aid, it was because I felt her fear. I knew it was Jonah who was in direct danger, because her terror was greater than it would have been for herself."

Jonah took a step forward as Mina continued in that same quiet voice, her features strained with the effort. She focused on some portion of the air over their shoulders, as if she couldn't bear looking at any of them. David turned suddenly and picked up the cloak she'd left behind as a dragon, which he'd had no time to bring to her before now. When she reached out her hand to take it, instead he spread it over her himself, saving her the effort. Blinking at him, she looked as if she might snap at him for doing what she could do for herself, but then she pressed her lips together and shifted her gaze to Jonah.

"She was completely selfless, keeping nothing for herself, though I'd never seen her want something as much as she wanted you." She worked the cowl up on her head, disguised her features in her normal way, and her voice strengthened. "She said she wanted to die with a heart full of hope, and she did."

That powerful grief suffused Jonah's features, and then it was gone, pushed away somewhere none of them could see, but David could feel it vibrating from him.

"She had another form, didn't she?" Jonah asked it thickly. "She never told me, but she mentioned it."

Mina flinched as though he'd hit her. David squatted at her side. He didn't touch her, though she leaned away from him as if she expected him to do so. He wondered if all the fire in

Lucifer's Underworld could warm the cold desolation he saw in her face.

"It was a phoenix," she said at last. Before the hope could flare too brightly in Jonah's eyes, she added. "But it won't help. The ash, what she did there at the end. She gave her last energy to me, the energy that would help her rise again."

"Talk about a wasted effort." Orion's murmur couldn't help but carry. David tightened his jaw, but nothing flickered in Mina's dark eyes. Maybe she hadn't heard it. But Jonah apparently had.

"She lived her life fully," the Prime Legion Commander said, casting Orion a quelling glance before shifting his attention back to Mina. "Anna would want to give you the chance of embracing the same gift. I hope you don't squander it. Only then would I find it in me to despise you."

He looked then at the small remaining pile of ash Mina had carefully scraped together from what was within her reach. "We'll take those in the sky and scatter them over the ocean when we're done here today. Mina can show us the best place. We need to take her home."

He paused, looking back at Mina for a long moment. In his face, David saw a compassion there that surprised the other angels, who looked like being on this ledge close to the Dark Spawn was about ten miles closer than they wanted to be. "When a being dies," Jonah said, "a type of angel called the Gatekeeper comes to lead the soul to the spiritual realm. They don't speak to us, but I felt her Gatekeeper come for her, Mina. She is safe, and at peace. I hope that comforts you."

With that, he returned to the sky, taking most of the angels on the ledge with him, leaving just David and several of his men. He saw Mina's gaze lift, following Jonah's trail through the sky, and heard her murmur, "Will that be enough to comfort you?"

David leaned in closer. "Mina . . ."

She turned with visible effort to look at him. As she did, David unexpectedly recalled her bravery in approaching the line of Dark Ones. The fierce way they'd come after her, when they knew the larger battle was lost, their burning red eyes and bared fangs focused on the young witch. Just remembering it made him check that his daggers were still close at hand.

It occurred to him that today was not the end of it for Mina. Whether she liked it or not, someone would have the thankless task of keeping a close eye on her. The Dark Ones did not forget what they would perceive as treachery from one of their own.

He didn't bring that up now, however, sure she would not take the news well. Plus he could tell she was somewhere far away from this place.

"What are you thinking?" he asked quietly, surprised when she answered.

"Anna was right. He is the leader she said he was. When he went into battle, even I felt the energy that pours out of him. But as a man, he is grieving sorely. It . . . I hope she's somewhere where she can know how much he loved her."

Twenty-six

THERE was work to repair the rift, as always, and it was a large one, such that a new nebula existed around the star when it was done. As they hovered in the dark vastness of space, bathed in the new star's bright light, Lucifer glanced toward Jonah. "I think this one should be named for you."

It was an honor often accorded to one of the soldiers who'd shown particular valor during a battle. It was not the first time Jonah had been offered the honor, but it was well-known he'd never accepted it. Nor did he feel that inclination this time. He was tired, just ready to be done.

"Arianne's Hope," he said shortly. Lucifer nodded.

Despite his weariness, Jonah looked around at his captains. While he didn't allow his usually commanding mien to change, he made sure he met each angel's gaze before he said his next words.

"I ask your forgiveness," he said. "For losing faith. It won't happen again."

"You will see her again, Jonah."

Jonah looked toward Lucifer. "When she'll have no memory of me but perhaps a lingering smile. Or sadness." He shook his head. "It doesn't matter, Luc. I will honor her memory by never straying from what she brought me back to. I never deserved her to begin with."

"No one deserved her more," Luc rejoined. But Jonah was already winging away into the darkness.

"He goes to mourn her," one of the captains said. A request for reassurance. "Can't we—"

Lucifer placed a hand on the captain's shoulder. "He'll be all right. He doesn't know it, but he flies into the Lady's arms, even now. Let Her take care of him."

THERE was a place in the universe Jonah preferred for his meditation after battle. It had a vantage point of the Milky Way, and he hovered there now, willing his mind to clear as he stretched out on a dense blanket of energy to hold him. He made his muscles ease, one by one, but the act allowed other things to sweep through him, over the shields against his emotions.

Anna, before his sword. Soft hair blowing around her, unafraid, even as he stood there like a Grim Reaper. Blood on her face from his fist, the power of his energy used against her. The rising cries of his captors egging him on. *Kill her. Kill her.*

He knew what he must have looked like, caring not who or what he killed. His eyes red fire, his heart no longer his own, a specter more terrifying than the army of Dark Ones behind him.

She'd opened her arms to him, her gaze seeing him, seeing past it all. Wisdom he'd known, but somewhere along the way the blackness of his soul had painted over it. The hope of the world was not in the complex theories of the philosophers or the politics of men, but simply in this. The power of love and creation, a touch of love and forgiveness waiting just a step away . . .

He'd felt it pervade him, her life essence, all her love for him. She'd given him another unbearably poignant gift. He understood that wisdom again; the blackness washed away. He knew why the Goddess had done what She'd done. A spark could grow into a flame, and when that light spread, all darkness would be warmed by it.

He remembered what Anna had said about Ix Chel and the underwater caves, how the Mayans had seen the openings to the caves as tunnels to the Underworld, to rebirth. Healing.

When Anna's blood had mixed with his, light had exploded through him, through his empty chest. He'd roared at it, at the feel of her mortally wounded body in his arms, even as her magic and the magic of the seawitch rushed through him. Dark Ones around him screaming in agony, scattering before that light. Anna's light became his as the coffin carrying his heart simply turned to dust in the hands of the one carrying it, and he felt its power and weight flood his chest again. The power to feel, to ache, yes. But also the power to love, which he now knew was greater than any agony, any loss.

Her smile . . . her touch . . . her faith in him. He couldn't lose faith. No, he wouldn't. For her. But his heart, the one she'd restored or given, felt so empty. To be able to hold her, press his face in her hair, smell it . . .

Her hair. He recalled the bracelet he wore for the first time, and it choked him to find it still there. The knot in his chest was so painful he pressed his wrist to his forehead, trying to feel past the loss. Burying his hands in her hair. Her laughter. She'd been a miracle.

A gift.

Her energy surrounded him, replacing his incorporeal bed with the substantial coils of Her presence, a warmth and comfort, but filled to brimming with all the grief and loss he'd experienced. Such that it was the easiest thing then to turn on his side, pull his wings over his head so he would not shame himself before Her, and let it take him.

He didn't think, didn't wonder why things couldn't be different, didn't imagine anyone to blame. He simply felt, loved and grieved.

The harsh sobs that wracked him went on for a long time. Perhaps a day, a week on Earth . . . one thousand years of pain unleashed. Her light built around him, charged with Her compassion, holding him, rocking him.

When at last he was done, She had him completely encapsulated, carrying him, cocooning him. Until Her gentle hand eased back a wing to see his face.

"My handsome, weary angel. You have suffered much for me, Jonah. Even angels who are warriors are beings of light, of life. To be immersed in death and destruction for so long, with such evil, it wears upon you, the soul, the mind."

He saw it in Her eyes, what Lucifer had tried to say about Her. "We all suffer, my Lady. For evil is something that will always be with us."

"But then why do you fight?"

"Because we must." He thought of the row of pictures in Anna's cottage. "She ended up dead, just as they did, but it wasn't that she feared. It was dying without hope, without light or purpose. Mina was right. The condition of the spirit will ever be the spark. The spark is You. And me. All of us."

He felt Her soft smile. "You said the witch's name rather than calling her Dark Spawn. There is hope for my stern and immovable angel yet."

In that one gentle moment of humor, his heart poured open to Her. He felt Her within him, himself in Her, and there was a stillness to him that made the sadness that much more acute and bearable at once. And She saw that as well.

"You've given me so much, Jonah. You've earned the honor of Full Submission long before now."

He considered that, straightening up to sit cross-legged on the bed created by Her energy alone, since all of his had gone into his grief. "Perhaps it is a male way of thinking, my Lady," he said slowly, "but I am charged to protect You, as I was to protect Anna. Because I was hers and she was mine. It's a part of what You are, but more than that, I don't wish to abdicate the ability to see right and wrong, to protect You when You need it."

"Even when I do not think I need it? I *am* at least over four billion years old, Jonah." At his uncomfortable shrug, her amusement surrounded him. "You are right, my Commander. It is very male thinking. No wonder you and my Lord get along so well."

"Lucifer."

"Yes." Myriad emotions curved around him. "He is my balance, as you know. And yet, that balance is strong because it shifts, grows, struggles . . ."

"Are You saying the two of You . . . argue?" He could not get his mind around such a thing, but then he remembered standing on a Sea of Glass, challenging Her, and a flush rose in his cheeks.

Her laughter was the winds, moving the stars and spinning them so they glittered like diamonds.

"I remember a bitter moment, after Ronin's death, when you mocked the text that said God made man in His own image. You thought there could be no greater insult to me. But what was in that one spark *was* the deepest essence of my image. An extraordinarily complex ability to love, so complex it wars with the dark side of human nature constantly. It is the greatest gift I can give, and I hope that spark will never allow the darkness to gain dominance in the human heart, for their sakes as well as my own."

She grew serious then, the stars stilling, only flickering. "The Dark Ones have never understood, not since the beginning. I could tell them, but I don't think they would ever understand. It is their greatest weakness, as well as ours. It is also our greatest strength against them. You were more right than you know. Because even if they have an angel fighting at their head, if that angel is there because of a sacrifice of love, not because of a true surrender to evil, then love can call him back and turn the tide.

"You were so close at one point to proving that wrong . . ." She materialized enough for him to see the hint of a woman's face, so beautiful and timeless it made him miss Anna all that much more, even as he could not help but feel the peace She had to offer. It also made him remember how the poison had intertwined with his rage and grief and brought him to ugly places in himself . . . the red anger of Anna's back . . . his avoidance of the Joining Magic, of anything that would lead him back into the Lady's embrace . . .

Her gaze saw and knew it all. "But it was Anna's love that called you back to yourself, kept calling you back to yourself, until you were ready to step back onto the path yourself. It is always the way of it. We none of us do this alone.

"Anna's gift was that she was a complete balance. Through her shape-shifting, she was connected to all elements—fire as the phoenix, water as the mermaid, air as the fairy, and of course her flesh is of the earth. That is also why the magic was even stronger when you brought love forth in her."

Her tone softened. "Lucifer was also right, what he said about you deserving her. You did deserve her, Jonah, for all your many years of service. That's why she is my gift to you." She paused, and the universe turned around him, dark and light, all the planets and the stillness that existed out here, as well as within him.

That's why she is *my gift to you.*

Jonah's heart pounded up into his throat. "My Lady?"

"She waits for you in her ocean. Why do you make her wait, sitting up here talking to an old, old, old woman?"

"But . . . she died. And the laws of death . . ."

"Are unbreakable." That hint of a face again, this time with a fall of hair that contained showers of rain and fire together, twining together like ribbons while stars sparkled through the flawless skin of her face. "Unfortunately, Anna upset the balance herself. Mina was the one that was supposed to die, Jonah. Anna sacrificed her energy as the phoenix to her."

A shadow moved over Her expression. "What will come of that is not yet clear. But there are laws that must be obeyed, and laws where the consequences of breaking them are worth the risk, if the love is great enough." Her eyes darkened. "Once, I risked the fate of all Creation to break a rule, to imbue darkness with a small spark. To give humans a chance at salvation, a purpose beyond violence and hate. How could I not do the same for my Prime Legion Commander, who has loved me so long, and one simple mermaid, whose faith has put us all to shame? You are my Prime Legion Commander, Jonah. You are also her lover, the soul mate you both need for the universe to stay strong and keep its balance. Do you disagree?"

He felt that nudge of amusement then, a sense of humor infectious enough to recall his own, lethargic though it might have become in the past years. Until prodded back to life by Anna.

"I admit it will make it very difficult for me to criticize You for breaking Your own rules in the future. Unless I want to be accused of being hypocritical."

"*Hmmm.* I'm sure I never would have thought of that."

Jonah smiled then, brilliantly, his joy surging up through him such that he knew he could make it from here to Earth with all the fierce brightness of a shooting star. "You are female, my Lady. That is my answer to that."

The explosion of adrenaline left Her laughter in his wake. He shot through the stars, upsetting their axes. The Lady quickly steadied them as Her usually careful and conscientious commander rocketed out of the skies toward Earth like a fledgling. She just hoped he remembered to slow in time to keep from creating a wake that would bring a second flood upon the continents. She sent a warning to the weather angels to be prepared with interference as needed, even as Her smile grew. It sent a wave of sensual, loving warmth out that enveloped Her universe in a precious moment of peace and calm.

It pervaded every heart and soul, in every place. The darkest prison, the highest mountains. Down into the bowels of Hell itself, giving an ebony-winged angel a moment's pause and a smile of His own that sent searing pleasure through Her heart.

Twenty-seven

ANNA floated on the surface of the water, riding the waves. For a while after she'd awoken here, she'd watched the sky, lazily propelling her arms through the cool silk of the water. But then she'd closed her eyes and, despite her best intentions, she'd turned to warm, inviting thoughts of a silver and white winged angel with firm lips and dark eyes. Hands that could bring shivers to her body. But even more than that, he had a *presence* that simply made her feel complete . . . whole. His voice, his closeness at her back while she slept. She just couldn't describe what she felt for him in words.

But that was done. She wasn't entirely sure yet what had happened, but for some reason, she'd been given back her life. Perhaps it would even be a long life now. She needed to see the beauty in that, embrace that gift, knowing that her brush with an angel was only one part of what would be many joys, and try not to ache for more. She'd known he couldn't be hers. So she would try not to miss him, to feel this deep, penetrating loneliness for that presence. His touch. There were mermen. Humans. For heaven's sake, she had the males of two species to choose from.

Bother. Yes, she was crying again, but it would pass. She'd felt pain before, knew it would go. She would disappear beneath the waves, stay away from the sky a little while. Seek out a pod of whales, or sit among an underwater garden. Or maybe she would go to her cottage, watch the ocean rush to shore with her feline companion purring on her lap. Avoid the bed where he'd lain with her, which likely still bore his scent. *Oh, Goddess, help me.*

As if echoing the turn of her thoughts, clouds had obliterated the warming light of the sun. She opened tear-filled eyes to find the angel in question hovering horizontally just above her, his dark eyes devouring her face. It was his spread wings that had blocked the sun, not the clouds. He had his muscular arms crossed and a mock forbidding look on his face. His body was mere delectable inches above her.

Jonah.

They stayed that way some time. She couldn't think of one thing to say, so many memories of just a handful of days filling the air between them, clogging her lungs. His mouth softened, as if realizing she wasn't up for teasing. If he reached out to her face, she would be lost. She couldn't bear for him to leave her. She just couldn't. She'd had the courage to face the Dark Ones for him. She didn't have the courage to ask him why he was here, or the strength to drop beneath the water and try to escape him before he shattered her.

"You great big silly bird," she said at last, though her voice shook. "I thought I was done being pestered by you."

Still not speaking, he reached down, tracing her lips, the line of her eyebrows. Anna sucked in a sob and his eyes flickered. While her body was floating, she felt as if everything inside of her was frozen, warring between cold fear and spiraling heat at that single touch. She hadn't recovered her wraps and so her breasts were bare, yearning for his touch like every other inch of her.

"Mine," he said softly. "Mine forever."

He was going to shatter her anyway, only with an explosion of happiness too enormous to contain. She knew his choice of words had been deliberate. In the caves, at the beginning, when she had lain next to him in those first few hours, he'd heard her. When she thought him unconscious, she'd laid her hand upon his chest and thought it. Perhaps even said it.

Mine forever.

A fantasy, now a wish come true. He was giving the gift to her, letting her know she finally belonged with someone, to someone. As he belonged to her.

She let out a soft cry that was breathed into his mouth as he landed upon her. His hands wrapped around her waist as he held her close to him, so tightly she could barely breathe, but she didn't care.

"Take me in the air," she whispered, and wondered if he'd understood she'd meant both things, even before she thought of the double meaning herself.

She helped him by transforming, allowing the glittering scales of her tail to become a pair of slim white legs that hooked around the backs of his thighs as he spiraled upward, taking her into the clouds, her bare skin pressed against his hard muscles, the cool metal of his belt, the silk of his half tunic. The dark blue of the ocean spread beneath them like a sparkling blanket. Seagulls passed around them, a line of pelicans so close in their singular formation she saw one turn its eye toward her.

His arms tightened, holding her closer against him. Burying her face in his neck, she felt his hair brush over her temple, her jaw.

"Goddess, I love you, Jonah. I'm sorry I love you so much, but I do."

He drew her head back by winding his hand in her hair, and his eyes were fierce with desire, his mouth held in that firm line that made her want to nip at his lips. "Why does that make you sorry?"

"Because I can't imagine you have much use for a mermaid who is completely besotted with you."

A smile tugged at those lips, and now she couldn't resist. She scraped her teeth over him and his grip increased at her waist, his fingers spanning her hip, caressing her buttock as he tilted her head and plundered her mouth, biting her back, only with a sensual intent that speared right through the center of her.

"You're the one who's going to be sorry, little one. Because I want you besotted with me. I plan to take advantage of your devotion. Often."

"Now," she said urgently. "Please."

It was so close, how near a thing it had all been. Losing him to the Dark Ones, watching him cut out his own heart to save her. Feeling the bite of his blade into her stomach, the rage in his face as he broke her arm. The malevolence of the Dark Ones . . . She needed his light, to feel the warrior who served the Goddess, to know they'd truly done it and he was in fact hers forever.

Jonah cupped her face then, gave her a look he knew was torn between fierce desire and exasperated tenderness. If his mermaid understood what a gift she was, she would recognize his besottedness eclipsed hers to the point he was her slave. "Hold on to me," he murmured.

She complied, shifting her arms higher around his shoulders, burying her fingers in his feathers as he lifted her away from his body enough to get the front panel of the battle skirt out of the way and guide himself into her tight but blessedly wet opening.

Bringing her down on him on a spiraling turn, he earned a gasp from her that made him laugh with the sheer joy and pleasure of it, which turned to a groan as an excruciating spasm of her inner muscles wrenched the sound from him.

Her hair rippled around them, landed like strands of silk on his shoulders as he went higher, faster, supporting them both as he slid deep inside of her, letting the movements of their bodies drive them higher, keeping the edge just out of reach so it could be savored, this searing sensual tension that warned of the explosive pinnacle to come.

When he saw tears in her eyes again, he bent to kiss her throat, her chin, tasting her skin. Then he possessed her mouth once more as he held her so close. It wasn't close enough. He wanted to prove to her he intended to possess her. Keep her. Care for her. Be with her in all ways. Always.

Simple words with the power of the highest magic, because they were backed by the most serious oath he'd ever taken, even beyond that he'd taken to serve the Goddess. For it was one and the same, and he understood that in a way now he hadn't understood then, centuries ago. Even a week ago.

He took her off the Earth and into climax so quickly Anna was almost dizzy with it, crying out at the release, feeling his sure, possessive hands on her hips, the roundest part of her buttocks.

As she gripped him inside, Anna willed him to come with her. He had his fist in her hair as they spiraled down, a sudden, stomach-jumping drop, and then he caught them up, teasing her so that she gasped, caught between laughter and desire. But as she felt him about to release, she brought her mouth to his ear.

"Hold . . . nothing back . . . my lord. Let me give you a child."

The flash of heat in his eyes was almost enough to send her over again. But he hesitated. "I don't want to lose you."

"That is for the Lord and Lady to decide, but I no longer fear the curse. We are stronger than that curse. Our love is."

He was thinking of her ancestors, she knew. How the mothers died soon after childbirth. "I'm not afraid," she said, her lips curving, pressing her face into his strong throat. "You're an angel. You'll protect me."

She wanted the warm seed to flood her, the life energy it would bring to her, intensifying the Joining Magic. Despite her own tiny voice of fear, she wanted him to do it. She wanted to give them both the gift of life between them. Eternal proof that it existed, that it could not be denied.

"I love you, Anna," he said, his voice a whisper of heat in her ear.

Then, as he had from the first moment he met her, Jonah let her faith take away his doubts.

And gave her what she wanted.

Read on for a special preview of the
seductive follow-up to *A Mermaid's Kiss*

A Witch's Beauty

Available now from Berkley Sensation!

"SHE doesn't need protection," Marcellus pronounced. Despite the fact most angels only had solid black eyes, no hint of white or colored iris, there was no mistaking the murderous intent in the captain's narrowed gaze. "She needs a cage. Manacles. A gag."

Affront accompanied every ripple of muscle and sinew as he stretched out what should have been two impressive wings. Marcellus's feathers were a glossy green so dark as to be almost black, except for an iridescent shimmer of color, caught by the beams of sunlight filtering in through the Citadel's arched open windows. One wing still displayed the plumage. The other was now leathery black and vestigial. On closer inspection, it was obvious it had been transformed into a bat's wing.

David had halted respectfully at the doorway to the main hall, but at Jonah's glance, he took a step in. He was smart enough not to interrupt an audience between the Prime Legion Commander and one of his upper-echelon captains. But the wing was flapping back and forth in an uncontrolled manner, as if it had a mind of its own and was trying to free itself from Marcellus's back by flagellation.

"At least she changed it to a fruit bat's wing," David ventured. "That's the largest bat species in the world. The hognosed bat is only about three centimeters long."

From Jonah's searing look, David suspected the commander

knew he wasn't trying to be helpful. If truth be known, he was hoping to instigate.

Marcellus, however, ignored him. "Raphael said he would fix it *when* he stopped laughing. Which meant I should come back after the next cycle of the moon."

Jonah's lips twitched. "Raphael does tend to view life more comically than most."

"Well, perhaps that's because he hasn't had to stand over the bodies of the four angels that have been killed in this pointless effort so far. Unfortunately what she did to them was beyond his healing skills."

"You can't blame her for that," David protested.

"David." Jonah sent him a more than searing look this time. "You're early, which I expect was deliberate. So if you don't stop speaking without leave, I'll send you to the training field until I'm ready for you."

Marcellus leveled a hard glance at the young lieutenant to reinforce the message, then shifted it back to the commander. "Let them have her. It's no more than she deserves. She's one of them anyway, isn't she? She's not of the Goddess's creation; that's for certain."

The amusement flickering through Jonah's gaze had died away at Marcellus's reference to the four they'd lost. Now there was a trace of steel there his angels all knew, well enough that Marcellus appeared to recall himself.

"Ah, by the bloody maze of Hades, Jonah. I don't mean any disrespect, but none of us believe she came to your mate's aid three moons ago to save you. The witch is bound by curse to protect the descendants of Arianne. If it weren't for that, she'd have turned on Anna, too."

David held his tongue with effort, but couldn't stop his fingers from closing into fists at his sides. From Jonah's sharp glance, he knew he'd caught it, and he tried to make himself relax. It was hard, for Marcellus hadn't run out of steam yet.

"There's never been a Dark Spawn who survived past five years old that didn't turn into a full Dark One in the end." The vestigial wing slapped against his shoulder as if underscoring his point. "If the Dark Ones had to take some of ours, I wish to Goddess they'd taken her down with them. Then we'd be done with this."

At his commander's silence, Marcellus sighed. "I serve you, Jonah. You know that. But this is almost too much. I speak only the truth of it."

Jonah studied him a long moment. Then he inclined his head. "Go see to your wing. I'm sure Raphael will restore it now. Tell him I have need of you for other duties in the morning, and that will hasten him."

David managed to stand without further expression as Marcellus bowed and took his leave. On the way out, the captain cast an almost pitying look toward him. The way one would look at the village idiot, David reflected. Still, he managed to wait until Marcellus had awkwardly winged off into the blue and white sky before he spoke. "So we just let them have her, like he said?"

"David, do me a favor. Shut up for a minute." Jonah sat down on the sill of a large open window and eased his silver white wings out to stretch them fully in the early morning air. As the breeze fluttered through the tips of his primary feathers, he closed his eyes.

Outside the window, a rainbow stretched over a green valley, diving behind a silver ribbon of river. The silver and ivory spires of the Citadel, piercing the seven layers of Heaven, were a gathering place specifically for the warrior class that fought the enemies of the Lady. Right now, they were in Third Heaven, Machanon, which overlooked the Garden of Eden. To plan battle strategy with his captains and lieutenants, Jonah would typically go down to Shamain, the layer of Heaven closest to Earth. The Machanon level of the Citadel was an oasis of sorts, a place for the angels who regularly had to fight the Dark Ones to take their ease. To remember, in such a serene setting, what they fought for.

Of course, like today, less tranquil business often came here to find Jonah. It was one of many reasons David did not envy the commander his position. He regretted adding to that burden, but he was sure of his duty. He could not shirk it, particularly in this matter.

For the moment, however, he went to a squat, traced the etchings on the floor tile with a finger. The design displayed a circular formation of angels, fighting the various shapes that evil had taken over many millions of years. Three symbols marked the outer boundaries of the circle. Courage. Loyalty. Commitment. The *Semper Fi* of the Dark Legion.

"What's your attachment to the witch, fledgling?"

David lifted his head to look at his commander. "I'm not sure I understand the question."

"I'm fairly certain you do. I assigned this responsibility to Marcellus's battalion, making it clear you were not to be involved in it. Yet over the past three months, he tells me you've badgered her security detail for frequent reports, and shadowed them when your other duties allow. Why do you champion her, David, when no one but you and I will?"

David straightened, feeling uncomfortable under the shrewd gaze of a born angel well over a millennium in age. Whereas he'd come from a human soul and was only thirty years old. Barely a child to most of this company, but enough of a fighter that he'd been made a lieutenant of one of Jonah's frontline platoons. Over time, that had become a source of quiet, fierce pride to him. But that desire wasn't what had brought him here in the beginning.

Regardless of skills, most angels had to undergo myriad trainings before getting their first assignments. Learn about being Watchers and Messengers, or participate in the heavenly choirs. But from the moment he'd crossed the Veil, David had needed something to fight. What he'd wanted was the oblivion of eternal dust, not an afterlife.

He often suspected that was why he'd been placed under Jonah's wing. The angel had not only trained him to fight. He'd broken David down, torn him open to let the rage and bitterness bleed out, built him up when despair would have taken him. Taken care of him until he could take care of himself. He'd given him a good-against-evil struggle with clear lines.

So he loved Jonah. He couldn't think of him as a father—too many horrible memories attendant to that—but he could think of him as an older brother. A friend, and a leader he respected more than any other.

A few months ago, he'd had the honor of rescuing Jonah from an army of Dark Ones. Or rather, David helped Anna and Mina rescue him. Because of the things he'd seen the witch do, he sure as hell wasn't going to let Marcellus talk Jonah into abandoning her.

"It *isn't* the curse. That's not why she helped you," he insisted. "When I first found her, and thought she was involved in your disappearance, I hurt her to get information." He didn't like the memory, that struggle on the sand, his daggers punching into her flesh to pin her to the ground, her cries of pain, but he faced it now. "It didn't matter. She wouldn't give you up."

Of course, Mina was contrary enough to hold her tongue just because someone wanted her to talk. It wouldn't matter if the subject was the secrets of Heaven or the color of the sky on a clear day.

Angels could share thoughts, but he didn't need to expend the effort in this case. Jonah's arch look told David the commander had likely had the same thought.

Jonah didn't give in to spontaneous bursts of humor, but David had seen more moments like that since he'd taken a mate. Anna, a mermaid of royal blood, a daughter of Arianne. A young mermaid to whom laughter and joy were as easy as breathing. She believed in Mina, too. Which bolstered David's argument considerably. He wasn't too proud to take advantage of it.

David pointed to the floor. "From what I've seen, Mina has all of these qualities. Courage, loyalty and a tremendous amount of commitment."

"We just don't know to what. Or whom." Jonah studied the ceiling, which, true to the tastes of the wholly male population that frequented these halls, depicted a lush and sensual scene of young women bathing. "She doesn't seem to want our protection, any more than my angels want to protect her."

"Yet four have died because of the necessity of providing her protection against attacks she couldn't have handled herself."

"Well, according to her conversation with my mate, she could have. They simply 'got in the way.'" His expression darkening, Jonah turned so his feet were propped against the opposite side of the window frame and one wing was curved under his body.

"Where is she now?" David ventured.

"We don't know. Which is why I called you. You're the only one with a blood link to her."

"Oh." At David's expression, Jonah's brow rose.

"Why did you think I called you?"

A muscle flexed in David's jaw. "Let me protect her, Jonah. Before you say that I'm too inexperienced, hear me out at least."

Jonah inclined his head. "You're always welcome to speak freely, David. You know that. Before I say no."

David's eyes narrowed. "A whole detail is an easier target to find than one angel and one—"

"Dark Spawn."

"Girl."

Jonah shot him a look as David lifted his chin. "She doesn't deserve what Marcellus said about her."

"David, you're still close enough to your human life to think that morality is always relative, shades of gray. This Legion has fought Dark Ones since before the skies were created. Not a one of my angels, and that includes me, has *ever* met a Dark Spawn worth saving. They're either wholly evil, the true children of their sires, or so physically deformed they don't survive. She is Dark Spawn, their child. Daughter of a mermaid, for certain, but that mermaid was a seawitch, from a line of seawitches who were known to embrace the Darkness far more often than the Light. And her personality does nothing to convince us she's different," he added dryly.

"Everyone in this Legion has a preconceived notion of Dark Spawn, no room for the possibility of a rare exception—"

"Because there's never been one."

"That's why they're called exceptions," David argued. "I'm not saying there's no darkness to her. But no one, not even Marcellus, can deny there's something different about her. Maybe she *can* protect herself and just needs someone to watch her back. But if they do take her, they'll have to go through me. Worst case, you'll only have lost one of many lieutenants, rather than more members of your higher-ranking platoons."

"You're not listening. Typical young idiot." Jonah shook his head as David opened his mouth again. "I don't like her, David. But I love you well; you know this. You're baiting me, and I'm likely to bash your head in for it."

David's lips twisted. "You and Luc are always threatening me with bodily harm, and neither of you ever follows through."

"Would you like us to?"

"No." David put up both hands in surrender, allowing a small smile. "Training under you is punishment enough. But, Jonah, let me do this. I've felt a connection to her from the beginning. I think it should be me. Anna senses it, too; you know it."

Jonah rolled his eyes, an odd effect for the solid dark orbs, then pushed off the window to stand again. "She's been badgering me for a week about it. Though her methods are far more persuasive."

David pressed on. "We've been protecting Mina without trying to understand her. That's the key to keeping her safe. Anna said even she hasn't been able to get very close to Mina. And she knows more about her than anyone. She's given me everything she thinks may help me."

"So that's why you've been spending so much time with her. I was beginning to wonder if my young lieutenant had a crush on my mate."

That brought David up short. His gaze strayed to the bracelet, a thin braided strip of Anna's golden brown hair, Jonah had worn since the Canyon Battle. "Jonah, I wouldn't . . . couldn't . . . I mean, Anna is beautiful and truly I love her. But not . . . I mean, I don't *love* her . . ."

Jonah's lips quirked and he waved a hand. Goddess, the boy was young. On Earth, he might have been married by now, a father, but up here his age made him practically less than an embryo to the others.

He'd grown to physical manhood in the skies, though, and brought a rage so strong from his human life Jonah had at first wondered why the Lady had made him an angel, rather than simply reincarnating him into another soul to lance those boils in the earthly realms.

Then, underneath all that, he'd found the shock of a serene and steady soul, a levelheadedness far beyond David's years. He was more than a capable fighter. Using his wits at all times, no matter how thick the fighting got, he came up with ways to defeat greater numbers in hand-to-hand that had earned him the respect of the captains and extra duty to teach his techniques. No one could match his artistry when fighting with two daggers. Jonah had let him stop carrying a sword into battle some time ago when he realized the longer weapon was merely a hindrance to the young angel.

When the lieutenant of his platoon fell, David took over the command, brought them through a fight where they were outnumbered three to one. He'd served as acting lieutenant while Jonah looked for a replacement, but several battles after that, the commander realized he'd already found him.

However, it was in battle that he still saw remnants of what David had brought with him to the gates of Heaven. He preferred to be close to his enemy when he took him out, though Jonah suspected David wasn't seeing a Dark One when he plunged his knife in for the killing blow. Despite how far David had come, a darkness still lingered in him. It no longer ruled him, but it had not yet been resolved. That was what most concerned him about David's desire to take guard detail over a witch who might be ruled by darkness entirely.

But Anna had drawn his attention to other attributes David could bring to the protection duty, which had little to do with his intelligence and fighting skills. When Anna had teased him about David's handsome face and body, he'd retorted that he didn't believe her prickly Dark Spawn friend even noticed such things.

"Oh, she notices," Anna had said, the twinkle in her blue violet eyes replaced by something more serious. "She definitely noticed David. That's why it should be him."

"The boy has little experience with women," he had replied. "She will drive him to insanity."

"If that's the problem, I'd be happy to educate him further, my lord. Purely to help him serve you better." She'd dived beneath the ocean waves then, laughing and evading his grasp, though he knew they could both look forward to the ways he would exact retribution later.

There was no denying David was a striking man. All angels were, but human-born angels, unlike born angels, retained the human characteristics of the eye, complete with iris. David's eyes were a rich brown, and his hair was a pleasing complement of brown and chestnut streaks that fell to his shoulders. He had a tensile strength to him that Jonah could evaluate with a commander's eye. The lad wasn't overly bulky, but his shoulders had a good breadth for the knife work he did. The fine length of arms and legs were well integrated with smooth, toned muscle.

He'd always liked the character in his lieutenant's face, even in the beginning when he was little more than a train wreck in the vessel of a fourteen-year-old's soul. Sharp-bladed nose, well-cut chin and jawline, high brow. Then there was his most impressive trait—his silence. David was serious, quiet, which made his sudden fierceness in the thick of battle so at odds with his contemplative nature and the flickers of humor that could ease the occasional tensions among the angels.

When David finally investigated other heavenly skills, it was found he was a deft musician, with impressive skills in magic wielding through the playing of instruments and singing. But he'd been clear that his preference was staying on the front line, fighting the Dark Ones until a higher purpose appealed to him. Jonah was glad to have him there, though at times he had an equal desire to send him into the safer climate of composing music. He'd become very fond of him.

"If this witch gets you killed, I will not think well of her."

"You don't think well of her now."

"True," Jonah admitted. He sighed. David's thinking on the matter was sound, even if there were things that made Jonah uncomfortable about it. He was running out of options, pure and simple. And he reluctantly admitted that David's reticence on so many things made his outspoken support of the witch even more significant.

"If I agree to your request, I need to be sure you can accept my terms."

David straightened. "I accept."

"Young idiot," Jonah repeated irritably. "Listen first. As much as I love Anna, there's a larger reason we're expending resources on protecting the witch. Over the Canyon, we saw evidence that the powers she can command are formidable. From the energy I felt when the Dark Ones had me, I believe she's only tapped into a tenth of her capabilities."

David's attention sharpened. "She was hiding her full range of power?"

"Anna said her mother died when she was seven years old and she's been on her own ever since. She may lack training, confidence. A goal." Jonah gave him a pointed look. "So far her goal appears to be survival. Much more might be possible if she has a greater aim."

"And that worries you as much as it gives you a reason to protect her."

"It worries me *more* than it gives me that reason to protect her," Jonah warned. "Anna insists Mina's heart is good. Much as I don't wish to admit it, you're right. Your connection with her might provide us valuable insight on whether she is an ally, an enemy or"—he held up a hand at David's expression—"could be used by our enemies."

David's eyes flashed. "So I could be the doorway to her death warrant."

"If she grasps that power and turns it to an evil purpose, she'll be the one who opened that door. You'll simply be the messenger."

David went back to a squat on the tiles and stared at the design. "Nothing's ever easy here, is it? Never like the storybooks, where you can just ride in, swinging your sword, save the day and the girl."

"No. You know that as well as any of us." Though Jonah regretted saying it, particularly when he saw David's head bow, the pain that crossed his face. Moving across the room, he laid a hand on the young man's shoulder, offering simple comfort for the unintentional prick at an old but nearly fatal wound. "Can you accept the task?"

"If we leave her alone, she might focus only on surviving and never grasp any potential, good or bad. Neutral."

"When it comes to power, there is no neutral. If the Dark Ones take her, they *will* force the decision."

"So we watch over her until she decides. If she makes the wrong decision, we kill her." David rose, facing his commander. "I guess I thought there was another reason we were protecting her."

"I've told you the reason this Legion must protect her. We serve the Goddess." Jonah's tone was sharp, all commander again, and David automatically shifted to respectful attention. "I've no problem with your desire to protect her for her own value. But if I order you onto this detail, it will be because I'm certain you can focus. Beyond the swinging of your sword."

David had the grace to flush and take a step back. "That's not—"

"It is some of it. There's no shame in wanting a female, and certainly not in wanting to protect her. Unlike Marcellus, I don't wish any harm upon the girl, though I wish she was a problem we didn't have." Jonah's expression hardened. "But no matter the personal feelings any of us have—you, me, Marcellus or Anna—it doesn't change the fact she has the power to be a strong ally for the Dark Ones. If she can become our ally instead, she'll be a lot safer. That I can promise you."

The Prime Legion Commander pinned David with his dark, direct gaze that could see through any lie, rationalization or half-truth. "Will you be able to stay clear enough to make the right decision? Can you accept the responsibility that comes with her protection? For you to get the answer you want, I need the answer *I* want."

JONAH had over a thousand years of wisdom on his shoulders. On many things, he was unambiguous as a sword point, but expressions like "the right decision" could have multiple levels, David knew. Like one of those flaky biscuits he'd liked to split open and eat, layer by layer, when he was a mortal child.

Ah, Goddess, over sixteen years and he could still smell the things. Well, in truth, he kept the memory fresh by sometimes hovering over one of the fast-food restaurants that made them in the early dark hours of dawn. Angels didn't eat human food because they couldn't taste it, but oh, the smell . . . It hurt and pleasured at once.

When he was six years old, he remembered reading *The Littlest Angel*, the tale of the young angel who longed to be a human boy. Had Mina ever wished for the life of a normal mermaid child? What did mermaid children do that was the equivalent of human children's wish to wade in a creek or play ball?

He didn't miss it, really. Not the way that poignant little angel had. The last eight years of his human life had been a taste of Hell that eradicated much of the pleasure of the first six. But being the youngest of the Dark Legion and a made angel, he sometimes longed for the familiar, something that was a true part both of who he'd been and who he was now.

Something to tie those two things together and fill the emptiness that still existed in the lingering part of his human soul.

Maybe what drew him to the seawitch was his belief that Mina faced a similar struggle. He was tired of hearing she wasn't worth saving. That disastrous first time he'd met her, he'd tried to heal her after his attack, and she'd scathingly refused his aid. But there'd been such a stunned look in her eyes, as if no one had ever offered her such a kindness, a look that only grew more confused when he told her she could call on him if she needed aid.

Call me if harm threatens you . . .

On the other hand, he suspected she'd never take him up on it, even if the Dark Ones captured her and promised her a thousand years of torture.

"An eternity of hugging and having to share her feelings with someone," Anna had remarked. "*That* would be Hell to Mina."

Despite Anna's wit, he knew she worried about Mina. She'd been able to give him *her* sense of Mina, but little that was solid and concrete about or from Mina herself. So whether David liked it or not, Jonah's pessimistic predictions couldn't be discounted.

Until his meeting with the Prime Commander, David hadn't realized leaving Mina to her own devices was no longer an option. Ironically, by revealing her power during Jonah's rescue, she'd identified herself as a strong weapon—for whichever side could use her.

David had no question that the service of the Goddess was for the greater good. Free will was vital as well. But now Mina had only two choices. Fight for the angels, or fight for the Dark Ones, and if she chose the latter, they'd take her out the same way they would any Dark One. She could be dead or cooperative.

No one would call Jonah a warm and fuzzy angel. He knew his enemy and wasn't going to risk Mina being used by them. He not only had a universe to protect, but also a mate pregnant with their first child. And the ferocity he could wield to protect them was formidable.

But he was fair. So David just had to make sure that Mina was given a good chance. Tightening his jaw, he focused on what he did know of her. She was a shapeshifter, capable of human and dragon form, as well as a somewhat aberrant mermaid, with two long and deft dark tentacles in place of a tail. She'd demonstrated shielding capabilities that repelled the archery attack of a Dark One army for an amazing duration, though that and Jonah's blade would have cost the witch her life had it not been for Anna's sacrifice on her behalf.

Her spell-casting abilities were impressive, for she'd proven herself a capable fighter when he tried to corner her. She'd combined magic with physical strategy in a manner that nearly kicked his ass. Marcellus's wing had been just a whimsical taste of what she could do.

"Potions," Anna had added, on one of his visits. "She does potions for the merpeople. Love spells, sleeping, good fortune, all the usual things. I'm not sure why she does them, but maybe it amuses her, or what passes for amusement to Mina."

"Like pulling the wings off flies," Jonah had murmured, earning a sharp look from his mermaid.

If she had to be executed, would David volunteer to do it, no matter how much it would tear him apart? Was it better to be murdered by the one who'd hoped to save you, rather than by someone who considered your existence a mistake?

Stop it. He couldn't keep vacillating between the worst possible outcome, which he saw far too clearly, and the best one, which was murky at best. *This is not a thinking matter.*

When he saw her, he'd know the best way to handle it.

A warrior's mission . . .
A woman's desire . . .
And the unnatural evil
that could destroy them both.

———

FROM *NEW YORK TIMES* BESTSELLING AUTHOR

ALYSSA DAY

ATLANTIS BETRAYED

What could Christophe, powerful Warrior of Poseidon, have in common with Fiona Campbell, prim and proper Scottish illustrator of fairy tales by day and notorious jewel thief known as the Scarlet Ninja by night? Answer: The Siren, a legendary Crown Jewel that Fiona has targeted for her next heist. It's said to be worth millions, but to Christophe it's invaluable, for the Siren also happens to be one of the missing jewels from Poseidon's Trident.

But breaking into the Tower of London is a two-person job, so Christophe and Fiona team up to commit the crime of the century. As newfound passions fire their motives—and cloud their judgment—they realize they aren't the only ones after the priceless gem. A dark force is shadowing their every move and threatening to shatter their trust with revenge, betrayal, and a haunting revelation about the past.

penguin.com

LOVE
ROMANCE
NOVELS?

For news on all your favorite romance authors,
sneak peeks into the newest releases, book
giveaways, and much more—

"Like" Love Always on Facebook!
f LoveAlwaysBooks

Penguin Group (USA) Online

What will you be reading tomorrow?

Patricia Cornwell, Nora Roberts, Catherine Coulter,
Ken Follett, John Sandford, Clive Cussler,
Tom Clancy, Laurell K. Hamilton, Charlaine Harris,
J. R. Ward, W.E.B. Griffin, William Gibson,
Robin Cook, Brian Jacques, Stephen King,
Dean Koontz, Eric Jerome Dickey, Terry McMillan,
Sue Monk Kidd, Amy Tan, Jayne Ann Krentz,
Daniel Silva, Kate Jacobs…

You'll find them all at
penguin.com

*Read excerpts and newsletters,
find tour schedules and reading group guides,
and enter contests.*

Subscribe to Penguin Group (USA) newsletters
and get an exclusive inside look
at exciting new titles and the authors you love
long before everyone else does.

PENGUIN GROUP (USA)
penguin.com